Blackthorn Winter

Sarah Challis

review

First published in 2003
by HEADLINE BOOK PUBLISHING

First published in paperback in 2003
by REVIEW
An imprint of Headline Book Publishing

1

ISBN 0 7553 0948 0

Printed and bound in Great Britain by
Mackays of Chatham plc, Chatham, Kent

HEADLINE BOOK PUBLISHING
A division of Hodder Headline
338 Euston Road
LONDON NW1 3BH

www.reviewbooks.co.uk
www.hodderheadline.com

Sarah Challis, whose father is the distinguished cinema-tographer, Christopher Challis, travelled widely with film units as a child. She has since lived in Scotland and California but is now happily settled in a Dorset village with three rescued dogs and three chickens. She is married with four sons. *Blackthorn Winter* is her third novel.

Also by Sarah Challis

Killing Helen
Turning for Home

For my parents, with my love and gratitude

Chapter One

It was Star Bishop, on her way to work at The Bugle, who witnessed the accident. It was a beautiful June morning and the narrow lanes were hedged high on either side by the banks of blackthorn, the vivid green woven with pink and golden honeysuckle and dog roses. She had been following the car all the way from Sharston and thought the woman was driving too fast. 'You can't see nothing round them bends and going like the bloody clappers, she was,' she told Monica, the landlady. 'She hadn't got a hope of stopping. Went slap into the tractor on that corner outside the village. Bloody lucky she weren't killed.'

Star had pulled up behind and got out to survey the damage while Greg Whittle jumped down from the cab of the tractor. 'Livid, he was,' said Star. 'Bloody effing idiot, he called her. Bloody maniac! Do you want to get killed or something, he said. And she just sat there, staring.'

'It would be the shock,' said Monica, knowledgeably. 'Shock can take you like that.'

Star nodded and went on, important in her role as storyteller. 'She came to, like, and got out and looked at the front of her car. All smashed up, it was, into the tractor. She doesn't say nothing, just stands there, looking. Greg's still carrying on at her but it's as if she isn't listening, and then she goes to the car, gets her bag out of the back, writes her name and address on a piece of paper and hands it to him.

' "Was it my fault?" she says. "I don't know what happened. Was it my fault?" Almost like it wasn't her that was driving. "I'm terribly sorry," she says. "I'm ever so sorry." You'd think she was born yesterday. Everyone knows you don't say sorry. Not after an accident. Your insurance tells you that. Shaking and white as a sheet, she was. "I don't feel too good," she says. "I think I'd better go home. You won't call the police, will you?" she says. "Not for a little thing like this."

1

' "We'll have to get her shifted," says Greg, pointing at her car. "Get her off the road."

' "Could you do that for me?" she says. "I'd be ever so grateful," and then she just walks off. Just like that. Walks off and leaves it there.'

'She never!' exclaimed Monica, suitably shocked. 'Who was her then? You didn't know her?'

'Never seen her before. Greg and me looked at the address and he says she's the woman who's got the Major's old place, up next to Mrs Durnford.'

'I heard someone had moved in there last week. Betty saw the van outside. What sort of woman was she, then?'

'Thin, tall. One of those beanpole types. No make-up. Middle-aged. Round the bloody bend, I'd say. I had to get in her car – rusting old heap it was – and Greg got it shunted back into the gateway. That's where we left it. Then I come on here.'

'Perhaps we should call the police, whatever she said,' suggested Monica, who liked a drama.

'Not bloody likely,' said Star, remembering her out-of-date tax disc. 'Don't want them snooping about. Greg said he'd tell Brewer. Get him to see to it.' She shifted her ample behind on the bar stool. 'Here, Monica,' she said. 'Give us a brandy, love. To steady me nerves.' She lit a cigarette. 'He's not half bad, that Greg,' she added. 'Got a nice little arse on him.'

Monica laughed. 'Give over, Star. He's only just out of school. Not much older than your Rosco. That's baby-snatching, that is!'

'Catch them young, I say. While they've still got a bit of go in them!' Star sniggered and took the glass Monica slid across the bar to her. 'I'll just have this and then I'll make a start. Shall I begin in here, Mon?'

'Anywhere you like, love. It won't go away, none of it.'

'Claudia Knight,' said Star later, pausing on her way to collect mop and bucket. 'That was her name. Claudia Knight.'

Not far away, at the top of the village, in an ugly yellow stone bungalow optimistically called Garden Cottage, Claudia stared at her pale face in the bathroom mirror. She saw the stain of blood from the cut on her forehead and relived the clutch of terror as she saw the tractor bearing down on her, her car brakes screaming and what seemed a slow-motion slide across the lane. The inevitable collision had been followed by a peaceful lull, both engines silent and the sound of birdsong from the open window. Claudia had opened her eyes and found she was still

2

alive and also unhurt and felt nothing very much. The fright had made her hands tremble and she could feel her heart thumping. A stocky young woman with bright red hair had appeared from somewhere and was staring at her as a man in a baseball cap and green overalls jumped down from the cab of the tractor and started to shout. He was quite young, in his early twenties, blue-eyed, suntanned. Claudia remembered studying his angry face and seeing little bubbles of white spittle at the corners of his mouth. He's foaming at the mouth, she had thought, interested. She had never realised that one actually could. She watched him shouting without listening to what he was saying but then growing tired of his tirade, tired of the whole incident, she had opened the car door and got out. The surface of the lane glittered in the morning sun and she had smelled the hot rankness of the long grass. She walked to the front of her car where the bonnet was crumpled into the maws of the tractor and stood looking at the damage.

What do I do now? she had thought. She cast around in her mind for guidance and then went back to her car and got her bag.

'This is where I live,' she said finally, finding a Biro and a piece of paper and scribbling down her new address and handing it to him. 'I'm terribly sorry. I accept it was my fault. I wasn't concentrating, I suppose. Just for a moment. What happens now? I don't know anything about accidents. There's no need to call the police, is there?'

The young man had stood holding the piece of paper, looking at it. His hands were cracked and dirty. The woman with red hair, her thighs heavy in her tight jeans, looked over his shoulder.

'That's where the Major lived,' he said to Claudia, almost as an accusation. He looked up at her and, noticing how pale she was, said in a different tone, 'Are you all right?'

'Actually, I don't feel very well. I think I should go home.' Claudia had felt a tremor in her voice and held a hand to her forehead. 'Could you possibly see to my car? I'd be so grateful.' She supposed he had agreed, she wasn't sure now, but she had to get away and it was close enough to walk back. It had sounded strange to call the bungalow 'home'. It did not feel like home. Not yet. The sun was unexpectedly hot on her face as she stood in the quiet lane and then, turning away from the smashed car and the looming bulk of the tractor, she had set off towards Court Barton.

It was running away, she thought now as she looked in the mirror. Stupid, because he was only a young man. Probably not much older than Jerome. He was shouting because she'd given him a fright. The truth was that she just couldn't face a conversation. That was it. An interrogation. Questions. Having to find answers, with that girl listening.

The lane ahead had wound round another bend and she had felt relieved to be out of sight of the vehicles left behind. She was just able to see the square grey of the church tower through the trees in the distance. A lark throbbed out its song from the glistening blue sky. She had squinted up, but the little bird was invisible in the high, shining air. On either side, the edges of the lane were deep and dense with pink campion and Herb Robert and thick with the cream froth of cow parsley. Biscuit-coloured cow pats, rolled flat by tyres, were crisping in the sun and black beetles scuttled away from her sandalled feet as she walked. In front, over the flat green top of the hedge, as wide as a table, she could see the blue hills, darkened by patches of woodland, rolling into the shimmering distance, and beneath the song of the lark the whole valley seemed to tremble with the contralto voices of the sheep and the plaintive bleating of their lambs.

It was a beautiful morning. As Claudia walked, she stretched her legs and swung her arms, feeling her muscles lengthen and her lungs fill with the clean air. The hot sun prickled on her bare skin and she breathed a rush of sweetness as she crushed a stem of honeysuckle in her fingers, plucked from the hedge as she passed. It seemed, she thought, inappropriate that it should be on such a particularly fine morning that her husband, Roger Barron, be taken away in a police van to begin his prison sentence.

Several months earlier when she had first found this village, tucked into a secretive fold in the gentle Dorset hills, she had loved its isolation and the radiating, meandering lanes which, apart from the road to Sharston, seemed to wander off to nowhere in particular. A row of council houses with pretty front gardens led the way into the village. Passing them, as she walked away from the accident, Claudia remembered that when she was searching for somewhere to live she had said to her sister-in-law, Minna, 'One of those would do. Look, lovely gardens and what a view!' This morning the street was quiet, children all in school, mothers and fathers at work, dogs shut up. Only an elderly face, waxy pale and grey-haired, peered from between the curtains of a living-room window as she went by.

She walked on, past an untidy breaker's yard where chickens scratched amongst the nettles and rusting wrecks, and then four or five substantial stone houses with mullioned windows and stone lintels standing behind low walls with beautiful and carefully tended gardens. The parish church was round the next bend, its yew trees darkening the lane. Claudia noticed the list of names on the war memorial as she went by. Three Winsor boys lost in the Great War, two young Roberts, two Gilberts. What sorrow, she thought, must have descended on this little green village so far away from the mud of Flanders where its young men had fallen.

Hastening on, hurrying to get home, she passed two farms, the first right on the village street, its yard a mixture of old barns with sagging tiled roofs like sway-backed cows, and modern units and machinery. Claudia could hear a tractor working somewhere but otherwise there was no sign of life. The other was Manor Farm, a handsome old stone house with a roof covered in golden lichen and set back across a small paddock in a stand of beech trees. Three black and white cows, each with a spindly-legged calf, were lying in the long grass by the gate, the tassels of their tails flicking at the flies which bothered their flanks.

Claudia was glad it was so quiet. She wiped her forehead and saw a bright smear on the side of her hand and felt alarmed. A stranger, walking up the street with blood on her face, was sure to be noticed. A car approached slowly from the other way and she ducked her head as it passed. Then all had been silent again. Cottages turned blank faces to the street and the neatly tended gardens were empty and still. A fat golden and white cat strolled from a gate and lay in the road ahead, twitching the tip of its tail. A bright pink rose with an egg-yolk yellow centre reared in great clusters over a porch next to the lane and a deep red and gold honeysuckle scrambled along a fence, climbing in and out of the posts and reaching waving tendrils up into the sky. The air was sweet with the toilet water scent of orange blossom and lime flowers, with a whiff of fried bacon from an open kitchen window where a radio played softly.

Claudia hastened on past the pub, festooned with hanging baskets, where back in April she and Minna had shivered over the coal fire as they ate sandwiches and drank half pints of potent cider in the little bar. It had been a bitterly cold day then, with a bone chilling wind and leaden skies. Even the sheep had looked miserable in the bleached fields, huddled round feeding troughs with tiny new lambs folded into little white scraps on the frozen ground. The lanes had been bright with daffodils and primroses and the hedges, still black and leafless, were wreathed with starry white blossom. An old man, nursing a pint in the corner had heard them complaining and called over, 'Blackthorn winter. That's what this is. Get a cold snap when the blackthorn's out and folks reckon it's colder than the winter proper. Won't be spring till the blossom's finished.' He'd been right, too, Claudia remembered. She'd been house-hunting then, looking for somewhere to live after the London house had been sold and things had been at their most grim.

Beyond the pub was the little triangle of green with the village noticeboard and the bench where she had never yet seen anyone sit. A flyer had been stapled to a telegraph pole announcing a missing spaniel bitch named Nutty. Owners desperate, she read as she passed. Especially Beth, aged eight. Claudia could not bear to think about it.

As she walked up the hill she passed the Old Schoolhouse, the Old Post Office, the Old Bakery, the Old Vicarage and the Old Forge – 'You should call your place the Old Lag,' Minna had suggested – then some pleasant modern houses in a close, more council houses, a scramble of thatched and tiled cottages, and then where the lane divided at the top end, two substantial houses behind high walls on the right-hand side. Nearly home now.

When Julia Durnford, her neighbour, called out to her from her drive, Claudia merely waved a hand and bolted on, towards the horrid leylandii, a tree she loathed, and the iron gate to the bungalow. It sat there squarely, back off the road, an uncompromising box of yellowy pink stone with two blank windows on either side of a frosted-glass front door. Sheltered behind a chestnut paling fence, it was further screened by overgrown trees and shrubs. The patch of lawn at the front was long and neglected and on it two black crows, which had been squabbling viciously over something dead, flapped into the air.

Claudia reached her front door at a run and fumbled in her bag for the unfamiliar key, the estate agent's label still attached. In a moment she would be inside and safe. Where was the bloody thing? Ah, here in her trouser pocket. The frosted-glass door slammed behind her and she had stood in the hall amongst the packing cases and covered her face with her hands. Thank God, she thought. Safety. Somewhere to hide. Nobody would follow her here.

Now as she leaned over the basin to bathe her forehead, Claudia wondered how she had received the cut above her eyebrow. Perhaps she had not been wearing her seat belt. She could not remember. Thinking back, she was surprised instead by a sudden flashback to a vision of a bold black and white horse, sharp against the green field across which it moved. Was it this that had distracted her just before the accident? She clearly remembered seeing the horse in the distance, galloping and jumping the hedges, but it seemed unlikely, an unreliable recollection. Recently she had found she could not trust the images her mind threw up. 'I'm losing my grip on reality,' she had complained to Minna, who was a doctor. 'It's stress,' Minna had reassured her. 'Stress does that. Gets things out of synch. You'll get over it when things calm down a bit.'

The cut was not deep and had stopped bleeding. Claudia let the red-stained water out of the basin and considered her face in the bathroom glass. She knew she had changed over the last nightmare months. She was thinner and had not bothered to maintain her haircut, which had lost its shape and now the roots were threaded with silver. Her London hairdresser was out of the question. She lifted the heavy dark locks from both sides of her neck. She should have it off. She used to be proud of it, so thick and glossy and subtly coloured in shades of chestnut and tangerine and mahogany. Now she thought, 'I'm too old for long hair. I've reached that watershed. My face can't take it any more.' Her brown eyes looked more deep-set, ringed with dark shadows, and there was a new tautness about her mouth. Not much to look at any more, she thought. Not much left in the looks department.

Thinking again about the accident, she regretted having been so feeble. She should have taken responsibility, said her insurance company would deal with the repairs, exchanged addresses, done the thing properly. Damn. Now she could expect a visit from an angry farmer. She dreaded the sound of steps on the drive, past where she would cower in the kitchen, the knock on the door, having to answer it, to face a stranger, act a part, remember that in this new life she was Claudia Knight, divorcee, and not Claudia Barron, whose husband had gone to prison.

She supposed there must be papers somewhere relating to the car. Roger's secretary had boxed everything up when she helped clear out the London house. The papers would be in one of the packing cases. Claudia glared at them stacked in the tiny hall.

There were more in the sitting room and garage. She would have to make a start on them, she knew, but she did not look forward to the task. When the children came back she must have at least made an attempt at creating a home, but that was months away. Jerome was in India until the end of August and Lila was working for a finance house in New York.

Claudia did not want to think about unpacking. The bungalow felt so unlike her home that she did not know where to begin. She preferred, for the moment, to camp here, waiting until things settled around her and she dared to start to put down roots. Her clothes still lay draped over her suitcase in the bedroom at the back, her make-up in a little heap on the floor, the light beside her bed without a shade.

Minna had told her that it was absurd to buy the bungalow without making an appointment to view it properly. 'What if you loathe it?' she asked. 'It's important to buy something where you'll feel happy.'

'Minna, you saw it. It's perfectly OK.'

'But you must look round. It's going to be your home, for goodness sake!'

'I can afford it, which is the most important thing, and I like its secluded position and the village is lovely. The agent says it was built in the kitchen garden of the big house next door and it has the original high walls on three sides.'

'Why do you want high walls? It's not you who's going to prison.'

'I like it, Min. I really do. It feels like the Secret Garden. I'll feel safe there.'

Now, on this bright day, the little rooms were filled with sunshine. Before she had moved in, someone from the village had been round to clean. The pile of circulars and junk mail had been neatly stacked in a pile inside the front door, and all the old Major had left behind was a smell of tobacco and a few whisky stains on the carpet. The sitting room, now a muddle of furniture and packing cases, had an open fire and a small glass extension with a door to the back garden. It would all need painting and had ugly old storage heaters that looked large and cumbersome enough to house a nuclear reactor each. The kitchen and bathroom were shabby and had an air of neglect. Masculine sort of rooms from the days before the New Man had been invented, with his apron and chargrilled this and that and his bathroom cabinet full of moisturisers. Claudia could imagine the Major shuffling about, poaching an egg or cooking a solitary chop, and wiping the steam from the bathroom mirror to shave with an old-fashioned brush and soap.

There were three bedrooms on the other side of the bungalow, which were described as double, although Claudia could not see how this could be, unless one climbed over the beds to get in and out, but they faced east and would be filled with early sunshine. She thought of her children. Even though they were old enough to be independent, they still needed somewhere to call home. At least when they got back they would find their boxes of stuff here. The paraphernalia of their teenage years. She had packed up their cassettes and CDs; the old, loved clothes; the magazines; the scuffed A-level notes; the letters and photographs.

Claudia inched round the furniture in the sitting room and unlocked the door to the back garden. She loved it out here where the high walls sheltered the bungalow and where overgrown roses and fruit trees scrambled against the old bricks. 'You could sunbathe nude out here,' the cheeky young estate agent had suggested when she had eventually looked round.

'Where does that door go?' Claudia had asked, ignoring him and pointing to a peeling gate in the wall.

'Next door, I presume,' he said. 'It must be the old gate to the Lodge. Like I told you, this was once the kitchen garden. In fact, I believe there was a lot of trouble over permission to build here. Contravened planning regulations and so on. Opposed quite bitterly by the people on the other side. Not that there's any bad feeling now,' he had added hastily, not wishing to cast any shadows over the prospective purchase.

In fact, this lack of ill will had been borne out that very morning when the opposition from next door had been round with a jar of marmalade and fired, Claudia suspected, by a keen desire to investigate the new neighbour. Claudia had held the door open, but stood resolutely in Julia Durnford's way, blocking her view, and received the marmalade with murmured thanks. Had things been different she would have welcomed the friendliness of the gesture but now she dreaded any kind of scrutiny, feared even neighbourly approaches which would lead to inevitable questions and evasive answers. Julia had introduced herself, speaking in little excited rushes, all the while craning to see in. 'I'm from next door,' she had explained. 'East End House. I expect you find this awfully small. I mean you've probably come from something larger. It must be so hard to have to get rid of things.'

9

'It's plenty big enough, actually,' said Claudia and, stepping out, closed the door, like an argument, behind her. 'I'm here mostly on my own, you see. My children are grown up. One in New York, one in India. It's big enough for me.'

Now, standing in her back garden she could just see the roof of the East End House over the wall to the right. Some sort of rambling rose scrambled along the top of the wall, raising apricot flowers to the blue sky. Then, just as she stood there, thinking about her neighbour, from the other side Julia Durnford's ringing tones floated up amongst the nodding blooms. 'Here, Tom,' came the voice. 'Over here. I want you to spray Lady Hillingdon. She's covered in greenfly.'

Down in the vale, below the village, where the hay had already been cut on the lush water meadows and lay in straight, silvery swathes, waiting to be turned to dry in the sun, where the roe deer sheltered in the thick overgrown copses and a pair of buzzards wheeled lazily in the high blue sky, a thin, brown-haired girl cantered bareback on her black and white horse. Through her worn jeans she could feel the heat of Jigsaw's body, the black patches hotter than the white, and the muscles across his shoulders and back bunching and stretching beneath her. Her skinny legs clung round his flanks and she sat balanced and easy, her body moving with the horse's powerful stride. She could feel her hair rising and falling on her back, lifted from her neck, and the cool rush of air on her face. Jigsaw was pulling. He was strong and keen. A big powerful horse. Jena knew from her dad that you didn't fight a horse. Didn't pit your strength against his. It didn't take a genius to see who would win that particular contest. Not when you were only eleven years old and weighed six stone and the horse was sixteen hands and strong and bold. No, Jena knew instinctively how to use her hands and seat to coax him not to set his power against her, to give her his head, to accept the snaffle bit in his mouth rather than snatch it away from her. In return she did not fuss him and let him go forward freely and the two of them fairly flew the track which had once been the old railway line. Up and over the embankment they went, clearing the rails at the top with an easy bound. Jena grinned to herself. She had watched members of the local hunt making a pig's ear of that fence last winter, going at it all wrong, too slow, not using their horses right. All but one or two, that was. The Master always jumped well. Jena knew that he'd been a jockey. Him and a young woman with blonde hair on a black horse who had skipped over neatly and was a pleasure to watch. She'd smiled at Jena where she stood watching, waved her stick at her and called, 'Where's your lovely horse?' and Jena had grinned back and shouted, 'Up the woods. Working with me dad!'

They cantered on, girl and horse, along the edge of a hay field. She could see a tractor and mower working along the far edge. She would keep away, out of sight. She was supposed to be in school but had convinced her dad she'd got asthma. If she concentrated she could make her chest contract, could bring on an attack of the wheezes until she gasped for breath and had to lie flat to get enough air into her lungs. He'd let her stay behind then, didn't make her walk up to the village to wait for the school bus to take her into Bishops Barton to the primary. She was off school a lot and he told her she'd have the truant officers down on him if she didn't go like she was supposed to, but she hated school, hated the bigger kids who pushed her around and called her names. She'd do anything not to go.

Pulling up, she slid off Jigsaw's back and led him down the steep bank, back onto the old railway line. She was out of sight here. The insides of her legs were prickly with warm horsehair and she brushed them off. Down on the line the overgrown verges were bright with flowers. Cranesbill and pink and white dog roses scrambled up the banks amongst the cow parsley. Her dad's woman, Heather, would be out collecting orchids and Hound's-Tongue for her remedies. When she got back to the vans she'd go and help her. Heather didn't care about school. Just laughed and said it hadn't done her no good either. Dawdling along, Jigsaw's reins looped over her arm, Jena wished it could always be like this. Just her and Jigs out in the sun and everything easy.

At five o'clock that evening, the telephone rang in Garden Cottage and the quiet voice of David Rowntree, Roger Barron's friend and lawyer, said, 'Claudia? They've moved him today. He's gone to Parkfield Prison in Staffordshire. It will be on the evening news, I'm afraid. I thought I should warn you.'

Claudia's breath was suddenly rapid. She could see her breastbone rising and falling sharply.

'Claudia? Are you all right?'

'Yes, I am. Thank you, David.' She had prepared herself for this moment. She had known it would come. 'Could you do something for me? Could you email Lila in New York and let her know. Warn her. It's hard to get her on the telephone at work, and difficult for her to speak in her office.'

'Of course. I'll do it right away. I have her address on file. Anything else? What about Jerome?'

'I don't think even Roger would be considered newsworthy in Delhi.'

'No, probably not. I saw him today, Claudia. He asked after you, said he's thinking of you. Wanted to know how you were managing.'

Resolutely, Claudia refused to allow herself to utter the words, 'How is he?' Instead she managed to say, 'Did he,' in a small, unresponsive voice that was not even a question.

'Yes.' There was a pause. David was waiting for her. Eventually, because she remained silent, he said, 'He's remarkable. Very brave. Almost cheerful. Full of optimism about the appeal.'

Claudia closed her eyes and with a conscious effort of will refused to be drawn into territory she had sealed off. She needed to bring this conversation to a close.

'Thank you, David, for telling me. It was thoughtful of you. Now I can warn Mother.'

'It was nothing. I'll keep in touch. Give you any news. Goodbye.'

When Claudia put the telephone down, her hands were shaking. Of course, she thought, Roger would love it. The drama, the press, being at the centre of things. But what about when the cell door banged shut behind him, when prison tedium set in, when the world he so loved to be part of was just a square of sky in a barred window? How would he survive then? She had speculated on this many times before, discussed it endlessly with Minna, but now it was a reality. He was there now, in the prison where he was to serve his sentence, perhaps on his own in a cell, apparently thinking of her. What was it David had said? 'He asked after you. He's thinking of you.'

Claudia went back to the last time she had seen her husband alone when he was released on bail. He had been living with Carla for months by then but the angry words they had exchanged and her bitterness had got the better of her. Roger had backed off, putting his hands up in mock defence and had smirked, 'At last I've got a reaction out of you. I'd forgotten how very attractive I find you when you're angry,' and she had struck him then, hit him hard, several times, with her fists, and he had caught her arms and pulled her to him and held her against him in a fast grip. It was the first physical contact they had had in months. Trapped, Claudia felt a surge of sexual energy. Horrified, she had tried to pull away but he held her tight and ran his hand over her bottom and ground his pelvis into her. God! She hated thinking about it, even now, how they had made furious, fantastic love; how she had bit and struck him and how he had torn at her clothes and she had cried to him to let her go and all the time wanted him more than she ever had before. Sitting here, in what is supposed to be my first independent home, she thought, having put me through all of this nightmare, he can still arouse me, make me want him. That was what he had had in mind when he said he was thinking of her. She knew it.

Before the early evening news she must telephone her mother, who lived alone in sheltered housing in Winchester, and warn her what she might see – Roger with a blanket over his head, or handcuffed and smiling, she did not know.

Olive Knight answered the telephone in a state of excitement. 'Darling, I've seen it already. I had the television on for that quiz programme. I must say he looked really quite well. He's lost a little weight and it suits him. Of course they didn't allow him to say anything, just bundled him off into a police van. Public school is supposed to be an excellent preparation for prison, so I feel confident he'll be all right. Of course, everyone here is riveted, riveted, by it all. I'm very discreet, darling, don't worry, but naturally they're all frightfully interested . . .' Claudia had to block her ears and think very hard of something else.

Before six o'clock she poured herself a glass of wine, grateful that she and Minna had had the foresight to smuggle several cases out of the cellar of the London house, and turned on the television. It was the last item on the news. Her mother was right. Roger did look well, turning and managing a brief smile at the cameras, handcuffed to a pleasant-looking prison officer who then got into a muddle getting into the back of the van because he stood back, almost deferentially, for Roger to get in first. It was a fleeting view, a brief item. The arrest, the trial, the sentencing, all fully covered at the time, was now stale news. Press interest had moved on. The man who had momentarily captured the attention of the nation because he was glamorous, a good-looking maverick whose trial had revealed breathtaking audacity and cunning, would be forgotten when he was locked away from its scrutiny.

Claudia turned off the television and sat on the sofa, thinking. That was the last time she had made love. Or had sex, would be more accurate. During the weeks that followed, two or three of Roger's friends had sought her out, taken her to dinner, offered support, and then assumed they could share her bed. She had kicked them all out, disgusted. Each one had a wife she thought of as a friend. After that she steered clear of people who offered a shoulder to cry on and became more reliant on the uncomplicated relationship she had with David Rowntree, who did not want to be either her friend or her lover, but only to steer her towards an independent life.

On the whole she had not missed the company of men. Distress and anxiety subdued sexual appetite – she had read that somewhere, and it was true. It was strange that the young man on the tractor today had made her remember what it means to be an attractive woman, or rather, reminded her of what she felt she had lost. Refilling her glass and thinking of Roger and that last time, she felt restless and disturbed. It wasn't exactly the absence of a sex life she regretted, more an awareness of the person she had been, for whom sex had been important.

Thinking of Roger made her also think of Carla and the details of their relationship which had been picked over in court and then plastered over the newspapers. Roger had been portrayed by the prosecution as a sexual predator, Carla as an innocent in awe of her powerful boss. Claudia had devoured every detail, succumbing to an insatiable desire to feed her jealousy. At first she thought it was anger that ripped through her as she read accounts of expensive trips to Paris hotels, urgent sexual encounters in the office, presents exchanged, promises made. Carla said in court she believed Roger was in the process of divorcing his wife and that they would marry. She claimed that Roger had outgrown Claudia, that in his meteoric success he had left her behind. Claudia read on and on, horribly fascinated, unable to believe that it was her marriage that was being dissected in the courtroom.

Looking back she had to admit that during the time of this affair, although she was unconscious of it, she had wondered if their marriage was over. It was a stubborn belief in the institution which made her plod on. Later, this might have been a comfort, this realisation that things had run their course, but instead she felt enraged by jealousy, peering at the photographs of the young blonde woman leaving court, once even stabbing away at the image of her face with a knife. It was frightening to feel like this. She did not want to know what it meant about how she felt about her husband. She feared that this rushing jealousy was like a chain, shackling her to the man who had betrayed and discarded her. She had seen enough abandoned women limping on through life, hobbled, by their jealousy and bitterness, to the man who had left them behind, and unable to strike out on their own. Unless she could cut it away, she would never be free of him. She had to learn not to care in order to stand alone.

Sitting there amongst the packing cases, drinking too much, she felt she had achieved this distance and had the scars to prove it. Sex, she found with relief, was no longer a weapon in his armoury. She could do without it. She could ignore his message, put it aside. She was not going to allow him to follow her here. Garden Cottage was the beginning of a new life.

Later, as she was cleaning her teeth in the bathroom before going to bed, Lila telephoned from New York, her voice trembling. 'Mum? I got the email. I can't bear thinking about him. Poor, poor Dad. I mean, what is this prison like? Will he be locked up all the time? I really want to come back over and see him. I've just written to him now. David gave me the address. He said he was being fantastic. Really dignified.'

Claudia bowed her head and listened. When there was a pause she said, 'Lila, darling, it would be much better to stay where you are and write him cheerful news. It's important to Dad to know that you are out of it all, busy in New York. It won't help him to have you weeping over him in prison and him unable to do anything. It's being powerless he's going to find the hardest thing.'

There was a pause while Lila considered. 'Yeah, I can see that,' she conceded but there was resentment in her voice. Claudia braced herself for the attack she felt sure was coming.

'But he hasn't got anyone else, has he?' Lila's voice rose. 'You've completely let him down, Mum, just when he needed his family most, and Aunt Min's always been on your side. You've seen to that.'

Claudia did not respond. It had become a familiar theme. She allowed her daughter to rail on.

'Sorry, Lila,' she said finally. 'I can see that it's hard, but you will have to accept that he left me. Not the other way round. I'm afraid there is no going back. I would be no good to him. It's better for us both this way.'

'Better for you, you mean. Can't you forgive him, Mum? He really needs you now.'

'Lila, I don't think that's true. He's got Carla, for one thing, and forgiveness doesn't come into it. There's no point in us arguing like this. I know how upsetting this is for you, darling, but remember, I'm here in Dorset and there's a room for you, always. It's important you know that. If you feel you really must come back and see him, come here.'

'Do you really think I would? It would seem as though I was taking your side. He told me that he begged you to meet the press with him but you wouldn't. You wouldn't stand by him.'

Claudia sighed. She must be patient. 'Please, Lila. He had left me. He was living with someone else. It was a charade he wanted. I couldn't do it.'

'Oh, I knew you would say that,' Lila cut in impatiently. 'Playing the injured party. Dad was just that sort of man, Mum. You must have known it from the start. Like all these powerful, charismatic men. Look at JFK. Look at Clinton. Dad needed women, but he was always for *us*. He was always for the family, and that meant you, too. You know that. These other women – they were just trash to him. He would have come back to you.'

'Some of what you say is perfectly true, darling. But you don't for one moment consider me. How he made me feel.'

'Here, we go!' said Lila bitterly. 'I'm supposed to be feeling sorry for you, am I? Well, I'm not. Not one bit. It's Dad I'm sorry for,' and there was a loud snuffling and sniffing.

'There's no need to take sides,' said Claudia calmly. 'I'm glad that you support him. It will mean a lot to him.'

Lila gulped. 'Sorry, Mum. I'm sorry. I'm just so *upset* by all of this. It's so terrible.'

'That's why we have to stick together.'

'Yes. You're right. I just wish you'd try again with him. Anyway, how are you, Mum? How's the horrible bung, as Minna calls it?'

'Not horrible at all,' said Claudia stoutly. 'I really like it, and I'm fine, darling. I'm fine.'

Poor Lila, so much her father's daughter, his golden girl. No wonder she idolised him. Claudia believed her impatience with the young men who attempted to love her was because they could not match up to Roger. They never lasted for long before they were rejected as pathetic or sad. 'God, Mum,' she would exclaim, explaining the fate of the latest casualty. 'He needed a nanny. I just couldn't be bothered with him.' Lila was lovely, too, tall and strong and golden, but Claudia knew she looked tougher than she really was and that the last few months had been terribly painful. She was better off in New York, a big, open-minded unshockable city, where Roger's notoriety would not be held against her. It would be easier for her there.

Jerome. What of him? Claudia missed him and longed for the comfort he would have been to her now. Only nineteen but wise beyond his years; tall, brown-haired, fine-featured, he was the opposite of Roger. Her son, who bore the imprint of her features and who would instinctively support and understand her. 'Just as well he's away,' she said into the dark, 'or I would have used him. I couldn't have helped it. I would have burdened him with all this mess. When he comes home I must be stronger, braver. I can't let him see me like this.'

Claudia lay in bed while the village slept. The last drinkers had left The Bugle hours earlier, the headlights of those driving home to Bishops Barton sweeping over the crumpled bonnet of her car where it remained abandoned in the gateway, silvered over now by the light of the full moon.

There was no point in trying to sleep. She was wide awake, staring open-eyed into the darkness. She got out of bed and drew back the curtain and opened the window. The night air brought her the scent of lime blossom and the brightness of the moon surprised her. The trees in the garden were cast with silver into mysterious shapes, standing in pools of black. She went through to the kitchen and switched on the light to fill the kettle and make a cup of tea. The night sky, framed in the window, turned back into a dark square.

Claudia unlocked the back door and went out in her bare feet and pyjamas. The grass was cool and damp. Beyond her barrier of trees she saw the moon with all its shadowy continents and seas, sailing as round as a silver coin in the starry sky. Across the lane the roofs of the cottages were white, the thatches sleek and shining like the pelts of crouching beasts. It was very still. Claudia felt as if she were the only living soul astir. Then, very faintly, from the dark house next door, came the sound of breaking glass.

Chapter Two

When Julia Durnford set off on her marmalade mission she was motivated by curiosity, and she was not ashamed to admit it. Anybody moving into the village was of general interest to her, more particularly so when right next door and a woman of her own age. She had glimpsed her new neighbour once or twice already and was struck by her tall, slim figure and shoulder-length hair, unusual on someone in her forties. Now she had met her face to face she recognised Claudia as the type of woman who had a certain distinction, regardless of age or class; an indefinable quality which set her apart from the commonplace. Perhaps it was in the fine bones of the face, which was neither pretty nor conventionally beautiful, but certainly compelling, with its high cheekbones, wide mouth and deep-set, far-apart eyes. The nose was too long and narrow, the eyes ringed in dark shadows, the hair, now that Julia was close enough to notice, streaked with silver. She carried herself in the old-fashioned manner of the deportment class, very tall and straight, and had a way of moving that was poised and deliberate. Dressed in a thin pair of loose cotton trousers the colour of redcurrants and a black T-shirt, she managed to look both glamorous and careless.

Julia, who was not unobservant, saw all this and was made vaguely uneasy. She herself had to work hard on her appearance, take trouble with make-up and hair and the choice of clothes to achieve what she thought of as a halfway decent result. Peter, her husband, jokingly called it 'scrubbing up' when she got out of gardening clothes and painted her nails and put on her inherited bits and pieces of unfashionable jewellery in order to go to a 'do' at her daughter's school, or some other social function. The end result, Julia knew, was perfectly acceptable and conformed to a dress code endorsed by the English countrywoman, but lacked any verve or flair, both of which rather alarmed her in others. It was unnerving to have a

19

neighbour who, she saw at a glance, displayed these qualities. Not in a thousand years would she have chosen to wear those old drawstring trousers in that shade of red. She had learned by now the type of flat-fronted, straight-legged trews that suited her and bought four pairs each year from an up-market catalogue. But Claudia had looked wonderful, graceful and feminine. And her shrunken black T-shirt emphasised a small, girlish bosom and slender waist. Julia was only comfortable in polo shirts in the summer, in various pretty, fresh colours, but how boxy and square she had felt beside Claudia. And her new neighbour's feet – slim and brown with pale, unpainted toenails in simple black sandals, so much more alluring than her own, with their neglected corns and calluses, shoved, as usual, into her every-day, second-best deck shoes.

She was sexy, this woman. That was it, thought Julia. Not in the sort of brash, obvious, big-tits-in-tight-T-shirt style of *The Sun*, but in the seductive, knowing, elusive way of foreign women. It was rather disturbing to have such a woman next door, although when she thought about it, she did not quite see why. After all, there were really no comparisons to be drawn between them, and it was she, Julia, who was the established one, living in the most important house in the village and having been born and brought up there.

It was easy to hand over the marmalade and be friendly and welcoming and at the same time establish a bit about the newcomer. From the way Claudia spoke and her assured manner, Julia put her in the same social class as herself, in which case it was odd that she should choose to live in quite such an unprepossessing bungalow with apparent equanimity. However, since the Lloyds crash, Julia knew several people who had fallen on hard times, and it was in this category that she decided she would place her new neighbour. She did not at all mind the briskness with which she was shown to the gate. In a village one should try to avoid the habit of prolonged chatting and dawdling, and anyway she had seen all she needed for the time being. She would report to Peter this evening and then take care to make Claudia Knight feel at home in what Julia thought of as her village.

And it really was her village, she thought, as she walked back to her own house, through the iron gates, up the drive and round to the back door. Living here, in East End House, the most distinguished house in the village, brought with it certain responsibilities and duties. Her mother had run the Mother's

Union and initiated the Wednesday Club for old people. She had opened the fete and organised the Flower Club and in many other ways underpinned village life. But things were so different then, thought Julia. In her youth there had been two daily cleaning women, dusting and polishing, Florrie, the cook, and a girl who came in to do the ironing, and at least two men to do the outside work.

These days, Julia ran the place almost single-handed. She had Star Bishop, whom she considered a rather bolshie young woman, who arrived in a car with her own up-to-the-minute vacuum cleaner and cleaned, after a fashion, twice a week. She banged the Hoover into the furniture and refused to empty wastepaper baskets, while Julia bit her tongue and said nothing, for fear Star would walk out and she would never find a replacement. Peter did the grass on his sit-on mower, and there was old Tom, from the village, who did the digging and some planting, but he was over seventy, slow and arthritic.

Recently Julia had felt burdened by the village responsibilities, which because of her position she saw as her duty to take on. She already did flowers for the church once a month and opened her own garden to the public in August. She was chairman of the Village Hall Committee, albeit reluctantly, because there appeared to be no one else willing to take on the job, and had recently been made secretary of the local branch of the Pony Club. She felt she had to do her bit while her daughter, Victoria, now sixteen, was still so keen on her riding, and as Julia explained to Peter, the longer she preferred ponies to boys, the better.

Things were frantic during the holidays when Jim, her son, was home from Durham University and Victoria back from boarding school. Julia tried to fit in tennis and bridge with her girlfriends and there was her Decorative Arts Society to keep up with. Often she felt she was chasing her tail, as she complained to Peter. Being up to ninety, he called it, and he was right. Hardly time to draw breath. She did not see why Claudia should not get involved. She would have plenty of time on her hands and something useful to do would make her feel less lonely and, of course, she should be aware of the need to contribute to one's community.

Getting something for supper out of the freezer and peering into its icy depths, Julia began to plan a little party. She needed to use up the salmon which had been loitering there for months. She would get Peter to rack his brains for a single man to make up the numbers and she would invite Claudia. Once Claudia had been a guest in East End House, she would appreciate Julia's position, understand where she and Peter stood in the scheme of things. After the cramped confines of the bungalow, the gracious rooms and good furniture and paintings would not go unnoticed and it would give Julia the opportunity to remark that three generations of her family had lived there. That will put her fairly in the picture, she thought, as well as being a neighbourly gesture.

Standing with a lasagne in her hands, she wondered whether it would not be wasted when there was only herself and Peter for supper. It would come in useful in the holidays when the children needed ballast, and Peter had complained the other day that he was putting on weight. She could put it back in the freezer and make him an omelette instead. There were some lettuces in the garden ready to cut, and he could have a salad.

Going back outside, she spied old Tom needlessly digging in the far border and sent him off to spray the roses for greenfly again instead; then with a knife and a basket, followed by Skye, her Border terrier, she worked her way down the rows of the vegetable garden. Things were coming along well. The peas would be ready soon, and the second early potatoes. Both would go nicely with the salmon. There should be some raspberries too. Perhaps she would make a summer pudding.

Straightening up from cutting two lettuces, Julia looked across the wall to the roof of the bungalow. It was still an aggravation, an eyesore, but that was hardly Claudia's fault. Peter had done everything he could to buy the plot and then everything to block planning permission, but that wily old bitch, Valerie Pomeroy, turned him down flat, and then put up such a persuasive case for infilling that it had gone through. It never ceased to rankle, even now, twelve years on. Poor old Major Burnside, who had bought it, had been all right. It was not as if Julia resented him personally. It was the spoiling of their end of the village she cared about, the encroachment on their own property, the feeling of suburbia to have neighbours so close. She had never forgiven Valerie and never would.

Later that evening, Peter Durnford, tall, balding and mild-mannered, was disappointed with the omelette. Coming home later than usual from his Dorchester office, and with only a grabbed sandwich to sustain him at lunchtime, he felt uncharacteristically aggrieved. Really, he thought, Julia's at home all day with bugger all to do, you would think she could rustle up something a bit more substantial. To compensate, he opened a rather good bottle of wine and drank most of it himself. Because it annoyed Julia, he spread the newspaper on the supper table and read the television guide, checking on the evening's viewing. He looked forward to a slump after dinner. Julia was banging on about supper parties, trying to get him to settle on a date to ask round the new woman next door. Peter pushed his glasses up his nose and helped himself pointedly to more bread.

'She's rather attractive, actually,' said Julia. 'About my age, I should think. Divorced with two children. Nineteen and twenty-two, I think she said, but they're both abroad. Peter! Are you listening?'

Peter had lost interest. He did not find women of his wife's age attractive. Not compared to what he called the hot totty who came and went as disgracefully inept secretaries in the solicitor's office where he was senior partner.

'Not really,' he said. 'You get on and organise it if you want. My diary's in my briefcase.' He stood up and, carrying the newspaper and leaving the remains of supper on the table, went through to the sitting room to watch *Big Brother*.

Julia sat on, annoyed. Peter could be maddening, and so selfish. It never occurred to him to offer to help. He did not seem to realise just how hard she worked, running this house and garden. Crossly, she slammed the plates into the dishwasher and turned on the tap of the sink. The water gushed fiercely onto the cutlery in the bowl. She was buggered if she was going to make him coffee.

Peter collapsed in his armchair, unconcerned, a whisky in his hand. The hostile atmosphere did not bother him. At least it meant he would be left in peace. Later he went to sleep where he sat and woke with a stiff neck long after Julia had gone to bed. She seemed to have left lights on and the back door open, which was irritating because he considered the routine they referred to as Last Thing to be her territory. He shuffled about switching things off and turfing Skye into the garden. He had a pee himself outside the back door. It was an amazingly bright night, the moon bleaching the garden with white light and filling dark pools of shadow.

On his way up the stairs he stopped on the half-landing where there was a long uncurtained window through which the moonlight flooded. From up here, his eye glanced over the wall, drawn perhaps by a movement from next door. Although the bungalow was mostly hidden, a section of the front garden was in view and a tall woman was standing on the grass, in what looked like pyjamas, barefooted, looking up at the sky. She appeared frozen in white light, like a graceful marble statue. Peter stood still, suddenly alert and interested. So this was the woman Julia was going on about. What the hell was she up to? Watching her like this was oddly arousing, secretive and furtive as it was. Like so many of the middle-aged women he saw in his professional capacity, she was clearly unhinged, wandering about in the garden in the middle of the night. Dear, oh dear. Frustrated probably. Either that, or pre-menstrual. Peter, who knew little about women and cared less, believed these two conditions provided a satisfactory explanation for most eccentric female behaviour. Or menopausal, of course. Although she looked a bit too young for that.

Fascinated, he continued to watch as she turned her head to look over the village, and then sharply, as if she had been surprised by something, towards the dark mass which was Valerie Pomeroy's house. A moment later she turned and went swiftly indoors.

Peter Durnford continued on his way to bed, where Julia lay far over on her side, snoring slightly, and managing, even in her sleep, to look reproachful.

What Claudia had gone inside to look for was something to put on her feet. The sound of breaking glass had been quite distinct and she felt no option but to check that her elderly neighbour was all right. She had learned from the estate agent that Mrs Pomeroy was in her seventies and lived alone. There was no point whatever in telephoning the police. She had discovered that the nearest manned station was over thirty miles away. Rapid response was not a feature of life here. She could go across the lane and knock at the door of one of the cottages, but she shied away from disturbing strangers for what might seem a flight of fancy on her part. No, it was up to her, and she was not surprised to discover she had little fear for her own safety. Bumping along the bottom of life, as she felt she had been lately, had left her with a careless disregard for what once might have seemed frightening.

Slipping on her sandals, she took up a hammer which she found in the garage, more as an aid to gaining entrance than as a weapon, and hurried to the door which led from her back garden into the rear of Mrs Pomeroy's property. The gate had clearly not been used for a long time and was grown over with vegetation and its hinges rusted. Claudia lifted the latch and pushed. The top part gave way and bowed inwards but the lower portion stuck fast in the frame. Shit, she thought, and tried again, this time simultaneously pushing with her shoulder and kicking the bottom to try and free it. The door groaned but would not give. Standing back, Claudia hammered the bottom edge sharply several times and then tried again. She was making so much noise that any intruder would be warned off, which was just as well. This time she was able to force it open a few inches and by pushing at the top to widen the gap, managed to slip through to the other side.

The moonlight gave her a clear view of the house which appeared to be in darkness. The drive to the front was empty and still. Claudia froze, listening. Nothing. No steps on the gravel, no sign of life. Relieved, she thought that having got so far she should take a closer look. As far as she knew, the old girl lived alone and there was always the risk that she might have fallen, breaking glass as she went.

The garden was neglected and long matted weeds and briars caught her legs as she grasshopped towards the house. The windows on either side of the front door looked into formal unused rooms – a drawing room on one side, a dining room on the other. Claudia worked her way round to the back, where there was an outcrop of domestic offices, and peered through what she realised was the kitchen window. She was about to turn away when something caught her attention. Although the room was unlit, the moonlight flooded the stone-flagged floor and illuminated a scene of domestic chaos. A large table over-flowed with clutter, which had also collected on the floor beneath. The sink under the window was full of pans and dishes, as were the draining boards on either side. An old-fashioned dresser on the opposite wall was similarly over-burdened. All this Claudia took in, while her attention was focused on a dark shape near the door. She was sure it was a human figure slumped on the floor, and the droop of the shoulders and lolling of the head spurred her to hasten round the corner to find a way in.

Valerie Pomeroy was drunk, but not so drunk that she was unaware of a woman kneeling beside her, sloshing cold water on her face, and speaking loudly into her ear. She lifted her head which felt as large and woody as a turnip and said, 'Who the hell are you?'

'Your neighbour. I live next door. You've cut your hand. It looks as if you fell on this broken glass.'

'Bugger.' Valerie looked down at the hand the woman was holding up to her. She felt nothing but saw a splash of red. 'Shove it under the tap. Nothing serious. How did I get down here?'

'I imagine you fell. Slipped.' Claudia was trying to be tactful. The woman on the floor was clearly drunk. The remains of a cut-glass tumbler were scattered in shards around her. She was a large lump, mountainous even, in a green cardigan and stretch trousers – her legs stuck out in front, her puffy feet still secure in Velcro fastened sandals. Claudia wondered how she could get her up.

'Don't know you. Never clapped eyes on you before,' said Valerie, peering up at her. 'How did you get in?'

'The door was open. I heard the glass breaking. Look, this bottle has broken too. That's what I heard.' Claudia stirred the shattered remains of a green gin bottle with her foot. 'If I get behind you, I'll put my arms under yours and try and give you a hoik up. I don't think you've broken anything. Are you ready?'

'Perfectly all right where I am. Bloody interference.'

'Well, I want to go back to bed and I can't leave you here. You would be on my conscience. I'll just get you into that armchair.' Claudia indicated a sagging chair piled with newspapers. She moved them onto the floor. 'Come on,' and from behind she slid her arms under the woman's armpits and heaved. The body she was holding felt soft and bloated and very, very heavy. She wanted to laugh and thought, I mustn't. I'm getting hysterical.

Valerie Pomeroy's feet scrabbled at the floor as she came off the ground and in a moment she was able to catch at the edge of the table and heave herself unsteadily upright. With both hands flat on the table she rested her weight and looked at Claudia through small, bloodshot eyes. It was the look of a dog about to bite. Her face hung in folds round her mouth and sagging chin. Her short white hair was madly awry. Claudia noticed, with surprise, that her fingernails were manicured and varnished red and her hands sparkled with some impressive rings.

'Bloody, bloody nerve,' Valerie said, glaring.

'Come on. Get into this chair and then I can go home.' Claudia took her arm but was thrown off. Valerie made her own way round the table and then transferred her hold to the back of the chair before collapsing lopsidedly into it.

Claudia went to the sink and, ignoring the mess, rinsed out a bowl and filled it with water.

'Have you any antiseptic? Dettol, or something?'

'Bugger off!'

'Here. Put your hand in this. We need to see if the cut is deep. There may still be glass in it.' She found a reasonably clean roller towel on the back of the door and proceeded to wash the wound, crouching beside the old woman's knees.

Valerie looked down at the top of her brown head and repeated in a less aggressive tone, more puzzled than cross, 'Do I know you?'

'No,' said Claudia, 'You don't.'

Gently, Valerie lowered her hand on the bowed head and absently stroked the soft hair. Claudia froze. It was a long time since anyone had touched her. Horrified, she felt a rush of emotion, a great uncontrollable mass of grief and pity and sadness and despair. Dropping her head into the old woman's lap, she wept for the first time since her husband had left her.

Waking the next morning with sunshine a square block on her bedroom floor, Claudia felt weighted down by dread. What had she done? What an appalling way to behave, to blub on the lap of a stranger. Thank God the disagreeable old woman was drunk and possibly would not remember. Claudia's loss of control was, fortunately, brief. Of course, she had drunk quite a bit herself – nearly a bottle of wine during the evening – and Mrs Pomeroy had taken her by surprise. That sudden absent-minded touch, like a parent stroking the hair of a child or a dog owner caressing a pet's ear, had caught her unawares. This unselfconscious gesture had, for a moment, undone her, and she had surrendered, like a hurt child giving itself up to be comforted.

She had recovered quickly, sniffed, wiped her nose on her pyjama sleeve, got up and emptied the basin – the second time she had dealt with bloodied water in one day, her own injury now forgotten – and put the kettle on the Aga. Mrs Pomeroy slumped back in the chair with her eyes shut. Claudia had been going to make tea, but glancing at the unconscious figure, gently snoring with mouth open, changed her mind. She would leave now while the going was good. Cut and run before she got involved. She took the kettle off the hotplate and shut the lid of the Aga. She closed the kitchen door quietly behind her, ran across the garden to the gate, climbed back through and was in her bed in a matter of minutes. She pulled the duvet around her and hunched up in a miserable ball. Utterly exhausted, she was asleep instantly.

Now, horridly awake, various unravelled thoughts crowded through her mind, each asking to be examined, sorted out, dealt with. Bloody hell, she heard an interior voice moan, and she wanted to put her head under the duvet and become oblivious, inanimate, a vegetable person that needed to be taken care of, wheeled away, treated kindly and firmly by competent people in charge.

I've got to get all this sorted out, she told herself sternly. I must think clearly. What would Minna do in this sort of situation? First of all, think about last night. There was a good chance that Mrs Pomeroy would wake this morning, surprised to find herself sitting in her kitchen armchair, her memory of the night before a blank. There need be no explanations and Claudia's moment of weakness would remain her secret. But it had taught her something. She could not allow herself to behave like that again, or she was done for.

If she was to make a fresh start, to leave behind the gossip and speculation which she had lived with in London, she must not give herself away. Here in this sleepy village she was just an ordinary, single, middle-aged woman, of no interest to anyone, and she wanted to keep it that way.

Her car. She must think about that. Yesterday she had walked away in panic, which was stupid. She should not have asked the young man to move it for her and this morning she must make the necessary arrangements to get it towed away and looked at in a garage with a view to getting it mended. Then there was the problem of cost and if her insurance would pay. She must search for the policy and discover what sort of cover she had. One of the advantages of being married to a man like Roger had been that he had dealt with these sort of details. I'm woefully ignorant, thought Claudia. I've been sheltered all my life. Now I have to learn to stand on my own feet. There's no reason why I can't manage perfectly well when I've got the hang of things. It was just that Roger didn't want me to. He liked keeping me in a state of dependence.

One thing was obvious and that was that living in the village without transport was impossible, so getting back on the road was first priority. She remembered when Roger smashed his car, somehow or other a replacement had been provided while the repairs were being carried out. That was what she would have to organise. So the first thing to do was find the insurance policy, which in turn meant making a start on unpacking the boxes.

Yesterday, when she had had the accident, she had been on her way back from Sharston where she had gone to photocopy some documents she was required to enclose with a job application form. Then, standing in the queue in the post office, she had found she had left the form at home. It was maddening, this absent-mindedness, and that was why she had been driving home in a fury.

The letter was still unposted and the copies of the originals were either in her bag or left on the seat of the car. Damn. She must find them at once and make sure that the application went off this morning. The first collection from the letter box in the main street was ten o'clock, so she had plenty of time.

She glanced at her watch. It was half past seven. She was surprised that she had slept so long. Recently she had been waking at dawn and was well-acquainted with the dread, dead hours of a sleepless early morning when the World Service occupied the air waves and only the early shift workers were out on the roads.

She must get up. She had things to do. Padding about in her pyjamas, she looked for her bag – an artful designer straw, shaped like a dog with a red felt tongue. She used to think it witty, but now it seemed ridiculous and she did not want to think how much it had cost, or how differently she would spend the hundred odd pounds.

Thank goodness the papers were there and the application form in its envelope was in the hall. She must have put it down on her way out when she was looking for her keys. Picking it up now, she noticed that her handwriting looked strange. Whereas it used to be round and bold and confident, it now looked cramped and angular. No doubt a graphologist would make something of that.

She had seen the advertisement for the job in the local free paper – a small mine of information which came out on a Friday. The sort of situations vacant to be found within its pages had given her hope. Mushroom pickers needed, egg collectors, unskilled helpers for old people's homes, skivvies in pubs and restaurants – all her sort of work, as David Rowntree had pointed out when she had asked his advice about what sort of employment she should seek now that she no longer had Roger to support her. She had ringed those that she considered possibilities. She discounted anything too far away which would cost too much in petrol and others which suggested cosy situations to which she did not wish to be exposed. She wanted to be able to keep her distance – do the work, take the money, no questions asked. There were several which might suit. A small, rather grand hotel wanted reception staff, a private girls' school wanted a matron, and a local primary school wanted a cook.

Although she had ringed the hotel, it made her slightly uneasy. The owner, to whom a handwritten letter of application had to be addressed, had a double-barrelled name which stirred a faint recollection of some of Roger's racing friends, a syndicate of owners, amongst whom she had heard either him, or his hotel, mentioned.

The girls' school presented the same problem. It would take her back into the social world she wanted to escape but the primary school would be different and it had the huge advantage of being in the next village. She wondered whether she would be considered properly qualified to do this sort of work. Probably not. She suspected that these days one had to go to a college and learn about nutrition and hygiene and Health and Safety, but it was worth a try. Cooking was the only area in which she had any real experience. It was what she had done until Lila was born, working with a schoolfriend in a small catering company in London, but that was years ago.

Fetching the local paper, Claudia read the advertisement for the school cook again. It came under the heading of Dorset County Council, but the replies were to be directed to the head teacher. It said nothing about qualifications, just 'experienced cook wanted'. In a way it sounded terrifying. Would she be up to it? She imagined wearing a white hairnet and overall, dishing out trays of shepherd's pie and vats of cabbage to lines of small children, each holding out an empty plate.

It had been a problem sorting out references, but she had eventually used the headmaster of her own children's prep school who had known her for years and who said that he was happy to write her a glowing character reference, and dear Felicity, the old friend who was still running the same catering company which was now most successful and employing over twenty people. She told Claudia that she had read the papers and had been horrified by Roger's trial and imprisonment and had been wondering how Claudia was coping. 'I'm glad to be of help,' she said. 'There's always a job back here with me, you know. You were a bloody good cook once.'

'I was once,' said Claudia. 'That just about sums it up. It's sweet of you, Felicity, but I'm trying to organise a new life down here in the country. A fresh start. Anyway, I don't think it would be at all suitable to have the wife of a man convicted of high-level fraud passing round the canapés at City parties.'

Ah, well. The primary school was worth a try. Apparently there were only two left in Dorset which still offered pupils cooked lunches. If she didn't get the job, then she would go mushroom picking. She imagined a dark polytunnel, pungent with the smell of fungi, with the little pale domes of button mushrooms poking through the compost. There couldn't be much skill needed and she had seen the white transit van collecting women pickers from the village in the early morning. At least the transport problem would be taken care of.

Collecting her clothes, Claudia went to run a bath. She found it hard not to think of Major Burnside in the bathroom. It was here that she felt his presence more than anywhere else. It was partly the disabled handrails, the fading cream paint and the plastic bath streaked and stained a dirty, septic green by a dripping tap. It was an old man's bathroom. She had even found a rusting razor in the cupboard. The floor was covered with cracking yellow vinyl tiles marbled with veins of red, as if a corpse had recently been dismembered after a grisly murder. She imagined the Major's once a week ritual, switching on the electric fire up on the wall, getting a good fug up, running a steamy bath and, with a tumbler of whisky balanced on the edge of the tub, lowering his old body into the water.

Claudia was grateful for her ridiculously expensive bath oil – she still had one bottle left – and her big fluffy bath towels, both of which helped to dispel this unfortunate image. This will be the first thing I do, she thought as she lay back in the scented foam, if I get a job. I'll buy some paint and do this bathroom up. Put a carpet on the floor. Make it look less like an abattoir. That will be a start.

She dressed carelessly in yesterday's trousers and T-shirt and made herself a strong pot of coffee. Extravagant probably, but coffee was her kickstart, what got her on the road every morning. Nursing her cup, she sat at the kitchen table and looked about her. The kitchen was all right – square and featureless, with old-fashioned units, but it had a large window and a door which opened onto the walled garden at the back. She sat now with the door open. It must have rained later in the night; there was a smell of damp earth and the sweet scent of roses and honeysuckle which grew rampantly over the walls. The sun shone from a washed-looking pale sky. It was very quiet, but overlaying the silence and the birdsong came the drone of the insects and the distant sound of sheep.

For the first time in many weeks Claudia felt a sense of peace. It's OK, she thought. I am really OK here. Lucky to be in such a beautiful place with my things around me. Lucky that the children are all right. Lucky that I am fit and well and able to look for work. Lucky to be able to sit here and enjoy the sun and this wonderful privacy. She could not help but think of Roger, swept along by now in the prison routine – slopping out, or whatever they called it, or performing some mundane task in a workshop, while she could sit by an open door, making decisions about her life. When she had finished her coffee, she would walk to the postbox and then go and look at her car. Later she might ask Julia Durnford if she knew the name of a reliable garage which might undertake the necessary repairs. Then she would start unpacking some of the boxes.

She put her cup and saucer in the sink and rinsed them. How pretty the Provençal china was. She had chosen the pattern years ago when Roger had been made chairman of his City finance company and they had bought the cottage in Oxfordshire. She thought it would look right in the country. Now she felt she was looking at it properly for the first time, appreciating the cheerful, naïve colours, the bold handpainting. Just setting it on the draining board lifted the dull kitchen, made it glow a bit.

She tried to think back. Had she been happy then? Having money made everything easy, of course. All her childhood the lack of it had been a constant backdrop to family life, a permanent anxiety which ate away at her parents. She remembered how her mother had tipped her purse out on the kitchen table, counting the last penny, making calculations about what they could afford to eat for the rest of the week. It was hard to make ends meet on a clergyman's stipend if one had her mother's notions of gentility. Married to Roger she never had to worry about paying bills.

Roger had wanted the cottage because it was near the children's prep school and she remembered happy weekends, taking out Lila and Jerome. If Roger came too, and he often did in the early years, they ate out and whirled about doing things, which Lila loved. If it was just her, they had quieter days, pottering about in the garden, making bonfires, eating off their knees. They had been good times, she knew that. The last years, when things had changed, cast long shadows back over the past, making her sometimes feel sadly that her marriage had always been a hollow affair, which she knew was not the case. It was important for her, and especially for the children, not to write it off as a disaster from the start.

The rot set in later, when Roger had become so successful and the solid things upon which she thought they had built their lives started to shift and crack until she could not rely on them any more.

With a start, Claudia who had been staring, unseeing, out at the garden, heard the crunch of gravel as a vehicle drew up and then the opening and slamming of a door. Peering furtively out of the window she saw a battered Land Rover parked outside, with a collie in the back, and the next moment there was a ring at the chiming doorbell. There was no time to hide.

Shit, she thought. Who the hell is this?

Rosco Bishop, pale, thin, gangly without being tall, got off the school bus and looked about for his mate Sean. They had arranged to meet just outside the school gates and when the coast was clear, skive off for the day. In his trouser pocket he'd got some fags and the ten quid note that he'd earned last Saturday off Monica, down at The Bugle in Court Barton, for clipping the hedge at the back of the pub.

The other children got off the bus and streamed across the car park and into school. Rosco hung back, his skateboard under his arm, a T-shirt in his bag ready to replace his school uniform. He didn't want no more trouble with his social worker for non-attendance. His mum, Star, she went ballistic when the Social came down on her. Where the hell was Sean? The teachers were arriving in their crappy old cars and would notice him.

Last night, while his mum was in the Nag's Head in Sharston, he and Sean had been out down the old railway track on Sean's bike. It was great, revving it up and flying across the rutted ground and skidding to a halt where there was a heap of gravel dumped to stop the travellers. Not that it did any good. There were vans down there again. A van and an old bus, anyway. The tinker kid went to the primary in Bishops Barton. Funny little thing she was, but fuck, she could ride. He'd seen her on the black and white horse of hers, fair flying along. Took some guts to ride like that. Bareback too.

After, he and Sean had hidden round the lanes looking for the car his mum had told him about. She'd helped get it off the road after some dozy woman driver had smashed it into a tractor. Sean reckoned there might be something worth nicking – but there wasn't. Just a load of old junk. Not even a decent radio. Where the bloody hell was Sean? If he didn't turn up soon he'd have to go in to school. He couldn't stand out here much longer. It was like having letters stamped across his forehead, reading 'Truant'. Ah! Here he was, shambling along, grinning his head off.

'Where you been, yer wanker?'

'Whaddyer mean, mate? Yer windy bugger. It's not nine o'clock yet. Where we gonner go then? Any ideas?' Sean, big and heavy and slow, his face blemished by a fresh crop of acne, rubbed his spade of a hand over his shaved head.

'Let's have a fag behind the precinct.'

Together they sloped away from the school gates and cut down the chainlinked footpath that led to the town. The day stretched long and pointless in front of the two boys but at least it was better than school

Chapter Three

When Peter Durnford went downstairs the following morning, Julia was up as usual. A load of washing was already churning in the machine in the scullery and Julia was sitting at the kitchen table wearing her reading glasses and looking at the *Telegraph*, while Radio Four droned in the background. Peter turned it off and sat down opposite her where she had sketchily laid a place for breakfast. She looked at him over her glasses.

'Egg?' she said.

'No thanks.' Peter was aware that he had drunk too much the night before. His head felt thick and ached dully. 'I'll just have toast.'

Julia got up and he took the opportunity of removing the newspaper from her side of the table and taking it for himself. She slammed two slices of bread in the toaster and put the kettle back on the Aga hotplate. The atmosphere between them was cordial, the discord of the previous evening now in the past. The tenor of their marriage was even, neither of them inclined to harbour differences, nor to experience either emotional highs or lows. Chugging along was how Julia thought of it.

The kettle boiled and she poured the hot water on the ground coffee in the cafetiere and pushed it across to her husband. Peter grunted and a few moments later reached from behind the paper to pour himself a cup. He could hear Julia unpacking the dishwasher. He cleared his throat and said casually, 'Did you find a date for that party?'

'What party?' asked Julia, her voice sounding compressed as she bent to collect the plates.

'That dinner party. Or supper. Or whatever it was.'

Julia stood up. 'What, you mean for Mrs Next Door? No, I didn't. I didn't get round to it. Have you got your diary? We could do it now.'

'In my briefcase,' said Peter, going behind the paper again. Julia would think it odd if he seemed too interested.

Julia went out into the hall and came back with Peter's old-fashioned briefcase, which had once belonged to his father. 'Here,' she said, plonking it down by his feet.

Peter went on reading. He left it several minutes before he put the paper aside and bent down to open the case and take out his small black diary. He put it on the table. 'There,' he said, picking the paper up again, but Julia had gone. He heard her opening the door of the washing machine.

'What?' she shouted from the scullery.

'Here. Here's my diary.'

'Hang on.'

Really, she could be maddening. Peter buttered his toast and reached for the marmalade. He thought about the woman he had seen the night before. There was something about her which excited and intrigued him. Perhaps it was the moonlight which had given her that mysterious allure, or perhaps it was just the idea of a youngish woman living on her own next door. He was used to old Major Burnside, eighty-four when he finally went into a home, with his bloodshot eyes and stained moustache.

Julia went outside to hang out the washing. Peter finished his toast and stood up. He could not appear too keen. He collected his jacket from the hall and picked up his car keys. He put his diary back in his case and went to the door.

'I'm off!' he called.

'Hang on!' Julia called back. 'I'll be in in a minute.' She was not being deliberately slow. Just slow. It was all part of the balancing act between Peter and herself. The necessity not to feel at his beck and call, sometimes even to be unhelpful.

'Can't. Must go. Goodbye. Give me a ring.'

Julia heard his car start and then swing down the drive. She stood under the washing line with a pair of his underpants in her hand. Victoria had given them to her father for Christmas and they were blue with little bunches of green holly with red berries. How odd, she thought. Just from his manner of leaving she knew he was irritated by her not getting on with finding a supper date. He was not usually that keen on entertaining. She pegged his pants on the line where they fluttered brightly in the breeze. Perhaps he was bored, going through that restless stage one was always hearing about. Turning to go inside, her attention was caught by the rose which tumbled over a trellis by the path. No longer thinking about her husband, she hurried off to examine Gertrude Jeykell for signs of scab.

At the bottom of the drive, Peter looked left and right before turning into the lane. He drove very slowly past the bungalow and was annoyed to see that the woman already had a visitor. Anthony Brewer's Land Rover was parked outside. What was he doing, sniffing around? he thought crossly. And at this time of the morning. Julia had annoyed him by being uncooperative but she was not going to provoke him into displaying more interest than was normal. He wasn't going to fall into that trap. He would make a point of not mentioning the supper date again. Then she would get on and fix it up.

Feeling unusually unsettled, he continued on his drive to work. At the last bend before the lane joined the main road he met the tinker's girl cantering along the verge on her black and white horse. She grinned and waved a hand to thank him for slowing down. Her long brown hair whipped behind her and she was riding bareback. Julia would disapprove, he thought. No hat, either. Not at all Pony Club.

The man standing outside the front door made Claudia wish that she had bothered more with her appearance. He was not very tall but square and compact, probably about fifty, with a handsome, rather jowly face. He was extremely suntanned – she could see a deep brown V in the neck of his checked shirt and then tender white skin which had not been exposed to the elements. His sleeves were rolled up and his strong forearms were brown and sinewy, the hairs bleached to a golden fuzz. He wore battered jeans and work boots. Clearly a working man. His eyes were very bright blue and when he took off his cap to speak to her, she saw that his thick, brown hair was going grey at the temples. His voice was a surprise. Claudia did not know what she was expecting – a soft Dorset accent probably – but he sounded rather grand and plummy. Quite an artsy sort of voice, which you might expect to hear talking about opera on Radio Three. The contrast with his appearance was intriguing. To go with the voice, his manner was assured and even slightly patronising.

'Good morning,' he said, and looking at her forehead, went on, 'I hope you've had that attended to.'

Claudia put her hand to the cut. She had forgotten about it. 'Oh, that,' she said, confused.

'It was my chap, Greg, you ran into,' he went on, 'and going far too fast, according to him.'

Claudia felt a nip of anger. She had no need of a lecture.

'Look,' she said, 'I'm really sorry. I did say so at the time, but that enormous tractor takes up the whole lane.'

'Exactly. That's why one has to be able to stop.'

Claudia felt wrong-footed and uncomfortable. She was too old, too tired, too something, to be ticked off on her doorstep by this stranger. The man was looking at her speculatively. She felt herself blushing. Then he smiled. He had good teeth, very white and even, and his broad smile showed them off. He put out a square brown hand.

'Anthony Brewer,' he said. When Claudia took the hand, it was very hard. The palm felt like a piece of old leather, lumpy with calluses.

'Claudia,' she returned, managing a smile. 'Claudia Knight.'

'The important thing is that you weren't hurt. Did you get that head looked at?'

'There was no need. It's nothing. I'm much more worried about the car.'

'Ah. I was coming to that. Now, I don't know what your husband is going to say, but I'm afraid it looks like a write-off. Greg, he's a good lad, you know, got it into Bishops Barton, to the garage. They reckon the axle has gone. Not worth repairing. Your insurance will probably write it off.'

Claudia closed her eyes with an expression of despair.

'Well, it can't be worth much, but they'll give you a few hundred for it, I expect.'

'A few hundred! I paid a thousand only two months ago.' She felt like bursting into tears.

There was a pause and then he said gently, 'I'm sorry to be the bearer of bad news. I was also going to say welcome to the village.'

Claudia put her hand to her forehead. She couldn't think beyond the demise of the car.

There was a pause.

'A bit of a blow, the car?' he asked.

'More than that. A disaster. I don't see how I can replace it.'

They stood together in the weak sunshine, the man watching Claudia's face and Claudia looking at the ground, where her toe worked a hole in the gravel.

'I'm sorry,' she said, looking up and giving her mouth a little sideways twist. 'Thank you, anyway. It was really good of your Greg to deal with it for me. Please thank him. I don't know quite what I would have done.'

She wished he would go but he hung on, seeking further conversation.

'I've got time for a coffee,' he suggested. 'If you need a shoulder to cry on.'

Claudia pulled herself together. 'No. No, really. I'm fine. It's fine. As you say, no one was hurt. That's the important thing.'

He smiled again, not offended, very easy. He leaned an arm on the frame of the door, forming a kind of crook within which Claudia stood.

'All right. Another time. I'm from the farm, Church Farm. If I can help with anything?'

'That's really kind. Thanks. Please thank Greg for me. I'm afraid I wasn't very, um,' she sought for the right word to describe her behaviour, 'businesslike, I suppose. It was the shock, I expect.'

'So he said.' Anthony Brewer's eyes twinkled and he dropped his arm and turned to go. The collie whined in the back of the Land Rover and wove up and down along the grill. He got in and slammed the door and put the gear lever into reverse. Then he seemed to think of something and turned towards her again and slid the window open.

'Are you on your own, Claudia?'

The use of her name sounded intimate, almost suggestive.

'Yes. Yes, I am as it happens.'

He smiled again, held her eyes for a moment. 'You'll enjoy the village,' he said. 'We'll get you round for a drink.' He paused and added with a grin, 'Since you won't give me one.' Looking over his shoulder, he reversed down her drive, and then shot off up the lane with a wave of his hand.

Claudia went back indoors. She felt dreadfully lonely. More than anything she wanted someone to talk to. Someone sensible and clear-headed but she knew she must sort this out on her own. She looked at the envelope on the kitchen table. What was the point of even posting it? Without transport, Bishops Barton was out of reach. How could she have driven so carelessly? It made it worse that she had no one but herself to blame. She picked up the envelope and held it in her hand. She thought of the form, neatly filled in, and the trouble she had gone to in acquiring references. Oh, damn it! She'd post the bloody thing anyway.

It had been tempting to blurt everything out to that man, to be feeble and get him to help her. She could tell he was the capable, managing sort and he had been kind and refrained from asking too many questions. He was attractive, too, fit and healthy. She wished she had not looked quite such a wreck herself. She imagined his wife, back in the kitchen at the farm, making cheese or doing something sensible and practical, pickling onions and potting jam.

The village was utterly silent and deserted as she went to the postbox. The school buses had done their pick-up and the gaggle of mothers who saw their children off were already back inside their houses. Claudia imagined them making beds, Hoovering, picking clothes off the floor, their day stretching before them, planned and predictable. Like mine used to be, she thought.

On her way back she heard the clatter of hooves, and a black and white horse came down the village street towards her. It had a very showy action, throwing up its knees and arching its neck. Claudia stopped as it went past. It was ridden by a skinny girl with long brown hair. It was too big and strong for her, Claudia thought. She looked only about ten and was riding bareback, leaning back, graceful and easy. She grinned at Claudia – a great wide gap-toothed grin. Claudia couldn't help but grin back.

'Hello,' she called out. 'That's a lovely horse!'

The girl pulled up with difficulty. 'Hello,' she shouted back. 'He's me dad's.'

Claudia, ridiculously, found she wanted to talk. 'What's your name?' she asked.

'Jena. What's yours?'

'Claudia. Where are you from?'

Jena laughed. 'I thought you'd know. Everybody does. The railway line. We're travellers.' The horse was bouncing across the road and Jena indicated she must go on. 'Bye!' she called, waving a hand. 'See yer, Claudio!'

Claudia could tell the cheeky little thing felt great up there, steaming along, looking down on everybody she passed, and the horse was splendid, so spirited, and beautifully marked. The pair of them thoroughly cheered her up and the sound of hooves brought clattering life to the silent village.

She had turned back towards the bungalow before it occurred to her. So she wasn't going mad, losing the plot. She remembered where she had seen them before.

Next door, at about the same time, Betty arrived as usual, on her bicycle, to 'do' for Mrs Pomeroy. She let herself in the back door and surveyed the mess in the kitchen. After twenty years it was what she had come to expect. It had been no different when Professor P was alive. 'She's no housekeeper, Betty,' he used to say. 'It's not her forte. Brought up in India, you see. Used to servants.' It was his way of apologising for the state they got in. He couldn't see she might take it wrong, be offended, to be thought of as a servant. She wasn't, mind, because the one thing about Mrs P was that she treated everyone the same – never hoity toity or talking down. 'I'm like a pig in muck, Betty,' she said. 'Don't notice my own mess.'

Pulling on rubber gloves, Betty made a start of the washing up. It always took her an hour or so just to get the kitchen straight, which meant she never got round the whole house and gave it a good turn out, as she called it. There was nothing Betty liked better than to pull all the furniture into the middle of the floor and do the skirtings, give everything a good going over. Few of the rooms were used these days. Only the little sitting room and Mrs P's bedroom, study and bathroom. The house was only opened up when her son, Christopher, came over from Hong Kong with his children – all four of them last summer. Oh, it was lovely then to have the whole place used and she'd come in every day to clean, like in the old days. Now she only did her two mornings.

She finished filling the dishwasher and put it on. Christopher had bought it last summer, thought it would encourage his mother to keep things better, but it was a lost cause. She never used it. Said she couldn't stand all that water gushing away, wasted. She just washed up what she needed when she needed it, and let all the rest pile up.

Betty finished doing the pans and put them on the Aga to dry. Taking rubbish out to the bin she noticed the wrapped newspaper parcel on the top. There wasn't much she missed. She opened a corner. Broken glass. A green bottle by the looks of it. Gin. Putting back the lid, she sighed. There was a lot of talk in the village about the drinking. Since they'd put the recycling bins down by the recreation ground at the back of the cottages in Long Lane there had been a lot of nosy parkers counting the bottles going in. You'd think Mrs P would be more careful, more discreet, but not a bit of it. Bold as brass, she'd sling them in, one after another. She was like that, though. Didn't give a toss about what people thought. There were some that took offence at that. Thought she was too outspoken, but Betty was used to it. You always knew where you stood with someone like that. That was the good thing.

You never saw her drunk, mind. She sort of topped up during the day. Only drove in the mornings when she was sober. It didn't do to telephone in the evening. She wasn't always too good then. And forgetful. You could tell her something, or she'd tell you, and the next day – nothing. Gone completely.

There were plenty that liked her. The vicar, for one. He was always calling, though half the attraction was the whisky she poured him. She could be kind, too, and generous. Well, if she wasn't, Betty wouldn't still be here, mucking her out, as Mrs P called it. She was more like a friend these days. Betty's mother, Freda, who had been in service since she was fourteen, would have been horrified at some of the things they talked about. No holds barred. But then, she was lonely, Betty thought, as she dried her hands. All that history she was always writing didn't make up for not having a bit of life going on round you. Betty was widowed too, but she'd got Pat, her daughter, only two cottages up, with three kiddies, so it was different for her.

She checked the morning's post which was in a pile on the table. Bills, mostly, but a nice postcard from Italy from Mrs P's friend, Guy. Betty read it slowly. Usual stuff about the weather and the food and some remarks that went over her head about his conservation work on the Gambottis, it looked like. Whatever they were. Betty put the card back on the top. Mrs P had plenty of friends, she thought, it was just that they all seemed too far away and busy with their own lives.

She pulled the Hoover out of the cupboard in the hall. The dust bag was full but she couldn't abide changing it, fiddling about trying to fit a new one, so she'd make do as it was. She heard a bucket being clanked down at the back door and Mrs Pomeroy came into the scullery, wearing a pair of old rubber boots.

'Morning, Betty!' she called. 'That bugger's been egg-eating again.' Something was stealing the hens' eggs out of the nesting boxes. Stephen, Betty's son-in-law, was supposed to come round with his rat traps. Valerie, huge in her green cardigan, padded across the kitchen to the basket where she kept the eggs. Betty scowled at the boots trailing dirt over her floor.

'I've just done that,' she said sternly.

'Ooops. Sorry.' Valerie put the kettle on. 'I'll make the coffee.'

'I'll just do the hall first. Here, what have you done to your hand?'

'Oh, dropped a glass. Last night. Nothing serious. Only a scratch.'

Mmmm. Thought as much, Betty said to herself, as she vacuumed the rugs in the front hall and let the Hoover roar over the floorboards.

Valerie Pomeroy looked at the large pink plaster she had put on the palm of her hand. She had woken up this morning in her kitchen armchair with dried blood on a cut and no memory whatever of what had happened. She had seen the glass on the floor and brushed it up before going to wash and change and spruce up. She had probably had too much to drink. Not that she cared. Over-indulging now and then was something she allowed herself as long as she was alone and at home and no nuisance to anyone else.

She made her own coffee and poured water onto Betty's tea bag.

'Yours is here, Betty,' she called. 'I'm taking mine up. I've got footnotes to start on. I'm not in if anyone calls.'

Shambling up the stairs, she caught a glimpse of herself in the glass on the top landing.

What a ghastly sight, she thought, pausing. She found it hard to associate her outward appearance with the person she felt she was beneath the cladding of fat. The age when she had developed a clear sense of herself in relation to everyone else had occurred when she was about fifteen and slim as a reed and startlingly pretty. She remembered polo matches in India when every head had turned to watch her walk with her sisters to the pavilion, and later, in London, when she had been considered the beauty of the Season. Now, nearly seventy, vastly overweight, it still felt shocking to inhabit this alien body. She would sometimes look at the texture of the skin of her arm or leg, pinch a fold, look at the red veins, feel the slackness of old age and wonder that this blemished sack of tissue and blood was actually her. Totally without vanity, the slow progress from girl to old woman was accompanied in her by a sort of scientific interest in ageing and decay. She remembered a very ancient great-aunt catching hold of her hand when she was about seventeen and saying, 'I feel just the same inside, you know. Just as young as you', and it had seemed obscene and pathetic. Now she could sympathise. One did feel much the same. Obviously older and wearier, but the same person. It was still a shock to see what had become of her body, this monumental baggage in which she lugged herself around.

She went on to her study, and put her coffee on the desk. The room was untidy but workmanlike, with crowded bookshelves and an advanced computer and word processor on which she was engaged in writing a paper on Hindu devotional poetry commissioned by an academic journal. She had chosen this room as a study because it was small and easy to warm in the winter and also because the deep window looked south over the rolling patchwork of fields and woods to Bulbarrow Hill in the distance. At least her brain was in good shape, she thought, as she sat down and switched on the computer. She could still rely on that.

Ten minutes later, just as she had composed her thoughts, she heard Betty humping the Hoover up the stairs, plugging it in and banging about the top landing. She knocked the door to the study open and roared in. Valerie stopped what she was doing. Conversation, thinking, anything, was impossible with that noise. She waited until Betty switched it off.

'You've got a new neighbour,' Betty announced as she flicked a duster over the books. 'Did you know?'

'So everyone keeps telling me,' said Valerie, dragging her eyes away from the screen. 'I've yet to meet her.'

'Divorcee,' said Betty. 'Middle-aged. Londoner. One of those,' she sniffed. 'Drives too fast. Went smack into Brewer's tractor yesterday. Wrote her car off.'

'My goodness,' said Valerie. 'Was she hurt?'

'Don't think so. Ever such funny behaviour, though. Just walked off and left her car in the middle of the road. Greg Whittle had to get it moved. He told Pat she didn't seem all there. Away with the fairies. Or drugs. Could be that Prozac, I said. All these women are on it. Especially them on their own. Well, it's the age, isn't it? Think they're over the hill. Get depressed.'

'What about us, Betty? We're on our own and over the hill. You'll be saying we're neurotic next.'

Betty stopped dusting and turned to look at Mrs Pomeroy with a laugh. 'Us? We're long past all that nonsense. We've had our lives, and thank God. We don't expect nothing. Not any more. Just the family. That's what we live for.'

'So we do. And sterner stuff, Betty. We're made of sterner stuff.'

But of course, thought Valerie Pomeroy, drink helps. Numbs the painful places.

By the time Betty had finished and bumped the Hoover back down the stairs, Hindu devotional poetry had become quite inaccessible and another morning's work was lost. Valerie went heavily down to the kitchen to make more coffee. Her new neighbour was of little interest to her and she did not speculate about the sort of woman she might be. If at all socially acceptable she would be swept up by Julia and Peter Durnford. If not in their league, there was plenty else going on in the village. She would soon find her own sort. Valerie did not judge her own company to be worth seeking, or offering, come to that. She was not beset by any feelings of neighbourliness.

Old Major Burnside had been an easy sort of man to have next door in the bungalow. To begin with he'd played golf and was out and about most days. Later on, when wheelchair-bound, he'd taken up campaigning: against the closure of the village post office, against street lighting through the council houses along Back Lane, against the cuts in the bus service to Sturminster Newton, against the introduction of the new Prayer Book – in fact, to this day the vicar' still used the 1662 Order of Service, entirely due to the battling Major. Valerie signed his petitions but would not campaign. 'Villages have got to change,' she told him. 'They aren't museum pieces. They're living communities with changing needs. It's all very well for the rich amongst us to want to preserve everything to look charming. We can all afford to go and shop in Waitrose and send our children to boarding school. But there's nothing here for ordinary young families or teenagers'. That's why the village will die.'

'Well, we must do something, Valerie. Not just mouth plati-tudes,' he had reprimanded.

'Not me, I'm afraid. I leave everything like that well alone. Sorry, Godfrey, I'm not a shaker and stirrer. Believe in things taking their course without interference from the likes of me. Like most other people, I would be motivated by selfishness. Take your bungalow. I wanted to sell the land and get planning permission to build. Needed the cash. But look at the furore that caused. You'd have thought I was putting up a block of flats. I've been persona non grata in some quarters ever since. It won't help your petition to have my name on it.'

Major Burnside had frowned. 'Not good enough, Valerie. We need people like you. Open-minded people.' But he had known she was a lost cause.

Valerie spooned instant coffee into her mug. As she poured on boiling water, she had a sudden jolt of memory. There had been a woman with her last night. Here in the kitchen, filling the kettle as she had just done. She could see her now. Tall, slim, a nice-looking woman. What was it she had said? She had heard the sound of breaking glass? Something like that. Valerie looked down at the plaster on her hand with a horrid wave of consciousness as a sequence of events replayed in her mind.

Bugger! She said to herself. Bugger. I could do without a bloody interfering do-gooder next door. Although it was true she did not care what people thought of her, she found she did rather mind what revelations this new person was sure to share with Julia Durnford on the other side, and anyone else, for that matter. What Valerie did in her own home she felt was her own business.

Ah, well. Nothing to be done. Damn stupid of her to have got so rat-arsed. Would take care not to get so again. Still, if this woman was from London and had had some sort of breakdown to boot, she wasn't going to be too concerned with an old dipsomaniac next door. She'd have other things to worry about.

Then, with a degree of pain, Valerie remembered the softness of the woman's dark hair and how, for a moment, she had cried, with shaking shoulders, into her lap. Strange. It had been a strange moment and one best left well alone. If there was one thing of which she was sure, it was that she did not want to go raking around in someone else's problems.

Anthony Brewer was brisk and matter-of-fact when he telephoned Claudia after lunch.

'Claudia? Anthony Brewer here. It occurred to me that you would be stuck without that jalopy of yours. I've got a rusting heap here that you could borrow for a week or two until you're sorted out. It's taxed and insured and just about roadworthy. No, don't bother to thank me. Wait until you've seen it. Let's think. Do you want to pick it up tomorrow? I'd better get Greg to check the brakes.' There was amusement in his voice. 'Call round at about eleven tomorrow morning. I'll have it ready for you, OK? Until then. Goodbye.'

As quick and as easy as that. Claudia's spirits soared when she put down the telephone and she felt greatly moved by this act of kindness and generosity. The kindness of strangers, she thought, and indeed it was exactly that. She could never imagine such a thing happening in London. Her only slight worry was that she was compromising her independence, denting her anonymity, by accepting Anthony Brewer's help, but what the hell. As soon as she had a job and collected a cheque from the insurance, she would replace her car and that would be that. Meanwhile she would make the best use of being mobile again. Picking up the telephone she dialled her sister-in-law's number.

'God, Claudia. Those little lanes are lethal. You can't go whirling about like Jehu, or whoever it was.' It was unlike Minna to sound cross but she had had a difficult morning trying to persuade young mothers to accept the triple MMR vaccine for their babies and she had an ante-natal clinic starting in ten minutes.

'Minna, I've been thoroughly ticked off already. I'm only ringing to ask you if we could meet for lunch tomorrow. It's your day off, isn't it, and I'm coming into Salisbury to buy some paint. I'm going to make a start on redecorating the bung. I'm getting tired of old Major Bloodknock's colour scheme.'

Minna ran her hand through her hair and began a complicated doodle on her telephone pad. Talking of lunch made her feel terribly hungry and she began to hallucinate about a thick ham sandwich.

'Well, of course I'll meet you. There's a nice pub in Hartington, which is about halfway between us. Let's say one o'clock, shall we?'

'Great, Min. I've got a lot to tell you. See you. Love to the boys. Bye.'

Minna put down the telephone. It was good to hear Claudia sounding upbeat and cheerful. The last few months had been so difficult and there had been times when she had wondered how her sister-in-law would cope with life without Roger. Not only that. Having an errant husband was one thing, but to have him also locked up in the slammer for four years was quite another. Minna was concerned that the piece of information which had reached her last night through David Rowntree would be another blow. She was going to have to warn Claudia, put her on her guard, and it was better to do that when they met, not over the telephone.

Claudia spent the rest of the day usefully, unpacking all the cases in the hall, lugging things out to store in the garage and making a large pile of stuff to go. There was something wonderfully therapeutic, she found, in stripping herself of all this unnecessary *garbage*, as she thought of it. Since packing a few weeks ago, she seemed to have divested herself of another skin, sloughed off another layer. In her new life she would no longer need twelve dinner plates – she would put at least six aside for Lila or Jerome. Vegetable entrée dishes could all go, along with the paella pan, the ice-cream maker, the pasta machine, the complicated juice extractor. The absolute minimum, that was what she would aim for. Soon the pile to go was larger than the items she stored in the kitchen cupboards. She repacked what she no longer wanted and lugged the boxes out to the garage to be dealt with later.

As she worked she found that ideas were starting to form in her head about her bedroom. At first she had thought she would paint everything in the bungalow white, but now changed her mind and thought that a soft violet – halfway between thistle and lavender – would be pretty in her own room. A colour Roger would have hated. Standing on a chair, she yanked down the Major's curry-coloured curtains which reached an extraordinary foot below the sill and two feet above the floor and stuffed them into a plastic sack. Somewhere she had packed a pair which had hung in the cottage, made of a soft, very pale grey French fabric. She would see if they would fit.

She began to put clothes away. The built-in wardrobe, which smelled of tobacco and mothballs, was adequate for all she needed. The lovely eighteenth-century twin tallboys that had been in their bedroom in London had gone to auction and in those days she had a whole walk-in dressing room as well. Now all she needed was somewhere to hang a few skirts and trousers, some shirts and jackets, and her winter camel coat. Her sweaters could go into the drawers on the side. A pile of clothing on the floor grew as she cast out more items she knew she would never need. She saw herself as a dinner lady now, a cook, and it was liberating to feel that the suits and sleek London outfits could be got rid of. They were all designer labels – and a fat lot of good they had done her. Once it had been important to look chic and expensively dressed. Roger had said so. She threw another beaded cocktail dress on the pile. Out with the lot of them. Anyway, she had never liked those twinkling evening dresses which Roger had wanted her to wear. She remembered the photograph of Carla which had appeared in all the newspapers. She was caught stepping out of a taxi in New York in just such an outfit, her wonderful American teeth bared in a smile. Add a string of fairy lights, Claudia felt, and one could dispense with the Christmas tree.

When the floor was finally clear she started on books and photographs. She had brought a small scrubbed table from the cottage to use as a desk and dressing table and she piled her few favourite books on this and then added photographs of the children, one which included Roger, one of her parents, and one of her younger sister, Kate, who now lived in New Zealand. She looked at Kate standing on a wooden veranda, squinting into the camera, with three mop-headed children clinging round her bare legs. She had her arm hitched on to the shoulder of her big blond husband, Harry. They made a square family unit and looked unassailable.

The photograph of Roger and the children was deliberately chosen. It did not include her and was therefore telling no lies about family unity. She supposed she must have taken it about twelve years ago in Oxford. The three of them were sitting on a wall, Lila sticking her head through the crook of her father's arm and laughing, Jerome sitting slightly apart, his trainers dangling. Roger was wearing an open shirt and pale trousers, the material straining over his wide thighs. He looked fit and well, smiling his lazy smile. Claudia wiped the glass with the front of her T-shirt and put the photograph down.

Struggling through the furniture still piled in the sitting room, she pulled out a bedside table and a couple of lamps and extricated a small armchair. With these in place, her room looked much better. At least the carpet was a solid blue, and she had covered some of the mysterious stains with a cream cotton rug which she had managed to smuggle out of the cottage. With some of her favourite things set around her, and with so few of them left that each one seemed weighted with significance, Claudia felt somehow more centred, less adrift, as if she was coming back to herself. She had had to fight for her silver hairbrush, for example, point out that the initials were those of her maiden name and nothing to do with Roger.

The small seaside painting which she had nailed up over the bed had belonged to her father. He had loved the wide, windy beach, bright with canvas awnings and scattered with children and donkeys. It reminded him of his childhood in Norfolk, where he, also, had been a child of the vicarage. Claudia loved it too. It made her think of a time when the beach was a paradise of freedom and wonderful raw sensations – hot sun, cold sea, rough sand on skin which had grown thick and dull in heavy woollen school uniform. One forgot the tar, the smell of the seaweed from which black clouds of vicious looking flies swarmed, the agony of being rubbed with a rough towel over sandy wet limbs, the cold, the rain, the long haul back to cars when handles of beachbags cut into children's soft fingers and wicker baskets swung and banged against bare legs.

It was the only painting she owned. Standing back to look at her work, she felt pleased. Now she had about her the things she loved. Everything else she could do without.

Sarah Challis

She was struggling out to the garage with another load when she heard her name being called. 'Claudia! It's me, Julia Durnford. From next door. I've come to see if you are all right. Star tells me you've had a prang. Here, do you want a hand?' Julia's shape blocked light from the door. Claudia heaved the box onto the packing case wall she was building. God, she thought, news travels fast.

'That's very kind of you, but I can manage. Yes, I did have a bit of an accident, but I'm perfectly OK. Only a stupid bump on the head.'

Julia scanned her face anxiously. 'Are you sure? It was Anthony Brewer's tractor, so I hear. I'm always complaining at the speed they go through the village.'

'No. It was my fault. Entirely.' To change the subject, she indicated the boxes. 'I've started having a bit of a sort-out.'

Julia nodded sympathetically. 'It must be awful. Goodness knows what we will do when the time comes to move. Of course, one hopes it won't ever happen but we won't be able to manage at East End when we're older. Far too big and expensive to run. What are you going to do with all this?' She waved a hand at the boxes.

'Oh. Get rid of some of it. Let the children have a root through. Charity shops, I suppose, after that.'

'We have a wonderful Riding for the Disabled Christmas Fair in December. Could you hang on until then? What's this?' Julia pulled at the paper in a packing case. 'You don't mean to say you're getting rid of this china? My dear! It's Copeland.'

'Yes, I am and yes, I know. I've no room for it all. I think I'll keep half.'

'But it's a terrible shame to split it. Why don't you sell it? I know the most wonderful man in Sherborne . . .' This was typical of Julia, Claudia was to discover. She always had a better idea, knew someone, had just the person, often what she called 'a little man'. Maddening, but also tremendously useful. Claudia scratched her forehead. The cut had already started to itch.

'That's a thought. I don't even like it very much. There's masses of it – the full works.'

'Look. Leave it with me. I'll get on to my man and let you know. He'll give you a valuation.'

'I think I'd like to get rid of it all,' said Claudia. 'It's a very good idea. I'm keeping some pottery stuff. Simple, I don't need much. Just the basics. I had some Quimper, but that went . . .' She tailed off vaguely.

Now Julia had had a chance to have a good nose she could see that Claudia had once been a woman of some substance. She glimpsed a designer carrier bag stuffed with formal looking clothes and another bearing the name of a ridiculous London shop where shoes sold for hundreds of pounds. She had obviously been used to a very different sort of life. It was odd that she gave so little away, with no hint at all of her past.

'Now,' she said briskly. 'I've also come to ask you to a kitchen supper. Peter longs to meet you and I've got hold of a few locals. Can you get your diary and see if you are free on Saturday week?'

Claudia felt cornered. She did not want to go back into the bungalow with Julia at her heels. She cast round wildly for an excuse and eventually had to say, 'Well, thank you. No need to look. That would be lovely.'

'Good. Eight o'clockish? Don't dress up. Very informal. Literally in the kitchen. Are you sure I can't help you?'

'No, really. I'm just pottering but I'd be very interested to know about this china man.'

'Oh yes. Don't worry. I won't forget. I'll be in touch. Must go. I've got to get the horsebox in to be serviced before the holidays.' She glanced at the overgrown garden as she made for the gate. 'You'll have to start on this next,' she called over her shoulder and with a cheerful wave she was off.

Claudia could not help but feel amused. Julia Durnford clearly belonged to that dying breed of Englishwoman who could, given enough scope, sort out most of the world's troubles. The dreadful refugee camp she had seen on television last night with filthy tents and no water and gaunt silent mothers cradling crying children, Julia would have them all rehoused, cleaned up and sitting down to a square meal with no elbows on the table in no time at all. And at least she doesn't hang around, thought Claudia. Now she was in a more positive mood, she did not hate the idea of the supper quite so much. Selling the dinner service was a wonderful suggestion. She might even raise enough to buy another car.

Wandering about her garden searching for her spectacles and fearing that she had dropped them from her cardigan pocket when she had been poking about looking for eggs, Valerie Pomeroy heard voices and glanced up. She would know Julia's foghorn anywhere. She always talked as if she were calling the cows in. So she was in there already. In with the new woman next door. Thick as thieves. Valerie had guessed as much and made up her mind to keep well away. Let them get on with it, she told herself. As she stood, short-sightedly peering at the green blur of the garden, she noticed that a little droop of sadness tugged at her heart. Ridiculous old thing, she told herself sternly. Why would she want to be friends with an old fool like you?

'What's all this?' Ivo Brewer asked his brother, throwing his car keys down on the dresser in the kitchen of Manor Farm. 'Why the philanthropy? She must be good-looking!'

'Really,' said Anthony smoothly, 'you might allow me some finer feelings. The poor woman is obviously on her uppers and I have to admit to feeling slightly to blame. Greg does go like the clappers, you know. I've had quite a lot of complaints from people in the village.'

'But is she good-looking?' persisted Ivo, opening the fridge and taking out a bottle of white wine.

'Hmm,' Anthony considered. 'Yes, definitely. A bit haggard. Needs a bit more flesh for my taste, but not bad, not bad at all.'

'There you are!' said Ivo triumphantly. 'I knew you wouldn't be quite so obliging if she was sixty, with a moustache.' He poured out two glasses of wine and passed one to his brother. He ran a hand over his face. 'Jesus! I've had one hell of a week. I'll have to go back up to London tomorrow. I've really only come home for a change of clothes. That auction in Geneva was a complete cock-up. Half the lots had been withdrawn and the other half failed to meet their reserve.'

'You know you love it,' said Anthony unsympathetically. 'Two days down here and you're restless. Are you seeing Sally tonight? There must be some reason for coming here from Heathrow.'

'I am, as a matter of fact,' said Ivo, leaning across to refill their glasses. 'Remember Dad's expression? There's nothing relieves a man like a pee or a poke!'

'I don't know, Ivo. How could you use the poor maiden so?' Anthony sat at the scrubbed table and flicked open *Farmers' Weekly*.

Ivo laughed. 'Hardly qualifies as a maiden,' he said, 'and remember, please, it was Sally who despatched that poor husband of hers and cast her roving eye on me. In that order and not the other way round.'

Anthony looked up and smiled. 'Of course,' he said. 'I forgot.

Saint Ivo. Are you serious about her?'

Ivo pulled a face. 'Fond of her, but she's too neurotic and intense. She's getting tired of me, I suspect. Started saying she's moving to Tuscany to paint or grow organic lavender or something barmy. No, give me a nice, straightforward country girl every time.' He refilled his brother's glass again. 'Here, we might as well finish this.'

Chapter Four

When Star Bishop heard the horse's hooves clattering past The Bugle, where she was wiping down the tables in the saloon, she stopped working and glanced out of the window. She thought as much – that tinker kid again. Star could not count the number of times she had seen that girl out and about when she should have been in school. It made her sick when she thought of the trouble she had with Rosco playing truant. Social workers, the headmaster, even the police, she had had the lot down on her, snooping and prying, while this kid got away with it. Mind, she'd given them what for. She wasn't going to be put upon by that lot. Let them try and do something with Rosco. Nearly sixteen, and at the High School in Stur, he'd only got a few weeks to go before he left, and the sooner the better as far as she was concerned. It was a waste of time him being there. The teachers reckoned he wouldn't get a GCSE above grade F and that was their own fault, as far as Star was concerned. They always picked on him, or ignored him when he'd got his hand up to ask a question, and when he got stroppy, they threw him out. He spent more time out in the corridor or the 'cooling off' room, they called it, than he did in class. He'd got his car mechanic NVQ a year early because he was interested in that and Mr Busby, the teacher, took a bit of trouble over him. Made him feel worth something.

He could be difficult, mind, a right little bugger, and that was his dad's fault. Billy'd never had the time for him, and only saw him a few days a year since they'd split when Rosco was a few months old. She had packed Rosco off last summer to stay with him – Billy was living in a commune in Cornwall – but the little bugger had hitched home after three days and turned up on the doorstep, just when she had been glad to see the back of him.

That was when she had been with Ken, the animal feed rep, and he'd wanted the kid out of the way, but that hadn't lasted anyway. He was a right bastard, that one. Star sighed. She had an unlucky streak as far as men went. When it came down to it, she thought, you had to look after number one, because if you didn't, no one else would.

She picked up the cloth and started to clean the shelves behind the bar. That kid on the horse made her see red. Typical it was, those bloody travellers. Got away with murder while law-abiding people like her copped it at every turn. Bloody scroungers. She threw the rag back into the sink and went to get the Hoover.

I've worked my arse off, she thought bitterly as she plugged it in. She had had two brief years between fourteen and sixteen, before she'd fallen pregnant with Rosco, when she had felt free. That was when she had changed her name from Stella to Star and had bummed around pop festivals, smoking pot, lying comatose in the backs of vans, but that was it. She'd had to grow up then. She'd ended up in Taunton, pregnant and homeless. The council had found her a place but it was disgusting, one dirty room and a bathroom up on the next floor, shared with five other tenants. Her own mum wouldn't have her back. Not that she'd have gone anyway.

After she'd had the baby, and fed up with being stuck in that dump, she'd wanted to go back to the country, where she had grown up. She wanted to be able to open a window and smell the earth, to leave the back door open and hear only the rattle of a tractor and the cawing of crows. It was in her blood, she supposed; her dad and granddad had both been farm workers. She applied for a housing transfer and had jumped at it when they offered her a place in Sharston. It was in a close of council houses on the edge of the little town, between where the old station had been and the light industrial estate. From the upstairs windows there was a lovely view, right over the fields to the hills, and they all had gardens. Mind, hers was nothing to be proud of. She'd never had the spare to buy a mower, so the grass wasn't up to much, although next door mowed it every now and then, if she let him feel her tits when his wife was out. 'Here, Star!' he'd call over the fence. 'Your grass could do with a bit of a cut. Shall I pop round?' She could have got the whole garden done if she'd let him have more of what he wanted, but she wasn't that desperate. Dirty old man. He was off on the sick, too. Said he had a bad back.

Star moved the stools onto the tables so that she could get underneath with her nozzle. She liked it where she lived. Liked the tight community, the chat in the butcher's queue, the post office, the little supermarket where she sometimes did a bit of overtime on the till, the garage, the two pubs, one dusty and quiet, the other raucous with pop music until the early hours. There was a chip shop run by a Chink family, a newsagents and chemist and ironmongers. A war memorial stuck out conveniently into the high street where milk tankers meeting head on caused traffic to come to a standstill. Although it was quiet compared to a proper town, it still had an air of bustle and life about it.

It had been a good place even when Rosco was little and she was more or less stuck there, although Billy couldn't stand it. He'd sat around in a haze of dope and then disappeared and Star couldn't say she missed him. He didn't contribute anything anyway. But she had been happy there from the start. She could push the pram up to the doctor's clinic and down to the post office to collect her giro, and in the evening her neighbour would baby-sit while she went down the pub. Saturdays she caught the bus to Yeovil, and hung around with her friends in the shopping precinct, trying on clothes and passing Rosco round like a parcel. They'd have fish and chips or a pizza, share a joint and catch the bus back. Soon as she could, she got her neighbour to agree to have Rosco in the mornings and she started back at work. Ever since then she'd stood on her own feet, saved for the car, bought a suite and a satellite dish, even gone on holiday to Spain with her girlfriends. She felt proud of all this, Star did. Never had a penny off her mum and dad, and never lived off a man.

She'd got nine cleaning jobs now, and since she'd got her own transport, was able to get out and work in the villages. She did the two jobs in Court Barton, the pub every morning and Mrs Durnford up at East End House twice a week. She enjoyed it up there. Big old place where no one could see where she'd been, and Mrs Durnford just let her get on with it. Of course Star had made it clear from the beginning that it was her who chose the jobs, not the other way round, and Mrs Durnford knew she was lucky to have her. Cleaners were like gold dust in the villages. Everybody wanted one. All the cottages and houses where ordinary people, working people, once lived had been bought up by incomers who didn't do their own housework.

She put the Hoover back and filled a bucket with hot water to do the outside lavatories. It was a proper country pub this, with the privvies out the back in a whitewashed lean-to. Clean, though. You couldn't fault it, even though it was perishing out there in the winter, when the water in the cisterns froze.

She finished sloshing out the gents with a good slug of bleach and started the ladies, polishing up the mirror with a bit of spray. Her moon-like face glimmered back at her, pale and startling with the bright red candyfloss hair. She liked to look a bit different, create a bit of a stir. She didn't bother with the nose rings and studs she used to have. Not any more, but she was proud of her tattoos, all across her shoulders, with one or two in more intimate places. She'd shown them off last New Year's Eve at the millennium party in the Nag's Head in Sharston. That had really got them going. The landlord, Ted, had never allowed her to forget.

'When are you going to show us again, Star?' he was always asking.

'You dirty bastard!' she laughed back. 'Special occasions only!'

She swilled her bucket down the lavatory and pulled the chain. That was her done. She glanced at her watch. Monica, the publican's wife, would have the kettle on by now, so she'd go and sit in the kitchen and have a fag and a coffee before she went up the lane to Mrs Durnford.

The yard behind the pub was bright with sunshine and barrels filled with petunias and geraniums. Star wondered for a moment why she felt a residue of tetchiness. Oh, yeah, that bloody gyppo kid. She'd go and tell Monica. She felt the same way about the tinkers. Blot on the landscape as far as she was concerned. It was Brewer who let them on the old railway line with their stinking caravans and buses. He left his gateways open and they got through with their vehicles and then you couldn't get them shifted. They'd had the police out to the last lot in the end.

'Here, Mon,' she said, going into the kitchen where the publican's wife was moving boxes of crisps to replenish the bar. 'That kid's just gone by again. Bold as brass on that horse when she should be in school. It's always the same with them bloody gyppos. They get away with murder.'

Monica, a tall stately woman with swept-up grey hair, stopped what she was doing. She was used to Star's rantings. She was always on about something or other, but there was no denying she was a worker. She reminded Monica of a bullock the way she went round the pub, crashing about, bumping into things, her big knees flat and white beneath the shorts she often wore in the summer, her hair in red curls on her forehead. She was strong too – if ever she needed a hand with moving barrels or getting the cider up from the cellar, Star would make it look easy.

'It's a different lot this year though,' she said peaceably, filling the kettle. 'Ron told me Brewer's let them camp on the line because the man's a hedger. He can cut and lay beautiful, he said. The woman does herbal stuff, remedies and that, and there are the three kiddies. It's not the same lot that were moved on for thieving last time.' She passed Star a mug of milky coffee and watched as she spooned in the sugar and settled her large backside onto a stool. No wonder she was putting on weight.

Star sniffed. She wasn't going to be done out of her outrage. 'They're all the same, Monica. What sort of people live like that? Like animals. Look at the filth they leave behind them when they do get moved. They're an insult to decent, hard-working people and they get away with everything. Don't pay a penny of tax, don't have vehicle licences, no insurance, nothing.'

Monica, who knew very well that Star made sure she was paid in cash, no questions asked, didn't argue. She also knew that all the trouble with Rosco had left Star critical of people she thought escaped censure. Monica had seen enough life pass through the doors of her public house to understand a thing or two about human nature.

'Here,' she said, pushing over a box of crisps from the cash and carry. 'These are past their sell-by date. Take them for Rosco.'

'Ta, Mon,' said Star, lighting up a cigarette. 'He's a devil for crisps. He's still a little kid like that. It's hard to believe he'll be out in the big bad world come July. He's working today, mind. Study leave they call it, but it's just an excuse for them teachers to have a doss, if you ask me, as if they didn't get long enough holidays.'

'Where's he working then?' asked Monica.

'Down the industrial estate on the old airfield. At that tyre and exhaust place. That's like your mum, I told him – tired and exhausted.' Both women cackled. 'He started Saturday mornings, and goes full-time when his exams are over. Thinks he's the dog's bollocks now he's earning. He's saving up for a motorbike. Don't look at me, I told him. I can't afford to buy you one. Buy it yourself.' Star stubbed out her cigarette and heaved herself off the stool. 'I'll be off then, Monica. Up the road to Mrs High and Mighty. See you tomorrow, love.'

Claudia, slapping white paint over the Major's gloomy walls, cursed when the telephone rang. She had already finished doing the bathroom, painting over the hideous abattoir tiles and putting a pretty cotton rug she had bought for a few pounds over the offensive lino. She felt quite cheerful and optimistic. Minna was right. Getting on with things, cracking on, as her sister-in-law called it, was the best way.

As she picked up the receiver she noticed she had splashes of paint all over her hands, little splattered dots like tiny, white freckles, and was just about to speak when she remembered Minna's alarming words. 'You must get yourself an answer machine. Don't answer the telephone yourself when you don't know who is on the other end. Not until all this had died down.' She paused and a woman's voice said, 'Hello? Hello? Mrs Knight?' With relief Claudia noted the gentle, local accent.

'Hello. Yes, sorry. Hello. This is Mrs Knight speaking.'

'This is Mrs Peck from Bishops Barton Primary School. I have your application here for the post of cook.'

'Oh yes. Thank you for telephoning.' Claudia's heart fluttered with expectation.

'There's a letter on its way, but I thought I would ring to explain. I am afraid that we have already filled the position.'

Claudia was hit by a cold draught of disappointment. Damn. She felt physically knocked back and as if this rejection was weightily important and significant. A real blow. She realised that she had foolishly allowed herself to believe that she would get the job, that with her glowing testimonials she could not fail. I've lived so long in Roger's climate of success that I thought I could get what I wanted, as he always did, she thought. I've got used to dispensing patronage, not begging for it.

'Actually by the time that ad was run we already had someone lined up. A lady who worked here previously, who suited us very well.'

'I see. Oh dear. I have to say that I'm really disappointed. It would have been perfect for me, you see. And you don't have anything else? I'd do anything. Dinner lady, cleaner, anything.'

Mrs Peck heard the desperation in her voice. 'I'm afraid not. Not at the moment. But we'll keep your application on file. You never know. Vacancies come up from time to time. We're unusual, you see, in that we're one of the very few primary schools left in the county which still provides school dinners. We're entirely self-financing in that department and so our kitchen staff are very important to us.'

'I see,' said Claudia. 'I hadn't realised. Tell me,' she added, bracing herself for the truth, 'would you ever have considered me anyway?'

Mrs Peck hesitated. She was a kind person, used to encouraging small children, looking on the bright side. 'Well, your qualifications are a little unusual. We're more used to dealing with City and Guild diplomas, but you would have got an interview, and in a small village school like this, if the face fits . . .' She tailed off. This woman sounded an unlikely candidate but she could hardly tell her that.

'Thank you,' said Claudia, 'and please do let me know if anything else comes up. I really do need to find local work.'

'I'll do that. Thank you for applying. As I said, a letter is on its way but I usually try to speak to applicants personally. I'm sorry to disappoint you. Goodbye, Mrs Knight.'

'Thank you. Goodbye.'

Claudia put down the telephone and sat on the stool on which she had been standing to paint. Now it had slipped through her grasp, the job seemed even more desirable – it would have been an answer to prayer. She and Minna had discussed it when they had met for lunch, which had been a jolly, laughing occasion to begin with, with Minna glad that Claudia seemed positive and on top of things, and Claudia cheerful and optimistic.

Minna had arrived early at the village pub where they had arranged to meet and taken a lager out to the garden to sit under a tree at a pub table, enjoying the sunshine and the prospect of her afternoon off. She closed her eyes and mentally switched off from the concerns of the practice and the merry-go-round of family worries. She was broad-shouldered in every sense and attracted other people's burdens and was expected to hoist them aboard, like crates onto a cargo boat, afloat on a choppy sea. Occasionally it was necessary to give herself a break.

After five minutes or so, a chugging diesel engine alerted her and she glanced up to see an extremely battered white pick-up truck turn into the car park and stop with a jerk. Claudia, in dark glasses, was at the wheel. She had a faded red Castrol baseball cap pulled over her eyes. She laughed when she saw Minna sitting under the tree and called, 'Well? What do you think? Classy, eh? I stink of something called Udderment that I found in pot here in the cab. Do you think I could rub it on my chest for bigger tits?'

'If you did, and it worked, we'd have it made!' said Minna. 'Is this the borrowed vehicle? Sorry, Claudia, I can't help but smile at the contrast with your former swanky cars.'

'It's great! I love it!' laughed Claudia. 'I drove all the way here with my elbow stuck out of the window, listening to a Country and Western tape and chewing gum. It makes me feel quite frisky. I had to stop myself eyeing up male drivers.' She got out and slammed the door. 'Greg said he'd cleared it out but it'll still full of binder twine and about three inches of straw.' She chucked the cap onto the floor through the open window and brushed down the legs of her jeans. She and Minna embraced. Claudia felt the sturdy warmth of her sister-in-law's body and was reminded of Roger. The same flesh and blood, she thought, and yet one straight and the other crooked. I've loved them both but this one I would trust with my life.

'Actually, Minna, I'm just terribly grateful to have wheels of any sort. I would have been utterly in the schtook without it. Of course, when I read my policy I found my insurance didn't cover a replacement vehicle and the old banger is a write-off. I can't afford to replace it until I get a job.'

'No, I can see that. Wonderful, Claudia, to find a benefactor. I want to hear all about him, but first, what will you have to drink? I'm having another lager. Let's go in and order some food. I'm ravenous as usual. You've lost weight again so I insist you have a vast ploughman's, or something hefty.'

'A vast ploughman might be a good idea,' said Claudia, grinning. 'To go with the truck.'

Later, eating ham, eggs and chips, Minna said, 'So tell me about this man. The farmer chap. Your knight in shining armour.'

'Hardly that. Filthy, battered Land Rover and rather well-worn work clothes is more accurate. He was a bit of a surprise actually. Fiftyish, good-looking in a rugged way and very, very smooth. Used to be a picture dealer, I gather, and took over the farm twenty years ago when his father died. I admit I'd quite looked forward to seeing him again this morning. He had sort of implied on the telephone that he would be there to hand over the truck, but when I pitched up, there was no sign of him, just the tractor man I'd run into, who was very nervous and jumpy. He clearly thinks I'm a dangerous woman. he made very sure he wasn't standing anywhere near when I drove off!

'Anthony had asked him to clean up the truck for me and check it over. Apparently it's a sort of workhorse when they have sheep turned out on the hills in the winter, and it stands a bit idle in the summer. I had a peer round the farmyard. It's all very picturesque and predictable. Someone works very hard on the garden. The house looked lovely. The sort of place one would dream of living in the country. I wondered whether I'd get invited in by the wife – a cup of coffee or something – but no one appeared. I asked a few leading questions and it turns out, to my great surprise, I have to say, that Anthony Brewer is a bachelor and that he shares the house with a younger brother, Ivo, who runs the picture business.'

'Homosexuals, I'd guess,' said Minna.

Claudia looked at her and laughed. 'You're just like your brother,' she said. 'That's exactly what Roger would have instantly assumed. As it turns out, I don't think so. Anthony exudes testosterone, for one thing. It's just an arrangement which suits them, I imagine. Greg said that the farm was left to them both, equally, but that Ivo isn't interested in farming. I think he said he had been married at some time. I can't remember all the details.'

'Do you realise, Claudia, just how lucky you are to have bachelors like them on hand? Available, straight men are tremendously hard to come by, you know. The country is stuffed with single middle-aged women desperate to get hold of one. And desperate to be stuffed too, come to that. My goodness, tongues will wag! They will have started already.'

Claudia laughed. 'Nothing to wag about. I'm just eternally grateful that he was kind enough to help me out. You know I'm not in the man market, Minna. I've had quite enough of men, but I admit it is quite nice to feel that there is another single person out there, amongst the cottages and cows. And a very personable male, to boot.'

'Talking of Roger,' said Minna, inaccurately, 'I'm afraid I've got a bit of bad news. Something I must warn you about. No, don't look like that. Nothing startling, really, just that David Rowntree telephoned the other night. There has been a development of sorts. It seems that Roger has been contacted by a Sunday newspaper which wants to serialise his life story. Much more in-depth than the garbage that was churned out at the time of arrest and trial, and to be ready for the time of the appeal. He says that the word on the street is that the appeal will be unsuccessful but that the sentence could be commuted to three years. Roger is more than willing to co-operate, of course, making a very public donation of the proceeds to charity. David says that childhood, early life and marriage will feature in the first two instalments. That will mean wedding photographs, snaps of the children, everything, I'm afraid. And probably an analysis of your marriage. Sorry, Claudia. Fucking horrible, I know, but nothing that we can actually stop. The photographs are all in Roger's possession. They are his. He can do what he likes with them.'

Claudia sat, her heart a heavy weight in her chest. The pub garden which had seemed sunlit and attractive now seemed like a baited trap. Was the nightmare never to stop? She picked up her glass and swallowed the last mouthful of lager before answering. 'God, Minna. I wish I wasn't driving. I could do with a stiffer drink.' She sighed, twirling her empty glass. 'You know, I sort of half expected something like this. It wouldn't be in his character to go quietly.' She leaned back in her chair and stuck her legs out in front of her, studying her feet meditatively.

Minna admired her calm. She could not imagine what it would feel like to have one's personal life and most intimate relationship analysed across the front of a newspaper, to be smeared with Sunday breakfasts, kicked about on the floor of sitting rooms in thousands of homes, before being put out for the binmen. Unthinkable. And Claudia, sitting here, looking completely ordinary and unremarkable, had to endure it all.

'You'll get through it. Of course you will. You'll ride it out. But you need to be prepared. For one thing, you must expect to be recognised in the village. You've got to think of that.'

'Yes, I know. Of course I realise that. When do we think this will be?'

'Two, three months. It's hard to say. We can appeal to Roger's better nature but I don't think that will work, do you? Given the raw material? He might, of course, change his mind about co-operating with the newspaper, but no doubt they could publish something anyway if they felt it was newsworthy.'

'If you leave me out of this, you'd think he'd want to protect the children, wouldn't you? He loves them, Minna. You know that.'

'He apparently feels that they will come out of it rather better. He's confident that the newspaper will provide a platform for him to not exactly clear his name, but portray himself in a more flattering light.'

'Has he gone mad? Why in heaven's name does he think that?'

Minna shrugged. 'It's hard to say. I actually wonder whether he's suffering from delusion. It can happen with men like him. Men with over-inflated egos.'

'Can't David stop him?'

'Claudia, who has ever stopped Roger from doing anything?'

'What about injunctions? Things like that? Can't I try and prevent this happening?'

'I don't think so. Legally, there is nothing to stop the newspaper from doing a profile of him. Nothing at all. It in no way prejudices the outcome of the appeal because they intend to run it after the hearing. Of course it's only with Roger's co-operation that family photographs and other really personal stuff can be used, but the paper will be able to access other material – archive photographs of you and Roger for instance, which they can use without anybody's permission.' Minna put a hand on Claudia's arm.

'The other thing,' she went on, 'is that David said that the newspaper will quite likely seek you out, that it won't be difficult for a journalist to find you. Reverting to your maiden name isn't exactly covering your tracks. And the sooner you get an answer service on your telephone line, the better. It won't stop them finding you, but at least it will be a first line of defence.'

Claudia covered her face with her hands. 'Oh God, Minna. I feel embattled again. Just when I thought things had calmed down.'

'Let's hope it doesn't come to anything, Claudia. David says that everything depends on what else is happening in the world at that moment. Roger might be the stale news we feel he is, if something more exciting comes along. After all, he had no real public persona, not like a disgraced politician. He was only well known within the City.'

'Yes, of course,' said Claudia, 'but think of it. Think of the timing. Jerome will be about to start at university and Lila may be back in London. It would be so awful for them. I just can't believe it of him. He loves them like I do. Why can't he see what it would do to them? I could kill him, Minna. I could kill him.'

'According to David he feels it's a way to have control over what they print. That with his co-operation they'll allow him to dictate the tenor of the piece.'

'As if! Newspapers aren't like that, are they? They'll print whatever suits them.'

'Exactly. You're not the only one, Claudia. I'll be in this, too, you realise. I'm not looking forward to seeing chubby-cheeked sister, Minna, aged five, clutching pet rabbit, all over the inside pages.'

Claudia looked at her and had to laugh. 'Oh God, Minna.'

They fell silent. The sun shone and the pub garden was peaceful. It was hard to feel threatened.

' "Sticks and stones may hurt my bones, but words will never hurt me",' said Claudia. 'That's what my mother used to say to me when I complained about someone being unkind to me at school. I feel I should take comfort from that now.'

'I bet it wasn't much help at the time,' said Minna. 'The principle is correct though, isn't it? My work is taken up with people who have far worse things to bear and whose courage and fortitude are humbling. I must say, though, I'm grateful that my parents aren't alive. I don't think they could have stood it. I know I can. I have a wonderful husband, great kids, a job I love. It can't touch me. Obviously it's much worse for you and Lila and Jerome.'

'We'll be OK,' said Claudia stoutly. 'Let's hope it won't happen. Let's hope Prince Charles chooses that weekend to elope with Camilla. But if it does, we'll be OK.' She smiled wryly at her sister-in-law. 'God, Minna, why didn't you warn me off your bloody brother?'

'You were mad about him, remember?'

Now, sitting on her painting stool, feeling the weight of this new blow, the disappointment about the job at the school, Claudia caught sight of herself in the mirror she had hung in the hall. She saw a long, mournful face, downturned mouth, drooping hair. It was a shock to glimpse herself like that, caught unawares. This is how I appear to other people, she thought. God Almighty, what a miserable cow. She got up and marched through to the kitchen to look for scissors, then went back to the mirror. Without a moment's hesitation she began to hack off her hair, which fell to the carpet in thick brown chunks. Half elated and half horrified, when she finished she saw a pale face staring back with a ragged cap of uneven urchin hair. She practised a smile and found she looked younger, chirpier, and utterly and completely different. No chic banker's wife. More like a bloody mushroom picker, she thought, shaking her head like a wet dog. And it went well with the truck.

'Good Lord! What have you done to your hair?' asked Anthony Brewer as he drew up alongside her in the lane the next day. 'And you've located the brakes, I see.'

Claudia laughed back. She banged both hands on the steering wheel. 'It's great, this vehicle. Thank you so much. I am hugely grateful.'

'And the hair?'

'A brainstorm. Felt I needed a change.'

'It's certainly that.' He looked at her speculatively. Claudia feared she might blush. 'I rather like it. It suits you.'

A car drew up behind, blocked by his Land Rover. He glanced in the rearview mirror and raised a hand in recognition of the driver before turning his attention back to Claudia. 'We're meeting again on Saturday week, I believe. At the Durnfords'. Party in your honour, I gather. I'll see you then. Yes, I like the hair,' and he drove off.

Claudia waited while the following car squeezed past her. With a start she recognised the driver as the woman from next door. The old drunk. Valerie Pomeroy. Steering carefully and looking straight ahead, Mrs Pomeroy did not give her a glance. She wouldn't know me now anyway, thought Claudia. Not with my new barnet. She found that she was pleased that Anthony Brewer said he liked her hair, although he was too smooth by half. Cheeky, really, to make observations about her appearance when they hardly knew one another. He was an appalling flirt, but God, how a bit of innocent flirting lifted the spirits. She drove home with a smile flickering round her mouth. To Valerie Pomeroy she gave not a second thought.

Turning into the gate of Garden Cottage, she hardly registered its ugliness. The place was growing on her. The warm weather and the pleasure of having doors and windows open and of sitting in the afternoons on the long soft grass at the back where the old walls were high and reflected the heat of the sun, all this had restored her spirits. There were some fruit trees and rambler roses which scrambled over broken trellis work. The neglect and rampant greenness gave the place a secretive, undisturbed air and Claudia felt comfortable and safe. It's like a sanctuary, she thought, where no one can find me. Minna's bombshell had shaken her, it was true, but she realised that somehow she had expected something like this to happen, and that a sort of uneasiness had been lurking in her consciousness. In a way it was a relief to know the worst. If this whole ghastly business was going to blow everything wide open, then it was important to make the most of this peaceful interlude and not let the threat of it spoil the present.

She had dragged a trestle table from out of the shed and

recently ate her meals sitting in the sunshine, swigging the last
of the wine. She watched yellow and blue butterflies dance from
shrub to shrub and tried the acidly unripe gooseberries which
covered the thorny old bushes. There were currants, too, black,
red and white, and some raspberry canes grown wild and
covered in soft, pink fruit. My little garden of Eden, she thought.
I love it like this, grown wild. I don't want to change it.

The open country on view from the front of the bungalow,
although it was beautiful, held little appeal. She did not want to
go and explore the sweep of hills or the dark patches of
woodland. She knew there were footpaths and bridleways and
ancient tracks to be discovered. Minna had pointed them out to
her on an Ordnance Survey map but she did not feel ready to
set out on her own. She felt something threatening in this
landscape which she did not know, and on the one short walk
she had attempted she found herself hurrying and glancing
furtively behind, convinced she was being followed. The path
became overgrown and tangled with brambles and nettles and
there was a rank smell of decay from a tumbledown barn where
she imagined an animal must have died. The sense of being
watched, overlooked, grew intense and she had stopped and
stood silently, her heart thumping, then turned and fled back
the way she had come. When she reached the wicket gate to the
lane and, feeling less vulnerable, looked back up the hill, she
thought she saw a man move into the trees from where she had
come. I'm going mad, she told herself. One stop closer to
Barking. She had not walked alone again.

Inside the bungalow she was halfway through painting the
sitting room. Her trip out in the car had been to get more white
spirit from the ironmongers in Sharston. A couple more hours of
work and it should be done, but first she would have a break in
the garden before taking up her brush again. Without intending
to, she found she was thinking of Roger, shut up like a bull in a
pen. She imagined his cell had a window but that it looked out
onto a blank and featureless brick wall. How he would hate not
being able to see beyond. He would love to walk this country,
taking its miles in his long stride, uncovering its lonely places,
reducing its mysteries, revealing her fears to be silly fancies.
Claudia imagined herself hurrying along in his wake as she so
often had in the past, walking in his shadow, her feet following
the steps of his boots.

Then, from inside the bungalow, the telephone started to ring.

★ ★ ★

Valerie Pomeroy had recognised Claudia instantly. She had already noticed the pick-up parked outside the bungalow and knew that it belonged to Anthony Brewer. In a village served by tortuous narrow lanes one got to know every local vehicle and to whom it belonged. Betty, too, had told her about the loan and that Greg had reported to his mum, who lived two down in her row of cottages, that he thought Brewer was up to his usual tricks.

The woman must be stupid to be taken in, thought Valerie. Stupid and vain and likely to have her head turned. Not that she disliked Anthony. On the contrary, she found him charming and cultivated and one of the few people locally who shared some of her interest in oriental art. Oh no, he was in many ways a delightful man, but so obviously a seducer. One could observe him work a room of women, not allowing himself to rest until each and every one had succumbed to the merciless onslaught of charm. Once he had them captivated, like most hunters he lost interest in his prey. The chase was all. Valerie could not begin to count the number of broken hearts which littered the surrounding countryside and that was not counting the flocks of girls he imported from London and elsewhere. Silly women one and all. Now her new neighbour was set to join their bleating throng.

Valerie was rather sorry, because she had expected better of her. She did not know quite why, but there was something a little determined about Claudia's isolation, something about her looks, her style, which marked her out as being different. But just now she had caught the exchange of smiles, the secret, sly look from under the eyelashes which a woman shares with a man who finds her attractive, and Valerie could see that Claudia would be another victim. Oh well. It was none of her business.

Part of her own determination not to allow the events of her recent debauched night to come to the surface made her drive past with no acknowledgement. The woman was a stranger and would remain so. Meddling Julie Durnford had already swept her up and no doubt organised something for her, some sort of welcome to the village. There was no need for any gesture on her own part. One of the benefits of being elderly and single and generally regarded as difficult was that one was usually left out of these social charades.

On the back seat of her car, in a padded envelope, was her manuscript which she was taking to the post office in Sharston. She was pleased with her work. It was a scholarly article and she had thought of little else for weeks. Now that it was out of the way she could turn her mind to other things. She wished that Christopher had another visit planned for the summer. She adored his company – adored his children. She wondered when her old friend, Guy, was due back from Italy. She could do with some different company. When she had posted the package she would go home and telephone and maybe arrange a few days in London. Catching up with old friends always did her good.

Driving over the railway bridge she saw the old van parked on the disused line. She had heard complaints in the village about the travellers, but the family living there now were rather different. There was the girl who rode about on the black and white horse, a couple of dirty little boys and the parents. Jem, the father, was an interesting man. She had employed him to clear out the ditch which ran along the bottom of the field behind her house and she had discovered he was remarkably knowledgeable about ancient hedgerows. He had told her how one could date a hedge by the types of plants and trees to be found within it. Heather, the woman, was a lightweight by comparison, and talked a lot of nonsense about herbal shamanism. A load of rubbish, thought Valerie, whose own field of study had introduced her to true mystical religions. The woman made money out of it, selling potions and cures to a New Age shop in Glastonbury, which just went to show how half-witted people could be.

Valerie had become interested in the family and had discovered that the surname, Loader, was an old local name. It appeared on a 1543 muster roll of the village, and was one of the few surnames to reappear in the 1662 list of tithings, and again in 1709. After that it seemed that the family suffered some downturn in their fortunes, lost the cottage and piece of land and became itinerant tinkers, sometimes roving shepherds, drystone wallers, ditchers and hedgers.

Valerie thought that she might stop on the way home and walk down the line to see if she could see Jem Loader. He was always worth talking to. Which was more than could be said of some in the village.

Chapter Five

Lila Barron often power-walked from the apartment she shared in Greenwich Village to where she worked as a junior investment banker at First City Bank in New York's financial district. Wearing tracksuit bottoms and trainers and with headphones blaring out a dance tape, she enjoyed overhauling other walkers, feeling her long limbs stretching and lengthening, her strawberry-blonde hair in a ponytail swinging against her bare shoulders, an expensive calfskin backpack containing her work clothes bobbing on her back. In one hand she carried a water bottle from which she periodically suckled, in the other her stopwatch with which she checked her progress along her route.

Exercise was important to Lila. Even in this most steamy and sultry of New York weather she had so much energy that unless she burnt it off competing against herself, she started to feel tetchy and irritable. She needed a constant challenge and not being particularly academic she chose to set herself physical goals. She was already playing Ultimate Frisbee at weekends and mixed handball twice a week and in both games she was a merciless and aggressive competitor. There was nothing she enjoyed more than burying the opposition.

In most respects she was a popular girl, noisy, fun and vivacious. Great, a fun girl, the young men in her circle called her, with her wide humorous mouth, her ability to see the funny side, to muck about, to drink them under the table. She was refreshingly uncomplicated in her relationships with the opposite sex, having been brought up in the tough world of a co-ed boarding school, but some girls, those from amongst whom she did not choose her friends, found her over-confident and loud.

Her laugh practically blew doors open along the corridors at work. She put her feet up on desks, chewed her nails, and made little effort to conform to the ideals of smart city dressing. She had never had a manicure in her life, nor worn a pair of high heels. Her long golden legs were covered with a fair fuzz of hair which had never suffered wax or razor. She was scandalously, unnaturally, au naturel.

What was more irritating to those of her female colleagues who were less than enchanted by her was that in the face of this shocking disregard of the rules of good grooming and ignorance of fashion dictats, Lila was considered extremely attractive by some of the most eligible men at work. It had to be admitted that she had a good, athletic figure, with big round breasts and legs like a racehorse, but she was surely too large and powerful. Standing next to her in the crowded lift to the twenty-second floor, one of her female colleagues complained to a friend that she had been practically engulfed, with her nose pressed to the third button of Lila's shirt, but annoyingly, it seemed even the smallest men declared they would be happy to suffocate in her cleavage. While the smartest of the city girls whittled and honed themselves away to perfection, Lila tucked into cream cheese bagels, drank pints of beer and had never heard of body brushing. Trained in interpreting the cipher of designer labels, they could not understand the juxtaposition of a gold Piaget watch – an eighteenth birthday present – and the old V-necked grey school jumper which Lila sometimes wore knotted round her neck, complete with neatly sewn nametape and chewed sleeve ends. Or the shabby First XI tracksuit from her co-ed public school, in which she jogged to work on winter mornings. It was disconcerting that she did not seem to care or even notice their fresh manicures and spa-cleansed complexions, their Kelly bags and neat pencil skirts worn with a witty twist, such as a vintage baby-doll chiffon blouse which cost a month's wages.

Her detractors judged that what she had in abundance was the arrogance of the expensively educated English who errone-ously believed their careless confidence, born of money and a misplaced sense of superiority, was enough to be successful in New York. Too often it disguised lack of talent and idleness.

Carelessly attractive, not in the least ambitious, even lazy at work, treating men with casual disregard, Lila was a bundle of contradictions, for underneath it all she was anxious to be liked and could be easily hurt. A sharp word or a dismissive remark could puncture her air of self-confidence and she would then want to gather her friends around her to reassure and reaffirm. Those she liked could count on her loyalty and support and in return were called upon to offer unconditional comfort and sustenance when required, for Lila's life was a series of pitching highs and lows and her friends needed to be robust to survive.

She shared a charming apartment with two English flatmates, Tara, a junior fund manager like Lila, and Alice, a trainee valuer at Christies auction house. The three girls had created their own familiar environment, eating toast and Marmite and reading *The Times*. They might just as well have been in a New Town flat in Edinburgh or a house in Shepherd's Bush. American culture largely washed over them. Their accents remained untainted although various Americanisms crept into their vocabulary, which they felt made them sound stylish and cool when they talked to friends at home. They dated a variety of international men but at the back of their minds was the belief that they would marry their own kind. New York was just a rite of passage.

This particular morning Lila was unconscious of the stream of odd humanity which bobbed past her. As she pounded along she could think of nothing but her father. The day before, she had received an email from David Rowntree, to keep her up to date, as he put it, as if he knew that part of Lila's deep unhappiness stemmed from the loss of contact with Roger since his imprisonment. After his arrest they had spoken almost daily and she had been home to see him twice. He had begged her not to attend the trial and she had acquiesced, knowing that the sight of him being taken down between two policemen was more than she could bear.

Here in New York his arrest and imprisonment was a mere passing mention in the Wall Street pages. London was not the epicentre of the developed world and yet another case of City malpractice was hardly newsworthy. Lila was telephoned at work by a gossip columnist, who ran a brief mention of her existence at First City – and that was that. Nobody would have noticed had Lila not made such a public spectacle of her misery, breaking into noisy sobs at meetings and requiring much hugging and comforting by her handmaidens, who mopped at her fat, sliding tears and patted her broad, unmanicured hand.

Lila's emotions were gusty things, like unruly winds blowing up a storm, fleeting and hard to escape from. This openness and inability to hide her feelings was both her strength and her weakness, and could be equally engaging or tiresome. This morning her exasperation with her mother was fuelling her emotions. David Rowntree had mentioned Claudia's decision to sue for divorce. She could at least have waited, fumed Lila, until her father was out of prison and given him a chance to demonstrate that he was a changed man. Her understanding of her parents' marriage was so shaped by her own needs that she could not trace the course of her mother's unhappiness or see the marks she bore from her father's long-term infidelities.

To Lila it was simple. Her father was a big man in every sense and it was her mother's job to play a supportive role. She was not unaware of his faults; in fact their relationship was often stormy and she had grown up used to his impatience, his inability to listen, his bullying advice which you accepted or were damned, but these were nothing compared with the truly great things about him. He was the most fun of any of the fathers she knew, the most generous, the most courageous, the best looking, the most brilliant. The fact that he was unfaithful to her mother was something Lila did not dwell on. She felt in a vague way that this was something her mother should have resolved, as if it was a shortcoming on her part, rather than her father's. Lila took as an example various high profile European men, great, powerful men, some industrialists, some statesmen, who were quite openly womanisers, but whose wives dealt with the whole thing sympathetically and elegantly and generally came out of it all rather well. All this martyrdom her mother went in for – Lila had no patience with it, and now this decision to divorce. Lila was outraged. What about the family? What about her and Jerome? They wanted, needed, to have both parents together. It was what Lila had always relied on, like a solid block beneath her feet.

It had been Claudia's decision to shield her children from the existence of Carla and later, when Roger left the family home and moved in with his mistress, she had resisted the temptation to rally them behind her. As a result Lila, away in New York, had never really understood the sequence of events and carried on believing that her mother had thrown him out, leaving him to fall back into Carla's arms. On a flying trip to New York, he had even asked Lila out to lunch to meet Carla. He would have enjoyed being seen with an attractive young blonde woman on each arm, but at this Lila drew the line. 'Dad!' she had protested. 'I don't want to meet her. Why should I? Keep your tarts to yourself.'

Her father going to prison was a terrible, terrible shock and blow to her, but her loyalty and faith in him remained untouched. Other people were to blame. People who had let him down, people who had misjudged his motives, seen a crime where there was none. A little bending of the rules, maybe, a brilliant manoeuvre which went slightly wrong, but not a crime.

Tara, with whom she had also been at school, had annoyed her greatly by obstinately taking Claudia's part. 'I really like your ma,' she had said. 'I have to say, I always thought your dad was a bullshitter, but I envied you your mum. She seemed to be the one who supported you and really took an interest, not looking around for someone more important to talk to. I can't see how you blame her for wanting to finish it. Why should she put up with that sort of blatant infidelity? Can't you see how undermining and humiliating it would be?'

Lila had turned on her. 'How dare you judge my parents! What the fuck do you know about it?'

Tara had shrugged and made a face. 'Only what you've told us, which is almost everything, down to the smallest detail. Ad infinitum. If you don't want to know what I think, then shut up about it,' and she had gone into her bedroom and slammed the door.

Later she and Alice, the other flatmate, had discussed Lila. Alice was kinder. 'She needs our support, Tara. We can't begin to imagine how terrible this is for her.'

'What do you mean? We don't have to imagine anything. She tells us. Every bloody minute of every bloody day. I'm sick of it. Having a wheeler-dealer father who's in the slammer where he belongs and a downtrodden mother who's at last seen the light and is getting the hell out is not one of life's tragedies. Frankly, I'm surprised her ma stuck it so long. My mother always thought she had a hell of a time.'

Alice, a gentle, sympathetic creature who tended to be influenced by the person she was talking to, nodded. 'To Lila everything is black and white,' she observed. 'She can't seem to see it from her mother's point of view at all.'

Tara made a face. 'There's only one point of view as far as Lila is concerned and that's her own. I can remember her taking part in debates at school. She was incredible. She never listened to the opposition, just kept repeating her own views. She is totally and utterly single-minded. I mean, I love her dearly, I really do, but she is so dogmatic and impervious to argument that she sometimes drives me mad. Anyway, that's the last time I'll make any kind of contribution to her monologue. Why bother? But I tell you, Alice, it's her mother I feel sorry for. Not that shit in prison.'

Alice made a noise of agreement. It did seem that Lila's mother had drawn the short straw, but then when she listened to Lila she couldn't help agreeing that it was awful of her mother to abandon her husband when he was sent to prison. It was all such a muddle and so unlike anything she had ever experienced. She thought of her own parents in their neat house in Gerrards Cross and how her father got ticked off for leaving a teaspoon in the sugar or putting the milk bottle on the table. That was the scale of offence committed at Oakdene.

What Lila looked for was unquestioning, uncritical support and endorsement. After the row, she had pointedly stopped talking to Tara about her parents and turned the full beam of her attention on Alice who could be relied on to listen with patience and sympathy. Tara's problem, thought Lila, was that she had recently ditched a boyfriend whom she had discovered was two-timing her. No wonder she supported Claudia. Tara was in 'all men are shits' mode.

Arriving at work, Lila attacked the swing doors of First City and waved a hand at the receptionists manning the front desk. Up on the twenty-second floor she stalked between the workstations, glancing neither right nor left, knowing if anyone asked her how she was doing, she would scream. When she reached her own desk, she threw her bag under her chair and sat down heavily. Across the aisle her departmental boss, Marianne Freymann, glanced up from an email she was reading. She was getting a little tired of histrionics and, very early on in Lila's apprenticeship, realised that her new assistant had a dilettante approach to her career in fund management. Marianne was used to having dead keen, dedicated graduates, ready to lick her Manolos if she asked them to. If Lila had not been foisted on her by the vice-chairman, who was, apparently, a family friend, she would have had her moved long ago.

Lila was now glancing round, looking for someone to notice her mood. Marianne felt a pang of sympathy. Of course it was hard for the kid with all that shit happening at home. Lila caught her eye and when Marianne did not look away, got up and came to her desk.

'Can I talk?' she asked.

Marianne deleted the email and turned to her. 'Sure. Is something wrong?'

'It's my mother,' exploded Lila. 'I just can't believe what she's doing. She's serving divorce papers on Dad, which I really don't think is fair on him just now, and she's turned her back on all their friends who would have helped her, and buried herself in some godawful place in the country. I telephoned her this morning and found out that she has got herself a job – picking mushrooms. I just can't believe it. I mean, what's she trying to do? Humiliate Dad even more?'

Marianne, whose intense interest in fashion meant that she could not hear of any situation without wondering what she would wear, pictured a long dark-brown suede skirt, perhaps with a ragged hem, and a cobweb knit sweater in moss green. Over her arm she would have a woven basket into which she would drop the delicately coloured fungi. With a wrench she stopped herself worrying about footwear, and said, 'Picking mushrooms? What on earth do you mean?'

'It's the job she's got. She said she had to work, that she had no money and it was the only thing she could find. But it's just ridiculous. There are loads of Dad's friends who would have got her something to do, something more suitable. She does it to make it worse for him, to make him feel more ashamed. You know she was offered free places to live in London when the house was sold, but she wouldn't take any of them. She goes to live in the back of beyond in some godawful hovel, and takes a menial job picking mushrooms. It's to rub the message in that she's been brought so low by Dad. To make it worse for him!' and Lila broke into noisy tears.

Marianne rather liked the sound of Lila's mother. 'Now look here, Lila,' she said firmly. 'This really can't go on. Upsetting yourself like this. You can't do your work and frankly, you are no use to me in this state. I suggest that you get on the net and book a flight home. These things are always worse from a distance. You need to talk this over with your mother and go and see your father. You can take ten days' compassionate leave. What do you say?'

Lila lifted her wet, red face. 'Dad didn't want me to, but I think you're right. I must go. I must see for myself.' She wiped at her tears and gulped. She's like a child, thought Marianne. A big baby. Lila managed a smile. 'Thanks,' she said. 'What about the work I'm doing? How will you manage?'

Better without you, thought Marianne, but said, kindly, 'Just put that stuff I gave you on a disk and let me have it. I'll find someone to take it over.' Already she had a bright girl in mind. She would get her moved over from the South American desk.

'OK. Well, thanks again.' Lila tried a brave smile. 'I'll ring Mum now and tell her.'

After Lila had gone to her desk and was busy on the

telephone, Marianne turned back to her own work. Then she had a flash of inspiration – shearling boots would look wonderful. That was her mushroom picking outfit complete.

If Claudia had imagined that she could remain anonymous by driving herself to work and not making use of the mini-bus service provided by the mushroom farm, she could not have been more wrong. She was torn between saving the money on petrol and the thought of having to stand with a gang of village women every morning, waiting for the bus to collect them from outside The Bugle. I can't do that, she thought, without them asking about me, wanting to know where I live, where I'm from, speculating about me. If I drive myself, I needn't talk to anyone. I can keep myself to myself.

It was Anthony Brewer's pick-up which gave her away. In a small village, familiar cars are easily recognised even in unexpected places, and on the very first day it was spotted in the parking area at the farm when the ladies climbed out of the bus.

'Here. That's Brewer's truck, isn't 'er?' said Angie, nudging her friend Maureen. 'What's it doing here?'

'Didn't you know, Ange? He's got a part-time job.' Both women cackled at the absurdity.

'He's lent it to that new woman. The one who's moved into the Major's place,' said Jenny. 'You heard about her, didn't you? She ran slap into Greg's tractor, up Top Lane. Wrote her car off. Greg says she's not the full shilling.'

'She must have something else, then,' said Angie. 'Bit of a looker, is she?'

'Greg didn't say. But she's not young. She's not a girl, like. He said she was a bit peculiar.'

'So what's Brewer up to?'

'He'll be hoping to get in her knickers in return for the loan of that,' Maureen indicated the truck. The three women laughed.

'Beat up old thing like that,' said Jenny. 'I wouldn't be seen dead in it.'

'He'd say the same about you, dear,' said Angie. Laughing, they went into the shed to clock on.

At lunchtime next day, down at The Bugle, Monica wiped over the bar where she had spilled the beer she had just pulled for old Tom Atkins. It was always quiet of a Thursday and she had only got the four in today, all propping up the bar, with Tom's old collie, Scamp, panting under his stool. Tom wiped the froth from his mouth with the back of his hand. The other three were pensioners from the council bungalows, who sat in companionable silence, glad to be out from under their wives' feet, glad of a bit of peace and quiet.

They all looked round when a tractor roared up the street and stopped outside the pub. 'That's Greg come for his pint. Best get it pulled, Monica,' said Tom.

Slowly Monica took down Greg's beer mug from where it hung over the bar and pulled the handle on the Old Speckled Hen. The dripping mug was standing full on the counter when Greg ducked in the low door, his hair flat and dark with sweat from where he had taken off his cap.

'All right, son?' said Tom. The three pensioners said nothing but nodded a welcome.

'All right, Tom. How's things, Monica?'

'Not so bad, love. How's your mum?'

'OK as far as I know.' Greg slid some coins across the counter. 'Went back to work yesterday.' He took a long swig of his beer. 'That woman who ran into me, she's working up the mushroom farm. Give over, I said, you must have got that wrong, Mum. She was a right posh bitch, 'er was, but Mum said Brewer's pick-up was there in the morning and she and Angie saw her picking. Bloody slow they said she was an' all. She won't earn much at that rate.' All five listened with rapt attention.

'What's she working there for?' asked Monica. 'She can't need the money. Not a woman like that.'

'Must do,' said Greg. 'Otherwise she wouldn't do it, would she? And I'll tell you something else,' he added. 'She's cut off all her hair. Looks like a bleeding man, according to Angie.'

There was a silence while this piece of news was digested. Then Tom drained his pint and stood up and Scamp tottered to his feet.

'You tell that Angie she's a lying cow,' he said. 'That woman's a darn sight better looking than she'll ever be, or ever was, come to that. And I should know. I've seen 'er in 'er garden in 'er bathers.' With a wink at Monica he went out. He got on his bicycle and, with Scamp trotting behind, wobbled slowly up the hill towards the Durnfords where he had a bit of hoeing to do in the vegetable garden.

'That woman next door,' said Betty to Valerie Pomeroy. 'She's started work up at the mushroom farm.' She watched to see the reaction to this remarkable piece of news. Valerie put down the cloth with which she was wiping eggs before putting them in a basket on the kitchen table.

'Surely not. Where did you hear that from, Betty?'

'Maureen told Pat. There's a few of them work there, you know, from the cottages. They've seen her every day this week. Never talks though. Keeps herself to herself.'

'Really? Well, I am surprised. I wouldn't have thought a woman like that . . .'

'But you've not met her yet, have you?'

'No, not, properly, but I've seen her. She must be hard up, mustn't she? Single women often are, of course. I take my hat off to her. There's nothing to be ashamed of, working there.'

'No, but it's not what you expect, is it? Not the likes of her. Keeps herself to herself, Pat says. Comes and goes and doesn't talk much. You'd think she'd want the company. Lives on her own and doesn't know anyone in the area.'

'How do you know?'

'Greg told Pat. She was quite chatty when she collected the truck Brewer's lent her.'

'There's Julia Durnford. They seem to be friends already.'

'There you are then! You don't expect Mrs Durnford's friends to work up the mushroom farm, do you?'

'No. I grant you that. Hmm. Interesting.'

Betty smiled and nodded, satisfied that her bit of news had been well-received. She refrained from passing on Tom's comment which she had heard from Monica. Mrs Pomeroy would not want to know that her nextdoor neighbour had been spotted sunbathing. Some were saying topless, which would not surprise Betty. Well, you never knew with these London types. Anything was possible.

'That's me done, then,' she said. 'See you Friday.'

'Thank you, Betty. Yes, I'll see you then.'

Alone in the kitchen, Valerie sat in a chair at the table and gazed thoughtfully out of the window. How very odd, she thought. As a rule, incomers to the village were well-off people who chose the country as an antidote to busy working lives making money. They usually wanted thatched cottages in which to pursue their rural idylls, not rather ugly modern bungalows, but Valerie had automatically put Claudia in the same bracket. So she was hard up. And living alone. She wondered what had brought her to Court Barton. People on their own generally chose to live where they had friends or family or some sort of connection. This woman apparently had none of these things.

Slowly Valerie got up from the table and fetched an egg box from the pantry. Selecting the brownest eggs she filled the box, collected her stick from behind the door and made her way out of the back door and down the drive. It was a lovely June morning and the air was filled with birdsong and the scent of roses. The village street was deserted as she came out of her gate and turned into Claudia's. Checking that there was no vehicle parked outside the bungalow, she walked through her neighbour's unkempt garden to the front door. Stooping, she left the eggs on the step and without so much as a curious glance through the windows made her way back home.

When Claudia returned that evening she felt stiff and tired and dirty. She had picked solidly for six hours but even so, when her trays were weighed, she was far behind the other more skilled women whose fingers fairly flew over the crumbly dark compost, lifting the little white creamy buttons from their bed. She, on the other hand, fumbled and sometimes broke the fragile caps, hesitating over grading them for size into the different trays. She frequently dropped the knife she used to cut off the stalks and however hard she tried, seemed to be getting no more skilful. She emptied her mind of anything else but what she was doing and stared hard at the dark beds over which her hands moved until mushrooms started to float across her retinas and she began to feel sick. She gave herself half an hour off for lunch, and went and sat in the truck and drank some water and ate a roll she had brought with her.

The good thing about this work was that you could pick at your own speed and avoid other people as much as you liked. The polytunnels had two double rows of compost bags running down the centre and on either side there were three tiered shelves of growing mushrooms. The pickers sat on trolleys constructed like desks with sloping surfaces on which their trays were placed and as they picked rolled themselves up and down the rows. So far she had managed to avoid having a proper conversation with any of the women other than to exchange a few pleasantries. They were a cheerful lot who were anxious to help and encourage her by saying that they were as slow as she was when they started. It's a knack, they said. You'll soon get your speed up. Ever done anything like this before? They asked. Live round here, do you? No, and yes, she replied and managed to leave it at that.

She sat for a moment in the pick-up, looking at her fingernails rimmed with black, despite the rubber gloves, and feeling the muscles in her back protesting. She wondered if she might experience the satisfaction of honest toil and all that claptrap but felt instead only physically tired. She had earned £36 – the sort of sum Roger might have spent on a bottle of wine or she might have forked out for a pot of skin cream without a second thought. Still, it was cash in hand and, as she felt for where she had folded the notes into the pocket of her jeans, she realised that it was the first money she had earned herself for twenty-three years. She could work six days a week if she wanted and do overtime if necessary. The other women called it pin money – a funny old-fashioned term, Claudia thought. She had no idea of the national average wage or what income their families might expect to live on. She had heard programmes on the radio about rural poverty and unemployment but when she looked round the village at the neat, well-tended cottages and tiny gardens, or at the children waiting for the bus in the morning in their clean clothes and new-looking trainers, it was hard to identify deprivation. Of course it's so picturesque, she thought. It's difficult to imagine hardship when it wears such a pretty face and the backcloth is rolling hills and fields and not tower blocks and concrete.

As she got out and slammed the door behind her she thought again of Lila. She would be home in three days and Claudia's heart was filled with joy at the thought of seeing her daughter. She knew that it would not be easy and that there would be all sorts of scenes and eruptions but the prospect of holding her in her arms and having the Bung filled with her noise and mess and laughter made Claudia smile to herself in anticipation.

When Lila had telephoned completely out of the blue the afternoon that Claudia was finished the painting, Claudia knew that there was no point in trying to dissuade her. At first she had said that she would visit Roger and stay with friends in London and Claudia had had to quietly allow her that choice if it was what she wanted, but then she had telephoned back and in a typical change of mood had said, through tears, 'Sorry, Mum. Of course I want to stay with you. I can't wait to see you. Even if it means coming down to wherever it is you've buried yourself. Is there room in the rabbit hutch for me?' and Claudia had felt her own tears gathering as she had replied, 'Lila, there's always room for you.'

Claudia was thinking of this when she put her key in the door and noticed the egg box on the step. Bending down she picked up the box and opened it. The eggs inside were so astonishingly brown she wondered if they were real. There was no note to tell her who they were from. How kind, she thought. Someone knows I am new and has bothered to call and bring me these as a welcome present. She wondered who it could be. Julia perhaps. Claudia was sure she kept chickens. She looked the type. She turned the key in the door and as it opened she saw a note had been pushed through the letterbox. Putting down the eggs, she picked it up. In large handwriting she read, 'Claudia, The china man says not very fashionable at mo. But could prob sell over the net if you are int. Give him a ring on 01398 564722. Good luck. Bye, Julia.'

So it was Julia who had left the eggs. A small gesture like that was greater than the sum of its parts. The fact that she had thought of her and had bothered to come round and leave them on her doorstep meant a lot. Claudia decided to have a long bath and then enjoy proper country eggs scrambled on toast for supper.

Star Bishop helped herself to a squirt of Victoria Durnford's scent. She always liked poking around Victoria's room as she cleaned. This morning Mrs Durnford had asked her to give it a good turnout and change the sheets because Victoria would be home from school for the weekend. She was a tidy girl, mind. Star couldn't complain, and it would be a waste of time looking for anything incriminating like cigarettes or condoms. She seemed a bit retarded like that, for a girl of her age. Star had been pregnant at sixteen, whereas Victoria still had pictures of horses stuck on her bedroom wall and a teddy bear wearing a knitted jersey on her bed. Of course, Star thought, as she pushed the Hoover nozzle under the bed, it was different for a kid like this. She sometimes looked at the books on Victoria's shelf – poetry and history and a lot of the famous stuff they did on the TV that Star had heard of but never read, and realised what a lot she had missed when she was growing up. It was a different world, she thought, my childhood. Like being on another planet. It wasn't that her mum and dad hadn't done what they could for her, but stuck in the village with no car, there wasn't much life for kids growing up. No wonder they got into trouble, her and her friends, hanging around with older boys who had motorbikes. That was the start of it really.

She'd liked English at school. It was the one subject she enjoyed and for a while she took books home to read but there was no peace in the cottage where they lived and if her mum saw her sitting down she'd call her a lazy sod and find her a job to do. That and the telly always being on. Star picked a book off the shelf. *Sense and Sensibility.* She'd seen that film with Kate Winslet. It was lovely, made her cry. Amazing that that story was all here between these covers. The print was small and off-putting though and she couldn't make head nor tail of the first few sentences. She didn't know what half the words meant. She put the book back on the shelf and ran a duster across the rest.

It wasn't that she resented how other people lived. You'd got to have brains and work hard to make the money to live in a house like this and send your kids to boarding school. Mr Durnford, he was a solicitor, and she hardly ever saw him. He was always at work. She knew sometimes he wasn't home until after eight o'clock. That was the trouble with most of the men she knew, they were bone idle, one and all. No wonder they didn't get on in life. She wished she had given Rosco a better start, but she'd done what she could and the little bugger didn't help himself. Being out at work all day meant she didn't have the time to supervise him properly. She knew that, but what else could she have done? He'd got his wild side from them both, from her and from Billy, but he wasn't lazy like his dad. He wanted to leave school so as he could get a proper job and start earning. He'd done Saturday jobs since he was twelve. Even the social workers had to give him that. When he was in real trouble last year and they talked about taking him into care it was this which had saved him, the fact that he could hold down a job and that Mr Martin at the garage put in a good word for him.

Star finished dusting and looked round for the last time. It was a pretty room for a girl, with pink wallpaper and matching curtains and a patchwork bedspread. No telly though. Rosco had had his own TV up in his room since he was seven.

After a quick go round the bathroom she glanced at her watch. It was nearly time to finish. She'd stop off down The Bugle for a cider and a sandwich and then she had to be over at Bishops Barton to do the holiday cottages. As she was putting her cleaning things away in the cupboard under the stairs she heard Mrs Durnford talking on the telephone in the kitchen.

'No, don't thank me. I only put the note through the door. I expect they were from Valerie Pomeroy on the other side. She keeps chickens – Marans, they lay those dark brown eggs. Have you met her? She's not one of my favourite people, I have to say. She can be very, very difficult. We had real trouble with her over . . .' Julia hesitated. It seemed inappropriate to mention the bungalow in this context, 'over planning permission,' she finished. 'Anyway, how are things? Did you telephone about the dinner service? Oh good, I'm glad he can help.' She saw Star standing in the door, waiting to be paid. 'I must go. I have someone here. Don't forget Saturday. We're looking forward to seeing you. About eight o'clock. Remember it's only a kitchen supper.'

Julia put down the telephone and turned to Star. This morning she felt really rattled. There was so much to do. Victoria's horse needed shoeing, she couldn't get hold of the farrier and she had a million and one jobs stacked up, including a Village Hall Committee meeting in the evening. She pushed her hand through her hair.

'Thank you, Star. How much do I owe you? Did I pay you last time?'

'No. You owe me for the two mornings,' said Star, thinking Julia looked a sight. Hair all on end, no make-up, and a pair of trousers she wouldn't been seen dead in. Julia started a frantic search for her bag and then her purse. Finally she found that she did not have enough money anyway and asked Star if she would mind a cheque.

Star stood and waited. She was used to this performance. She took the cheque and folded it into her pocket. 'I'll be off then,' she said, and then as she turned to go added, as an afterthought. 'Her next door's working up the mushrooms. Monica told me.'

'What?' said Julia. 'Claudia? The woman from the bungalow? That was her I was just talking to. You must be mistaken. She never said anything.' She stood, hand on hip, arrested.

'Well, she is. Started Monday.'

'How very extraordinary,' said Julia. She sat down at the kitchen table.

Star picked up her car keys. 'See you Friday.'

'Yes, all right Star. Thank you.'

Julia could not make head or tail of it. She would have thought Claudia would have mentioned having taken a job and why on earth was she picking mushrooms? It was the sort of work teenagers did, or women with no skills. It wasn't even an organic farm or something like that. It was unthinkable for what Julia thought of as PLU – People Like Us. Some of her friends had had to find employment but did so within clearly defined areas – making curtains, garden design, interior decorating, bed and breakfast, that sort of thing. She can't be that hard up, she thought, remembering the carrier bags in the garage, the evidence of high consumerism not so long ago. She had clearly once been a rich woman. Where on earth had the money gone? All sorts of ideas began to form. Perhaps she had been a very rich man's mistress and the liaison had come to an end. Perhaps she had lost everything in some dramatic business failure. It was all very mysterious. The thing to do was to ask her outright. Just say, why on earth are you working on the mushroom farm? Much better to be direct about it and avoid speculation. Julia made up her mind to put the matter straight at the first opportunity.

Claudia, who had come home for lunch at midday to avoid having to talk to other people at the farm, took her coffee and sandwich out to sit in the garden. If Julia was right and the eggs had been left by Valerie Pomeroy, then common courtesy demanded that she thank her. Really it was a bloody nuisance because it meant creating another opportunity for that unfortunate night to be recalled. Damn. This was a silly, niggling complication. She would have to get it over with, maybe just drop a brief note through the letterbox and creep away. She would do it now, on her way back to work.

She finished her lunch and carried her plate and mug inside. With the sun shining and the new white paint, the bungalow looked so much brighter. What will Lila think, she wondered, when she comes in a day or two? It's not what she's used to. It might look better with a coat of paint but there is no disguising that her room is a small square box. She'll be appalled, I expect.

She found a card, a Turner landscape, among boxes packed with the personal papers and stationery from her London desk and wrote a brief note. 'Was it you who left the lovely eggs? If so, many thanks for the kind thought.' She scrawled an indecipherable signature and, collecting her bag, locked the door and got in the pick-up. Pulling off the lane outside Valerie's gate, Claudia ran as quietly as possible up the drive. In the sunshine the house looked attractive, a solid Edwardian villa, rather stately and imposing. It was the sort of house associated with croquet on the front lawn and housemaids bringing out trays of tea. The windows at the front were shut and the front door was closed but the little silver car was parked outside. Damn, so she's in, thought Claudia. Very quietly, she managed to slip the card through the heavy iron letter box and saw it fall onto the mat.

Valerie stood frozen in the hall on the other side. She saw the flap of the letter box lift and the flash of a brown hand as something was pushed through. If she remained very still the person would think she was out and go away. She had no idea who it might be. She only knew that she did not want to see anybody. She waited a few moments but when there was no knock on the door she thought she was probably safe and lumbered over to pick up the card. She glanced at it perfunctorily but could not make out what it was about or who it was from. Going through to the kitchen she put it on the table next to a nearly empty bottle of gin, and sighing, slumped into the armchair and closed her eyes.

Claudia skittered back down the drive and got into the truck. Blimey O'Riley, she said to herself. What to make of that? For, quite clearly, as the flap of the letter box opened and shut, she had seen a pair of women's feet in Velcro-fastened sandals, side by side, as if planted, on the other side of the door. Mrs Pomeroy had been standing there, a few feet away, and Claudia had the strong impression she was hiding. How strange, she thought. She's trying to avoid people. Just like I do. I wonder why.

She was musing on this intriguing fact when she saw a familiar horse in the lane ahead. Slowing up behind, she wound down her window and called, 'Hello, Jena. You again!'

The girl half turned, resting a hand on the horse's quarters. 'Hiya,' she said, and then, remembering her name, 'Claudio!'

'Claudia. It's Claudia, with an A.'

'Oh yeah. Hi, Claudia.'

'Where are you going? For a ride?'

'It's me job, to exercise Jigsaw.'

'Why aren't you in school?' Claudia saw that this was tactless as soon as she had said it.

'Who's asking?' said the child suspiciously. 'I've got a cold,' she said, and added, for good measure, 'Bronchitis. On me chest.' She gave a little hollow cough and then grinned.

Claudia grinned back. 'Don't worry,' she said. 'I don't care. Lovely day like this, I'd rather be out on a horse.' Jigsaw started to swing about from side to side, impatient at being held up.

'D'you want to get by?' asked the child. The lane was narrow. Too narrow to pass. On both sides ran a ditch and a high overgrown hedge, thick and green, with banks of creamy cow parsley. Jena turned the horse across the lane in front of the truck and with a kick of her heels put him at a set of rails which

Claudia had not noticed on the left-hand side; they had been used to fill a hole in the hedge. The horse bounded forward, ears pricked, Jena sat back and with an unorthodox flapping of the reins to urge him on, leapt the ditch and the rails, and disappeared on the other side.

Claudia watched, open-mouthed. My God, she thought. After the sudden stab of fear for their safety, she was deeply impressed by the courage of the child and the talent of the horse. She had never seen anything like it. To jump out of the lane like that, barebacked and hatless, was foolhardy in the extreme, but there was something wonderful and thrilling about it, a sort of showing-off, look-at-me disregard for safety that she warmed to. Smiling at the thought of what she had just seen, she drove on to the mushroom farm to spend the afternoon in a polytunnel.

Chapter Six

On Saturday Peter Durnford was annoyed to discover that Julia had invited Anthony and Ivo Brewer to supper. It was not that he disliked them – in fact, he counted Anthony among his friends – but on this occasion he could have done without their particular brand of charm being lavished on the woman from next door. He was not mollified to learn that Ivo could not accept Julia's invitation. Quite a bit younger, Ivo had his own set of friends, mostly from London, and of the two of them, it was Anthony whom Peter considered the greatest threat to his claim on Claudia.

Peter had looked forward to the party with mounting excitement. He had even lain awake at night with Julia gently snoring beside him and fantasised about the course the evening might take. He would make sure that Claudia sat beside him and he would turn to her throughout supper and discover they had many things in common. With no effort he would be witty and charming and she would meet his eyes and smile into them in a way he found very stimulating indeed. He knew, of course, that this was all a piece of nonsense, based probably on some absurd television advertisement for coffee or after-dinner mints, but nevertheless he had enjoyed playing it through in his mind. There was no room in this piece of fiction for Anthony Brewer, smooth-talking and handsome, sure to be seated by Julia on Claudia's other side, rendering himself clumsy and tongue-tied by comparison.

It was too bad of Julia. He had suggested several other men to make up numbers and had assumed that she had invited one of them. Ted Garfield for instance, nearly sixty, divorced, overweight, who would talk the hind leg off a donkey on the subject of fly fishing, or George Casterton, a red-faced auctioneer who, though a nice enough chap, would never set the world alight. But not Anthony Brewer.

Peter remembered going to a dinner party at Church Farm

when Anthony had a particularly stunning girl staying for the weekend. Anthony had got up to collect more wine from the sideboard and as he passed the back of the girl's chair, Peter had seen how he trailed a finger lightly across her shoulders while still talking across the table to someone on the other side. Peter had watched the girl's almost greedy expression, the secret smile of pleasure as she looked up at Anthony over her shoulder. When he moved behind her again to fill her wine glass, Peter saw that she slipped a hand off her lap and caressed his thigh. Then she had turned her eyes, caught Peter watching and he had blushed and looked hastily away. He had never forgotten. It was like a glimpse into a world which he had never felt himself qualified to enter – the sexually charged, seductive world of handsome, buccaneering men and beautiful, available women, all looking for adventure.

Now, thanks to Julia, Anthony would have the opportunity to ensnare the woman Peter had wanted for himself, in his dreams at least. It was too bad. In a grump he had put away the better wine which he was going to serve and found some mediocre bottles he had bought in a Calais supermarket the last time they were in France. He had even decided which of his wardrobe of bow ties he would wear, but this now seemed a wasted effort.

Peter felt it was the one vanity he allowed himself, his collection of colourful ties. He saw them as his trademark and he admitted it gave him some satisfaction to look in the glass and see his unremarkable features and rather weak chin brought to an abrupt end by a wonderful and arresting tie; giant butterfly wings of explosive eye-catching colour. He knew his face was long and sheep-like, lately further elongated as his nondescript hair began to recede over his high forehead. Getting ready for a party, freshly shaved and pink, his glasses a little steamy from his bath, he would try on various patterns and designs. What he lacked in looks he could make up for by his neckwear, and he noticed that ladies, in particular, took notice and paid him compliments.

He had allowed himself to imagine Claudia remarking play-fully on his choice of flamboyant tie, and had thought up a witty reply. All wasted now.

Julia was in a bait, too. She was up in the bath with a gin and tonic, having slammed round the kitchen, banging cupboard doors shut because she had overcooked the salmon. She had been out all day with Victoria at some Pony Club do, and the horse had not gone well. Poor Victoria had been crying, he had seen the smears on her cheeks. She had hoped to be selected for the A team but Vinnie's jumping had not been at all reliable. He had stopped several times, putting Victoria on the ground at a quite simple tiger trap. Julia was carrying on about getting his back looked at, but Peter could tell that Tor thought it was her fault, that she didn't ride him as she should. She was up in her room now, on her mobile to a friend. It was a shame really that Julia had planned this party on her weekend out from school. Peter thought how nice it would have been to have had supper on their knees, watching television. At least, he thought that now he knew Anthony Brewer was invited.

Peter glanced at the clock in the kitchen. Seven thirty. The guests would be arriving soon. He looked for a lemon for the gins but found that Julia had used the last one for decorating the salmon. He poured himself a whisky and went into the sitting room, not noticing that the new potatoes in the sink still needed scraping and allowing the cat, who had been eyeing the salmon all day, into the kitchen where it managed to knock over the waste bin and drag the discarded fish skin all over the floor.

'Oh! Bloody hell, Peter!' Julia shouted, coming down in her pink linen trousers which had become too tight and sliced into her crotch. 'Really, you are the limit!' She kicked the cat out of the back door and started to scoop up the mess on the floor. Bending down was torture. She had to go down on one knee as if she was being knighted. The floor glistened with a fishy film. She mopped at it with the dishcloth from the sink.

What she needed was another drink. 'Peter!' she shouted again. 'Please! Get me a glass of wine before I murder you.'

He appeared in the doorway, holding the newspaper and looking at her over his glasses. 'What?'

'Get me a drink, immediately. I have absolutely had enough. These bloody people will be here any minute and I haven't done the potatoes or made the salad.' She went through the hall. 'Victoria!' she shouted up the stairs. 'Come and help, darling. I need you!'

Peter took a bottle of white wine out of the fridge and opened it with a corkscrew. He took a glass off the table which was already set for ten. 'Not off the table!' said Julia crossly. He put it back and got another out of the cupboard.

'Calm down!' he said, handing her the glass and retreating into the sitting room again.

Victoria appeared, tall and gangling in a T-shirt and stretch breeches with feet in pink socks. Her dark hair was caught in a rubber band. 'What's the matter?' she asked, her mouth full of the metal train tracks clamped on her teeth.

'Wash the lettuces for me, darling. Look, there they are.' Julia pointed at a bundle of muddy green crowns lying on a newspaper. Victoria obediently put them in the sink and began pulling the leaves apart. 'Yuk! Mum, these are gross. They're full of slugs and things.'

'Of course, they are. They're from the garden.'

'Why don't you get salad in bags, like other people? You only have to chuck it in a bowl then.'

'Just do it, will you, darling.'

Victoria began delicately fishing slugs out of the water on the tip of a knife and dropping them onto the muddy newspaper. She took a sip out of her mother's glass.

'Who's coming, anyway?' she asked.

'The Millards, the Turners, Ros and Julian. Claudia, the new woman from next door, and Anthony Brewer.'

'What's she like? From next door.'

'Hard to say, really. No, perfectly nice, I think. A bit mysterious.'

'Why mysterious?' asked Victoria, interested.

'Oh, I can't tell you now, Tor. I must get on with this,' and Julia dashed out to the larder for the mayonnaise. 'Are you joining us? If so, you must get out of those clothes.'

'Can't be arsed,' said Victoria, dropping the lettuce into the salad spinner.

'What? What did you say? Darling!'

'Oh honestly, Mum,' said Victoria in tones of despair and taking another slug of wine. 'I'm going back to my room.'

'Do come down later, Tor. Just to say hello and get something to eat.'

'Maybe. I've got some work to do.'

Victoria sloped off, sliding her socked feet over the floor. Up in her room she lay on her bed and twiddled her hair round a finger. She resisted the temptation to suck her thumb, a habit she had never really grown out of. She felt infinitely sad and lonely. Most of her friends were going to a party tonight, invited by an older girl in their year. Victoria had not been asked and she knew it was because she wasn't considered cool, just like Antonia Frost who was fat, and Elspeth Torrence who wore glasses and did nothing but work. Somehow, Victoria felt she had become an outsider while her friends started to be interested in boys and talked endlessly about sex and parties and who they had got off with.

Victoria wondered what was wrong with her. She had periods and tits and all that, so she must have hormones like them, but she couldn't even pretend that she wanted to hang about in town hoping to meet boys from the boys' school, or dye her hair or smoke or wear shoes with massive platform soles. She just thought it was all so silly. Such a waste of time. She didn't care at all about not going to the party. She knew she would have hated it, but all the same, being left out, being excluded, did hurt. They had all been such good friends up until about a year ago and then something seemed to have happened, something disturbing which swept them away from her on a tide of heightened excitement, of giggling and smirking and stupid remarks and endlessly discussing whether completely boring boys liked them or not. The very thought of it all depressed her. They practised French kissing on each other's arms and counted the number of boys they had snogged as if it was a competition. They called it 'tongue sandwich', which made Victoria feel sick; worse than sharing a toothbrush with a stranger.

Then Vinnie going so badly. The instructor had not said so, but Victoria was sure that she was doing something wrong, that she had put him off jumping by catching him in the mouth when she got left behind over fences, which had happened a few times recently. When they had bought him last year he was her dream horse, sixteen hands, dapple grey, a three-quarter thoroughbred who had already won several small events. So what had gone wrong? Tears started to prick behind her eyes and she sniffed them away. In a minute she would telephone her friend Lucy again. Lucy's mother hadn't allowed her to go to Gina's party, so that put them in the same boat, almost, but only because Lucy had a weird mother and not because she wasn't invited.

From downstairs she heard the doorbell ring and then her father's voice greeting someone in the hall. Victoria was grateful that her parents had a supper party to keep them occupied. It meant that she would be left alone and not have to answer their questions all the evening. She might go down later on. She liked Anthony Brewer. He talked to her as if she was a grown-up and there was something about the way he studied her face that made her feel a bit funny. He was really, really old but she'd rather spend five minutes with him than all the stupid boys at the party put together.

Getting up, she went over to the window to get her diary from her desk. It was comforting to write down how she felt.

Sarah Challis

Glancing out, her eye was caught by two people in the garden of the Major's bungalow. A tall woman with very short hair was walking to the gate, arm in arm with a blonde girl, deep in conversation. They turned towards each other and hugged and then the woman went out of sight and the girl stood for a moment looking after her, before moving back towards the bungalow, walking through a golden pool of evening sunshine. She had long hair loose on her shoulders and wore jeans and a T-shirt. Victoria thought she was beautiful and knew that if she could choose, at that very moment she would rather be that girl than anyone else in the world.

By eight fifteen all Julia's guests had arrived and there was a swell of noise in the drawing room. Goodness, thought Claudia, people in the country do shout. It must be because they are for ever bellowing for dogs or hailing one another across windswept acres. She nursed her gin and tried to concentrate on Ann Millard, a large woman with steel-grey hair held back by a hairband. She wore a striped shirt with turned up collar festooned with strings of pearls, and a calf-length, full denim skirt, bunchy around her waist. So far she had addressed no questions to Claudia, embarking instead on a long description of a recent fishing trip to Scotland. Claudia knew enough about Scottish rivers to keep her going with judicious prompts. Also listening patiently was Ros Caswell, a gentle woman with a faded prettiness and a nervous habit of making little encouraging noises in her throat.

The party seemed to have divided on a gender basis – the men all gathered in a corner round the drinks table, and the women round the fireplace, although there was no fire lit but a large and beautiful flower arrangement in the hearth. Jo Turner and Julia were discussing the Pony Club rally, at which, Claudia gathered, they had both had children. Jo was tall and very slim with blonde hair, skintight suede trousers and rather a lot of make-up. Claudia had been told that she and her banker husband divided their time between Dorset and London and she immediately shrank from talking to her.

They had gathered in a pretty room with long windows and a lovely honey-coloured wooden floor scattered with good Persian rugs. It was furnished in an English country style, with battered faded chairs and sofas, some very good antique furniture and rather gloomy portraits on the pale green walls. It had a comfortable lived-in air, with piles of magazines and books

94

and photographs. She's a good homemaker, Claudia thought, looking across at Julia, and, she would bet, a good wife too. Peter Durnford had a well-fed and cared for look about him, with that ridiculous yellow and red bow tie fixed under his receding chin. He had been rather jittery pouring her gin, rabbiting on about no lemon and not able to look her in the eye. He must be shy, Claudia thought, because he seemed quite normal with the others, whom of course he knew.

Anthony Brewer, who arrived last, had kissed all the women on both cheeks and Claudia noticed how easily he moved between them, perfectly at home with each. He wore a blue shirt, which intensified the impact of his startling eyes, and cream cotton trousers. He looked fit and well, more so than any of the other men who had all spread a little in middle age and become slack-paunched to varying degrees. He's a man's man, too, she thought as he took up a position with the husbands, and began a clearly very entertaining story about someone they all knew. She felt slightly disappointed that he hadn't lingered by her side or given her any special attention. For some reason she had supposed he might have done.

Peter Durnford broke away from the men and started to refill glasses, which gave Ros the opportunity to turn to Claudia and ask how she liked living in the village.

'Oh, I love it. Well, I'm still very new, but I like it very much. I've always been happy in the country.'

There followed an exchange about the virtues of various counties, and how unpleasant it was to live in London. Jo Turner joined in.

'The worst thing is to have to migrate between the two. People think one gets the best of both worlds but not in my experience. I flog up and down the motorway shipping meals one way and leftovers the other. I once had a red cabbage which clocked up about eight hundred miles. I long to live down here full time. I can't wait for Adrian to retire.'

Claudia noticed that no one asked her about her husband. Julia had done a good job on briefing her friends that she was divorced. Anthony Brewer now appeared by her side, whisky in hand.

'Are these girls looking after you?' he asked jokingly.

Claudia nodded and smiled.

'Old banger going all right?'

'Oh yes. Thank you so much.' She could not exaggerate her gratitude.

'You know that Claudia here took on one of my tractors?' Anthony turned to the other women, teasing. They simultaneously adopted expressions of amused concern.

'Wrote my car off, I'm afraid, and I was totally stuck without transport,' Claudia explained, 'and Anthony very kindly lent me his pick-up. It's meant I can get to work and—'

'Oh yes!' broke in Julia as she passed behind them with more ice. 'Now, Claudia, is it true you are mushroom picking? My daily told me and really I couldn't believe it.'

'Yes, absolutely,' said Claudia firmly, determined not to look uncomfortable. 'Why?'

'Well!' said Julia, and her voice made Peter turn to listen. 'I was just terribly surprised. There must be other things you could do. It must be so boring for one thing, and don't you have to do it in the dark? Now, Ann does silk flowers. Terribly clever. Don't you need some help, Ann? You're always flat out doing the shows in the summer.'

Before Ann could reply, Claudia said, 'I quite enjoy it, actually. It's well-paid for unskilled work and I can do what hours I like. It suits me very well until I find something else.'

'Have you worked before? I mean, have you had some sort of career?' Julia persisted. She wanted to get to the bottom of this.

'No. Not really. I used to cook a bit, but not since the children were born. I really am unskilled in every sense. Actually, I'm not going to pick next week anyway, because my daughter's home from New York for a few days and I want to make the most of her visit.'

This piece of information was sufficient to secure a change of direction. It was easy to speak of Lila and what she was doing in New York, which led to universities and degree courses and a general exchange of experiences related to grown-up children. Julia got no closer to finding out exactly why Claudia was now hard up. She had to go through to the kitchen to drain the potatoes, swilling wine as she went; goodness, she felt completely pissed already. She cascaded the potatoes into a serving dish and slapped a knob of butter in their direction. It fell short and dropped onto the floor and Skye, waiting optimistically by her feet, was on to it in a flash.

Julia poured dressing on the salad and tossed it about haphazardly. Several leaves fell from the bowl onto the table and she chucked them back in.

'Come through!' she shouted at the open door. 'Peter! Bring everyone through! Sheepdog, Peter!' She leaned across the table to light candles and the kitchen was glowing in soft light as her guests started to drift in from the drawing room. 'You should have brought your daughter,' she said to Claudia. 'We would have loved to meet her.'

'She was very tired. She only got here yesterday. I think she was going to have a bath and early bed.'

'Peter. Do the seating, darling. It's quite beyond me by this stage. Jo, give me a hand with these plates, would you? Claudia, you're at the other end. Next to Peter. And then Anthony.'

At last they were all seated and Julia began passing plates of salmon down the table. Now, in the soft gloom of the candlelit room, Peter could look at Claudia properly. He thought she was lovely. Her hair was a shining chestnut colour and the short cut emphasised her long elegant neck and the fragile bones of her face. Her eyes looked large and dark – tired, really, but the shadows somehow suited her. She was dressed very simply in a short-sleeved black T-shirt and a pair of black trousers with a rose-coloured scarf tied somehow at her throat. There was a stillness and quiet about her which he found most attractive. She was leaning across the table to catch something John Millard was saying.

'Yes,' she said, 'I moved out of London. We lived there for years, so it's a wonderful escape to come to a village.'

'Who is "we"?' John asked.

Goodness, Claudia thought, people in the country like to get to the bottom of things.

'My family,' she said simply, and turning to Peter remarked, 'This is a lovely house.'

'It's Julia's,' he began, but his wife was now rebuking him from the other end of the table.

'Peter! Don't go to sleep! The wine, darling, for goodness sake!'

'Excuse me,' he said to Claudia and got up to put bottles on the table, and to fill the women's glasses. Conversation was further interrupted by the potatoes and salad being passed down the table.

'My dear,' said Anthony to Claudia, 'I insist you have more potatoes than that. You're like a reed as it is.'

Large Ann Millard on his other side was conscious of having helped herself to rather too many. Bloody man, she thought, vigorously buttering her bread, smarming over that new woman who was disgustingly thin.

'How long have you been on your own, Claudia?' he asked,

97

as their heads were bent close over the dish.

'Quite a time,' said Claudia, taking the dish from him. To Peter who was at the other end of the table doing his duty with the bottles she said, 'Shall I serve you, Peter?'

'Oh my dear!' murmured Anthony in her ear. 'Make his day!'

Claudia ignored him and spooned some of the rather dirty-looking new potatoes onto Peter's plate.

'You are being very mysterious,' Anthony persisted. 'Tell me about your ex-husband.'

This was it. Claudia had known this moment would come and she had rehearsed what she would say. She turned to look him straight in the eye. 'I'd rather not talk about him, if you don't mind. It's something I don't discuss.'

There was a moment of silence suspended between them. Anthony raised his eyebrows and looked solemnly into her face. He nodded. 'Of course,' he murmured. 'Forgive me.'

Next door, Lila sat with her eyes closed in the last of the evening sun, a glass of wine on the grass beside her. She had that prickly-eyed feeling of too little sleep but all the tension she had felt in New York had evaporated in the mildness and calm of the English countryside. It was strange to have no home, to accept that she couldn't walk down their familiar street in Chelsea and let herself in through the glossy front door of number 46 and run up the stairs to her bedroom. Although she hadn't lived there properly for years, that house still occupied the space marked HOME in her head. Now she would never go there again. Nor to the cottage, where they had had some of their happiest times as a family. The odd thing was that after all that angst in New York, now she was back she found it did not matter; that this funny, ugly place was as much home as anywhere. The familiar bits of furniture helped, and her mother had done a good job in saving the things that mattered to her. The little bedroom here was full of them – her boxes of photographs, letters, tatty old clothes, even her rabbit hot-water bottle had survived the crisis. Her mountain bike was in the garage. Tomorrow she would go for a ride and explore the countryside, stop and have a drink at the pub, get her bearings.

She had to admit that although she remained deeply disappointed that her mother could not be galvanized into saving her marriage and had taken up a role which Lila found exasperating, on the whole she had done a good job. It wasn't such a bad idea to come to the country. Lila could see that to be penniless in London would not be much fun, and the mushroom picking, now her mother had explained her reasons for doing it, no longer seemed like a provocative gesture. The bungalow was fresh and bright with new paint, and with just the two of them there, felt a bit like sharing a flat with a girlfriend. She had had a happy first evening, helping her mother henna her hair, and then going into the little town to get fish and chips. It had been fun and felt oddly carefree.

It was only on the subject of her father that Lila saw her mother stiffen and tense.

'I can't telephone him, Mum. They're not allowed incoming calls, but apparently he can buy phone cards and call out. Why can't I give him this number? Why won't you speak to him?'

'Lila, there is no point, and on no account are you to give him this number. If you do, I will have to get it changed. We don't have anything to say to each other, darling. We have said it all. Over and over. There is no point in stirring everything up again. We both need a chance to, I don't know, realign our lives, or something. When he comes out, according to David, he intends to live with Carla. You must accept that.'

'Why should I?' Lila had blazed. 'Why should I accept it? My father with a, a . . .' she could not find the word she wanted, 'a tart like that,' she finished. 'It's you he needs, Mum. He always did and he will again. You shouldn't accept it either.'

Claudia sighed. It was impossible to get the message across to her daughter.

'When will you see him?' she asked.

'I'll go up to London in a day or two, and I'll go from there. I can get a train to Stafford, and then a taxi. He's only allowed visitors twice a week, so I'll go twice and then I must back to work, I suppose.'

Claudia had wondered whether this was the moment to bring up the threat of the newspaper story but decided to leave it alone. Let Roger tell her. She would find it easier to accept from him.

Lila picked up her glass and yawned. Half past nine and the shadows were lengthening but the air was still warm. Time for bath and bed. She could just hear the sound of voices from next door. They must have all the doors and windows open on this lovely evening. She hoped her mother was enjoying the party.

The summer pudding was being passed round, followed by a jug of cream, and the conversation had turned to horses at Julia's end of the table. She was complaining loudly about Vinnie and the people who had sold him to her. 'I'm certain they knew he wasn't genuine,' she said. 'It was only a matter of time before he started to go wrong. He's got a real nap in him. He was a beast today. Poor Tor, she adores him.' There was a murmur of sympathy, but not from Jo, who knew the horse was perfectly all right and that the fault lay elsewhere.

'When Tor's at school, what happens to him?' she asked.

Julia pulled a face. 'What do you think? Muggins here has to keep him ticking over. I really don't have the time, but someone has to do it.'

Jo, who knew the standard of Julia's horsemanship, said, 'But doesn't he get schooled? Don't you get someone to jump him?'

Julia pointed the serving spoon she was holding down the table at Peter. 'He wouldn't hear of it. Goodness, keeping a horse is expensive enough. We can't afford jumping clinics, trainers, and all that malarky.'

Jo raised her eyebrows as if to say, well, that explains the problem.

Claudia, who caught the end of this conversation, said to Anthony, 'Have you seen that girl and the black and white horse? I'm intrigued by them. She seems to live round here.'

'The girl from the railway line? Yes, they turn up all over the place. The horse came from Ireland, I believe. Her father uses it sometimes when he's wooding.'

'It's a terrific jumper. They jumped a ditch and a set of rails out of the lane the other day. I couldn't believe my eyes. Absolutely flew.'

Jo was listening now. 'Who's this?' she asked. She was always looking for talented horses for her daughters.

'A child of about ten who rides bareback round the village on a coloured horse. They jumped out of the lane in front of me – stiff rails and a ditch, out of a trot.'

'Goodness. Where are they from, did you say, Anthony?'

'The railway line. They're travellers of sorts. The father does some hedging and ditching for me.'

Julia had also picked up on this conversation. She had drunk more than usual and her face was flushed and shining rosily. 'Ah! Anthony! I want to tackle you about that. It's causing a lot of upset in the village, you know, you allowing them back on the line. After all the trouble we had last year—'

'Julia, dearest,' Anthony cut in smoothly, 'these are not the same people. The father, Jem, grew up round here. Really they're a local family, and he's a very skilled man. There aren't many left who can lay a hedge the way he does.'

'That's all very well, but others don't see it like that. Where you get just one of their dreadful vans, it attracts others. They'll all be back before you know it. We simply don't want people like that living on our doorstep. Nothing feels safe in the village. Garden sheds, garages get broken into, and look at the mess they make, the rubbish they leave, and that child is a disgrace. She's never in school. Charging about on that horse which is far too strong for her, and without a hat. One of these days I am going to call the Social Services. Do I gather Claudia has seen her jumping rails out of the lane? It really must be stopped before there is an appalling accident. You must talk to the father. It's utterly irresponsible.'

'Shut up, Julia, you're being a bore,' said Peter, so suddenly and loudly that it made Claudia jump.

There was an awkward moment before everybody laughed and Claudia saw that Julia took the rebuke cheerfully, saying to Jo in an unrepentant tone, 'I'm very sorry, but you know me, when I get a bee in my bonnet . . .'

Claudia turned to Peter. 'Do tell me about my neighbour on the other side. Mrs Pomeroy, I think?'

Peter muttered, 'For goodness sake, don't let Julia hear. Valerie Pomeroy is another of her bugbears – she can't stand her. The bungalow, you see. Your bungalow, in fact. It caused a terrible row when it was built. Valerie claimed she needed the money and Julia was determined to stop it going ahead. She feels it ruins this house, which it does to a certain extent.' Peter was becoming uncomfortably aware that he was being tactless but could not see how to extricate himself.

Claudia saw his predicament and was amused. 'Well, it is an eyesore, isn't it? I can quite see Julia's point. I think I would have felt exactly the same if I'd lived here.'

Peter smiled, relieved. Fortified by several glasses of whisky and quite a lot of wine, he said earnestly, 'I've been meaning to say, you know, being neighbours, if there is anything I can do, ever, please, don't hesitate. If you are nervous on your own. Any time.' Again he had the uncomfortable feeling he was being run away with. There was too much emotion in his voice. His tone sounded, even to himself, as if he were deeply moved and offering something heroic, when he had intended to be casual, but Claudia was still smiling at him.

'That's really kind of you. Very comforting. Thank you very

much.' Unexpectedly, she patted Peter's hand where it lay on the table next to her own.

In a flurry of embarrassment Peter got up to fetch more wine and only when he had sat down again could Claudia continue. 'And Mrs Pomeroy? What is she like? I find her rather intriguing as well.'

'She's quite a character. She and her husband were both academics. He was a professor at London University – SOAS, I think, and she did some sort of research. They've had that place next door for about thirty years I should say and then retired down here. It wasn't long after that her husband was diagnosed with some sort of galloping cancer and he only lived a few more months. Valerie nursed him to the end, I believe. Wouldn't let them take him into hospital. All in all, they were that rare thing, a truly devoted couple.

'After he died she got crabbier. She was always a bit short with people, and she stopped having drinks parties, stopped going out much, and then she dropped this bombshell about building in the garden. Said she was short of cash. You know the rest. There's one son who comes over from Hong Kong periodically. I've no idea what he does. Got a tribe of children who hurtle about the village for a few weeks and then they all disappear back again and all goes quiet.'

'Ah,' said Claudia thoughtfully.

'She's a fascinating person, actually,' said Anthony, who had been listening. 'An expert on Indian poetry and art, and Frank, her husband, was delightful. She's gone downhill since he died. I used to persuade her to come to supper occasionally, but she won't stir any longer. I hardly see her these days.'

'Are you talking about Big Val?' said Julia, collecting pudding plates and plonking down a wedge of cheddar on a wooden board. Claudia nodded assent. 'Has Peter told you that she hits the bottle? Peter! Don't look like that! Everybody knows! Are you going to get the port, darling?'

In the ensuing bustle of coffee cups and port glasses, Anthony turned to Claudia and said quietly, 'Our hostess will get us to change places in a moment. She always does, and I must have a moment with you before I get evicted.' Claudia sensed what was coming and wondered how she would handle whatever invitation or proposition she was going to receive but at that moment the kitchen door opened and a lanky teenage girl came in, a large tabby cat in her arms, wearing stretch jodhpurs and a grubby T-shirt.

'Tor, darling! Come in! Get yourself a plate!' called Julia from the Aga where she was making coffee.

Victoria buried her face in the cat and slid into her father's vacated seat. Claudia smiled at her.

'Hello,' she said. 'I'm Claudia.'

'Hi.'

'How's my favourite girl?' asked Anthony. 'God! They must keep you well watered in Gro-bags at that school of yours. You've shot up.'

'Four inches this term,' said Victoria shyly. 'I'm nearly the tallest in my year.'

'It's all right to be tall these days, isn't it?' said Claudia. 'I mean, girls all want to be. It wasn't like that when I was at school and grew like a weed. I wished more than anything to be little. My daughter's tall, too. Nearly six foot with size nine shoes and she loves it.'

'Was it her I saw? Next door? Has she got blonde hair?'

'Yes. That's Lila. She works in New York so it's quite a treat to have her here for a few days.'

'Sorry to hear about the horse,' said Anthony. 'You'll be old enough to drive soon so I should get rid of it and start saving for a red sports car. Much more fun.'

'Anthony!' protested Victoria. 'I love Vinnie. It's not his fault. I wish Mum hadn't told everyone.'

'It's hard to keep him going well, I expect, when you're away at school,' said Claudia. 'Lila was lucky. She used to take her horse with her.'

'Does your daughter still ride?' asked Victoria. She was sure the golden girl did everything brilliantly.

'Not regularly any more. She was rather good at it at one time. She had a young horse when she was about your age, which she brought on to be an intermediate eventer. Her father wouldn't let her ride full time when she left university and I think, by then, she'd had enough anyway. She sold her horses before she went to New York.'

Victoria helped herself to a corner of cheese and a biscuit. 'I'm going to put up some fences in the field tomorrow and see if I can get Vinnie going any better. I know he can. That's what's so depressing.'

'If you like, I'll ask Lila to come and give you a hand. Only if you think it might help.'

'Do you think she would?' asked Victoria doubtfully.

'Of course she would. I expect she'd love to be around a horse again. She'll be bored stiff after a day or two with nothing to do. Shall I ask her?'

'Oh yes, please. That would be so cool.'

'What time shall I say? Ten o'clock? If it's no good for any reason, I'll get a message to you.'

'It would be really great if she would. It's so hard to know what I'm doing wrong.'

Claudia smiled and said, 'Between you I expect you'll sort out the problem.'

Julia began to tap a spoon on her plate and when there was less noise, told the men that they were to move places to drink their coffee and port.

'I told you,' said Anthony to Claudia, 'and I've hardly had a chance to talk to you. I'm very inclined towards open rebellion.'

'Come on, Anthony. Marching orders. You can't monopolise Claudia,' said Adrian Turner, appearing behind them. 'It's my turn. Or you either, of course, Ann.'

Victoria got up to make way for Ros's husband, Julian, and went to hang over the back of her mother's chair and pick at the summer pudding. Anthony sat between Jo and Julia, and Claudia noticed Jo immediately engaged him in some private and intense conversation. He looked down sideways at her plate while she talked, and then, noticing Victoria, broke off the conversation with Jo and leant back in his chair to talk to her instead. Jo sat back, looking rather put out.

Claudia finished her coffee and refused port. Her head had started to ache and she wanted to go home. She knew none of these people but the whole ritual of the evening was so familiar and seemed so pointless. She was here on a totally artificial basis, pretending to be a quite different person than who she was. These couples with their safe, predictable lives could not have guessed her secret and it felt deceitful to thus mislead them. As soon as she possibly could she would make her excuses and leave. She wished now that she hadn't got involved with Victoria. It was stupid of her to offer Lila's help which was sure to lead to complications.

She listened to her two male companions talking about house prices, then said, 'Will you excuse me? I really must go.' She got to her feet, dropped her napkin and bent to retrieve it, and found that her movement had caused a shift round the table and the other wives were also getting up. For a moment a look of relief passed over Julia's face, before she said, 'Oh! Must you? I'm sure it's terribly early!'

There was a period of stand-up talking then, giving thanks to Peter and Julia and saying goodbye to one another, kissing and laughing, before they spilled out onto the drive and made their way to their cars. Claudia managed to slip away into the darkness of the drive and escape any further conversation with Anthony other than a called goodbye across the kitchen. She bolted through her gate and ran across the front garden to the bungalow. The lights were on in the hall and sitting room and she thought, with pleasure, that Lila was there.

Peter Durnford poured himself another glass of port which he knew was quite a serious mistake and would give him an appalling headache the next day. The evening had been such a muddle, he thought. He couldn't decide whether it had been a disaster or was mildly hopeful. He had not totally disappointed himself in that he had at least had one or two conversations with Claudia, but not about anything very memorable, and when he had said his bit about being a neighbour and there for her if ever she needed him, he had sounded a complete twit. Completely over the top. But then she had patted his hand and looked really sweetly into his eyes. So much so that he had jumped up in a fluster.

The good thing, the really excellent thing, was that Anthony hadn't had a look in at all. In fact, Claudia had turned to speak to him more than she had to Anthony. All in all, he would give himself about seven out of ten. Certainly a 'could do better' performance, but not a disaster. He rolled up his sleeves, put on Julia's apron and began to wash up thoughtfully. Victoria drifted in and put her arms round him from behind.

'How's my girl?' he asked.

'OK,' she replied. 'I suppose.'

'Cheer up, old thing.' He squirted washing-up liquid in the sink and gave the water a whirl about. 'Nothing seriously wrong, is there?'

'Oh, Dad, don't be silly,' she said with a sigh. 'You always sound as if I'm going to say I'm on drugs or pregnant or something.'

'Good God! You're not, are you?'

'There are other things to be, you know. I mean, other than preggers or a druggie.'

'Of course there are,' said Peter, although he hadn't the foggiest what she was on about. It was probably a teenage thing. Feeling a bit down. Victoria laid her head on his back between

105

his shoulder blades. How tall she was getting. 'It's quite normal to feel fed up at times, you know.'

'Is it?'

'God, yes. Sorry to have to tell you, but it's how most people feel, mildly, most of the time. At least, I certainly do.'

'Poor old Dad.'

Peter put a saucepan to dry on the rack and turned round and put his arms round his daughter. 'Not poor old Dad. Lucky old Dad.' He kissed the top of her head. 'Here, I know. Have a glass of port. That'll do you good.' He poured her out a glass from the decanter on the table and gave it to her. They leaned their backs on the rail of the Aga and clinked glasses. 'Sod the lot of them,' said Peter.

'Dad! What do you mean?'

'You know. Them!'

'Yeah,' said Victoria, in a little voice. 'Sod them.'

They smiled at one another.

'Where's Mum?'

'I sent her to bed. She's fair beat.'

'I'll help you clear up.'

'No need, old thing. I'm a lazy slob most of the time. Won't hurt me to do it for once.'

'It's OK. I don't mind.'

Together they shuffled about the kitchen in a companionable way, stacking the dishwasher and washing glasses and putting things in cupboards.

'What did you think of Mrs Next Door?' asked Peter, casually. It had taken him quite ten minutes to get the moment right.

'Claudia Thingummy? I thought she was cool. Don't you? She's pretty, isn't she? Sort of different looking.'

'Mmmm.'

'Her daughter looks fab, I saw her out of the window. She's got this wonderful blonde hair. Dad, do you think I should have streaks put in mine? Everyone at school is doing stuff like that.'

'Shouldn't bother, old thing. You've got lovely hair. Shiny and lovely. Well, that looks as if we've done.' He flung the tea towel onto a chair and looked round the kitchen.

Victoria yawned. The port had made her feel heavy and tired. Together they turned off the lights and went up to bed.

Claudia was surprised to see that Lila was still up. When she pushed open the sitting-room door she could see her sitting on the floor, leaning on the sofa, smoking a cigarette.

'I thought you would have gone to bed, darling,' she said, and then Lila turned and Claudia saw that her face looked very white and strained and knew instantly that something was wrong.

'What is it? Lila, what's the matter?'

Lila's face collapsed like a crumpled paper bag. 'Oh Mum!' she said in a trembling voice. 'It's Jerome. There's been an accident.'

Chapter Seven

Victoria had been working Vinnie in the paddock for at least twenty minutes. She kept glancing at her watch and it was now well past ten o'clock. She had set up some jumps and put up the poles over a few fences her father had built for her in the field. She knew that Lila wasn't coming. The sun was already getting quite hot and dark patches of sweat were spreading on Vinnie's neck. She hadn't got the heart to start jumping him on her own. In a minute she would pack it in and take him back to the stables.

'Hi!' said a voice. 'I couldn't find anyone to ask where to find you, so I've just barged in. I'm Lila.' The tall, blonde girl was coming through the gate, wearing jeans and a white T-shirt, her hair tied back in a slide under a baseball cap.

'Hi,' said Victoria, flushing, and yanking Vinnie round. 'This is really, really kind . . .'

'Sorry I'm late. We had a bit of a crisis last night and there were one or two things to see to this morning.'

'Oh dear,' said Victoria. She didn't like to ask what. 'I hope . . .'

'My brother,' said Lila, coming to pat Vinnie's neck. 'He's had an accident in India. Broken his leg quite badly in a bus crash. Eventually we got through on the telephone and he's all right. He's being flown home. There was quite a bit to organise.'

'Oh dear,' Victoria repeated. 'I'm really sorry.'

'He's in Delhi on his gap year, so that's spoilt, but at least he's had most of it. He was teaching at a school for blind children. Of course, Mum got really hyper about the whole thing, but she's calmed down now. She was better when we got through to the hospital and she spoke to some doctor who'd been trained in Birmingham. Anyway, enough of all that. So this is Vinnie? He's rather nice.'

'Yes, he's lovely.'

'Mum said you were having some trouble. I don't know

109

whether I can help. I'm a bit rusty but I had good teachers when I was competing. If I can remember anything, that is. Why don't you just go on doing what you were doing?'

Victoria continued circling the horse, first at a trot and then at a canter, changing rein so that she was going in one direction and then the other.

'OK,' said Lila. 'Pull up a min. He's been well-schooled, hasn't he? And he's well-balanced. I see you've put up some poles. Do you want to do them just as you would normally? We can see what happens then.'

'OK,' said Victoria, beginning to canter again. Vinnie knew these jumps well and he popped over them in a bored way, rolling the poles on two and then swerving to the side of the last. Victoria nearly came off as he ducked to the right.

'I see!' called Lila. 'Naughty boy!' She walked over to where Victoria had pulled up. Her face was red and upset but she patted her horse's neck.

'I'm sure it's me,' she mumbled. 'That it's my fault.'

'Bit of each, I think,' said Lila. 'What I think you're doing is going in a bit fast with quite a long rein and then when you get to the stride when he's about to take off, you kind of drop everything and just sit there, and he thinks, oh, she's out for lunch, and he does what he feels like.' Victoria listened hard, trying to take in what she was being told. 'I also think you're riding too long in the leg. That's why you're getting left behind and then you drop the rein so that you won't catch him in the mouth. Let's put these leathers up a couple of holes. Now get into a jumping position. See? Your weight will be over his shoulder now and you'll find it easier to keep your seat when you're jumping. Now shorten your reins and go much more slowly. He could jump all these out of a trot. Shorter than that. Shorter still. That's better. Now try again.'

This time Vinnie felt completely different, thought Victoria. He felt as if he knew she meant business. He hopped over the fences easily and when he tried to swerve out again at the last, she was able to straighten him up and make him jump it, even though it wasn't very well or tidily done.

'Great! Miles better. Doesn't it feel better?'

'Yes, much. I really see what you mean. Shall I do them again?'

'No, I wouldn't. He's fairly bored by them already. I expect he does them all the time, doesn't he? What have you got in the field? That little hedge? A post and rails? Do you want to try those?'

Lila walked beside her as Victoria rode Vinnie through the gate into the field.

'Circle him in front, very quietly, and then when you feel ready, just pop him over. Don't let him have time to decide he's not going. Shorten your reins again. You've got in the habit of riding much too long. Don't worry about catching him in the mouth. You won't get left behind in that jumping position and you can always let them run through your fingers if you think you are.'

Again Vinnie went much better and Victoria came back beaming. 'Thank you so much. It makes all the difference doing it like that. Would you like to try him?'

'Would you mind? I'd love to!'

Victoria jumped down and the two girls swapped hats. Up in the saddle, Lila let down the stirrup leathers. 'Poor Vinnie. He wonders what he's got on his back.' She gathered up the reins. 'Come on, my lad. Let's see what you're like.'

Victoria watched as Lila circled Vinnie and then popped him over the obstacles. She could see what a competent rider she was.

'You can jump the big hedge if you want,' she called. 'I'll take the wire down.'

'Where? Over there? OK, great. He's got a lovely jump!'

Victoria ran to the hedge and unhooked a strand of barbed wire and stood back to watch.

She hadn't noticed the man walking across the field towards her until a voice said 'Hello, Tor. I thought it was you on the horse.' She turned to see Anthony Brewer approaching, dressed in his farming clothes and holding an envelope. 'I came to give this to your ma,' he went on, waving it in the air. 'To thank her for last night. Couldn't find her in the house. Who is that riding?'

'They've gone to church,' explained Victoria. 'It's Lila. Mrs Whatsit's from next door's daughter. She's a wonderful rider. She's been helping me with Vinnie.'

'Is that who it is?' said Anthony, interested. Together they watched the horse and rider sail over the hedge and canter round to pull up next to them.

'He's great,' said Lila, patting Vinnie's neck and jumping down. 'Thanks, Victoria. I really enjoyed that.'

'This is Anthony Brewer,' said Victoria hastily, before rushing on, 'Vinnie was wonderful with you. That's how he used to go.'

'Hi,' said Lila, brushing down her jeans and taking off the

riding hat. Her hair fell loose from the clip and she squinted up into the sun at the man who stood watching her.

'Hello,' said Anthony. 'Now, that was a pleasure to watch!'

Claudia sat on the floor beside the telephone, talking to Minna. She picked nervously at the fringe of the rug at her feet. 'So what do you think, Min? It's a compound fracture, apparently, and he was unconscious for quite a while after the crash. Is it really the best option to have him flown home? It's one hell of a flight and I just don't know whether I've made the right decision. I could fly out to be with him, but I'd much rather get him back here if I could.'

'I think you will have to be guided by what the doctors out there have to say. You got hold of someone who spoke English?'

'Eventually I did, after a very long time. A doctor who was trained over here. He said that it was a kind of spiral break and that it was going to need a plate put in as soon as the swelling has gone down a bit.'

'Yes, that sounds right. Did he say that he thought Jerome was fit to fly? He'll have to issue him with some sort of certificate of air worthiness before any scheduled airline will take him as a passenger.'

'He's going to do that. He couldn't see that flying presented any risk. Thank God, Roger had taken out massive insurance which will cover sending medics home with him. I rather gathered from the rep of TeachWorldwide that it would be just as well to get him out of that Delhi hospital – risk of infection and all that sort of thing.'

'We have that here, too, you know,' said Minna. 'Our hospitals are full of it. Where will he get taken to, this end?'

'The insurance company have agreed that he go to Salisbury, to that orthopaedic man you said was brilliant. I spoke to him this morning. He said he would hope to operate in a day or two of his getting back and that if all went well he'd be home in a week.'

'Let's hope so. You can come and stay with us. You don't want to do that journey back to your village twice a day.'

'Thanks so much. I was going to ask you that. The really awful thing is not to be able to see Jerome right now, or even to speak to him. I have to take other people's word for how he is. It was a bloody awful crash, I gather. People died, Min. It took hours to cut the bodies out, so the doctor said.'

'We have a lot to be grateful for, then. He's young and fit.

He'll recover quickly.' After a pause, Minna added, 'Have you told Roger?'

'Min! Of course! He *is* his father. By the time I got back from this ghastly party next door, Lila had already telephoned the prison and left a message with the night staff. They wouldn't let her speak to Roger but said they would tell him immediately. She nearly came round to get me from next door but thought better of it. She decided it was best that I heard the news here at home, privately. I was surprised at how thoughtful that was. Unlike Lila, really, who usually needs instant reassurance herself. It's every mother's nightmare, isn't it? Those ghastly words "there's been an accident".'

'It's the distance that makes it worse. As you said, not being able to see for yourself. Can't they get Jerome a telephone so that he can speak to you?'

'The hospital didn't sound up to anything quite so sophisticated. I don't think they have telephones on the wards and then making an overseas call would be very difficult, I imagine. We'll just have to sit it out. They will let me know what flight they can get him on and then I'll go to Heathrow and come back in the ambulance with him.'

'How's Lila been?' asked Minna, knowing her niece's penchant for drama.

'Actually, she's been great. Selfishly, it's been wonderful to have her here to share all the anxiety. She's been quite calm and sensible and got me through all the ghastliness of last night when we were trying to find out just how badly Jerome had been hurt. She's next door now, helping out with the daughter's horse. She's going to London tomorrow and then to see Roger, then back here to see Jerome, then back to New York. Not exactly a rest.'

'Lila will be all right. She's tough. It'll help her stop thinking about herself. This puts Roger and his shenanigans into perspective, doesn't it?' said Minna.

'It surely does. And all that worry about that newspaper article coming out. I almost couldn't care now. Jerome is so much more important. I'll tell you something else, Min. The bungalow will be ideal when he's let out from hospital. No stairs to cope with. London would have been a nightmare with everything on different floors.

'That's true,' said Minna. 'Look, sorry, Claudia, but I'm going to have to rush. I've got to collect the boys from Swim Club. I sent poor old Johnnie even though he's got an awful cold.

113

Doctors' children have to understand from an early age that they're not allowed to be ill. Let me know any news, won't you? Give tons of love to Lil. See you soon. It will be lovely having you to stay for a bit. I'll get Chris to muck out the spare room. He uses it as an office extension.'

'Don't do that. I don't care what it's like. I'm quite happy to climb over his stuff.'

'No, it's a matter of principle. He keeps trying to extend his sphere of influence.'

'Well, I don't want to disrupt everything. He's had a hell of a lot to put up with from the Barron side of the family one way and another.'

'Yes, he's a good man. I know I'm lucky. Must go, Claudia. Speak soon.'

Claudia put down the telephone and yawned. She felt terribly weary after a nearly sleepless night, but at the same time her nerves felt taut and strung tight. Her thoughts kept turning to Jerome and now as she sat by the open door looking out into her garden, instead of the overgrown lawn she saw a white hospital bed in a long ward with fans whirring from the ceiling. She saw Jerome lying still, bandaged heavily, his eyes closed, his hands arranged tidily on the sheet. The upsetting thing was that she could not picture his face. Every time she tried to catch an image of it in her mind, it slid away and she found herself unable to assemble his features. It was the same last night; she had had to go and get a photograph of him and hold it in her hands, trying to imprint that dear face on her mind. Then it became unbearably painful to look at him, laughing at a table outside a London pub, beer mug in hand, while he was lying injured so many thousands of miles away, and for all she knew uncomforted and homesick.

She heard the sound of the gate, then footsteps and through the open door she saw Lila striding up the drive. Thank God for Lila. Claudia got up and went to meet her. Wordlessly, she put her arms round her daughter and felt her strong body, warm from the sun, the skin of her cheek the colour of a slightly brown egg. Jerome was so slender to hold by comparison, so narrow and bony. How she longed for him. She felt a hard lump pressing against her throat and tears began to well in her eyes. Lila allowed herself to be held for a moment before breaking free, saying she was gasping for a drink of water. Claudia followed her into the kitchen, still fighting back the stinging tears. With her back to her mother, running water into a glass at the sink, Lila said, 'No more news?'

'No. I've spoken to Minna. I'm going to stay there when we get Jerome back and into hospital in Salisbury.'

'That'll be nice for you.' Was there an edge to Lila's voice? Claudia thought so.

'Lila? What is it?'

Her daughter turned round, holding the glass of water. Her face was hot and red. 'I just can't believe you, Mum. At a time like this I'd have thought you could have relented and spoken to poor Dad. Don't you think what it's like for him, shut up in prison, not able to do anything to help Jerome?'

'Of course I've thought of him, Lila. I know he loves Jerome like I do. I'll keep him completely informed of what's happening. What else can I do?'

Lila burst into noisy tears and pulling out a chair slumped at the table. 'You can treat him like someone you've loved,' she cried. 'Share it with him, or something. At least speak to him. Let him get in touch with you.'

Claudia sighed. What had brought on this change of mood? she wondered. The tears which had threatened had gone, beaten back by her daughter's outburst. She remained standing by the door while Lila sniffed and snuffled. Something complex, which could not be resolved, seemed to stir in the silence between them.

I can't say what she wants to hear, thought Claudia, much as I would like to ease her pain.

Why can't she see how it's up to her to put things right? How easy it would be if only she would try, thought Lila. She sniffed again and pushed her hair back.

'I'm going to ride the horse again tomorrow morning,' she announced. 'Victoria wanted me to take him out if I had time. Then I'm going to London. That farmer's giving me a lift.'

'What farmer?'

'The smarmy one who lent you the pick-up. The one who thinks he's sex on legs. I met him just now. He's sorry, by the way, about Jerome. About what's happened. He said to tell you.'

'What do you mean, giving you a lift?'

'What's the matter with you, Mum? It's plain English, isn't it?' said Lila rudely. 'He's driving up to London tomorrow afternoon and said he would take me. OK?' Her tone implied that she was addressing someone very simple-minded.

Claudia said nothing. The atmosphere had become so hostile between them that it was better not to speak. She wondered if something Anthony Brewer had said had upset Lila.

Lila got up and went out. It was Claudia's turn to sit at the table. She just sat, not feeling anything very much, except the drag of anxiety. What was it Minna had said? That they had much to be thankful for. She must hang on to that. Much to be thankful for. Jerome was alive. Jerome was going to be all right.

Of course she had not needed Lila's admonishment to make her think of Roger. One could not wipe out twenty-five years of married life like that. She had thought how hard his punishment must seem, being locked away and unable to get on the telephone and fax to sort things out in India as she knew he would have done in any other circumstances. It would have been all systems go. His secretary would have been galvanised into action. There would have been telephoning of airlines and hospitals and embassies; no stone left unturned, no connection unexplored or unexploited. Certainly Claudia would not have been allowed to deal with any of it. But now things were different and she could see no point in speaking to Roger directly, as Lila wanted her to. He had already been passed all available information and she would continue to make sure he was kept up to date, as the situation developed. He could trust her to do that.

The problem was that Claudia knew how easily her defences would be swept away if she spoke to him directly. She could not trust her reaction to the sound of his voice. She was not yet strong enough, independent enough.

The other anxiety, she realised, had been stirred by what Lila had just told her, that Anthony Brewer was giving her a lift to London. Could she trust Lila to be discreet? It would not take much, just a little gentle prodding for Anthony to uncover everything and Lila was in no mood to be asked to be careful.

Getting up, Claudia filled the kettle and switched it on. She would make some strong coffee. At midday she was going to telephone the hospital. Dr Banderjee had given her his number and promised to be there to speak to her. She longed to hear some reassuring news of Jerome. She needed to be told again that he was going to be all right.

She could hear Lila shouting something from the bathroom. 'Mum! Can you get me a towel? I've washed my hair.' Obediently Claudia fetched one for her and, opening the door, passed it to her, where she stood bent over the basin. Lila looked round, her face still half upside down. 'Sorry, Mum. It was wrong to go at you like that.' She stood up and wrapped the towel turban fashion round her head. Her face looked shiny and very young. 'It was because of that lot next door. That's what set me off. Victoria's father, he came out to see how we were getting on with the horse and he was so, well, concerned and everything, and it reminded me of Dad and how things used to be. I know it's not your fault. I'm sorry, I really am. God, I do balls things up.'

'Oh, Lila!' Claudia sat on the bathroom stool. 'It's all horrible, I know. But as Minna said, we must be grateful Jerome is going to be all right and that is the only thing that matters now. As for Dad, it will mean a huge amount to him to see you next week and you can reassure him in person.'

'Yeah, I know.' Lila sat on the lavatory. 'It's just that I find it so hard to accept that we're not a family any more.'

'We are!' said Claudia fiercely. 'As much as we ever were. We've still got each other, but in a slightly different configuration. A bit imperfect, but still a family.' They managed a smile at one another.

'I'm making coffee,' said Claudia. 'Want some?'

'Sure,' said Lila, in a small voice. 'Thanks, Mum.'

Later they sat opposite one another at the table, nursing mugs in their hands, Lila wearing Claudia's dressing gown. 'So, you've been offered a lift to London,' said Claudia conversationally.

'Yeah. Nice of that bloke, really, but God, doesn't he fancy himself?'

Claudia laughed. 'I suppose he does. He has been terribly kind, though. Quite beyond the call of duty.'

'Yes, I'll give him that. He needn't have offered me a lift, either. He asked me how long I was going to be around and when I told him I was off tomorrow, he just said that he was driving up there after lunch.'

'He's quite nosy, Lila. He'll take the opportunity to ask you a lot of questions.'

It was Lila's turn to laugh. 'Don't worry, Mum. I won't let your cat out of the bag but you'd better make sure I know what story you've been putting around this village.'

'I haven't got one. All anyone knows is that I'm on my own, although I have implied that this has been the case for quite a long time.'

'OK. I don't suppose we'll talk about you or Dad anyway.'

Claudia had to smile. That, she thought, puts me in my place. She glanced at her watch. In fifteen minutes she would ring Dr Banderjee.

★ ★ ★

Waking the following morning Lila experienced the strange sensation of not knowing where she was. She lay looking at the strip of bright light showing between the curtains, trying to remember, and then as things started to take place in her mind she thought of Jerome. By now he would know when he was being flown home and that in only a little more than twenty-four hours he would be landing at Heathrow. Yesterday Dr Banderjee had somehow managed to get him to a telephone and she and her mother had both spoken to him, his voice as clear as if he was speaking from London although there was a time delay on the line which created odd little pauses and made them blunder on and speak over one another. It had been such a huge relief, this evidence that he was all right, that Lila and Claudia had both cried and had to pass the telephone between them in order not to waste a moment with gulping and sniffs. There had been something in his voice, though, a sort of restraint, which they had both noticed.

'Of course he's been in a horrific accident. There's sure to be some reaction. He's in a state of shock,' Lila had said, as an explanation for something which had troubled them both.

'We don't know if he was with anyone, and if he was, if they survived or not,' said Claudia.

'The man from TeachWorldwide said he wasn't with any other volunteer. I asked him,' said Lila.

'But he could still have been with friends – a friend,' said Claudia. 'He knew a lot of local university students. He taught some of them at evening classes. There was a girl, Jabeena.'

'Mum, don't speculate. What's the point? Wait and see. We'll soon be able to find all this stuff out.'

Now, lying warm and drowsy in her bed, Lila thought of her brother whom she loved very deeply, different though they were. She hoped he was not in any pain other than the physical discomfort of his leg. He was so intense, so given to brooding and agonies of spirit. For all their sakes she hoped there was no other, more complicated damage done.

Not given to pointless introspection, Lila climbed out of bed and opened the curtains. Another lovely day. She could hear her mother up and about, already in the bathroom. If she was going to school Vinnie again, as she had promised Victoria, and maybe go for a hack, she had better get moving. It was good to have something to do. Physical activity cleared her mind most wonderfully, and there was nothing she enjoyed more than riding.

118

★ ★ ★

It was hot by the time Lila finished doing some flat work in the paddock and Vinnie had started to sweat. He was a well-schooled horse who responded obediently to her commands and Lila realised that it was only Victoria's lack of conviction and determination which had allowed him to become sloppy and evasive. She, of course, hadn't said this to Victoria, but she had every intention of telling Mrs Durnford that her daughter needed some lessons to build up her confidence. When she had finished riding she would go up to the house and see if she could find her. She could see the roof of East End House with its lovely grey stone tiles rising above the trees which bordered the paddock. White stock doves tumbled from its ridges, cooing gently in the warm sun.

First she would take Vinnie for a ride. She had had a quick look at her mother's OS map and worked out a circuit taking in a couple of bridlepaths. It would be lovely to explore on such a beautiful morning. After the clamminess of New York, the air felt light and clean. As she halted Vinnie at the gate, before turning onto the lane, Greg, going past on the tractor, slowed down. Blimey, he thought. Who's that? He had enough time to take in the length of long thigh in the faded jeans and the hefty bosom and the swag of pale hair down the back. A tasty piece all right. Certainly not that droopy Durnford girl, who was only a kid anyway.

The girl on the horse waved a hand in thanks and he signalled back. Have to keep his eyes open for her, although knowing his luck with women, she was probably only passing through. It was always the same with a bit of class crumpet like that.

Betty, dismounted from her bicycle at the side of the lane before crossing into Mrs Pomeroy's drive, also saw Lila go by. What a big girl she was, and no mistake. Great strapping thing, with legs on her like a man. That's what they were like these days. Girls just grew and grew. Her granddaughter, Lauren, was only thirteen and already towering over her. So that was the new lady's daughter. Betty had already seen the two of them out in the pick-up together and Angie had been behind them in the queue in the chip shop on Friday night. Angie wasn't sure Claudia would speak, being a bit stand-offish, but no, she'd seemed quite pleased to see her and had a little chat, Angie said. The daughter was over from America and Claudia had said she wouldn't be going picking while she was staying.

Betty pushed her bike round to the back door, which stood

119

open. Mrs P must be outside somewhere. Doing the chickens, no doubt. The kitchen was in its usual state and, tying on her apron, Betty started on the washing up.

Out by the chicken run, Valerie heard the horse go by. It would be that child again. Jem's girl on the piebald horse. She ought to be in school. She'd told Jem as much but he had said she was unhappy at the primary school in Bishops Barton. Got bullied because she was a traveller. Valerie had not liked to hear that. She had been a governor of the school for a number of years and she felt she should take the matter up but Jem had said no, leave it be. She was due to move up to the secondary school in Stur next year anyway and there were only a few more weeks of term left. As it was, Valerie had no great faith in formal education. The child would learn more valuable things around her father than in any classroom doing what they called 'project work' which was just an excuse for not teaching properly, as far as she could see.

She filled the water dish from the tap and set it down for her hens. They were laying well and the egg thief seemed to have been deterred. She had collected eight brown eggs in her basket. Naomi, her favourite, came to her feet and murmured in a conversational way, cocking her head with its red cheeks and comb, her eye a bright yellow bead. Valerie bent down and stroked her slippery speckled back. It was a beautiful morning and the other chickens were busy with dustbaths in the sunshine, fluffing up their feathers and settling down in the dirt.

Turning towards the house she saw Betty going to the dustbin by the back door. 'Morning, Betty,' she called, 'and what a lovely one!'

Later, having a cup of coffee together, Betty remarked, 'Next door's got her daughter staying. She lives in America, according to Angie. I saw her go by on Victoria Durnford's horse this morning.'

'Oh, is that who it was? I heard the horse and thought it was Jem Loader's child.'

Betty shook her head. 'Her daughter's a great tall thing. A big, blonde girl. Not like her mother. That Greg nearly had his tractor in the ditch giving her the glad eye.'

Valerie chuckled. She enjoyed hearing the village gossip via Betty. Although she hardly saw anyone herself, Betty kept her in touch with things.

'That Star Bishop's boy's in trouble again,' said Betty, taking their mugs to the sink to rinse. 'Got caught Saturday night breaking into a workshop on the industrial estate. Right little vandal he's turned into. He'd got a job lined up for when he leaves school, but it looks as if they won't take him on now. Shame, isn't it? I don't like to see a boy go to the bad like that.'

Valerie murmured agreement. Children. She thought of Claudia with her big, blonde daughter and imagined them sharing confidences, laughing together. She looked the sort of woman who would have easy, satisfactory offspring. She thought of Star and that unfortunate son of hers – she remembered her yanking him around by the arm when he was younger, giving him a clip round the ear in the supermarket queue. The poor young woman had done her best to keep him straight. She thought of her own son, Christopher, who had been suspended from his public school on two occasions, she couldn't even remember what for, and who had grown his hair to his shoulders when he was at university. He had caused her and Frank considerable worry at the time, but look at him now, a highly respectable company director and the widowed father of four children. Their mother, Karis, hardly more than a child herself, had died when Rose was born and Christopher had brought up his girls single-handed. Being motherless, they were even more special to Valerie and she allowed herself to believe that she was important to them. Thinking of them, that dear bright-faced family, reminded her that it was only a few weeks before they would be over again to spend a month with her, and her heart gave a leap of pleasure. At least that was what she hoped it was. She had felt these odd tremors frequently of late and old Dr Gillespie had given her some pills and a warning about her weight and unhealthy lifestyle. 'For God's sake,' she had told him. 'Save your breath, David. I have no intention of changing at my age. I'm far too old to start all that health nonsense.'

Betty had gone to get the mop and bucket and was telling her to get out of the kitchen while she did the floor. Although she still felt a little odd, she stood up, and that was the last thing she knew, a lurching sensation, before her view of the kitchen dissolved into a murky blackness.

When Lila was not back from her ride by twelve o'clock, Claudia started to worry. She could not help but imagine possible accidents and she thought of Victoria's horse galloping home riderless, the stirrups flying and her daughter's body slumped somewhere on the road. It was therefore with great relief that she heard the iron gate clang and Lila's feet pounding up the drive.

'Hi, Mum!' she called in a breathless, happy voice, her face and shoulders appearing through the open kitchen window. 'I've had the fabbest time. A really great ride. Then I called in on your friend Julia, and told her that her daughter needs some lessons to get the horse going properly for her. I didn't realise I'd been so long. Hang on!' and with a quick heave she hauled herself onto the sill, swung her legs up and jumped through the window, clean over the kitchen counter.

'Lila!'

'What's the matter? Not the usual way in? Who cares! I went across what is called Broadmoor Common and I met that gypsy kid you told me about, with the horse. She came with me then, showed me where she jumps the hedges and we had a wonderful time. God, that horse can jump. She calls it a "lepping horse", said her dad bought it from a dealer in Ireland. It was just what Vinnie needed, a bit of fun and following something really bold like that. She's a great kid. She said she knew you. Called you Claudio.

'When I got back, I put Vinnie out in the field and went to find Victoria's mother. She was picking peas or something, wearing a pair of overalls which made her look like a refugee from Kosovo or somewhere. I don't think she was at all pleased to hear what I had to say. She said they couldn't afford to give Victoria more riding lessons and that she had been very well taught and didn't need them anyway. She said it was the horse's fault. I couldn't have that, so then I gave it to her straight.'

'Lila! It's hardly your business!'

'But that horse is wasted, or will be if she doesn't sort her daughter out. Poor girl! How can she be expected to get it right on her own?'

'What did she say?'

'Something about she would have to talk to her husband. But at least she knows now. I told her about that fantastic gypsy kid. That didn't go down too well either, I could see. What's the time? God! I must get a move on. Any more news?'

'I've got Jerome's flight details. He arrives at four thirty tomorrow afternoon. I'll catch the train up to Woking and then get the airport bus and come back in the ambulance with him. You can give Dad the details when you see him. Look, I've written down the flight, the hospital and the consultant's name, and the appropriate numbers.'

Lila swept the piece of paper up and shoved it in her jean's pocket. 'By the way,' she said. 'There's an ambulance outside your neighbour's house. No, the other side. The old drunk. The one you found on the floor.'

'Mrs Pomeroy? Goodness. What can have happened? I wonder if I should go and see.'

Lila was already running a bath and throwing off the clothes she had worn riding. She came out into the hall, her toothbrush stuck out of her mouth. She could hardly bear to give just one activity her full concentration and was always combining tasks – talking on the telephone while stirring a saucepan, or reading a book while pedalling her legs in the air as part of some exercise regime.

'Blimey, Mum, are you hoping to be nominated for Neighbour of the Year award? You'll be cycling round the village in a district nurse's outfit soon. Why don't you go and find out? I'll make myself a sandwich before I leave. Anthony Thing is coming for me at two.'

Claudia thought of what had been said about Valerie Pomeroy's isolation, how she had cut herself off. Maybe now was the time she needed someone. 'Perhaps I will. I won't be long, darling. I'll just see if there's anything I can do. She'll probably send me away with a flea in my ear.'

Running up the drive next door, Claudia could see the ambulance with its doors open but no sign of any activity. The front door of the house stood open and she knocked and looked in. The hall inside was also empty but she could hear voices from off to the right and, following them, went through into the kitchen where there was a theatrical scene being enacted. Two paramedics were working over a body on a stretcher on the floor, there were oxygen cylinders, a mask, a drip, all sorts of paraphernalia which suggested something serious had happened, and standing on the other side of the table looking ashen-faced was Betty. Claudia went over and stood beside her.

'What's happened?' she whispered. 'I'm Claudia Knight from next door. My daughter saw the ambulance.'

'She's had a heart attack,' Betty whispered back. 'Ever so sudden. I'd just got the mop and bucket.' She indicated the mop on its side on the floor, the water in the bucket, still steaming faintly. 'I rang the doctor and he got an ambulance here.'

'How bad?' asked Claudia, thinking of the son in Hong Kong.

'They say she'll be all right. They got her heart started again. I didn't move her. I didn't know what to do. She was in awful pain. Terrible fright it gave me.'

123

'I'm sure you did everything right,' said Claudia.

One of the paramedics stood up and turned to them. 'We're going to take her now. We've got her stabilised. Did you get that bag ready?'

Betty showed she had packed a small tartan zipped holdall.

'Are you coming with her?' he asked.

Betty's face took on a look of agitation. 'Oh! Do you think I should? I don't know whether I can. Not without telling my family. How would I get back?'

'I'll go,' said Claudia, impulsively. 'Don't worry. I'll just nip home and tell my daughter and get my bag.' She turned to Betty. 'Do you know Mrs Pomeroy's son's number in Hong Kong? Can you write it down for me and I'll telephone him from the hospital.'

A few minutes later she was sprinting back up the drive, her bag slung over her shoulder and a cardigan tied round her waist. Mrs Pomeroy was being carried out on the stretcher and Betty was standing by the door holding the tartan case and looking fearful. Claudia took it from her and waited until she was told she could climb into the ambulance. For the first time she had a chance to see Valerie Pomeroy's face, partly hidden by the mask. The eyes were open and seemed to be looking at her beadily. She reached for her neighbour's scaly old hand. It felt cold and stiff. She held it in both of her own and tried to rub some warmth back into the crooked claw with its hard lump of rings and its red painted nails.

'Mrs Pomeroy,' she said softly. 'I'm here. I'm here with you. Claudia. It's Claudia.' Again the eyes seemed to seek her face and a look of bewilderment passed across them. She doesn't know me, thought Claudia. She doesn't know me from Adam.

Julia Durnford had not had a good morning. First, Star had not turned up and that, on a Monday morning, was the last thing she needed. In the end, she had telephoned Monica at The Bugle and had heard from her that Rosco had been in trouble and that Star was taking the day off to go to his school to see his social worker. Julia could see that this was an emergency but still felt she could have been told, and surely it would not take the whole day to sort the boy out. Star could well have come on later, and this was what Julia would have suggested if she had had the courtesy to telephone.

The house was a tip. After the late night on Saturday she hadn't felt like doing much on Sunday. She had taken Tor back to school at nine thirty in the evening and wasn't back until nearly eleven. This morning she and Peter had slept late and had a rush, which was never a good start. Now she had two friends coming to lunch, which was why she was picking peas when the young woman, Lila, had turned up to berate her about Tor's riding. Really it was a cheek, especially as Tor had only allowed the girl to ride Vinnie because Claudia had told her that Lila would be bored next door with nothing to do.

At the back of her mind was the nasty nagging thought that Lila had been right, that Tor did need some help. In the Pony Club these days she was always coming up against these beastly competitive mothers who bought ridiculously expensive ponies and got their children coaches and trainers, and Julia felt strongly that it shouldn't be about that sort of competing. It should be more as it was in her day when children could pull a hairy, unfit pony out of the field and have as much fun as anyone, doing picnic rides and popping over straw bales. Of course, she knew times had changed but she resented this professionalism, as she saw it, creeping in and spoiling everything.

However, Tor wanted to compete and they had spent a great deal on her horse, and it was extremely unsatisfactory for him to go as badly as he had on Saturday. Julia felt pushed into a corner. It was a pity that Lila wasn't going to be around. According to Tor, she was a good teacher and could have been persuaded to come across and give some free tuition in return for the opportunity to ride.

Crossly, Julia whisked a broom round the kitchen floor and swept the dust out of the back door. She would have to start on the washing up and tidy the place before making a quiche for lunch. Upstairs the beds were unmade and the washing was still in the machine, waiting to be pegged out. She would have to go and change and do something with her hair. She wished she had not let herself in for this lunch with the Mackenzie sisters, Penny and Rosemary, with whom she had been at school, but they had fixed the date weeks ago and it was too late to cancel.

It was when she was halfway through changing, buttoning up a hastily ironed shirt, that she glanced out of the window and saw the ambulance pulling out of Valerie Pomeroy's drive. Julia was not unkind and even though she disliked her neighbour intensely there was no satisfaction in the thought that she had been taken ill. It was then that she remembered about Claudia's son. Victoria had been full of his accident at lunch on Sunday. It had sounded rather grisly – a bus crash or something, in India. With a genuine pang of guilt Julia realised that she had never asked Lila how he was, or indeed telephoned Claudia to say how sorry she was. Glancing at her watch she decided she would do so when her guests had gone. Really, she could be an altogether nicer person if there were more hours in the day.

Chapter Eight

Star and Rosco drove home from the meeting at his school in hostile silence. They had done all their shouting, first in the early hours of Sunday morning when the police brought him to the door, then later after they had gone. Star chased her son up the stairs to his room, where he barricaded himself in. She thumped on the door with her fists and screamed at him until she was hoarse. When he opened the door and pushed past her to go to the bathroom, she caught hold of his arm to land him one and he turned on her and gave her such a mighty shove in the chest that she fell back against the wall, winded, and realised that she could no longer hit him. He'd got beyond that stage. She cried then, bawled her eyes out in anger and despair, slumped on the landing, and through her sobs and gasps wailed out her reproaches, even after Rosco had reappeared, stepped over her and gone back into his room, slamming the door.

Later she'd dragged herself downstairs and poured a brandy from the half bottle Monica had given her last Christmas and dropped on the sofa, putting the telly on for company. At first she'd been defensive with the police, hoping they hadn't got anything on him, but when it became clear that he'd been apprehended – caught red-handed – and spent the last hours of Saturday night in a police cell, she went ballistic. She would have killed him if the copper hadn't restrained her. She'd screamed at him, 'That's it. I've had enough. Out! Get out! I never want to see you again,' with a good deal of effing and blinding as punctuation. The WPC had tried to calm her down, suggested she made a cup of tea, that they all sit and talk it through, but Star was past all that. She'd had a bit to drink down at the pub. Had a happy evening, in fact. There had been live music and a sing-along and she hadn't been home for more than half an hour when there was the knock at the door.

'But, Mrs Bishop,' said the WPC, in a patient tone which managed to be patronising and unsympathetic at the same time, 'didn't you wonder about your son? Weren't you concerned about where he was?'

Star knew what they were getting at. Neglect. They were trying to prove that she neglected Rosco. All that pretending to be understanding and friendly, 'Shall I make us all a nice cup of tea?' it was just to catch her out.

'I knew where he was,' she snarled back. 'With his mate, Sean. Sean's mum gave them their tea. They were staying over at his place.'

'I'm afraid that's not the case,' the WPC had said sadly, taking out her notebook. 'Sean's mum's away for the weekend. Sean was supposed to be at his grandma's.'

'Well, how was I to know that?' exploded Star. 'He's a lying little bastard. That's what he told me. They were going to work on their bikes together. Come here, you. I'll kill you, I will!' All the time Rosco had lounged on the sofa, one leg hooked over the other, picking at the sole of a trainer, his face pale and thin and expressionless under the shadow of stubble on his shaved head, his gold earring glinting.

'I thought the last time Rosco was in trouble that we had agreed that you would supervise him at weekends. There was to be a curfew, Mrs Bishop, which you agreed with his social worker.'

'Oh yeah! You try and give him a curfew. It's all my bleeding fault now, is it? I'm sick of you lot, you know that? Sick of the lot of you. The school can't do nothing with him, the police can't do nothing, his social worker can't do nothing, but I'm supposed to be able to. Well, you tell me how. Take the little bleeder away and lock him up. Go on. That's what he deserves.'

It had gone on like that until at last the police had got up to leave, and then she and Rosco had fought it out between them. Now Star felt washed up and exhausted. She tried to think more calmly about what she should do, how she should handle him, but she didn't know where to turn with Rosco. All she knew was that she had done her best while always feeling that it wasn't enough, that there was something missing. When she thought back on her own childhood, cramped in the council house in the village, living on a farm worker's wage, she knew there was something in that cottage where her mother lit the fire every night and there was always a cooked tea on the table and where her father kept his fowl and grew his vegetables out the back that she had not been able to provide.

God, they'd been poor enough, and her dad had a temper and

her mum was always ill in the winter with asthma, but there was something there which she hadn't been able to give to Rosco. It was there in the saucepan of potato peelings and scraps put on to boil every morning for the chickens, the smell of which had made Star and her brother and sisters hold their noses and pull faces; in the cramped bedrooms with the textured wallpaper which they punctured with their fingernails, lying, bickering backwards and forwards, in their bunk beds; it was there in the boredom, the messing about with friends in the woods; in the rhythm of life in the village. God knows, Rosco had far more than they had ever dreamed of, but he'd missed out on something. Star couldn't work out exactly what it was. Her mum and dad had certainly not made anything of them when they were growing up, none of the closeness that kids had these days with their parents, and the home she'd made was far superior to that cottage, with her kitchen units and her microwave and her coal effect gas fire and her tumble dryer. The little bastard should be more grateful. He didn't know how lucky he was.

But there was an emptiness in him which Star could not understand. Sloping around, head nodding in time with his earphones, he hardly seemed to connect with anything around him. That was why she was so pleased that he had an interest in the bike. Now, that had got him into trouble. They'd broken into a workshop to steal tools, him and Sean. Of all the dumb things.

He could still be a sweet kid, lovable and loving, but he never seemed to think what he was getting himself into and he seemed not to care. She thought, lately, he was doing better with his Saturday job and his mechanics NVQ, and now he'd blown it. It made her want to bloody weep. She could hear him upstairs putting on his music and then the thump thump of heavy metal. They'd be knocking on the wall from next door in a minute. She hardly had the energy to shout up for him to cut it out. The next minute she heard him on his mobile, talking to Sean, and laughing. The pair of them were laughing. That did it. Fuelled again by anger, Star got off the sofa and started to yell. 'Get off that phone, you little bastard! It's not bloody funny! I'll swing for you, I will.'

Now, driving back from the school and the meeting with the social worker, there was plenty to think about. Rosco sat sullenly with his head averted, seeming to watch the green countryside slip by, the hedges overflowing with cow parsley and tumbling briars, the fields full of fat, grazing black and white cows. How much had he taken in? wondered Star. Had he heard that she would be fined if he offended again, that he was on probation for six months and if he re-offended he would be given a custodial sentence? That he had to report weekly to the police station in Sharston? She couldn't stand that copper, a real wanker, he was, always hanging round the pubs at closing time trying to catch the drinkers in the car park, and that tight-arsed bitch of a WPC. Star had her pride, and it smarted at the indignity of it all.

The only good thing that came out of it was that Mr Martin at the garage was still going to hold the job open for Rosco. Star's heart went out to the man. It was the only bit of help she reckoned she'd had from anybody, the only bit of generosity. You could keep all that mush from the social worker, who had no kids of her own and was bespectacled and flat-chested and always had a cold. Star and Rosco should communicate more, she had suggested, try to establish a 'growing' atmosphere, and a lot of crap like that. Star despised her as much as Rosco thought she was sad.

Turning the last bend before Sharston, Star glanced across at her son. There was something about his averted profile, a softness about his chin and a childish tilt to his nose which reminded her of him as a baby. Somehow he could still move her. She loved the little bugger. There was no denying it.

'Here,' she said, 'look in my purse and get out that tenner. We'll stop at the chippie on the way past. You'd like a cod and chips, wouldn't you? We could have some onion rings and all.'

Later, as they pulled back out into the main road, with the warm newspaper parcels on Rosco's knees, a smart navy blue Mercedes turned out in front of them from the lane to Court Barton. Star recognised the car – Anthony Brewer's. She saw the back of his head and then his profile as he turned to chat to the woman in the front passenger seat. She was a young woman with a fall of straight blonde hair, a tall girl, as tall as Brewer.

Oh well, thought Star, it was all right for some. She tried to imagine what it would be like to swank off in a car like that, sitting next to a man like Anthony Brewer. In your dreams, girl, she told herself. In your dreams.

Lila, in fact, had made very little effort to please one of the most eligible men in the county. Wearing jeans and a shirt of Claudia's, her hair still damp from the bath, she had slung her bag on the back seat and hopped in without waiting for

Anthony to get out and follow his usual courtly routine of
opening the door for a female passenger.

'Hi,' she said, flicking her hair back with a broad brown hand
and feeling under the seat for the lever to slide it further back to
make room for her legs. 'You're very on time!'

'I like to be,' he replied, looking at her, amused. What an
unlikely daughter this was of Claudia's.

'Me too. I can't stand waiting for people, can you? It really
gets on my tits. Right, let's go.'

'Your mother OK?' Anthony looked at the bungalow, wondering whether Claudia would appear to see her daughter off.
There was no sign of her. 'What news of your brother?'

'Both OK. Jerome's being flown back tomorrow. Mum will
feel much better when she can get him back under her wing.
He's always been her baby. I think she felt something like this
would happen if she let him out of her care to go off to India. It
just confirms her view that he needs constant looking after.
Actually, she's off on another mercy mission as we speak. The
old girl from next door's been shipped off to Yeovil with a heart
attack. Mum went with her in the ambulance. Never a dull
moment, is there, in this village?'

Anthony Brewer was concerned at this news. His expressed
fondness for Valerie Pomeroy was genuine and he often felt
guilty that he let the weeks slip by without bothering to call in
and see her. He knew she would enjoy pouring him a drink and
having a chat about art or travel or books – something beyond
the confines of the village. Now, his failure to express this
concern and affection until it seemed it was too late made him
ashamed.

'That was very good of your mother. She hardly knows her, I
believe.'

'That's Mum for you,' said Lila. 'She likes lame ducks. Prefers
them, really, to properly functioning ducks. You know what I
mean?'

'No, not really.' Anthony was intrigued. He was glad of this
opportunity to probe a little.

'Oh, you know. When people are fully up and running, she's
less interested in them.'

'Why's that, do you think?'

'I don't know. Something to do with Dad, I expect. He was so
dynamic that he didn't have time to notice those sort of people,
so Mum tended to take them over.'

'I see. Is he dead, your father?'

'No.' Lila's answer was so short that Anthony glanced at her.

'You talked about him in the past tense.'

'Did I? Slip of the tongue. I'm going to see him, as a matter of fact.'

'Where does he live? In London?'

'Yeah.' It was easier to lie.

'Oh, where?'

'Do you know New York, at all?' asked Lila, smoothly changing tack.

Interesting, thought Anthony. It's the same with mother and daughter. Neither like to talk about that particular subject.

'Yes, quite well. When I was in the art business I went back and forth a good deal. I had a New York girlfriend once. Carly.' The similarity of the name to her father's mistress's gave Lila a jolt. She recovered quickly.

'Extraordinary, isn't it, what American parents wish upon their children?' she said. 'With names like that, even quite sophisticated people sound as if they spend their whole time line dancing in check shirts or gingham dresses.'

She prattled on easily, then sorted through the tapes Anthony kept in the car, discarding most of them, and slotted an Eva Cassidy album into the player. She had not asked permission. 'Is this OK?' she said, almost too late.

Anthony smiled. 'Of course. Not entirely my choice, I have to say. Easy listening, though.'

'Not yours, then?'

'A girlfriend's, I think.'

'So, why haven't you ever been married?' asked Lila, sitting back, unabashed.

Anthony smiled again. There was something refreshingly direct about this large young woman.

'Where shall I start?'

'The beginning will do.'

In Yeovil Hospital Claudia found herself largely redundant. There had been a bit of form-filling when Valerie was first admitted when she was able to supply name, address, next of kin, age, date of birth, details from the small pocket book which Betty had put in her hand as the ambulance men slammed the doors and prepared to leave. She gave the son, Christopher, as next of kin, but that was as much as she could do. She had no idea who was Mrs Pomeroy's doctor, or whether she was on any other medication or had any history of heart trouble. Now the hospital had taken over and she was asked to wait in Accident and Emergency, in a bay of plastic chairs and out-of-date magazines, as the medical staff completed blood tests and organised a heart trace.

She had gone to the pay phones and tried to ring Hong Kong but a monotonous engaged tone suggested there was something wrong with the telephone or the number. She tried to work out what the time would be out there. Forward or back? God, she was so stupid. Going east was surely flying into the day. The sun rose in the east, so Hong Kong time must be in advance of the UK, but by how much?

She went down to the shop on the ground floor and bought a paper to help pass the time, a bottle of lemon barley water and two apples and a packet of biscuits. These were the sort of things Valerie Pomeroy might be glad of when she was feeling better, and provided Claudia with the small change to have another onslaught on the telephone. She dialled the operator who put her through to international calls, from whom she discovered that there was a seven-hour time difference. That would make it nine o'clock in the evening. She tried to imagine this son, Christopher. Would he be out at a cocktail party, a dinner party, a reception – leading the sort of life she believed ex-pats enjoyed in Hong Kong?

She dialled the number again and this time it rang and was answered promptly by a youthful female voice saying 'Hi' in an offhand tone.

Guessing, Claudia said, 'May I speak to your father please?'

'Sure.' There was a short pause then she heard, yelled to somewhere off stage, 'Dad! Phone. Some woman for you.'

When he came to the telephone the first thing that Claudia noticed about Christopher Pomeroy was that he had an extremely pleasant, deep voice. The sort of voice which gave her confidence in a man. 'Hello? Christopher Pomeroy.'

Her explanation, which she had rehearsed, was as short and precise as possible and she had in her hand the hospital and ward telephone numbers and the name of the specialist. The news of his mother's collapse clearly shook her son. Claudia found herself being reassuring. 'Really, there doesn't seem to be any suggestion that she is in danger. Fortunately, Betty was with her when it happened and very quickly got an ambulance.'

'Thank God for Betty. Should I fly back?'

'I can't give you an opinion on that. Why don't you wait until you've spoken to a doctor?'

'I'll do that. It might be better to come later. That is if she really isn't in any danger. This is so kind of you, to be with her. Did you say you are a neighbour?'

'Yes. Claudia Barron.' She said it before she remembered. Damn. In his distress, this man would not notice her slip. 'Claudia Knight, that is. I live in the bungalow. The Major's bungalow.'

'It's so kind. I worry about her being so isolated. She seems to have cut herself off . . .'

'Don't worry. I'll stay for the moment and when they've made an assessment, I'll telephone you again. Either from here, which is a bit difficult, or when I get home. Now you have the ward number you can at least keep in touch yourself.'

'Yes, of course. I'll ring again this evening. Is there anything I can do? Has she got everything she needs? It's such a huge relief to know she had someone she knows with her.'

'Betty packed her bag. Hang on, here's the doctor now. Would you like to speak to him? I'll see if I can nab him. Wait a minute . . . shit.' The pips sounded and Claudia was cut off.

It proved impossible to get a reconnection and Claudia had to be content with hearing the doctor's prognosis. She wrote what he said on the back of an envelope to relay to Christopher Pomeroy later.

'You can come and see her if you like,' the doctor said. He was a nice young man with thick, untidy brown hair and a crumpled white coat. Claudia thought he looked about fourteen.

She followed him back to where a bed was surrounded by screens. Valerie Pomeroy lay attached to tubes and with an oxygen mask over her face. She was in a hospital gown, her own clothes folded on a chair. Claudia put her purchases on the bedside cabinet and moved the chair to sit beside her. She took the hand which lay on the sheet and gently held it. She hoped that the touch would be comforting but Mrs Pomeroy turned her head and fixed her with that same doggy, provoked look that Claudia remembered from the night in the kitchen.

'Mrs Pomeroy. It's Claudia. From next door. I came to the hospital with you. I've spoken to your son. He sends his love.'

Hampered by the mask, the old woman could not speak but Claudia saw her trying to say something. She patted the hand and found that in response her fingers were clasped in a surprisingly tight grip.

'Thank you,' Mrs Pomeroy whispered through the plastic, 'thank you.'

Claudia smiled back. She thought of Jerome and hoped there was someone beside him as he prepared for his long journey home. Someone to hang on to like a lifeline, a hold on the present. While she watched, Valerie Pomeroy's eyes closed and she drifted off to sleep.

When Claudia got up to leave, as the afternoon lost its brightness and nurses started to bring round trays of supper, she picked up the newspaper, a trashy tabloid – the only one left in the hospital shop – and her eye caught a small story on the front page. Her heart jerked in panic. 'Fraudster's son in Indian bus horror.' Standing beside the hospital bed, beside the sleeping figure of Mrs Pomeroy, Claudia read the paragraph, one hand to her mouth, her heart thumping. It was all there. The story of the crash, the twenty-five people killed, Jerome's name in full, a reminder of Roger's crime and imprisonment. What bastards, she thought. Were they never going to leave them alone? The old sensation of needing to bolt, to find somewhere safe, came flooding back. She had to get out, get out of this hot, stuffy ward to somewhere where she could think.

Pushing past a nurse who was trying to persuade an elderly man that he should get back into bed for his nice macaroni cheese and that he could not go home to see to his pigeons, she left the ward without a backward glance.

Outside the hospital, finding a taxi took only a moment and she was thankful for the uncommunicative driver and the opportunity to sit in silence. It seemed that now everyone would know her secret, that her fragile anonymity would be blown to pieces and that the shred of protective cover she had hoped to establish for the children would be destroyed. Someone in the village would read the paper, would put two and two together. For all she knew there would be a barrage of press flash bulbs when they wheeled Jerome from the aircraft tomorrow. The fact that he was an innocent did not matter at all. When she got home she would ring David Rowntree and ask if there was any hope of getting some sort of protection for this purely private event. If anyone knew how to fix that sort of thing, he would. She should warn Lila, too.

Paying off the taxi outside the gate, she realised that in her anguish she had hardly given Valerie Pomeroy a thought and guiltily remembered that she must ring Christopher when she got in. It was three in the morning in Hong Kong when she got through and his voice sounded heavy and slow with tiredness.

'I can't thank you enough,' he said when she had told him

what the doctor had said, that his mother would be kept in coronary care for two days and then if all went well she would be transferred to an ordinary ward and would be home within a week. 'I haven't been able to get through to the hospital. I'll have to try again in the morning.'

'I'm not going to be able to go in to see her again,' said Claudia. 'I would have done, but I'm going away for about a week.'

'Oh, I see. A holiday?' Why was he making conversation? The connection between them did not require this form of politeness.

'No. My son is in hospital too. Or will be. I'm going to stay with my sister-in-law nearby so that I can go and see him each day.' She found it was a relief to be able to speak to this stranger. I would like to tell him everything, thought Claudia. To share this rising panic, to be reassured as I reassured him about his mother, but I must not.

'I'm so sorry to hear that. You never mentioned it before. It makes your going in with Ma doubly kind.'

'Not at all.' Claudia felt suddenly tired. She wanted to cease the effort of considering someone else. She wanted to concentrate on her own fears. 'Not at all. I'll see her when I get back, when I bring him home.'

Victoria Durnford was stuck in prep, putting the finishing touches to notes on a biology experiment on osmosis. She was a neat worker and the page was carefully written and the diagram drawn with coloured ink. The evening light coming through the prep room window was still golden and inviting and she wished very much that she was at home. She imagined sitting at the kitchen table, with Pushkin, the cat, a warm lump on her knee, while her mother bustled about making something for supper. The door would be open to the garden and the radio tuned to the evening news. It would be quiet but comfortable between them. She could almost feel the rough and smooth patches of the flagstone floor beneath the socked feet she always had at home, and the silky surface of the kitchen table as she traced the grain of the wood with a finger.

At home she could be herself with no conscious effort. The space she occupied at the table was her space. She was defined by everything about her. Her pottery mug with Victoria written on the side would be on the draining board, her jodhpurs drying on the rack above the Aga. On the door jamb were the pencil marks measuring her and her brother's growth each year, next to those of her mother and her sisters when they were children. At home she had a physical presence. She knew who she was at home.

At school she was starting to feel insubstantial, a non-person. She hated this prep in front of her on the desk – done properly and neatly in her careful round schoolgirl handwriting. Glancing across at Claire, who was writing notes to Lisa, she saw her carelessly scrawled page, its untidiness and lack of attention making clear that boring old Bilge was something not worth bothering about. Claire had put fake tan on her legs and they glowed honey-brown in a shaft of sun. She was sniggering about something, her head dropped sideways on her desk, cradled in one arm, her face averted from Victoria. Her newly dyed hair was streaked with daffodil yellow. Lisa was laughing too, snorting into her hand and glancing occasionally round the room, keeping an eye open for their headmistress. In ten minutes prep would be over and they would be free to hang around on the games field, shrieking and gossiping, sneaking a crafty smoke and maybe meeting up with boys from the boys' school.

Victoria would not be among them. She hardly spoke to her old friends these days, knowing that her conversation marked her out as a pariah. The thing that really hurt was when she had overheard Lucy mimicking her telephone calls of Saturday night. 'Really,' she heard her saying to Berthe, 'Tor is so sad, she just talked about her horse all the time. She's such a *child*!'

The time between prep finishing and when they had to be back in House was almost the worst. She would have liked to go and have a bath and get into her pyjamas and old dressing gown and curl up and read somewhere but that was considered peculiar and the younger girls would come and pester her, already learning to be scornful and mocking. Sometimes the housemistress asked her and Elspeth to take her dog for a walk, and that was all right because Scottie was a sweet little white Highland terrier and she liked throwing a ball for him, watching him career about doing handbrake turns, but the rest of her year, hanging about with girls from the fifth form, had started to make comments, saying that she and Elspeth were sucking up and that Scottie on his red lead looked like a Tampax.

It had been so easy with Lila. Lila hadn't made her feel peculiar or immature or any of the other things that she knew she was. She had chatted to Lila and hadn't felt shy and hadn't had to worry all the time about being uncool.

The house bell rang and there was a clattering of chairs as prep ended. Victoria put her work away in her file and watched as the others slung their books on the shelves and streamed out. Lucy turned back at the door. 'You coming, Tor?' she asked. Victoria blushed. Not after what I heard you say, she thought.

'No. I'm going to . . . I've got to wait for a telephone call . . .'

'Clear up for me then, will you?' asked Jane, who was supposed to be on duty to tidy the room. 'You might as well do it if you've got to stay in anyway.'

'God, you're a lazy fucking bitch,' said Rowena in the vernacular of the public schoolgirl. Laughing, they trooped out.

Victoria sat for a little while looking out of the window. Her father would be home by now. She imagined his car drawing up on the gravel and her mother shouting into the hall as he came in, 'Hello, darling. Good day?' She so wanted to be there that it hurt.

'Where am I going to take you?' asked Anthony Brewer as he crawled along in the traffic of Cromwell Road.

'You can drop me at the corner of Exhibition Road, if that's OK. It's only round the corner from there,' said Lila.

Anthony glanced at the time. They had had a good run and it was only a little after four o'clock. Not a good time to suggest anything like going for a drink, and tea seemed somehow inappropriate to offer to this very modern young woman.

'Are you going out this evening?' he asked.

'Yup, of course. I haven't been in London for ages. I want to see everyone.'

'Of course,' he said, feeling put in his place and elderly. He wished that he had something planned to do as well. He supposed that he and Ivo would wander round to the Italian restaurant for dinner as they usually did. Of course, he could go through his address book and find a spare woman, but somehow he couldn't be bothered.

Lila leant forward to look for something she had dropped on the floor. Anthony glanced at the stretch of her broad shoulder nearly touching his knee and the swing of pale hair. Raising one finger from the gear stick he allowed it to catch in the pinkish yellow strands which were so soft that the rough skin of his finger did not register the sensation. Lila straightened up.

'Take my London number,' he said. With one hand he reached for a Biro and a scrap of paper. 'You never know. You might need it.'

'Why?' asked Lila. 'I don't see why. Look, this will do. I'll get out here while the lights are red. Thanks a lot. It was great to get a lift,' and she was flinging open the door and getting her bag off the back seat and a moment later was waving cheerfully to him from the pavement.

Anthony felt thoroughly wrong-footed. There was nothing left but to wave and smile back before the lights changed and he was forced to move on with the traffic. Glancing in his mirror he saw her, a tall, striding blonde figure, turning the corner, her bag slung over her shoulder. Good God, he thought, whatever sort of man takes on a girl like that?

David Rowntree was as helpful as he could be when Claudia telephoned him. He pushed away his plate with its half-eaten chop and listened in silence. 'The press agencies will have picked up the story from the Indian papers,' he said when she had finished. 'Reuters will have got out a list of any English passengers hurt in the crash. Some sharp-eyed hack must have picked it up. Normally, hundreds could perish on the subcontinent and it wouldn't merit but a line or two over here but the Barron name is still worth a paragraph.'

'Do you think it was only in *The Post*?'

'I'll check that for you. I didn't see any mention in my paper, and I'll get on to the airport authorities right away. I don't see why Jerome can't be put into the ambulance on the runway and avoid any journalists or photographers altogether. I'm not sure that that doesn't happen anyway.'

'God, I do hope so. Honestly, David, how long is this going to go on for? I would have thought we would have been old news by now.'

'I think that depends what else there is to throw mud at. The next big case will wipe you off the front page once and for all, I should think.'

'Not if Roger goes on with this Sunday paper deal. I didn't tell Lila by the way. She's going to see him tomorrow. I thought he could tell her.'

'Ah. I wonder how Roger will feel about Lila seeing him in prison. Did you prepare her for it? It's quite an experience, you know.'

Claudia felt instantly guilty. She had, of course, wondered how it would be for Lila, and had offered, before the Jerome crisis cropped up, to go with her to the prison and wait outside, but Lila had scorned her concern. 'It's not me you should be worried about, Mum. No, if I feel I need any support, I'll get a friend to go with me. Anna, probably. She's out of work at the moment, so she'll be free.'

'Of course, I realise that,' Claudia said to David, irritated that he always managed to make her appear heartless. 'We've talked about it endlessly, but she wanted to go on her own. Frankly, David, I've got to concentrate on Jerome for the moment. What Lila chooses to do is up to her.'

'I'll see what I can do with the airport,' he replied, changing the subject, 'and ring you back.'

So, thought Claudia, after she had put down the telephone. Both Lila and I face an ordeal tomorrow, her seeing her father and me getting Jerome back. We both do it out of love. If those photographers and journalists are there in full force like before, then the whole thing will be opened up again and village life will become intolerable. Poor Lila has got to face the dreadful reality of seeing Roger humiliated and powerless, but by this time tomorrow it will all be over. Both of us, in a way, will know the worst. Jerome will be safe in hospital in Salisbury and Lila will be back with her friends in London.

The telephone rang twice that evening. The first was David to say that the airport authorities would allow the ambulance to collect Jerome directly from the aeroplane and that no journalists were allowed to be present.

The second call was from Julia.

'Claudia? Hello, it's Julia. I'm so sorry to hear about your son.'

Claudia leaned against the wall. So this was it. For a moment she could not speak.

'Claudia? Are you there?'

'Yes, sorry. What about my son?'

'The accident. We're so sorry about the accident. Victoria told us. Lila told her on Sunday. I meant to ask this morning, how he was. Any news? And is there anything we can do?'

So Julia hadn't read anything in her newspaper. It had been Lila, talking to Victoria. Claudia found her voice again. 'Tomorrow. He's coming back tomorrow. I'm going to meet him. We think he'll be OK. He has to have an operation, a plate in his leg. I'm going to stay with my sister-in-law in Salisbury, to be near.'

'Who will be doing the operation?' As with all such things, Julia was definitive on the subject of the best specialists. 'Oh, that's good. Mr Simpson is considered one of the top men. He did Jim's shoulder when he broke it. When do you think you'll get him home?'

'In about a week, I hope.'

'Well, we'll be thinking of you, Peter and me. Hang on, Peter's saying something. Oh yes. Another thing I meant to ask. How is Big Val? You went to the hospital with her, which was very good of you. I heard it all from Betty this afternoon. A heart attack? I can't say I'm surprised with all that weight she carries, and the drink. Peter's making faces at me, I'd better shut up. Claudia, we're here if you want anything.'

Julia put the telephone down thoughtfully. 'It's very odd,' she said to Peter who was reading the newspaper with a pounding heart. It seemed that even his wife talking to Claudia on the telephone made his blood race. 'She was most strange to begin with. Very distant, as if she didn't like me asking about the son. Peter, there *is* something odd about her. She's so unforthcoming.'

'For heaven's sake, Julia, the poor woman. She's got a lot on her plate and she's on her own, too. She's not used to living in a village, to sharing her business with everybody.'

'I am hardly everybody,' said Julia, annoyed. The telephone rang again and she picked it up.

'Tor? Hello, darling. How's things? Darling, you don't sound very bright. What's the matter? Well, do try to sound a bit more cheerful if there's nothing wrong.'

The following morning, the spell of warm weather broke. In Yeovil hospital on coronary care, Valerie Pomeroy was aware of a grey wet film clinging to the window. She had asked to have it opened but the woman who brought round the early tea didn't seem to think she had the authority to do so and the nurses were too busy. Valerie found the heat oppressive and longed to take a draught of cool, damp air but she had to lie still and behave as one of the nurses had told her yesterday. 'Now, behave!' she had said as Valerie had tried to complain about the noise of the television from the sitting room. She spoke to her as if she were a disobedient child, not crossly, but playfully, in a joshing sort of manner. Really, it was intolerable, but Valerie was helpless and weak and tired so that mostly she drifted in and out of sleep. They had taken away her oxygen mask, for which she was grateful, but she was still attached to a drip. The noise of the television filled her head. Soaps, game shows, explosions of laughter, thunderous clapping, all blasted out from across the corridor. I've become so used to silence, she thought. That's why I can't stand it. I just want peace. I don't want to die with all that racket going on in the background. I don't want the last thing I hear on earth to be a conversation from *Brookside* or whatever it was called.

As she lay, she thought of her dead husband Frank. I was near to joining him, she thought. I might have made it if Betty hadn't been there. Dear Frank. She thought of his kind and intelligent face with its bushy eyebrows and silver beard. She imagined him waiting for her at a kind of customs barrier, in a white robe and sandals. Ridiculous, really. Now she was going to be all right, they told her, and she thought of Frank turning away as if he had come to the station to meet the wrong train. Sorry, darling, she told him. False alarm.

She had spoken shakily to Christopher from Hong Kong, able to croak a few words of reassurance while the nurse held the telephone. 'No, don't come now,' she had told him. 'Come when I'm better. Want to enjoy having you. Not be sick.' He'd put the girls on then and they'd all shrieked down the telephone, 'Hey, Gran, we're so sorry. Get well, Granny,' and the youngest, Rosie had said, 'Gran, if you die, can I have the chickens?' and her sisters had pulled the telephone from her and Valerie heard her voice complaining, 'I only said *if*. What's wrong with that?'

Vaguely, she thought of home. Betty would see to everything, she knew. She would see that the fowl were fed and locked up from the fox at night. She would draw curtains and leave on lights to deter burglars. Not that I care, thought Valerie. It's the fuss of it all that would be a nuisance. She thought of Claudia and her heart was moved by the kindness she had shown in coming into hospital with her. If I had, in fact, been dying, she thought, I would have been comforted to have her there. Not entirely a stranger, but also not someone I would have to worry about, like poor Betty, who would have been upset. Christopher had told her on the telephone that Claudia's son had been in an accident and that he would be in hospital for a while. She thought he had mentioned India, but maybe her mind was wandering. Poor Claudia. So much worse when the patient was a child, even if practically a grown-up one.

Soon, she knew, when she was feeling a little better they would set the therapists on to her. She had already been warned about the lifestyle therapist and the cardiac rehabilitation nurse who would tell her not to eat butter and lose weight and give up drink. Bloody interfering so and so's, the lot of them. Ah, drink. She wondered, idly, if she would like one and was relieved to find that the morphine seemed to have wiped out that desire.

Closing her eyes again on the grey morning, she drifted off to sleep.

For Lila, on the train crawling out of Euston, the dull, grey morning suited her depressed spirits. She had been up clubbing until the early hours and now had a splitting headache and the dreary sensation of having been through the motions of having a good time without having really done so. It was hard, she supposed, to slot straight back into her old set of mates, many of whom she had not seen for over a year. So much had happened in the intervening time. There wasn't only her move to New York, but also her father's trial and now Jerome's accident. It's me that's changed, she thought sadly, unable to resist dressing her role in the cloak of tragedy. I've suffered so much, been through such a lot that it has changed me. She stared gloomily out of the window at the rows of back-to-back houses with their scarred patches of garden. I would have done better to have gone out with Anthony Brewer, she thought. Giving the old lech a thrill would have been more enjoyable in the long run.

The refreshment trolley trundled past and scrabbling in her bag for the money to buy a cup of coffee she pulled out an unfamiliar piece of paper and turning it over realised that it was Anthony's telephone number which he had forced on her in the car. Maybe I'll give him a ring, she thought, as she emptied several sachets of sugar into the murky liquid. He could take me out tonight instead. I'm going to need cheering up.

The coffee made her feel even more queasy and she wondered if it was partly because of how much she was scared by the prospect of the prison. In the end she had not asked Anna to go with her. I need to do this on my own, she had decided. I need to suffer the whole thing on my own. It has got to be my experience, not coloured or softened by anybody else. I want to feel it slicing into my bones, deep into me, so that I know what it's like for Dad.

What Lila had not been prepared for, when she was finally let into a meeting room to see her father, was the sight of a much slimmer, quite youthful looking Roger, wearing a navy prison tracksuit and trainers, his hair cropped close to his head. But the most astonishing thing was his expression – not dejected and subdued, far from it. Her father, in fact, had an air about him which she could only describe as jaunty.

The same grey mist hung over Heathrow, not sufficient to delay flights but enough to cling to the windscreen of the ambulance as it waited on the runway. Sitting in the front with the driver, Claudia kept wiping the glass with her sleeve, but the moisture was outside in beady drops which collected and rolled down the windscreen.

The radio contact crackled from time to time and every few minutes Claudia looked at her watch. The last news they had was that the plane had landed and was somewhere out on the flat green stretches of the airport, awaiting the allocation of a docking bay. She found it almost unbearable that Jerome was out there and she still couldn't get to him. She could see ghostly silver shapes and coloured lights winking as aircraft slid past, harried by small yellow service trucks. One of the two ambulance crew had collected coffee for them all and she had burnt her mouth on the scalding liquid, gulping at it nervously, terrified that the leisurely activity of coffee-drinking would somehow slow up the process of getting her to Jerome.

'You OK, love?' asked the fatherly driver, Dick.

'Just a bit wound up, you know,' said Claudia. 'It's been nearly a year.'

'Won't be long now,' he said comfortably. 'Look, here comes our escort. We can go out with this lot.' The radio crackled to life again, giving instructions, and the ambulance nosed forward onto the tarmac. 'Five, ten minutes or so and you'll see your lad again.'

When eventually they drew alongside the aircraft and nudged beneath its giant silver wing, a small party was already waiting for them. A solicitous air hostess in a navy raincoat and pillbox hat was crouching beside a figure in a wheelchair. 'There he is,' said Dick cheerfully, 'safe and sound.'

Hardly that, thought Claudia, who was jammed between the men in the front of the vehicle and unable to reach the door and jump out, or even have her hand ready on the handle. She waved frantically but Jerome was looking at a sheaf of papers in his lap, unaware of their approach. His leg, encased in a half plaster from the knee down, rested horizontally on a support. He appeared to be dressed in a loose-fitting faded green night-shirt and someone had put a blanket over his shoulders. His arms were burnt dark brown and so thin and sinewy that for a moment Claudia wondered whether it was really him.

The ambulance came to a halt and the men got out and began to organise the ramp at the rear while Claudia flung herself from her seat and rushed towards the chair.

'Jerome!' she called. 'Thank God, darling! Oh, Jerome!'

The seated figure turned to look at her and for that one moment it was hard not to allow herself to show how shocked she was by his appearance. His face was dark brown and had become so thin that his eye sockets looked huge and shadowy and his mouth seemed stretched tight over his jaw. His hair was shaggy, bleached by the sun and dried into stiff looking ropes. He held out a long thin hand towards her.

'Mum!' he said. His voice was the same, Claudia noticed with a surge of relief. His lovely, gentle voice was unaltered.

Squatting awkwardly by the chair she gathered him in her arms, feeling the fragile rigging of his ribs as she stroked his back. With his free hand he smoothed her hair and when she lifted her head she saw that his eyes looked a deep brown in his dark face and there was something in their calm gaze that frightened her.

Down on the railway line the damp swallowed up the distance, blotting it out with grey pearly light. The long grass and bracken along the top of the old embankment was bowed with wet and the legs of Jena's jeans clung darkly to her skinny calves. She was hiding. She had promised her dad she would go to school and she had indeed walked down the lane to the village but the gaggle of kids swinging their bags and scuffing about at the bus stop had frightened her off. She watched them from a distance, their navy blue blazers bobbing about through the mist. Their voices drifted across to her, laughing, talking. She hung back, down by the sheds on the council house allotments, and when the school bus loomed out of the mist with its headlights two yellow orbs she had remained where she was. She saw the boys threading their way down the bus and to the back seats and Billy Hunter already there, collected by his gate at Carne Farm, wiping the window with his sleeve. She wasn't going to go, she knew that now, although she knew she should, and she thought she had intended to. When the moment came, as if she had lost the key to moving her limbs, her legs wouldn't take her forward.

The bus lumbered off and she breathed again. Her dad would be angry. She didn't dare go back yet. She gave a little cough, examining the tightness of her chest, hoping she could summon up the onset of asthma, but she knew it wouldn't work.

Where now? At the top of the cul-de-sac were the big houses on the lane out of the village. That Claudio lived in the bungalow up there. Jena thought with pleasure of the fun she had had with Lila, showing her how to jump the hedges on Jigsaw. She'd liked that girl. Liked the way she talked, liked the way she rode the horse. All easy, and laughing. Jena wondered if she might still be there. She crossed the road by the bungalow and looked up the drive. Everything was all shut up and quiet. Next door was the old woman her dad liked. That fat old witch. Jena wondered if she was in. She went a little way up her drive. There were lights on upstairs. She thought she might go and knock at the back door and see if she was about. The old woman never bothered about school and all that. She might give her something to eat. Once she had made her hot chocolate and showed her a lot of pictures in a book she said she was writing about. They were of horsemen in India, prancing along with spears in their hands. But there was no answer to her knock, and out at the back, Jena saw the chickens going up and down the wire of their run like prisoners. If Mrs Pomeroy had been around she would have let them out by now.

She'd have to go back and hang around the van, waiting until dinner time. She'd show up then, tell them she'd been sent home early.

Chapter Nine

Jerome Barron had shouted himself hoarse. It was so bloody hard to get anywhere on his crutches and the hope of getting Finn to come back by just yelling for him seemed a wasted effort, but he had to try. The puppy had been gone about an hour, he thought. He'd been lying like a log on his feet when he had been resting on the sofa but had suddenly sat up, ears cocked, whining, and then jumped down and vanished. Despite his mother's efforts with chicken wire to make the garden dog-proof, he'd got out somewhere.

Finn had been Lila's idea. She'd seen the litter under the old bus when she'd been out riding with Jena, the traveller's daughter. She'd fallen for the mother, a gentle, rough-coated bitch, a collie cross greyhound with melting toffee eyes, and had picked Finn out from his brothers and sisters. Later she'd cycled back down the railway track with a wodge of bank notes and bought him, asking Jem to deliver him to Claudia when he was old enough. 'He'll be great company for you, Mum,' she had said when she had visited him in hospital. 'For Jerome, too. An incentive to get going again,' and she had kicked at his good leg as he sat in a chair by his bed. 'Dad never let us have a dog, so I reckon now it's time we did.'

They'd had Finn for a week now, and although Jerome and Claudia loved him on sight, he was already proving a handful.

Part of the trouble was that Claudia now had a regular job and was out each day. Greatly to her surprise and delight she had had a telephone call from Mrs Peck, head teacher at the primary school in Bishops Barton, asking her if she could start work immediately, that the new cook had not been a success and that she was desperate to find someone to stand in until the end of term and possibly for a permanent position in September. Jerome could see how thrilled his mother was by what she considered a break in her run of bad luck. He would never have believed it, really, that she would be so grateful to have the chance to take up a fairly low-paid job. 'Skivvies' they'd called the kitchen staff at his public school. An awful word, he realised now, but then it was used without thinking – not meant as a term of abuse. So now his ma was glad to be a skivvie.

He manoeuvred himself out of the gate and hopped down the lane, shouting. It was very quiet and his voice sounded loud and violent as it broke the silence. He stopped and listened. He could hear a distant tractor working somewhere and the far-off sound of sheep, but otherwise nothing. An aeroplane droned gently above, a tiny silver speck against the grey summer sky. Glancing up, he was reminded of India and his abrupt departure. He still longed to be back, to have his senses blasted by the heat, the noise, the smell, the colours of the country he had grown to love. All this is so *bland*, he thought, looking at the even greenness on either side of the lane and the monochrome sky, so grey, so dull, so nothing. That bloody Finn, where could he have gone? He wondered whether he might have tried to find his way back to the old railway, to the other puppies. Did dogs do that sort of thing? The little scrap of grey fur and needle teeth and bright, blackberry eyes had seemed contented enough, sleeping in his room on an old blanket, chewing at the legs of the loose cotton trousers he had bought in India, but who knew what went on in a dog's mind?

Jerome hopped on to the corner where the lane turned towards Bishops Barton. He could see it snaking on between the high hedges but there was nothing to suggest the puppy had gone that way. The fields on either side were full of grazing cows, or cows lying down in the long grass with calves beside them. No Finn to disturb them.

He called again, a note of panic creeping into his voice. The puppy was a bloody liability. What if he was already squashed on the lane somewhere, beneath the giant treads of a tractor tyre, or tossed, injured, to die in a ditch beside the road? 'Finn!' he yelled. 'Finn!'

Silence. Then from quite near he distinctly heard the sound of frantic squawking and excited barking.

'Shit!' Jerome wheeled round and set off back the way he had come. He could guess where the noise was coming from. 'Shit!' In his anxiety he put his injured leg to the ground and pain shot up his shin. He reached Valerie Pomeroy's gate and hopped as best he could up the drive, his heart thumping, dreading what he was going to see. As he got closer, from behind the house came a flurry of chickens, wheeling on skidding legs, wings fluttering madly, with Finn in hot pursuit. 'Finn!' Jerome yelled. 'Finn!' The grey puppy swerved sharply and with a look of intense joy and concentration, pink tongue flapping, set off after another bird.

Swearing, Jerome hopped on, waving a crutch, maddened that he couldn't make a lunge and grab the little blighter. Then there was a further commotion and a small sandy object shot out of the henhouse with a bird in its jaws. As Finn wheeled past, Jerome managed to whack the puppy with his crutch and it rolled over, yelping. The sharp blow brought him to his senses and he crept forward, looking abashed, his whippy tail flattened between his legs. Jerome bent and scooped him up. He felt the little heart pumping beneath the frail ribs and he regretted having struck him, but it was too late for that and he didn't seem to have come to any harm. He wriggled round in Jerome's arms to lick his face. 'You naughty dog. You bad boy,' Jerome scolded, at the same time looking for the other dog, the one with the chicken in its mouth. He saw it now, its rear end and frantically wagging stump of a tail were protruding from a holly bush. Jerome hopped over and prodded its backside with a crutch. A mischievous dark face looked round at him, pale feathers stuck to its nose and lips and old man's eyebrows. Oh God, thought Jerome, knocking the dog out of the way. Bending down, he could see the limp body of the bird in a shallow dusty grave beneath the bush, its head beaded with blood. 'Oh hell!' He straightened up, not knowing what to do. The chickens had gathered in a nervous flock, all scolding loudly, ready to scatter. Feathers had drifted over the grass but he could not see any other victims. The little brown terrier made another dash for the bush, but Jerome knocked it back. He hooked the dead bird out with his crutch. In his arms Finn whined and struggled to get free. 'Stop that!'

Jerome stood and looked at the dead chicken. It was large, speckled grey and white with a red face and a surprised expression. Part of its neck had been torn away by the little dog and pinkish flesh and white cartilage were exposed. Somehow Jerome did not feel he could let the dog go on desecrating the body but he couldn't pick up either the dog or the bird with his arms already occupied by Finn and his crutches. He felt helpless and unnerved. There was probably some law in the country that dogs which killed chickens had to be destroyed. He wanted not to be here in a stranger's garden, to spirit himself and Finn away and leave the little brown dog to its fate. It was sitting now at his feet, looking up at him and whining.

From the house he heard a door opening. Shit! There was someone coming. He turned his head to see a large, elderly woman come out of the back door, cross the little yard and turn the corner by the privet hedge. She glanced up and saw him standing there; a look of first surprise and then anger crossed her face.

'What's this?' she demanded in an imperious voice. 'What has happened? What's going on?'

When Valerie came out into the grey morning, she was at first only anxious to take care on the slippery flags by the back door. Since her 'bit of a do', as she called it, she found herself more concerned to keep herself in working order. She did not want another trip to hospital, another session of being hooked to drips and bags and at the mercy of doctors. She was on her way . . . she couldn't remember where, because the next moment she saw an extremely tall, extremely thin young man standing by her chicken run with something in his arms. He was wearing loose pale trousers and a fine cotton shirt and was so gaunt and hollow-eyed, with an expression of such anguish, that for all the world he could be some suffering deity. Then she saw his trouser leg was torn open to accommodate a plaster cast and that he was balanced on crutches and that in his arms was a puppy. At his feet sat another dog and the body of one of her chickens.

It took only a moment or two to make sense of the scene, and Valerie compulsively laid a hand on her bosom as if to still the rapid beating of her heart. She began to shout then, whatever words came into her head, demanding an explanation. The young man did not move or speak. He looked ill, she thought, so thin, so somehow agonised. He had a small gold ring through one nostril and one bony wrist was encircled with beads and strips of leather. Long fingers were working through the fur of the puppy's neck and he fumbled with the spare hand to keep his weight steady on the one crutch he could manage.

When he did speak his voice was beautiful, educated, gentle. Valerie felt suddenly tremendously moved by him, this extraordinary thin and exotic young man standing in her garden. Then she remembered the chicken and cast her eyes down. It was Bertha, she could tell, who lay slaughtered and ripped on the grass. Thank goodness not Naomi.

'I'm so terribly sorry,' he was saying. 'I couldn't stop them. I shouted. I'm so sorry.'

'That's not your dog? That one?' she heard herself asking briskly.

'No. No. I've never seen it before. This one is, though, and he was chasing them too.'

'Too small to kill,' said Valerie. 'I know whose dog this is,' and she indicated the terrier. 'Next door's. That bloody woman's.'

'I'm so sorry,' he repeated. Looking at him, she saw that he was swaying. He was too tall and thin to be standing on one leg like that. Like a crane.

'You'd better come in,' she said. She bent down and caught hold of the terrier by its collar and dragged it towards the house. It resisted for a bit, sticking its legs out like props, but gave up and allowed itself to be bundled into an outhouse. When the door was shut, it began to whine and scratch at the wood.

'Come in,' she repeated. 'Mind the step. How good are you on those? Here, let me take the pup.' Finn was removed from Jerome's arms and he got himself over the threshold and sank gratefully into a collapsing armchair which was pointed out to him in the corner of the most untidy kitchen he had ever seen.

'Little bugger,' said Valerie to Finn in her arms. 'Now,' she said, looking at Jerome, 'I know who you are, don't I?'

'Jerome. You know my mother, Claudia. From next door.'

'Yes. I heard about you. About the leg.'

'I heard about you. The heart.' They looked at one another almost like comrades.

'India, wasn't it?'

'Yes.' Jerome, sitting in the armchair, felt curiously peaceful. There was no need to say anything else. 'Mum says you know India.'

'Without wishing to sound melodramatic, it is in my soul. Written on my heart. I was born and grew up there.'

'You can't shake it off, can you? Not once it has got to you.'

'No. Nor want to.'

The elderly, rather sick old woman and the young, emaciated man exchanged a look of understanding and appreciation.

It was Victoria who answered the telephone. She had been home from school for four days and already felt as if she was unravelling like the sleeve of her school jumper where she had chewed the wool at the wrist, coming apart with the pleasure of mornings sleeping late and mooching about on her own. It was a lovely, lazy, idle sensation. Soon, she knew, Pony Club stuff would begin and she had several pieces of coursework to

151

complete, but for the moment she was allowed to do nothing. She had been sliding around the kitchen in her socks and pyjamas, eating cereal and reading *Horse and Hound*. In a while she would catch Vinnie and go for a ride, but she was in no hurry. Her father was at work as usual and her mother was off on a decorative arts day course in Devon – something about repairing tapestry.

'Hello' she said into the telephone and the voice boomed back.

'This is Valerie Pomeroy. Who is that? Victoria? Is your mother there? Well, I think you had better come round at once. Your dog has slaughtered one of my chickens.'

Victoria skidded around then, getting dressed, trying to contact her mother who was not answering her mobile, or her father at his office, but he was in a meeting. There was nothing for it, she had to go and face the gorgon herself. How terrible, what a dreadful crime Skye had committed. Almost as bad as sheep-worrying. Would she be expected to pay for the chicken? To replace it? She had no money at the moment. Only about forty pence in the fluff at the bottom of the pocket of her jeans. Mrs Pomeroy was so scary, so large and loud with her red talon nails and bulldog face.

With trembling hands Victoria buttoned up her shirt and pushed her feet into her trainers. Not bothering to lock the door she ran out of the gates of East End House and along the lane the few yards to Mrs Pomeroy's drive. As she passed she glanced at the bungalow. If Claudia had been at home she might have dashed in there for support, but there was no pick-up in the drive.

As she ran, Victoria supposed it was her fault. She should have kept an eye on Skye, checked that he was shut in or, if he was in the garden, that the gates were closed. He had a habit of wandering, was an inveterate hunter, working along the hedges after rabbit, badger, deer, anything that aroused his natural predatory instincts. He was deaf then, when his sharp nose was racing along a rich seam of scent. You could shout as much as you liked but he didn't bother even to look up. He had other more important things to do. Please God, prayed Victoria as she reached the back door of the Lodge, please God, help me get through this.

She knocked timidly on the door. She could hear voices from inside – a male voice and Mrs Pomeroy's booming tones. She couldn't decide whether this made things worse or better.

Perhaps she had called the police. Perhaps it was Gripper, the gamekeeper, known for shooting stray dogs that upset his pheasants. For a ridiculous instant, Victoria even wondered whether Mrs Pomeroy had called in the vicar, like people did for tragedies. However, when Mrs Pomeroy opened the door, she did not look too furious and for a moment Victoria felt distinct relief.

'You'd better come in,' she said and then Victoria was standing in the kitchen beside a table so cluttered that she could not see its surface, and in the corner, in an armchair with a leg encased in plaster and stuck out to rest on a stool, sat a very thin, dark young man with a wonderful face.

'Hello,' he said. 'I'm sorry. It's awful. Our dogs, I'm afraid. They've run amok amongst the chickens.'

'Oh,' Victoria stammered, blushing. 'I didn't know . . . didn't realise Skye had gone.'

'I'm Jerome. From next door. This is Finn,' and he indicated a puppy he had on his lap, a small grey creature with a cream triangle on its chest and a sharp little face.

'Your monster, that terrier, was the ringleader,' said Valerie. 'He caught and killed one of my best layers as well as chasing all the others and, no doubt, putting them off lay.'

Victoria blushed again and screwed her hands together. 'I'm so sorry. I should have checked where he was. It's my fault. I'm so sorry.'

The tall boy intervened gently. 'I'm afraid we're in the same boat, you and me. I was supposed to be looking after Finn. One moment he was there, the next he'd gone.'

'Are you Lila's brother? I thought you must be. The accident. She told me.'

'Now then,' Valerie cut in. 'Your dog. What are we going to do with the little beast? I don't want this ever happening again. Can't you keep him in? At least on your own land?'

'Well . . . he always manages to get out if he wants to,' mumbled Victoria.

'I've shut him in the woodshed and I've tied the dead fowl round his neck. It's the only cure I know for chicken chasing. I want you to leave him there for a few hours. He can't get at the bird and he can't shake it off. Dogs hate it. It'll teach him never to go near a chicken in the future.'

Victoria flushed again. Poor Skye. It sounded terrible. A terrible punishment.

Valerie saw her expression and said, 'Now, don't be silly. It doesn't hurt him one bit. It will just teach him a lesson. You can go and see him if you like, but not if you're going to speak nicely to him. He needs a thorough telling-off from everyone. Then he'll learn.'

'Finn's under-age, a juvenile delinquent, or he'd have to go through the same treatment,' said Jerome. 'I've just been told that.'

Victoria pulled a face. What could she say? She did not seem to have an alternative. She mumbled something like an assent. Jerome smiled at her. His teeth looked very white and large because his face was so thin and dark. It was a lovely smile, though, and she found she could smile back ruefully and that she was bold enough to say to Valerie, 'I know that Mum'll replace your chicken. Or pay, or something. I'm really sorry about Skye being so naughty.'

'We'll see,' said Valerie, in a less barking tone and then added, 'Jerome and I are having a cup of coffee. Would you like one? Or hot chocolate? A winter drink, I know, but it's a beastly cold morning for July.'

Victoria hesitated. As the guilty party she wasn't sure she was in a position to accept.

'Go on,' said Jerome. 'You probably need one. If you feel anything like I do about poor Bertha. All the hens have names, which makes it seem even more like murder.'

'I've a friend at school called Berthe,' said Victoria and then thought, God, what a stupid thing to say. What had that got to do with anything?

However Valerie, not seeming to notice, said, 'An unusual name. Berthe Morisot – one of my favourite painters,' as she rattled about in a drawer looking for a teaspoon. The hot chocolate was stuck in the bottom of the tin in a brown lump 'Not been used, you see,' explained Valerie, banging at it with the spoon, 'not since the grandchildren were here last summer.' She chipped off a chunk. 'Here. You'll have to leave it to dissolve a bit first and then give it a good stir.' She passed Victoria the mug of brownish milk, floating with dusty specks of chocolate.

'We've been talking about India. Jerome has just come back. The wretched accident meant the poor boy could not travel when his teaching term was over. I'm telling him a little of what he missed.'

'My brother went through India on his gap year,' ventured Victoria, shyly. 'I'm not sure he liked it that much. I think he had curry tummy or Delhi belly, or something like that, the whole time.'

'It's quite different being a tourist. Jerome lived and worked there. That's what gives you an understanding of a place.'

Victoria looked crushed and Valerie felt conscious of having been dismissive.

'Jim went on to work in Australia, didn't he?' she asked to make up for it.

'Yes. He worked on a sheep station for six months and then did all sorts of jobs all over the place before travelling back.'

'In India,' explained Jerome, 'I worked in a school for the blind and taught a few night classes for students my age.' His face darkened and he bent over the puppy on his lap. Victoria could see that there was something he did not want to talk about. She gulped at her milk, which barely tasted of chocolate.

'How is Lila?' she asked, grateful to have found something to say. 'She was so great when she was here. She helped me with my horse.'

'She's fine, as far as I know,' said Jerome, lifting his face. 'She seems to like New York. It's big enough and noisy enough for her. I'm not sure she's that keen on her job, but that's Lila. She gets bored easily. She was in Paris last weekend. She's always off on jaunts.'

'Will she be coming back here this summer?'

'I don't know. I don't think deepest Dorset is probably her scene. What about you? Are you off somewhere exciting this summer?'

'No. We never go away. Oh, Cornwall for two weeks, but that doesn't really count.'

'You must come round and see me then. I'm so stuck with this effing leg that I'll need distracting. You could count me as the social service for your Duke of Edinburgh award.'

'How did you know I was doing D of E?'

'All girls do, don't they? From your sort of school, at least.' They grinned.

Victoria lent down to rub her leg and said casually, 'Of course I'll come, if you want me to.' Her heart raced. This most beautiful of boys – hardly a boy, a man really – had said he would like to see her again.

Valerie, who had shuffled out of the room, returned with an old photograph album in her hand. She told Victoria to pile some newspapers on the floor and make a space on the table so that she could lay it down and open it.

'Look,' she said, 'this is what I mean. British Indian secular architecture. Adapting European classical style to the subcontinent. See the confidence. The railway stations, the public buildings, the Victoria Memorial in Calcutta, the Gateway of India in Bombay, the legislative buildings of Lucknow and New Delhi. All so very fine.' She passed the book to Jerome.

'Don't you think they are too grandiose and vainglorious? Disdainful of Indians, especially the poor?' said Jerome.

'Nonsense!' blazed Valerie. 'Look what has been built in free India. Hideous modern ugliness. Why shouldn't the impoverished be uplifted by grandeur and beauty? The brutality and crowding of modern buildings exacerbate poverty and misery. Grind people further into the dirt.' She flipped over a page. 'This is where I grew up – these bungalows built for officials in country districts were very pleasant in a tropical climate. We had this lovely wide veranda, thick walls, high ceilings and the most beautiful garden.' Victoria peered over her shoulder. A crooked, fat finger with a crimson nail was stabbing at a black and white photograph of a family group ranged in front of a large bungalow which was covered in a swarming creeper, the front shaded by a deep veranda. There were several adults – the ladies in large shady hats and white dresses, the men in pale jackets and collar and ties despite the heat.

'My mother and father and two aunts,' explained Valerie, 'and the manager of my father's company.' Four girls sat gracefully at the feet of the grown-ups, long legs slightly aslant, short skirts, loose hair, all fair and slender, all beautiful. 'My sisters,' she went on.

Victoria bent closer. Which one could possibly have grown into this old woman with her huge shapeless body and swollen ankles and jowly purple face?

'That's me,' and the finger stabbed beneath the prettiest of the young women – the one with a soft rosebud mouth and dreaming eyes. Victoria looked up, shocked. How awful. How could such a cruel transformation take place? All that youth and beauty come to this. Valerie caught her look.

'Changed a bit,' she said gruffly, amused. 'I was sixteen then. Your age.'

'You were terribly pretty,' Victoria said and then thought that this sounded rude, as if she was drawing attention to the fact that the looks were now all gone.

'I was thought to be. Lot of bother it caused at times. Made my parents want to marry me off and made it harder for me to come back to England to go to university. They thought it a waste, you see, when I could have been married well and set up in some grand establishment. Instead I chose a penniless life in a student bedsit in Bayswater.' She passed the book back to Jerome who, Victoria noticed, hardly bothered to look at the family group photograph. He was much more interested in the scenes of Indian life, the cities, the architecture.

Victoria finished her milk and started to wonder how she could leave. She was worried about Skye shut up in the punishment cell. She was worried that when her mother found out, there would be some awful row. She would come storming round and have it out with Mrs Pomeroy. Victoria couldn't bear that. Not now that they seemed almost friends.

'I'm going to have to go,' she said, re-looping the band that held her long hair at the back of her neck. She hesitated. 'When can I come back for Skye?'

'Come and get him in an hour or so. Just collect him from the shed. He'll have learned his lesson. Don't disturb me. I shall be working.'

'OK. I'd better go then.' She looked at Jerome who had put down the photograph album.

'I'll come with you,' he said. Victoria found a space on the draining board for the mugs which she had rinsed under the tap as he lifted his plastered leg off the stool with both hands and picked up his crutches.

'I'll take Finn,' said Victoria, collecting the puppy, who after the excitements of the morning had gone to sleep. She tickled the white patch on his chest and he yawned.

They said goodbye to Valerie. Victoria was grateful to be with Jerome who was so articulate in his renewed apologies for the behaviour of their dogs that all she had to do was nod in agreement.

'Apart from poor Bertha, I've enjoyed seeing you,' said Valerie gruffly, standing at the kitchen door. 'You must come again.'

After they had gone, Valerie turned again into the kitchen and sat in the armchair. What she would really like was a drink. Betty had cleared out all the bottles when she was in hospital but had overlooked the sloe gin at the back of the pantry.

No, she was not going to give in. Instead she would go and work. She had plenty to think about. Bertha's tragedy had ended well in the unexpected visit of that delightful boy. The girl was a nice creature too. Painfully shy and awkward but there was nothing wrong with that. Valerie remembered the teenager she had been as if it was yesterday. The photograph in the album had brought it all back. Sixteen was a difficult age. She remembered the agonies of confronting the adult world with all its complexities. What she also remembered was that while the photograph was being taken, Hugo Armstrong, her father's manager, seated behind her had been rubbing his knee across her back. She could remember now how it had made her feel. No, it was not easy to be growing up a girl.

At three o'clock Claudia had finished in the kitchen at Bishops Barton Church of England Primary School. She had given the stainless steel work surfaces a final wipe and hung the dishcloths to dry over the sink. Tomorrow's vegetables were ready to prepare in the morning and the mince taken out of the freezer for the shepherd's pie. She still felt anxious about quantities but the ring file of recipes was unequivocal. 'You'll soon get the hang of it,' said Mrs Peck, 'and learn what is most popular. We allow seconds if there is enough left over. Numbers fluctuate each day; we get more signing up for school dinners on days when there are chicken drumsticks or sausages, for instance. Chocolate sponge and chocolate sauce is very popular too.'

As she hung her white apron and cap in the office and took off the compulsory, white non-slip shoes, Claudia felt totally exhausted. She had only worked for a week and a half but she supposed the strain of taking up a responsible position so unexpectedly, and on top of the anxiety about Jerome, had taken its toll. The wonderful thing was that she loved every minute of it. From the very first day when she had received the emergency call to ask if she could help and had had to cook beans, chips and egg and bacon pie for ninety children, she had loved it. The cooking was routine stuff, her basic training stood her in good stead and, even more so, the years of feeding her own and other people's children. The raw carrot sticks she introduced – each child, if they wished, taking a handful as they queued for their plates – were a success, as was the way she did halved baked potatoes with the cut side slashed and buttered so that they browned and crisped in the oven. Mrs Peck had congratulated her on having so little waste and the children's enthusiasm was a reward in itself.

It was a happy and successful little village school where the teachers were mostly local women and the children were drawn from the surrounding farms and villages. School buses pottered along the lanes collecting and delivering those from outlying areas and Bishops Barton mothers walked their children to school along the village street, then stood outside the gates chatting and gossiping, with prams and dogs and pushchairs.

Claudia loved the busy, purposeful atmosphere and had already come to admire and respect Mrs Peck, a small bustling woman in her fifties. While she was explaining how the kitchen functioned, she had glanced through the plate glass window and spotted a child being pushed about in the playground and was off. She shot out of the kitchen and along the corridor like a rat up a drainpipe and Claudia watched while she sorted out the culprit and comforted the victim. The next moment a small, anxious girl was pulling at her sleeve to tell her that her mum had had a baby girl. 'That's lovely news, Amy. You must be very proud to be a big sister. Make sure you tell Mrs Armstrong and I expect your class will want to send them both a card,' Claudia heard her say.

It proved impossible to have Mrs Peck's undivided attention while the children were about. Claudia had to wait until after assembly when the children filed off to their classes before she could hear more about what was expected of her and be introduced to the kitchen staff – two large, cheerful women called Eileen and Susie, who were already peeling potatoes and making pastry in a huge mixer whose electric arm rotated through a golden ball of dough.

'Poor Donna,' said Mrs Peck, referring to the departed cook. 'It didn't work out with her. Domestic problems. She could be first rate when her mind was on the job, but she's going through a very tricky separation. We had scenes at school. Jealous husband, all that sort of thing. She's moved out now, I believe. Gone to the boyfriend in Ringwood.'

'Ah,' said Claudia, conscious that Donna's marital problems had worked in her favour.

'There's some paperwork to complete in my office and then I'm going to throw you in the deep end. It will be a bit of a learning curve at first, but we're all so glad you could step in at such short notice. I like to employ local women – it helps build the sense of community which is at the heart of village schools like this.'

Claudia double-checked her order for vegetables. Carrots, peas and potatoes were the obvious mainstays and these country children who grew up with allotments and vegetable patches were no more enthusiastic about their cooked greens than any others. Putting away her order book, she looked with satisfaction at her tidy files and paperwork. She enjoyed the sense of order and routine. After the last chaotic months it was reassuring to feel on top of things and to know that on Wednesday she would be cooking vats of mince and potatoes followed by apple crumble and custard, and on Thursday it would be sausages in batter. It all had such a nostalgic feel about it, like turning the clock back to a secure time when she was a child and ate this sort of food, while one day followed another in a steady, preordained succession.

Thinking about Jerome, as she often did, Claudia locked the kitchen and went across the playground to where the pick-up was parked. She had been prepared, she supposed, for him to look ill and traumatised, but not to be so thin and frail as to be almost transparent. The months in India seemed to have eroded him, worn him down to a hollow-eyed, listless skeleton. She remembered how, at the airport, she had hardly recognised her son in the gaunt stranger whose face had shrunk into hollows with the skin stretched across the bones so tightly that when he smiled she could see the knobbly structure of his jaw.

They had clung to each other and she had wept, but he had not. There seemed to be a deep well of feeling somewhere inside him which could not be accessed. Later, as they travelled together in the ambulance there surfaced between them much more that was familiar, but it shocked her that it was like getting to know someone again.

He had travelled home with a battered backpack, half empty. It contained a roll of faded cotton clothes, Indian style, in spice colours washed out by sun, a few tattered books, an exercise book nearly filled with his neat writing, and his camera. That seemed to be all. Where, she wondered, had all the stuff gone which she had so laboriously ticked off the list nearly a year ago? The sleeping bag, the towels, the sheets, the medical packs, the paraphernalia that accompanies westerners wherever they travel? Stolen? Given away? She did not know. Roger had insisted he took cricket whites and a bat. Jerome had been in the First XI at his school and his father had got him an introduction to a prestigious cricket club in Delhi. It did not seem that Jerome had moved in those sort of circles.

She had been shocked by his passivity, by his resigned acceptance of the discomfort from his injuries and by his lack of interest in his surroundings. She had fussed about his room in the private hospital. Was it too warm? Too cool? Did he want anything to drink, to eat? He had watched her with sleepy remote eyes, smiling a gentle smile but apparently indifferent. He had asked her nothing about his father, accepting what she told him without comment about her own condition – about how she was managing, where she was living, nothing. Slowly she fed him information to prepare him for what she felt would be a huge shock – all that he had left behind when he had set out year ago was now gone – but he seemed oblivious.

She spoke to the specialist, a brisk red-haired Scotsman who had a son much the same age, and he was reassuring. 'It's shock. Physical and cultural. Let him take his time. Slowly he'll come back to you.' Those words stuck in Claudia's head. 'He'll come back to you.' She told Minna, who agreed. 'Remember he's sedated for the pain and also it's the body's way of aiding recovery. Shutting up shop. Putting up the "Closed" sign for a bit. Don't worry. Not yet anyway.'

Lila had hardly noticed. She had made the hospital room seem small and overcrowded as she prowled about it, fiddling with the curtains, switching channels on the television, eating grapes. Claudia sensed her odd mood. Quite how she had found her father she could not make out. She had asked, of course, but Lila had fired back, 'If you're interested, visit him yourself!' Her restless energy sent her back to the village to ride Victoria Durnford's horse, to cycle and to run, and Claudia knew that her daughter's frantic activity was driven by something unresolved within her. How complicated they were, these two children who had both moved outside her influence, beyond her capacity to help, whom she could no longer patch up and put back on their feet after a fall.

Things had been easier when she eventually got Jerome out of hospital. He had hopped into the bungalow with no comment. Later he had said, 'This is OK, isn't it, Mum? You've made it nice. Homely.' She had looked forward to showing him the bedroom she had tried to make welcoming, but he had simply sat on the bed without even looking about him and said nothing. 'Is it all right?' she asked finally, indicating the room with a sweep of her hand, wanting praise, or thanks, she supposed, and he had said simply, 'It's fine, Mum. Fine. It doesn't matter, anyway.'

'Why does nothing matter?' she asked Minna. 'He used to be so fired up, so passionate about things. What has happened to him? He won't watch television or read a paper. He writes a lot but hides it with his hand if I am anywhere near.'

'You're too impatient,' said Minna. 'Give him time. Has he talked about the accident yet?'

'Not a word.'

'When he's ready he will.'

Claudia swung the pick-up out of the school car park. The Primary One and Two children were already leaving in little brightly coloured groups, shepherded along the road by mothers or climbing into the back seats of the cars pulled up outside. Some of them recognised her and waved and she waved back. The mothers smiled.

She saw Jena then. The skinny little back view was trotting down the pavement, the head turning to look round anxiously as cars swept past. She shouldn't be out of school this early, thought Claudia. She's on the run. Bolting.

She pulled up alongside and leaned across to open the passenger door.

'Here,' she said. 'Hop in. I'll give you a lift.'

'Don't want one,' the child replied and hurried on but Claudia had seen the white tear-streaked face and was not going to be put off.

'Get in, Jena. To talk at least.'

'Nah. Don't want to. Nothing to talk about,' but now she lingered by the door, fingering the handle.

'Come on,' said Claudia gently.

'OK.' The child opened the door and slid in. Claudia noticed that her jeans were dirty and the palms of her hands were smeared with grit and blood.

'What happened, Jena? Did you fall over?'

'Yeah. Something like that.' She began to poke about in the bits and pieces on the dashboard, not really looking for anything, just keeping herself occupied to avoid responding to Claudia.

'Jena? Do you want to tell me what really happened?'

Silence.

'OK. Well, come back with me. Come and see Jerome. I'm worried about him. I'd like to know what you think.'

Jena turned to look at her with wide, hazel eyes. She had never been talked to like that.

'What would I know?' she asked.

'I just think you might,' said Claudia. 'You're good with animals. You know how they are feeling and humans aren't so different. Come anyway. Finn'll be glad to see you.'

'OK.'

When they drew up outside Garden Cottage, the front door was open and when Claudia turned off the engine they could hear talking. Finn came running out, yapping in his puppy voice, and Jena bent to pick him up.

'I don't know who's here, but come on in,' said Claudia, leading the way into the sitting room where Jerome lay full length on the sofa talking to a dark-haired girl sitting cross-legged on the floor. It took a moment to recognise Victoria Durnford.

'Hello, Mum,' said Jerome, looking backwards over his shoulder. 'Hi, Jena! Don't be nice to Finn. He's in utter disgrace. He has been in serious trouble, hasn't he, Victoria? Led astray, I'm afraid. Got into bad company. Wait until you hear!'

Why, thought Claudia, he sounds almost normal.

Later that night she lay sleepless in bed. She could hear Jerome's music playing softly from his room – some kind of Indian music, silvery and hypnotic. He had had trouble sleeping since his return. After the drugged stupor of hospital and a return to a more normal routine at home, he had been restless and awake for long hours. She had heard him often, tap-tapping to the bathroom, and had at first got up to suggest a hot drink or to see if he wanted company. 'I'm all right, Mum,' he'd said. 'I'm OK. I'll just lie here. You go back to sleep.'

Apart from his leg, which was, as Minna pointed out, the least complicated thing to deal with because the operation had been straightforward and Mr Simpson was fully confident of his complete recovery, there was his dramatic weight loss. She had tried to interest him in all his old favourite foods but his appetite was very small. When she questioned him about how he had become so emaciated, he had replied, 'Everyone's thin in India. You don't notice when it happens to you. I was never ill but I suppose the school provided a very restricted diet. Loads of rice and vegetables, not much protein. I was hungry at first but after a bit I got used to it.'

'Why didn't you buy your own food – supplement what they gave you?'

'And eat more than the other teachers? Eat more than the children? Mum, I was perfectly all right. Perfectly healthy. People back here look gross to me now.'

The fact that he could remember nothing of the accident was another worry. He said, when she had tried, very gently, to open him up a little to reveal what had happened, 'There's no point going on about it, Mum. I simply don't remember. I remember catching the bus, sitting down and then nothing else until waking up in the hospital.'

'Who were you with? Friends?'

'I don't remember. Maybe. I expect so.'

'Where were you going?'

'Oh, Mum, what does it matter? Please leave it alone.'

So she had, but this withdrawal upset her. She did not like to feel there were areas of Jerome that she must not probe, where she was excluded. He had always been so open with her. They were so alike, she had felt that they could share anything.

His reaction to his father's situation was also surprising. Slowly, they had begun to speak more about the trial and his imprisonment and one day Claudia found a thick envelope on the kitchen table addressed to Roger in Jerome's neat handwriting.

'Do you want me to post this?' she had asked, weighing it in her hand.

'Please,' he had said, not looking up from a book he was reading.

'You know he's not allowed to take telephone calls? He's only allowed to ring out. If you want to speak to him we could get you a mobile. If you want to visit, just tell me and I'll take you to the prison.'

'OK,' he had said, still not looking up.

'Darling?'

'Yes?'

'You don't seem very, well, *involved*, somehow.'

He shrugged. 'I don't know how I *seem*. I know how I *feel*.'

'How is that?'

'Oh, Mum, please. Not now.'

It was Claudia's turn to shrug. 'There is one thing, though. You haven't put this address, have you? You know I don't want him to know where I am at this stage.'

'No, I haven't,' he replied wearily.

He had been far livelier this afternoon with Victoria and Jena. She'd made them a pot of tea and some toast and left them to it. Sitting in the garden she could hear laughter from inside. She supposed that they were undemanding company, those two, asking no questions, accepting him exactly as he was.

Now she was thoroughly awake she wondered whether to go and make a drink or read a few pages of her book. She thought about the next day at work, went through what she was going to cook, jobs she had to see to. At the end of the week she could collect her new car which the helpful man at Bishops Barton garage had found for her. Hardly new, but ten years old and with a low mileage on the clock. Then she would return the pick-up. She thought of Anthony Brewer whom she had not seen for weeks. It seemed strange that she had not bumped into him anywhere, that he had not telephoned. He had seemed really interested in her at that dinner party and she had felt sure he would subsequently ask to see her again. Then nothing. Men were so difficult to predict. She wondered what had frightened him off. She wondered then if she minded and found that she did. It felt a bit like rejection. The sort of thing she might have agonised over in the old days.

Her thoughts strayed to the events of the day. Jerome seemed to have liked Valerie Pomeroy despite the distressing circumstances of their meeting. She felt slightly guilty that she had not been in to see her more often but with Jerome at home and her new job there had been little opportunity. In two weeks when the school closed for the summer holidays she would do something about her.

Next door Victoria Durnford was also awake, sitting at her desk and writing in her diary. Her curtains were open and she could see over the trees to Garden Cottage and noticed that the light was still on in Jerome's room. She sucked the end of her Biro. With an absolute certainty she knew she was in love. It had happened to her as she stood in Mrs Pomeroy's kitchen and it had been like a physical blow that almost took her breath away. It had been when he had first smiled at her, really *at* her, and it felt as if all the air in her body had been exhaled in a rush, leaving a hollow emptiness in her chest. He was the most beautiful boy she had ever seen, and the nicest. She wanted to remember every single word he had said to her, especially when she had stood up to go and he had said, 'Must you go? Promise to come again, will you? What are you doing tomorrow? It's your neighbourly duty to come and entertain me.'

'OK,' she had mumbled, fiddling with her hair while her heart sang. She had felt like that all the evening, elated and fizzing with happiness. She found that she hadn't minded when her mother had got home cross and tired and had gone off the deep end about Skye. Of course, she knew that they hadn't a leg to stand on, that they were entirely in the wrong and that apologies were due to Mrs Pomeroy. Victoria could see that it was this that made her cross. She had not expected that it would be Claudia who was cast as a villain.

'It's too ridiculous to get a puppy like that. Lurchers are notorious for sloping off and of course they're killing machines. I mean, that's why the gyppos always have them. She'll never keep it in, and what about exercise when she's at work all day? Jerome will be gone to university in October. These London people have simply no idea about animals. I shall tell her she must send it back.'

'Oh, Mum,' Victoria had groaned. She didn't dare mention what Skye's punishment had been.

It was her father who had calmed things down when he got home, throwing his newspaper and briefcase down in the hall and swinging her off her feet although she was now so tall that he could only lift her a few inches.

'I'll need a forklift soon,' he said, 'to get you off the ground.'

'*Dad!* Thank you very much!'

Her mother had immediately started on him about the dogs but he had said calmly, as he went to the cloakroom to wash his hands, 'Don't be silly. You can't interfere like that. What dog she has is Claudia's business.'

'But it's sheer ignorance on her part. What does she know about lurchers?'

'Oh Julia, for heaven's sake stop it!' He had looked quite fierce for him and her mum had had to drop it.

Victoria looked at the yellow square of Jerome's window. She thought she could see his head moving about but it was hard to tell through the branches of the trees. But she knew he was there and that she would see him tomorrow and that he was going to lend her a book and help her with her English essay on *Wuthering Heights*. Apart from Bertha's assassination, which she still felt awful about, this had been an almost perfect day.

Chapter Ten

Lila loved Paris and the city had happy associations for her. She had spent a few months there as a student, staying with a respectable, wealthy banking family on the Rue de la Pompe – Monsieur was an associate of her father's. Madame had quite literally thrown up her hands in horror at the healthy size of the English girl – 'It is like sharing the house with a horse,' she exclaimed to her friends – but Lila had shrugged off all efforts to smarten her up and hone her down, refusing to enter the painfully chic boutiques patronised by Madame and her daughters. 'Nothing would fit me!' she explained cheerfully. 'I'd look ridiculous in your sort of clothes. You have to be French and dolly-sized to wear them, not a whopping great Anglo-Saxon like me.' She soon demonstrated her independence by finding her own friends, striding over the beautiful Pont Neuf to classes at the Sorbonne and afterwards to drink in the cafés and bars of the Left Bank.

She had her first altogether satisfactory affair with a Dutch student of architecture, a tall, bad boy, handsome and lazy, and in between epic bouts of lovemaking, wandered hand in hand through the streets of faded elegance, ate oysters, loitered in bookshops, sat in parks and argued about life. All the clichés about Paris she found were true, there was something in the air which seemed to promise an enhancement of all things pleasurable – love, food, drink, friendship, laughter – but not in the heavy, meaty style of other European fleshpots with their burger bars and sex shops. Here all was refinement and elegance, with the appetite heightened by the finesse and artfulness of the place. There was seduction in the little cups of hot chocolate, the creperies and cafés, the autumn leaves drifting into the Seine, which in the gloomy fading evenings was strung with necklaces of lights, in the patisseries with their luscious, gilded pastries and the chocolate shops where customers lingered unashamedly over the choice of each confection, for it to be lifted with

167

silvered tongs and placed reverently in a little golden box.

Even Lila, not the most observant of people, was struck by the special style of Parisiennes: the fantastically chic woman all in black with a baguette sticking out of her Hermes bag; the lovely girl bicycling home from her classes in a fifties Schiaparelli suit bought in a flea market; the gentleman, in a thoroughly English tweed coat, choosing a few perfect blooms in a thoroughly un-English way from a flower shop which spilled out onto the pavement and scented the street with lilies.

Now revisiting, four years later, in the clammy heat of summer, she was enchanted all over again. The man she was with was a surprise, their meeting one of those odd connections which just as easily might not have happened.

He knew Paris well, had also been a student there, and he took Lila to a hotel in Montparnasse and made love to her in a way which was so assured and confident that she, who often experienced boredom in bed, a sort of, 'for God's sake get on with it' feeling, for once felt wholly satisfied. He made love so beautifully, so sensitively, that afterwards she found her face wet with tears. He wiped them gently away with his hand and murmured, 'Darling, my love. *Ma petite mère. Mon petit coeur.*' It was not often that Lila was made to feel small and vulnerable.

They walked arm in arm through the streets, mile after mile, stopping for a coffee and to read newspapers in a café, then at a bar for a beer, then it was time to eat again in a cheerful packed café where they ordered saucissons de Morteaux au grille with mushy peas and mashed potatoes – the sort of robust food Lila loved – and dawdled over a cognac. Their eyes met and held in a sleepy well-fed languor and their fingers touched and they knew that the only place to be was back in bed.

He was satisfactory in other ways as well. Lila wanted to go to the Musée Quai D'Orsay where there was an interesting exhibition but rather dreaded what might turn into a lecture tour. People so often wanted to show off in such places, loudly knowing more than those about them, holding forth in a knowledgeable way and taking hours reading all the fiddly writing under every picture. Lila liked to zoom round, getting a rough feel, stopping when she felt like it, buying some post-cards, and pretty soon hiving off for some refreshment. She found with pleasure that the two of them were beautifully paced and he was quite happy to skim along on his own, bumping into her now and then in front of a painting to admire together in silence, or pull a disparaging face, and was ready when she was to drift out and find somewhere to have a beer.

When it was all over and he kissed her goodbye at Charles de Gaulle she hitched her bag onto her shoulder – she never travelled with more than hand luggage if she could help it – and strode off through passport control, feeling a curious lightness. It was such a casual affair and was accompanied by no heart-wrenching or agony. She knew he liked her and she liked him and that was that. They had met on neutral territory, arrived empty-handed, and that was how they parted. It was good to be able to walk away like that, Lila felt, unencumbered by a lot of emotional baggage and with no prisoners taken. However, as her plane took off and turned in the night sky to fly over the sparkling enchanted city, she looked out of the window and thought of him going back in a taxi without her, eating dinner on his own, spending a solitary night in the wide bed, and she wished she was still with him.

'This guy of Lila's,' Tara said to Alice one rare evening when they were both in together. 'Is he important, do you think? She seems very preoccupied since she got back from Paris.'

'She hasn't said much, which is unlike her, isn't it? I don't know anything about him.'

'I thought she might have told you. The other thing is, she seems to have dropped the "my father is an innocent victim" refrain. Have you noticed?'

'Yes, that's true. She went to see him, of course, when she was at home. She told me that in some ways it was worse than she expected and in some ways better. It must have been terribly traumatic for her, but perhaps just seeing him in prison has helped her accept it all. She said that his case was going to appeal and that he was hoping to be moved to an open prison and that he looked very well, considering.'

'Flourishing, probably, amongst his own sort,' said Tara tartly.

'And of course there was Jerome's accident. That was another thing she had to deal with at home. She's really fond of him, you know, and she said her mother was terribly worried about him.'

'He's OK though, isn't he? I mean it was only a broken leg?'

'Yes, but it's just another thing. Not much seems to have gone right lately. So I do hope this man will do her good.' Love was, for Alice, the panacea for everything.

'They don't generally, though, do they, Lila's men? They all start well and then get the order of the boot after a month or two. What is it she says? All mouth and no trousers? She's better at being mates than having a relationship.'

Alice considered. She thought Tara was being unnecessarily unsympathetic.

'But who is he?' persisted Tara, who liked to get to the bottom of things. 'Do you know? Why is she being so uncharacteristically secretive?'

'I haven't a clue. I've asked her and she just said someone she met by chance, through mutual friends. She met him when she was in London. Something like that.'

'Is he French?'

'I'm not sure. She said he'd been a student in Paris. Knew it well.'

'I can't somehow imagine Lila with a Frenchman. Usually they go for that rather untypical Englishwoman, don't they? Jane Birkin types. Very thin and neurotic who look as if they never see daylight. The sort who chain-smoke and have breakdowns. Not like Lila who you would think had been up since dawn, milking the cows and digging the potato field. It must be good sex, I think,' said Tara enviously, 'that makes her look so well at the moment. One long shagfest, I imagine.'

Alice laughed. 'I expect so. Well, let's hope he makes her happy, whoever he is.'

The long summer days dawdled over Court Barton. It was light by four o'clock in the morning – gentle, pearly damp dawns which crept over the hills and sidled into the valleys where the first silage and hay had been cut and the fields were already tall again with silvery grass. Jerome had made these early mornings his own. Walking more easily now, and supported by only a stick, he tramped about the lanes with Finn, enjoying the solitude and the empty secretive landscape in the peaceful hours before it was harried and probed by the agitations of tractors, farm machinery and milk tankers. In these silent, misty mornings he tried to find some solace for his aching heart and although no answers came to him from the dewy fields, the sentinel trees, or the glimmering brown stream under the wooden footbridge in the valley, he felt more at peace.

Grazing cows half lifted their heavy heads to watch him pass, their breath clouding the air, beads of water strung along their whiskers and eyelashes, and often he disturbed deer, who stood, frozen for a moment, before bounding off with flashes of white rump. He let Finn off his lead and taught him to walk at heel;

when his leg started to ache and he found somewhere to rest, the puppy would come and lean against him and lick his face, or climb onto his knee in an ecstasy of comradeship.

The only other person he ever saw on these early wanderings was Jem Loader, Jena's father, disappearing into the woods with his shadowy bitch at his heels, or already at work thinning and coppicing amongst the spinneys along the stream.

One particular morning Jerome found himself leaning over the brick parapet of the old railway bridge and looking down the straight thread of the track, now grown grassy, with brambles thick on the embankments. He had fancied a change from his more usual southern route towards the gentle hills where the sheep grazed. This morning he went east out of the village to where the land dropped to the low-lying vale and the summer pastures were full of cattle. The old turf was springy and dense and studded with wild flowers and the hedgerows thick with honeysuckle, clematis and dog roses.

Then Finn was gone. One moment he was there, sitting whining with impatience at his heels, and then off in a grey streak down the bank, in hot pursuit of the rabbits besporting themselves on the embankments. Jerome watched for a bit, amused, but when he called him back, the puppy was deaf to his shouts. After about ten minutes he started to curse. With his leg still in plaster he couldn't go after him down the steep slope to the track and he could not see another, easier, way. Disobedient Finn was hard at it amongst the brambles, appearing every now and then, a flying dog, leaping and dashing after his prey.

Jerome bellowed to no avail and, turning to search for some means of attracting Finn's attention, saw Jena, astride her black and white horse, coming out of the mist from the other direction. She spotted him and waved, and touching her heels to his sides, put Jigsaw into a canter.

'Hi!' she shouted, pulling up on the track twenty feet below him. 'You're up early, aren't you?'

'I can't get hold of Finn. He's down on the bank, chasing the rabbits.' He pointed. 'He won't come back.'

'Course he won't. He's a lurcher, en he? That's his job. Catchin' rabbits.' She looked up at him, laughing. His head looked funny, discmbodied, hanging over the edge of the bridge. Jigsaw swung about, excited by the raised voices and Finn's delirious yapping. 'I'll get him for yer,' she said.

She kicked Jigsaw on under the bridge and drove him up the bank to where Finn was dashing about. Jerome watched as she whistled and called. Suddenly frightened by the approaching horse, Finn's mind was taken off the chase and he paused and glanced round anxiously, suddenly aware that he might be in the wrong.

'Gerron! Gerron with yer!' Jena shouted and rode at him again and he scuttled down the bank and shot back towards the bridge and Jerome, who was now calling encouragingly. Pausing to locate his route back, he hesitated and then scrambled up the steep bank to reappear on the bridge, panting and apologetic, ears pressed to his head, his shaggy little body snaking in appeasement. Jerome caught him and clipped on his lead. He looked over the parapet at Jena on her horse, and gave her a thumbs up sign.

The sun was just breaking through the lavender coloured sky and the song of the hedgerow birds filled the air. Jena grinned and waved back, and looking down at her, her skinny legs sticklike against the black and white flanks of her horse, he was struck by the completeness of the moment – the happy, laughing child, the energy of the horse, the beauty of the morning.

'Wait there! We'll come up!' she shouted and he watched as she wheeled away and cantered across the adjacent field and, turning sharply, jumped the hedge onto the lane and came clattering up to meet him on the bridge.

'Thanks, Jena,' he said, as she pulled up. He patted Jigsaw. 'God, this horse really can jump. He's amazing. You make it look so easy.'

'He's great, he is. I taught him,' she boasted, her eyes sparkling, her nut-brown hair in tangled clumps. 'Anyway,' she added, 'how are you?' Ever since the afternoon when Claudia had asked her for her opinion on Jerome, she had had a special interest in him.

'OK. Slow. But making progress. I suppose.'

'What yer doin' up at this time?'

'I often go for a walk around now. I don't sleep all that well and I like this time of day. Nobody about. I slob around the rest of the time, as you know. What are you doing up so early?'

'We're always up early, me an' Dad. I can go where I like if I ride this early. Jump what I like. Sometimes me dad wants Jigs later – takes him out wooding.'

'Is that where you live? Down there?' He pointed down the track in the direction from which she had appeared.

'Yeah. Look, you can see the smoke now the mist's lifted. That's where the van is. Come and see, if you like.'

'I couldn't get there, could I? I can't do rough ground at the moment.'

'I'll come and get yer. In the cart. You could get up in the cart, couldn't you? Would you like that?'

'Sure. Yes, I would. It would be a blast.'

'Come tomorrer, then. Early, like this. I'll meet you here, on the bridge.'

'OK. Thanks, Jena. I'll be here. Thanks for getting Finn. He's so naughty. I thought he was learning.'

'He's only young. You'll see the others termorrer, and meet his mother.'

'Great!'

'How's yer mum? Missing school dinners?'

'No. I think she's glad term's finished. She enjoyed it though. Loves the job.'

'It's all right for the teachers. The grown-ups. It's different for them.'

'You don't like school, do you?'

'Lessons and stuff are OK. It's some of the other kids who are crap. They pick on me because I'm little and I'm off the railway line – out the van.'

'Can't the teachers stop it?' As soon as he said it, Jerome knew it was stupid.

Jena looked at him pityingly. 'Course not. I don't tell. I'd get it worse if I did.'

Jerome considered the wisdom of this. 'Maybe. But then they win, don't they? They always win, the bullies do.'

Jena shrugged. She couldn't see the bigger picture. 'I don't care. Anyway, I'm not going back there.'

'When you go up to the high school, will that be better?'

'Yeah. Reckon. It's bigger. A lot of different kids.' She thought a bit and then asked, 'You got friends?'

'Yes. Not around here, though.'

'Where, then?'

'All over the place. London, mostly. India, too.'

'That's a long way away. Tigers they have there. Mrs Pomeroy showed me. You lonely then? Not seeing yer mates?'

Jerome shrugged. 'Not really. I'm OK on my own. For the time being, anyway. I go to university in the autumn. There'll be lots of people there. I suppose I'll sort of start again.'

'Yeah, like me. You got a best friend?'

Jerome paused. Standing in the early morning English sunshine with this girl who was so young, a comparative stranger, he found there floated towards him the words that so far he had found impossible.

'I did have.'

'Whaddya mean, did?'

'She died. In the bush crash. When my leg got smashed.'

Jena looked down and wove a strand of Jigsaw's mane round a finger. 'Me gran died last Christmas. She was my best friend an' all,' she said.

'Was she? I'm sorry.'

'People said stuff like she was old and that, but that didn't make no difference to me.'

'No.'

'It's like having a hole in yer middle.'

'Exactly.'

Jena went on twisting the hank of mane while the big horse fidgeted. Jerome did not feel the need to say anything more. It seemed there was something shared between them which did not require any further raking over.

'OK, then,' he said eventually. 'I'd better get on.'

Jena unwound the mane from her finger and looked down at him and grinned. Talking about their grief had not made her adopt the solemn sort of understanding expression he couldn't bear.

'Yeah, OK,' she said cheerfully. 'I'll see yer tomorrer. Don't forget. Say hi to Claudio for me.'

'I will.' He raised his hand in a farewell salute and turned away and as he retreated from the bridge he heard her clatter off the way she had come.

As he walked back, he considered his condition. He had known after the accident, after he realised that Jabeena had been killed, that it was something too terrible to confront. It had to be contained inside him and was best kept there. He did not want his terrible, torturing thoughts to be picked over by people, who would want to offer comfort and compassion. It was best, he had unconsciously decided, to keep them locked like a pit of serpents in the dark, where only he could visit and poke at them and watch them writhe. That way he could stumble on with life and get by, pretending that he inhabited the old familiar world.

It had been easy to talk to Jena. Her simple acceptance of grief, without the need to offer solace or seek to dispel his sense of despair, was a huge relief. Sadness and loss, he thought, were something real to her, like the trees or the hills which existed as part of the landscape she was familiar with. Looking at the long blue shoulder of Bulbarrow Hill in the distance, he was pleased with this analogy. Jabeena would eventually become like that to him, a shape in the landscape of his life, but for now he couldn't immortalise her in that way. Instead, he remembered the silky softness of her slender wrist, how he had stroked it with the tips of his fingers as they both reached up to cling to the rail on the crowded bus. The last time I touched her, he thought. Her bracelets had slipped down her arm and her sleeve fell back as she hung on. She had been barely able to reach the rail above her head. She had swayed against him and they had laughed. This *nothing* moment was to be one of the last they had together, one of her last minutes alive. Despite all his resolutions, his eyes filled with hot tears. Stop it, he told himself.

He couldn't halt it, though, not now. He had gone too far and the thought of her warm, scented skin, her swift wide smile and gentle laugh brought memories of her whirling through his mind, taking possession of him. On the morning of the accident he had been grumpy for no particular reason. Moody and unresponsive. Her sweetness and passivity sometimes had this effect on him. In a certain mood he felt burdened, dragged down by her gentleness and the adoration she expressed for him. She had sensed his retreat from her and had been quiet. They had hardly talked as they waited for the bus and it was only because, when it came, it was so crowded that physical closeness was forced on them. Standing like that, squashed together by the crush of passengers, his chest level with her face, the softness of her slender body had moved him with tenderness when she fell against him. He had touched her wrist, kissed her hair. Tiny, unobtrusive gestures because after all they were in a public place. And that was it. That was her lot. She had looked up and smiled gratefully. A minute or two later the bus was hit side on by a runaway petrol tanker.

His leg hurt. He had walked too far and the early promise of sunshine had faded. The sky now looked a leaden grey. He pulled at Finn on his lead and limped slowly home.

Claudia sang on her way to work. Her new car, an elderly diesel estate, chugged along and although she missed the pick-up, which Lila described as her 'raunchy wheels' and which had certainly made her feel dashing, she was glad to be independent again. She had been able to supplement the measly cheque from the insurance company, which would hardly have stretched to a bicycle, with what she had got for the dinner service. She had Julia to thank for that. For a small commission, her china man had sold it very well. Since school had broken up for the summer she had started as a relief cook in an old people's home in Sturminster Newton, covering the holidays of the regular staff, and it suited her beautifully, this arrangement, earning extra money and having something to do.

Often, now, she looked back at her old life with no sense of regret or loss. Those days, especially in the recent years with the children grown up, had been packed with activity but it all seemed pointless now. All the entertaining and the being entertained, the shallow social life, the importance of networking, none of it had given her a purpose. She had been whirled along in Roger's slipstream, a passenger, with no real momentum of her own.

The school term had ended on a high note and she had enjoyed the end-of-year rituals, the leavers' assembly, the summer fair – to all of which non-teaching staff were warmly invited. Apart from anything else, she had gone to these things for Jena. Since she had taken her home that afternoon she had felt a particular interest in the child. There was something extraordinary about her, a contradictory mixture of resilience and vulnerability, of experience and innocence. Not only that, her parents never attended anything, according to Mrs Peck, and Claudia wanted, although uninvited, to be her supporter.

It was clear Jena was quite bright. She read fluently – Jerome had discovered that – but lacked confidence at school, sitting mute in class, with a pale, shut face. Claudia watched her moving between lessons like a little shadow, hugging the corners, always on the edge, never joining in the exuberance of the children in the top class who were making their presence felt in their last few weeks in primary school. 'Big for their boots, they get, at this time of the year,' Mrs Peck had said. 'Big fishes, small pool. They'll be frightened shrimps come September when they move up. It's the same every year.'

The morning after she had picked up the fleeing Jena and taken her home to see Jerome, Claudia finished the lasagne for lunch, washed her hands, and took off her overall and told her assistants she wanted to see Mrs Peck about something. Eileen and Susie, large, incurious women, nodded and got on with the apple crumbles.

Claudia went through the swing door and into the corridor. There was muted noise from one of the four classrooms and a sudden gale of laughter, but this was lesson time and there was nobody about. Pinned on the wall in the entrance hall was a display of leavers' work and an autobiographical profile of each child, accompanied by photographs, some, to judge by the stickers on the corners, taken from family albums. Claudia paused, scanning the display. Each child had written a summary of their time at Bishops Barton, what they remembered of their early days in Primary One through to how they felt about leaving and what they would miss. Jena's display was predictably sparse. Her photograph had been taken in the school playground and showed a featureless face that gave nothing away. In fact Claudia could have walked past it without recognising her. Her writing was surprisingly neat but also brief. She said she liked history and science but didn't like maths. School was 'OK'. She was looking forward to going to the high school, 'for a change'. She enjoyed athletics and, Claudia smiled, school dinners.

Finishing her inspection, Claudia went on to the office and knocked on the door before putting her head round. The secretary looked up from the photocopier. 'Any chance of seeing Mrs Peck? I only need a moment.'

Mrs Read consulted her watch. 'You may get her now, if you're lucky, but only for five minutes. She's got a lesson at half past.'

'Thanks, I won't keep her.'

Next door, Mrs Peck was kneeling on the floor of her office, surrounded by ribbons, certificates, cups and badges. 'Sorting the prizes,' she said, looking up and smiling a welcome.

'I'm surprised you're still allowed to award any. Isn't it too discriminatory by today's standards? Aren't we all supposed to be winners?'

'This is a Church school, as you know,' reminded Mrs Peck. 'Less red tape and interference. Children love rewards, love to see hard work and achievement recognised. As it happens, they all end up receiving some special praise during the year – I see to that, so they *are* all winners, but they do have to earn it. Now what can I do for you?'

'It's Jena Loader, Mrs Peck. She bolted out of school early yesterday and I saw her and gave her a lift home. She'd been knocked over, I think, was quite upset but wouldn't say anything.'

Mrs Peck hauled herself up from her knees. 'Hmmm,' she said. 'I've spoken several times to Mrs Dawson, her class teacher, and we are aware of the problem. There are one or two in that class who are already displaying some of the attitudes to be found out there.' She waved at the window. 'Bigotry, suspicion, small-mindedness, none of it very attractive, and what with puberty and hormones and bodies which are all over the place, and in some cases far from satisfactory home backgrounds, we do have social problems here, you know. It's not just inner cities. The rural community is in crisis as well with unemployment, poverty, low expectations.'

'Yes, I realise all that, Mrs Peck. I just wanted to make sure that you knew there was a problem and to ask if there was anything I could do to help. She comes from near where I live, you see, and I've got to know her a little.'

'Poor kid, she doesn't make things easy for herself. She's very secretive, very guarded, makes no attempt to make friends, even amongst the quieter girls. Poor attendance record. She knows they'll be moving on, you see, and she'll have to start all over somewhere new.' Mrs Peck started to sort through exercise books on her desk and then looked up to say, 'Take an interest in her, Claudia. That'll do her more good than anything else.'

'What about her parents?'

'Never see them. The social workers have checked them out and don't think there is any problem. No sign of abuse and she's well-fed and literate. The father's an oddball. Not a true gypsy, more a misfit. Self-educated. An interesting man. Hugely knowledgeable about the countryside. Knows more about flora and fauna than David Bellamy, according to those who employ him. Don't know anything about the mother. I think there are a couple of younger children, under school age.' The bell rang for the end of the lesson and Mrs Peck stood with her hand on the door handle. 'What's for sure is that with her background Jena has a hard life ahead. She's going to come up against prejudice all the time, isn't she? She's sure to.'

Claudia nodded. 'I don't suppose she's won any of those,' she asked, indicating the muddle on the floor.

'Don't you believe it!' exclaimed Mrs Peck, smiling. 'She's won the Environmental Studies prize. She's quite offhand about our wild garden, but there's nothing she doesn't know and she's the best runner and long-jumper by far. She's got a stack of ribbons here. She makes the other girls look like suet puddings. Which, of course,' she added mischievously, 'some of them closely resemble.'

After that, Claudia made a point of bumping into Jena as

often as she could. Most days she usually exchanged a quick word in the lunch queue and offered a lift to school if ever she saw her skulking in the lane. She made a tin of shortbread and suggested she might like it as her contribution to the summer fair, although Jena then produced a beautifully carved thumb stick with a horn handle. It had been crafted by her father and was much exclaimed over and admired, and later bought for £12 by the vicar.

Something like a friendship sprang up between them, which extended to Jerome and then to Victoria, who seemed to be around rather a lot, thought Claudia. She was a strange teen-ager, awkward and oddly old-fashioned. Jena could run rings round her as far as nous and vitality went, despite being four years younger. Victoria often appeared out to lunch, answering questions vaguely and with an air of abstraction. Jerome said she was bright, that they talked about books and watched videos while she was working, but the minute Claudia got home and joined them for a cup of tea or a chat about the day, she reverted to being dim and tongue-tied and it was never long before she scuttled home.

The two girls had adopted Jerome as a cause. It was evident that Victoria didn't have much to do. Her brother was abroad for the summer, and apart from riding her horse, she seemed to be at a loose end. Claudia wondered about Julia who, after the first rush of neighbourliness, she had hardly seen for weeks. 'She's always in the garden,' said Victoria. 'She opens it to the public in August and she practically weeds by torch at this time of year. Apart from that, she's out at meetings. She's on lots of commit-tees and things.'

Jena dropped by at odd times, growing browner and wilder as the summer wore on, with tangled hair and filthy fingernails. She liked making Jerome cups of tea and toast or rushing about in mad games with the puppy. She lolled over the back of the sofa while Jerome and Victoria talked about books but joined in silly paper games like Consequences and was a fiend at Racing Demon.

At least they amuse him and his guard seems to drop with them, which is surely a good thing, thought Claudia. In some ways he had made such a good recovery, his leg healing, becoming steadily more mobile and slowly putting on weight, but she was concerned at how he had cut himself off from his former friends, never telephoning or contacting any of them. Was that her fault, she wondered, because she had so resolutely removed herself from the old life and stuck him here in the outback, the boondocks, the sticks?

To rectify this she had gone into Yeovil with her first pay cheque and bought him a mobile telephone. 'Keep in touch with your friends,' she had said as she handed it over. 'Give the number to your father if you want. I feel bad about cutting you off from everybody.'

'Thanks, Ma,' he had said listlessly, hardly bothering to look up, and she had felt a rush of irritation. What was *wrong* with him? Why was he so unresponsive, and particularly, markedly, towards her? Before he went away they had been so close, sharing everything. Her mother and Minna counselled patience and she knew they were right, these were still early days, but why should he laugh and fool around with those girls but be morose and silent with her?

He also seemed to have grown close to Valerie Pomeroy. What with nursing him and starting full-time work she had hardly been round to see her neighbour and relied on Jerome's reports to keep track of how she was getting on. Valerie lent him books, chose video tapes for him when she went into town and allowed him to use her computer, but the thing that Claudia had to confess made her feel jealous and excluded was that Jerome evidently enjoyed her company.

I don't know, thought Claudia as she overtook a tractor, I've tried to spare my children so much of the strain of the last year, have really borne most of it alone, and neither of them seemed to understand or be grateful. Lila, for instance, had hardly been in touch since returning to New York. She had managed a couple of telephone calls in which she expressed little interest in life in Court Barton and had actually asked to talk to the dog instead. Jerome had held the receiver to Finn's ear, and Claudia heard a one-sided doggy conversation coming from across the Atlantic by satellite.

'You mustn't be hurt by it,' laughed Minna. 'They're not especially selfish or uncaring. You know that. It's typical of the self-absorption of the young.'

'Lila's old enough to be more thoughtful,' said Claudia.

Oh, well, despite all this she was still feeling happy. The threat of what Roger might spring on her seemed to have faded. There was even some doubt that he would win the right to appeal and she was ashamed to admit that when David Rowntree telephoned to tell her this, she was glad. She was earning money, living independently, driving her own car again, and tonight she was going out to dinner with Anthony Brewer.

Like Julia, he had disappeared from her life for at least three weeks and she hadn't even seen him about the village. When she returned the pick-up with a bottle of whisky on the front seat and a note thanking him warmly for his generosity, Greg was in the yard and took the keys, but she had expected some response sometime later from Anthony. None came and then, just when she thought that country people were remarkably fickle, he had telephoned one evening and asked her out. He was his usual charming self. 'Busy time for us poor farmers, Claudia, or I would have been in touch,' was his explanation for his silence.

'Thank you. I'd love to,' she had said and went out and had her hair properly cut in a stylish salon in Sherborne.

Now, glancing in the mirror, she liked what she saw. The things which worried her could not suppress her improved spirits. She felt good. Not her old self. No, something different, but definitely good.

Rosco lay on his bed and flicked through the pages of his Biker magazine. He knew what he wanted, a Suzuki GSX 1100. Beauties, they were, but even second or third-hand, more than he could afford. He had started to save, though, and he was getting there slowly, what with his wages and overtime and not going out with the Stur gang on Saturday nights like he used to. It was mounting up. The two hundred quid he'd got off the man from the newspaper helped.

That was a bit of luck. He still couldn't quite believe it, how the pieces had come together like a jigsaw puzzle. A couple of weeks ago he'd had a Saturday job down the Bugle, cleaning out the cellar, and he'd heard his mum and Monica gossiping as usual, minding everyone's business. Some old girl in the village had had a heart attack and been carted off, and the new woman, the nutter who'd gone slap into Brewer's tractor, her son had been in a crash in India and had been flown home in a special plane with a doctor in attendance. He hardly bothered to listen, and then something jogged his memory. He'd got a good memory, Rosco knew that. Anything he'd seen written down he could remember if he could be bothered. It was useful at work. He never needed to consult the list of what sandwiches the men wanted at dinner time. He always knew Kev ordered a double ploughman's and Dave wanted egg and bacon, and the cheese and pickle and the pie were for Alan.

When he got home he had found what he wanted in the kitchen bin. It was the newspaper from last night's fish and chips he'd bought on the way home from work. He spread it out, all crumpled and greasy on the counter and there it was, where he remembered seeing it. 'Fraudster's son in India bus horror.' He checked the date on the paper. It was six weeks old. Rosco read the piece again, moving his finger across the column. Taking the paper with him he had gone upstairs to his room and pulled the cardboard box from the top shelf of his wardrobe. It was full of junk, all the stuff he collected and didn't know what to do with, and somewhere in there he knew he had the final piece to complete the puzzle.

Here it was. At the time he didn't know why he had stuffed the postcard in his pocket when he and Sean were going through the glove compartment of the woman's car. They weren't really doing anything wrong that night. She'd left the doors unlocked and all they did was get in and have a look round and smoke a joint or two. The car had been pushed into a field gateway and just left there. Sean had nicked a cigarette lighter, but it was only plastic, not worth anything, and they'd shared a packet of mints and then he'd found the card. He remembered looking at it in the moonlight. He liked the picture on the front of a couple of kids on a beach, squatting down to peer in a pool of water. It looked real, but when you held it a bit closer you could see it was just splodges of colour. He turned it over and looked at the other side. It was addressed to Mrs Claudia Barron.

Rosco had sat on his bed with the postcard in his hand and the newspaper on his knee. The names matched. The accident, the broken leg and all. What did it mean? Her old man was in the slammer, that was one thing. She had changed her name, pretended to be someone else. She'd probably got the money he'd nicked stashed away and nobody but him knew her secret.

It hadn't been difficult after that. A few telephone calls, that was all. He'd met the reporter in a pub in Yeovil and he'd passed over the dosh, no problem. Easy money, that was, and more to come if he could give any more info. He'd asked his mum, but she didn't know anything worth passing on. The Barron woman was working at the Primary as a cook or something. Well, that wouldn't make much of a story, not like she was running a knocking shop or doing strippograms.

He'd not told anyone what he'd done. Not even Sean. It was one of those things best kept secret. Still, he was quite pleased with himself for being so observant. When he thought of the hot shit he was in for lifting a few rotten tools, that woman deserved all she got.

Valerie Pomeroy noticed that she was wearing odd shoes. This in itself did not bother her greatly because it hardly seemed to matter, not with her sort of life, but the fact that one was blue and the other brown and that they were both left feet did seem a little worrying. Since all the brouhaha in the papers about Iris Murdoch, she felt more aware of going dotty, and it was the sort of thing which would upset Betty.

In her hand she held a cup she had found in the fridge containing something brown and unidentifiable. She peered at the wrinkled surface. Gravy? Chocolate? Mince? She did not feel up to a decision and put it back where she had found it and shut the fridge door. She made a cup of instant coffee and slowly mounted the stairs to her study where, amongst her email messages to be attended to, was one from Christopher.

It had arrived yesterday and had caused her considerable agitation. In fact, she had thought about little else all day.

After the usual inquiries about her health came the nub. He was not after all bringing the girls over this summer. This decision, he said, had been reached after much debate. Debate, thought Valerie, was hardly the word for it. She could imagine the shrieks and protestations. But Alice had been asked to go on holiday with some friends, Emily and Laura had various things to do which they did not want to miss, and Rosie, well, Rosie was too young. Her views did not count. He had also considered whether this annual invasion was not now too much for her. Too much for me? thought Valerie. If it is, then life itself is too much. Instead he would come over alone for about ten days to see her and also to visit various boarding schools where he was thinking of sending the two elder girls.

Much as she loved and looked forward to seeing her son, it was the children Valerie most enjoyed. The gloomy old house was taken over by them. There would be wild arguments about the allocation of bedrooms and then, wrapped in duvets like a funny little nomadic tribe, they would swap beds and allegiances throughout their stay. They took over the sitting room, shedding their sweetshop coloured clothes, kicking off their trainers, piling up magazines and books and electronic gadgets she did not even have a name for. The bathrooms were filled with jars and tubes and tubs and bottles and the steamed-up

mirrors were embellished with drawings, messages and signa-
tures. They argued and cried and laughed and slammed doors
and pounded up the stairs and left cereal bowls under chairs and
plates of pasta on the floor. The house reverberated with their
pounding music and they danced and rocked and rolled and did
wobbly handstands on the lawn.

They zoomed about on the fleet of old bicycles she had
acquired for them, shrieking and calling to each other, and Em
taught herself to drive the little car in grasshopper leaps up and
down the drive.

Best of all, of course, they loved her, climbing into her bed in
the mornings, sitting on her lap even though they were far too
big, standing with their arms round her, clamped to her sack of
potatoes waist while she stroked their soft heads and felt the
beat of youth pressed against her.

Of course she had known this change would come, that they
would grow up and want more sophisticated ways to spend the
summer. Trips to Top Shop and Virgin Records in Salisbury
would be outgrown and picnics and days on the beach no longer
the fun they used to be. Christopher would feel it his duty to
come over now and then to poke her with a sharp stick, and
that was that. Poor man, he had enough on his plate without
feeling responsible for her as well. Damn and blast, what a curse
old age was. Lucky Frank, in a way, to have snuffed it early on
and got it over and done with. Not this dreary decline.

But no good moping over the lost summer. That would not
do. It would be lovely to see Christopher and have him to
herself. Perhaps they would go to London together, to the opera
and the British Museum and the National Gallery and Tate
Modern. There was a great deal to look forward to. And of
course there was Jerome.

When Betty arrived, just after nine o'clock, she found Valerie up
in her study contemplating her odd shoes and her two left feet.
Well, thought Betty, nothing would surprise me these days.

'I've got some disappointing news, Betty,' she said. 'The girls
are not coming over after all. They have other things to do. It's
just going to be Christopher this year.'

'Oh no!' Betty looked forward to their visit as much as their
grandmother. She stood in the doorway tying her apron strings,
her pleasant, unadorned face troubled. 'Why ever not? What
have they got to do more important than coming to see you?
They love it here.'

'They're growing up, Betty. That's the thing. They've lots of friends and activities out there. A busy life. We must seem very dull by comparison.'

Betty sniffed, considering. 'More like they're worried about you,' she said shrewdly. 'Worried they make too much work.'

'Perhaps, but that's nonsense, isn't it?'

'Well, they're a disruption, those girls. You know that. All the noise and mess. Never a moment's peace.'

'When have we ever minded a bit of noise and mess?'

This was true. But on the other hand Betty had been badly shaken when Valerie had had her turn and she couldn't help but think that Christopher was right to consider his mother's health. It was disappointing though. No doubt about that. The summer would not be the same. Still, life had to go on.

'Here, give me your mug,' she said, 'and I'll bring you up another coffee. Are you working in here this morning? Got Jerome coming round?'

'Yes, I'm going to tackle a book review. I must get started and have been putting it off until now. I suppose Jerome might come. He seems at a bit of a loss with his mother out at work every day and knowing no one round here.'

'Monica said there was someone asking for him, down at The Bugle.'

'Really? What, a friend of his?'

'No, Monica said it was a man from the papers. Or so he said. Wanting to do a piece about his trip to India or something. She didn't like the look of him. Didn't tell him anything except where the bungalow was. Thought he might have been one of them television licence spies.'

'When was this, Betty?'

'Yesterday dinner time. Asked so many questions that old Tom Atkins told him to bugger off. Excuse my French.'

Valerie had to smile. She could just imagine the scene. 'I'll tell him if he comes round later,' she said. 'Warn him. They send those bloody vans round, don't they, like a police state. Checking to see if you have your television on. Not that there's anything worth watching anyway. Saturday night was simply appalling rubbish. I suppose the programme planners think we're all out clubbing, Betty. Isn't that the right term?'

Miss Cavendish, Rosco Bishop's social worker, opened his file and flicked through the sheaf of papers before reaching up her sleeve for a wad of tissues. She had heard on the radio this morning that the pollen count was exceptionally high and violent hayfever had made her eyes weep and her nose run. Her head felt as if it was filled with porridge.

'So, Rosco,' she said, 'I see that your attendance has been better, so that's good, isn't it?' She tried to make her voice sound bright and encouraging which was doubly difficult given the contents of the file and how groggy she was feeling.

Sitting opposite her, swinging back on the legs of the plastic chair, Rosco scowled across the table. 'Yeah, well. It hasn't done me no good. I haven't learnt nothing.' He picked up a paperclip from the table and started to clean out his nails, determinedly avoiding eye contact.

'I'm sure that's not true, Rosco. I expect you've learnt much more than you think.'

'Nah. Me coursework's crap. I lost me English folder, anyway.'

'You lost it? How could you have lost it?' Miss Cavendish managed to sound surprised. In fact, she knew that most of Rosco's work had failed either to be completed or handed in.

'I dunno. I just lost it. Couldn't find it, could I.' He studied his nails.

'Well, what I've got here, Rosco, is your NRA.' Miss Cavendish put a printed form on the table between them. 'You know what it is, don't you? Your National Record of Achievement. It's for you to take away with you when you leave school. I want to help you fill it in. I'm afraid your attendance has to go down here, Rosco, and below seventy per cent doesn't look too good, but on the other hand we can put in your Design and Technology project and your Mechanics NVQ'.'

Rosco stared at the document with contempt. 'I don't need it. I've got me job starting full-time, as soon as I can leave here. Mr Martin, down the garage, he doesn't want nothing like that. He knows I'm a good worker.' He pushed the form back across the table.

'Well, I'm glad of that, Rosco, but a future employer will want to see it. Let's make a start, shall we?' She picked up her Biro, knowing that she was wasting her time. She doubted very much that after school classes formally finished for year eleven, Rosco would come near the place, let alone bother to turn up to take his exams. The sun was hot through the plate glass window and she swivelled in her chair to lower the blinds. She closed her eyes for a moment, wishing that she could go and lie down somewhere peaceful and quiet, but she had a job to do and so she turned back and patiently began to coax Rosco through the depressing task of listing his achievements.

'How are things at home?' she asked eventually when they had done all they could.

'All right,' he said.

'How's your mum? How are you getting along with her these days?'

'Don't never see her. She's always at work or down the pub.'

'You must see her sometimes. What about mealtimes? What about in the mornings?'

Rosco shrugged. 'Like I said, all right. She's all right.'

Miss Cavendish sniffed. She wasn't getting anywhere. The only comfort was that the lad seemed to be keeping to the terms of his probation and had kept out of further trouble.

In the corridor outside, the bell rang for the end of the session. Rosco, showing the first spark of animation, got to his feet.

'I'll be off then,' he said.

Chapter Eleven

'You've had two telephone calls,' said Jerome when Claudia got back from work. He looked up from where he was lying on the sofa. 'One was your boyfriend, saying he'd be around to collect you at seven thirty.'

'He's not my boyfriend,' protested Claudia. 'For heaven's sake, Jerome. It's not funny to say things like that.'

'Oh, Mum, don't be so touchy. I don't know what he is, do I? Your gentleman caller then. How's that?'

'OK, OK. What about the other?'

'Some woman. I wrote her name down. The Haunted Wives Club or something.'

'The *what*?'

'Haunted Wives Club, I thought she said. I thought maybe it was some sort of support group. They have Battered Wives, don't they? Something like that.'

'What was her name?' asked Claudia, baffled.

Wearily, Jerome reached for a piece of paper on the floor beside him. 'Ros Caswell,' he said, reading what he had written. 'She said she'd met you at a party next door.'

'Ah!' The light dawned on Claudia. 'The Hunt Wives Club, you mean. Yes, she did mention it to me. It's some sort of luncheon club for the non-riding ladies of the local hunt. She was keen I should join.'

'There you are then. Not such a mystery. Goodness, Mum, you are getting in with the nobs. You'll be having a lawn meet soon, saying, "Morning, Master," and doling out port and sausage rolls. Or is it a terrorist organisation? Wire-cutters and balaclavas?'

'Hardly. Anyway, I don't want to get involved in that sort of local thing. You can imagine the questions.'

'How long do you think you can keep it all under cover?' asked Jerome idly. 'Dad, and so on. It's sure to come out, isn't it?'

Claudia stopped tidying the mess he had spread around him, books and papers and mugs. She stood and looked at him.

'Why should it? I've filed for divorce, as you know. We're already legally separated. I need to put it all behind me, Jerome, and make a fresh start. Lots of divorced women revert to their maiden names, so I'm not doing anything unusual. Why should I always be seen as part of what happened, as some kind of accessory to the crime?'

'I'm not saying you *should*. Don't get so worked up. I am just saying that pretending it hasn't happened, denying the past, if you like, seems a mistake to me.'

'I'm not denying it! I don't lie about it. I avoid questions and I give evasive answers. Look, I had all the shame and humiliation in London. I saw my friends, for what they were worth, dropping off one by one. I had to endure the endless gossip and speculation, the quite appalling media intrusion. I've paid the price and now I deserve to have a bit of peace. All I want to do is live modestly and quietly and be allowed to put my life back together.'

'Of course you do. I understand that. I just wonder what it will be like for you when somebody here finds out. You see, Lila and I feel OK about being upfront about it all. Neither of us cares who knows. Our friends don't seem to mind and old Lil thinks it's quite glamorous to have a father who's banged up.'

'Well, I don't! I think it's disgraceful, shaming and humiliating. Added to which Roger left me for that other woman, remember, so I have no loyalty to him. Not a scrap. I'm as much his victim as all those people he cheated and swindled, and I will not, will not, go on carrying the can for him or having what he did besmirch my life!'

Jerome raised both hands in mock surrender. 'Shite, Mum! It's your decision, OK? But it's not over yet, is it? There's the appeal and then this newspaper article.'

'What do you know about that?'

'Dad told me.'

'*Dad* told you? When?'

'I've had some letters from him. Sent on by David, and I've talked to him a couple of times.'

Claudia stood thunderstruck. 'You've *what*? And you didn't tell me?'

'You've made it very clear you don't want to know. That you're through with him. You've just said as much. You can't have it both ways, Mum.'

Claudia sank down onto the sofa and stared at her son. 'You amaze me, Jerome. I would not have believed it of you.'

'What?'

'That you could be like this.'

'Like what, Mum?'

'I thought that you of all people would understand what I've been through. What this has *done* to me.' Claudia felt an awful wave of self-pity engulf her and knew she was going to cry.

'Wait a minute. Are you hurt that I've been in contact with Dad? But, Mum, you told me. You encouraged me. You pointed out he is still my father and it isn't as if I've deceived you. I even gave you a letter to post.'

Claudia knew this was true. She gulped. 'I know, but I didn't know you were having a *correspondence*. I thought you wouldn't want to. Not after what he's done. For my sake, I thought you wouldn't want to and that you would support me and help me to protect the future. For all of us.'

'Well, I'm sorry, in that case, but I needed to. I needed to contact him. It doesn't mean I condone what he did or how he treated you but as I've said, Lila and I don't think there's much to be gained by denying he is our father. You know, Mum, one thing India taught me is a kind of acceptance of fate, a way of transcending bad stuff, either in our own lives or other people's, and it helps, it really does.'

Claudia felt hot and angry. 'How dare you preach at me in that priggish way? What do you know about what I've been through? You weren't even in the country and neither was Lila. You don't know what it was like. Ask Minna. She'll tell you. I've been through hell, you know. Absolute hell, and all the time thinking of how I can protect you from the horror of it all. You know nothing, Jerome, nothing. Of course, you've broken your leg and been in an awful accident, but it's nothing to what I've suffered.'

'On the contrary, Mum,' he broke in in a quiet voice, 'I do know. I'm sorry we started this and I regret hurting you, but you must respect my right to have my own view even if it isn't in line with yours.'

His quietness and his composure after her outburst shook Claudia. She forgot what she was going to say and they sat in miserable silence.

'Do you want a cup of tea?' she asked eventually.

Jerome gave her a weak smile. 'OK. I'll make it.'

'No, I will.' She held out a hand to him. 'We mustn't quarrel, darling. We never have before.'

'No.'

Now she wanted to appear more generous, to go over what they had just said but colour her words a little differently.

'Jerome, I didn't mean that about being in contact with your father. It's the last thing I want, to keep you apart. You know that. It's just that it was a shock to discover that you had been in touch, without telling me. That's all.'

'OK, Mum. Let's leave it, shall we?'

'Before we do, there's one thing I think I have a right to know, because it affects me very much indeed, and that concerns this threatened newspaper article. Is he going ahead with it?'

Jerome stood up and gently put his hands on her shoulders. 'What he said, Mum, was that he would do nothing to hurt you, that you had suffered enough and that he bitterly regretted what he had put you through. Or words to that effect.'

'I don't believe you.'

Jerome shrugged. 'That's up to you. I'll make the tea, shall I?'

Lying in the bath, Claudia went over in her mind what had passed between herself and Jerome. In a way, she felt it was inevitable. There had to be a time when he engaged enough to offer an opinion, to show that he was even remotely connected to what had happened in their lives since he went away. She should be glad, because it seemed to mark a sort of turning point. What had the doctor said? 'He'll come back to you.' She supposed this was the beginning of his return.

What he had said, however, still nagged at her. Now she had time to think she could see why he and Lila felt that an open approach would be better. As his children, their involvement in Roger's downfall was so different from her own. They were deeply upset for him because they loved him but they in no way shared his guilt. She, on the other hand, was not absolved so easily. She remembered being asked on many occasions when his story rampaged through the newspapers, 'You're his wife, did you have no idea this was going on?' and she had had to reply, and honestly, 'No, I didn't.' But at the same time she had felt, acutely, that this must point to a shortcoming, a fault of her own. Blind? Stupid? Naïve? What had she been? Then there were the revelations about Roger's various sexual escapades which had given the impression that she knew about them and chose to ignore them, or that again, she was a total fool. Either way, it wasn't exactly that she had brought it on herself, but that, by being his wife, she was judged and found wanting.

Even her own mother had connived with this view, taking up Roger's defence and somehow implying that Claudia's moral impunity was challenged by the material advantages she had enjoyed as the wife of a wealthy man. The shadow of the vicarage, the threadbare years of scraping and saving and being denied even a modicum of comfort had to have some kind of reward and in Mrs Knight's case it was the permanent occupation of the moral high ground. Yet Roger, with his charm and admitted generosity of spirit, somehow managed to escape her censure. Claudia felt it had been heaped on her instead.

Once Mrs Knight had observed with a kind of grim satisfaction, 'It used to stagger me the money you got through. Can you remember, darling, when you used to take me to Harrods and say, "Choose anything you like, Ma"? In the long run all that money doesn't do one any good, you know.'

On that occasion it didn't stop you allowing Roger to pay for a Windsmoor coat and a lot of other things, she had felt like retorting.

There was no point, she thought as she lay back in the water, in going over all this again. In fact, she had believed she had put it in the past and that since moving to the country and beginning again she had allowed the wounds to heal. It was disappointing to find that they were still there, those scars, ready to break open again.

Her conversation with Jerome had reminded her of exactly why she had sought anonymity. She simply could not endure more public scrutiny. She would do anything she could to avoid it. Oh hell! she thought. I don't feel like going out this evening and making an effort to be cheerful and entertaining, to sing for my supper. She felt a strong temptation to ring and cancel. A headache? She thought she could feel one beginning, edging its way into her temples.

But if she did jack out, she was letting Roger win again, allowing him to muck things up just when she felt she had made progress. I'll have to go, she decided, I must, and I ought to shave my legs, on this my first date in twenty-five years with a man I find attractive. It was hard now to recapture the pleasure and sense of anticipation she had felt at being asked out by Anthony. It seemed that just by thinking about Roger again, she had allowed him to manoeuvre his way back into her life.

She could not forget the letters. Jerome said he had received letters from Roger. She could understand how she was unaware of their arrival because the postman called after she had left for work and she found the thought of missives from Roger arriving at the bungalow, her sanctuary, very unsettling. She could imagine pages of his bold handwriting expressing his thoughts, his observations of prison life and, most disturbing, some kind of discussion about his feelings for her. She was moved by a burning curiosity. Where had Jerome hidden them? She imagined, because he was usually very untidy and left his stuff everywhere, that he had carefully stored them away somewhere private. She was ashamed to acknowledge that she wanted to find them and read them. To read every weasel word. She would on no account allow herself to do so, but she had to admit that she wanted to.

Damn! She thought, getting out of the bath and reaching for a towel. The bastard still gets to me. That stuff about remorse was complete bollocks. He was at his manipulative games as usual. She would not fall for it. Not any more. Not only had she shaved her legs, she would varnish her toenails as well. A fiery, fuck-off-Roger red.

In the room next door, Jerome lay back with his mug of tea and closed his eyes. Why the hell did he do it? Why did he say those crass, insensitive things to his mother, whom he loved so much? I'm like Dad, he thought gloomily. A dyed-in-the-wool shit. I did it to Jabeena. Made her suffer when I was in a mood, and Mum was right about preaching. Here am I, who cannot begin to handle what has happened to me, telling her how to run her life. I still think she's wrong to try and hide but I can see that I've failed her miserably by contacting Dad. Why should it be that I find it much easier to express how I feel to him, when we were never close? If she knew, that would be just about the most hurtful thing I could have done. Why can't I be kinder, more understanding? God, I am a foul shit.

It's partly India. That's what Valerie Pomeroy says and she's right. It changes your perspective for ever to see all that mass of humanity whose hold on life is by a thread but who are free of any sense of personal drama. He tried to think of what he had learnt about Hinduism, that the whole world is seen as the divine activity welling up from the mysterious being of Brahman, which also pervades, sustains and inspires. He had seen for himself how the techniques of yoga made people aware of an inner world and how the disciplines of posture, breathing, diet and mental concentration could lead to enlightenment and illumination. He had talked about all this with Mrs Pomeroy and this was a path he intended to explore.

It had been natural and easy to go on from there and tell her

about Jabeena. She had sat listening in silence an̶
expected, offered no platitudes. Instead, she had nodd̶
as he stumbled to express his grief, and when he had ̶ ̶ ̶
she stood up to put the kettle on for tea and passing behind ̶m,
laid a hand on his shoulder in a gesture of wordless sympathy.
This was another thing he felt bad about. That he could
unburden himself to someone he hardly knew more easily than
he could to his mother.

It's because Mum cares too much, he thought. I can't tell her
because she will mind so much for me and that will make me
feel worse. She'll make such a thing of it, of being understanding, and then she'll want me to get over it. To recover. To forget.
And I can't do that. Not even to please her.

Perhaps Mum should take up yoga, he thought, but then
standing on one leg on a Tuesday evening in a dusty church hall
in Sturminster Newton would not be a very rewarding experience. He did not think he would suggest it.

'Peter, for heaven's sake, don't go and sit down. You've got to
come and help me tie up the roses. There's only ten days until
we open the garden and I'm beside myself trying to get
everything done, you know that.'

Peter put the newspaper back on the kitchen table and looked
at his wife over his glasses.

'What's the fuss?' he asked amicably. 'It looks all right to me.
Lovely, as usual.'

'No, it does not!' retorted Julia. 'Parts of it are a disgrace. The
Albertine has come away from the wall and is running wild, and
the border along the west side is full of ground elder. I know we
can't get rid of it but at least we can dig out what we can and I'll
put my salvia cuttings in to fill the gaps. All the paths need
weed-killing and all the edges must be done. Next week we
must deadhead like mad.'

'Don't people enjoy seeing gardens with ground elder and a
few weeds? I should have thought it was rather cheering.'

'Peter! Don't be annoying! There are standards, you know. It's
an honour to be a member of the National Garden Scheme and
I must have it looking its best. August is such a difficult month
as it is, with most summer things over and the Michaelmas
daisies not out. Now, come on. It's only just after seven. We can
do at least a couple of hours. You'll have to get the ladder out of
the barn. I want you to replace the wire on the wall, it's gone in
several places, and then we can tie the roses and the clematis

back up. I'm going to leave all this,' she indicated the supper things which were still on the kitchen table. Seizing her secateurs from the dresser and picking up her gardening gloves, she disappeared out of the back door.

Peter could see there was no escape. He knew when Julia was determined about something.

'Tor?' he called through to the sitting room. 'Are you coming to help, old thing? Mum wants us in the garden. You can stand on the bottom of the ladder for me.'

'What did you say?' Victoria asked, appearing in the doorway, eating an apple, her hair loose and untidy on her shoulders.

'Come and give Mum a hand in the garden. Stand on the ladder for me.'

'OK.'

They trooped off together to the barn where Peter found the ladder and Victoria took one end and he the other and they made their way down the path to the high east wall where the climbing roses scrambled in profusion.

'Would I be right in thinking you seem more cheerful these days, old thing?' said Peter as he raised the ladder and leaned it against the wall. The bricks were warm to the touch, he noticed, and glowed in the late evening sun.

'Dad, get up the ladder and stop asking me questions!' said his daughter, and then added, 'Well, I am actually.'

'Any particular reason?' he asked as he went carefully up the rungs and inspected where the nails had come out of the mortar.

'Not really. The holidays for one thing. Vinnie's going better, and there's Pony Club camp coming up.'

'Ah. Not bored then?'

'No.'

'Mum says you're round next door a lot.'

'Dad! I can see where this is leading!' Victoria protested. 'You're making a thing of it!'

'What sort of thing, Mouse?'

'Jerome, Dad. That I'm going round there to see Jerome.'

'What's wrong with that, old thing? Damn, I'll have to come down. I need some masonry nails and a hammer. Did you have the wire-cutters in the field?'

'I put them back.'

Peter got to the bottom of the ladder and stepped off. He put his arm round his daughter's shoulders. 'I'm glad you've got a friend, that's all. I can remember that being the bore about boarding school. That all one's friends lived miles away and one lost touch with the locals. I thought Jim abroad all the summer would make it a bit dull for you at home. You've had him around in the past.'

'It isn't as if we actually did much together, Dad. Jim thinks he's far too old for me.'

'I suppose four years seems a big difference at your age. Later on, it doesn't matter at all. How old is Jerome?'

'Nineteen.'

'What do you do when you go round there?'

'Dad! Stop it! What do you think we do? We don't have rampant sex, if that's what you mean. He's not my *boyfriend*!'

They had reached the barn where Peter pottered around looking for the bits and pieces he needed to complete the job and Victoria stood on the head of an abandoned wooden rake, holding on to the handle and rocking to and fro.

'Just a friend, eh?' he said, rootling about in a box of nails. 'Well, that's what I thought.'

Finding what he wanted, he gave a handful of nails to Victoria to put into her pocket and they went back out into the garden. In the distance they could see Julia bottom up in a flowerbed.

Back up the ladder he began to bang in some new nails and cut off the old broken wire.

'We talk a lot about books and stuff. He's going to do English at Cambridge,' said Victoria. It was easier talking up the ladder at the soles of her father's old shoes and his trouser legs, rather than face to face.

'Is he now? Clever chap, then, I suppose. Bit of a brain box.'

'He's fantastically clever, Dad. He's really helped me with my *Wuthering Heights* essay.'

'Well, that's good. And he's teaching you how to play chess?'

'Yes. I really love it. Would you like a game with me one evening?'

'Of course, Mouse. I'd love it. I'm not very good though. Haven't played for years.'

Peter went up a few more rungs to reach a wayward rose branch and secure it to the wire. From here, he had a view straight into the rear of Claudia's garden. She hadn't done much to it, he could see. The grass was overgrown and the roses on her side would give Julia nightmares. Some cheap white plastic chairs marked the place where she must come out and sit. There was even an abandoned wine bottle on its side in the grass. Peter imagined sitting there with her, glass in hand, on a peaceful summer evening. It was an enchanting thought.

Since the supper party he had only seen her to speak to twice and both times only in passing in the lane. A kind of resignation had come over him. It was no good, anyway. He couldn't get Julia to ask her round again. Since the dog and chicken incident she had rather gone off their new neighbour, quite unfairly, he thought, and it did not seem likely that Claudia would ask them. His only contact now was through Tor.

As he reached to secure the wire to the nail he saw Anthony Brewer's car pause in the lane and then turn into the drive. The door of the bungalow, which was out of his range of vision, must have opened and Claudia came out. Peter felt absurd, his head stuck over the wall like a voyeur, but was too insecure on the ladder to duck out of sight and too mesmerised to look away. For a wild moment he wondered whether he should call out a greeting and make his presence known.

Claudia was wearing her same black trousers and T-shirt, and a soft shawl thing. She looked lovely, Peter thought, so slim and graceful. Anthony had got out and gone round the car to greet her. He kissed her on the cheek and opened the passenger door for her and then they drove off.

When the car had gone, Peter felt his heart plummet. He looked down at the two white chairs and the bottle and felt infinitely sad.

'Peter! What are you doing up there? What are you staring at? Get a move on, darling!' Julia's voice came from down below.

'He's getting away from you, Mum,' said Victoria, pleasantly. 'Can't you see, the only place he feels safe is fifteen feet up a ladder?'

'I thought we would go to the sea,' said Anthony as he drove out of Court Barton. 'Would you like that?'

'Very much,' said Claudia, settling back into the leather comfort of the passenger seat. She felt all right now, she was relieved to note. Quite composed.

'Now, let's have your news. It's been ages since we've had a talk. Valerie tells me that she sees quite a lot of your son and that he's getting on very well, so that must be a relief.'

'Yes, it is. Luckily from the point of view of his recovery, he's got youth and fitness on his side. The surgeon didn't think there would be any problems. It's lovely having him at home.' It was easy to mouth these platitudes as they sped down the country lanes. There was no need to reveal anything more or go any deeper. 'But how do you find Valerie?' she asked. 'It's good of you to keep an eye on her when you're so busy. I'm afraid that I've been very neglectful even though she's my neighbour. Of course, Jerome goes round nearly every day and he reports back.'

'She seems all right. Confidence is a bit shaken by what happened. I don't know that she is following any of the lifestyle advice that she had meted out to her. She downed two or three hefty whiskies last time I was there. The house is too big for her, of course. I don't know how long she can go on living alone. I imagine Christopher will have to sort something out when he comes over.'

'What's he like?'

'Couldn't say I know him. A clever man and nice enough chap. A widower with four young daughters. Hong Kong has served him well in that respect. Live-in nannies and housekeepers and so on are easily come by, so the domestic side of life is taken care of much more easily than it would be over here.'

'Goodness, what a task,' said Claudia. 'It must be tough, bringing girls up on your own.'

'Well, nothing's easy, is it, on your own?' he said casually but with a sideways glance which Claudia chose to ignore. 'Anyway, tell me about how things are with you. Enjoying the village? Much to Julia's relief you've given up the mushrooms, I hear.'

Claudia laughed. 'Yes. I'm much more respectable now I'm a dinner lady. Funny, isn't it? I suppose making shepherd's pie and custard has that smack of voluntary work about it – you know, soup kitchens or meals on wheels, the sort of jobs women like our mothers might have done in the war. Mushroom picking is not the right sort of thing at all.'

'But gardening's OK, isn't it? One can be a very smart professional gardener.'

'Oh yes, that's quite different. I think it must be the polytunnels, don't you? I don't think they're at all acceptable. Too modern and factory like, and plastic, too, of course.' They laughed again.

'Have they been in touch, that lot you met at the Durnfords?'

'Ros has,' said Claudia. 'She kindly asked me to a ladies' hunt lunch.'

'Ah.' Anthony looked amused. 'The hunt Mafia. Will you go?'

'I'll be working, but it was very kind of her.'

'Women around here seem to fall into two camps. The

thoroughly good sorts like Julia and Ros, born and brought up locally who are the backbone of their communities, and the part-timers like Jo Turner, who lead much faster lives. Have you heard about the sex train?'

'The what?'

'The sex train. Wednesday, I think, it is, when they troop off back to visit husbands in London. Check them over. That's what they call it, anyway.'

Claudia laughed. 'No, I haven't heard of that one.'

'I must say, I wonder if they go to deliver the goods themselves, or check that the order hasn't been placed elsewhere.'

'You make them sound like pizzas. What about the other way round? Aren't the husbands at all nervous about what may be going on down here while they're in London?'

'No time for that. Too busy earning the dosh, I think. Now, here we are. I'll park here by the bridge. No self-respecting farmer ever walks any further than he has to.'

Claudia looked about her as she got out. They had arrived at a small seaside harbour, where rows of dinghies were drawn up on the hard, their tall masts and rigging clinking in the light wind. People were setting off to walk along the seafront, enjoying the mild evening air. She could see a long pebble beach strung with walkers and groups of children running in and out of the gentle waves. Behind them a narrow wooden footbridge led the way across a creek to a brightly lit building set on piles, which was clearly a restaurant.

'How pretty this is!' she said, delighted.

'The food's bloody good too. Hope you like fish.'

'I love it,' she said, leading the way onto the bridge.

Rosco Bishop had bought his mother a bunch of flowers. True, it was rather a lurid bunch from the bucket outside the petrol station, but Star didn't mind about that. She arranged them lovingly in her crystal vase and put them on the mantelpiece.

'Thanks ever so much, love,' she said over and over again. She gave him a hug but he ducked away.

'Shit, Mum. Leave off, will you? It's only one lousy bunch.'

'It's the thought, though,' she said, and it was.

It seemed to Star that the trouble Rosco had been in earlier had done him good in the long run. Pulled him up short better than she ever could, with all her nagging and going on at him. He was doing all right now, keeping to the terms of his supervision order, and getting on well at the garage. He was better, really, the minute he'd left school, like she knew he would be. He needed to be doing proper work, not being pushed around by them teachers. Mr Martin was pleased with him he said, and although Rosco complained that he was the one who always got sent to the catering van for the lunchtime sandwiches and pies and was for ever making cups of tea and coffee for the men, she knew he was enjoying it. He came home every night whistling and cheerful. He was saving up hard for the bike and that gave him something to aim for, a goal.

Star made herself a coffee and plumped down on the sofa. There wasn't anything worth watching on the telly. She was sick of those makeover programmes. She couldn't get excited about other people's front room being turned into a Balinese beach hut. That was the last programme she saw, and no wonder the poor buggers looked fed up, having to sit on a straw platform and look out the window at a street in Walsall. Or else it was gardening – never-ending decking and water features. The only water feature she'd got was when next door went outside to pee last thing. Or cooking. No thank you. She wished there was a good film on. Something romantic. But there never was. In a minute she'd get onto Ceefax and see what holiday offers came up. She fancied a couple of weeks of sun. She'd got enough saved to manage a budget break, and she'd take Rosco with her this year. He could put something towards it out of his wages and they'd choose a place with a bit of night life that they'd both enjoy. Her eyes fell on the flowers and she felt another rush of pleasure. He was a good boy at heart.

Upstairs Rosco lay on his bed listening to a thrash metal CD. It was sad how pleased his mum had been with the effing flowers. He only pulled them out the bucket to have a laugh with Sean, but then Mr Glasby had come out and shouted and he'd had to buy them. It's not that he minded spending a bit on his mum. She was all right, she was, although she could be a bit embarrassing, especially the way she was all over Mr Martin when they met him in the High Street the other day. She was right out of order, laughing too loud, pawing his arm, nearly pushing him off the pavement. He thought of other people's mothers, women you hardly noticed, in ordinary clothes with ordinary hair, who crept about doing the shopping and drove carefully through the village. His mum went round with her arm out of the car window, her pop music full blast, shouting cheerfully at people she knew and when she parked, usually illegally and causing a traffic jam, she'd get our wearing her leopard-skin jeans and her tight pink T-shirt, and she was like, well, you couldn't miss her. Everyone knew his mum.

Now she'd got this idea of going on holiday together. Rosco didn't know what to think of that. Kids his age didn't go on holidays with their mums, he knew that for certain, but it was the first time that he could remember that she'd wanted to do anything with him. Usually she was all for getting shot of him, first chance she got, like when he'd got sent off to his dad's, so he couldn't believe it when she'd said about the holiday. He would have thought she'd want to go with one of her mates. Not with him, anyway. She was always saying he was a pain in the backside, saying what she could have done with her life if she hadn't had him round her neck.

Rosco lay and looked at the ceiling, thinking about his mother. She'd been over the moon with the flowers, right enough. Suddenly, and with a pang, he wished that he had really thought to buy them for her.

Claudia leant back in her chair and sighed with satisfaction. 'That was so good,' she said. 'Absolutely delicious.'

'It's nice to see you eat,' said Anthony. 'You don't look as if you make much of a habit of it.'

Claudia smiled. 'I do. Like the proverbial horse. I must burn it off in nervous energy, I suppose. Treacle tart like that isn't often on the menu though.'

'Have a brandy with your coffee. Or a liqueur?'

'That sounds tempting. Yes, I will please. I'd love a cognac.'

Anthony caught the eye of the waitress and gave the order. 'Not for me, though,' he said. 'I'm driving. I'll have to wait until I get home.' He smiled across the candle at Claudia. 'How pretty you look when you're relaxed.'

'That's a bit of a back-hander!'

'I mean it as a compliment. You can look a bit strained, you know.'

Claudia felt rattled. She disliked personal remarks that seemed to her to require a form of defence or rebuttal. 'You've hardly seen me. Not for weeks, anyway.'

'Just an observation. You're not at all like Lila, are you? In some ways it's hard to believe she's your daughter.'

'She's more like her father. Jerome takes after me. I meant to ask, how did you get on with her? It was kind of you to give her a lift to London.'

'It was nothing. I was going anyway. Oh, we got on fine. She was most entertaining. Actually, she made me feel very elderly. Twentysomethings suddenly seem like a different race.' He paused and then added, 'She said she was going to see her father. It seemed to upset her rather.'

Claudia froze. 'Oh?' Had Lila been talking? She held her breath for what might come next.

'I gave her my London number in case she wanted a lift back to Dorset. She rang that evening and seemed rather low so I asked her to join a crowd of us for dinner. It turned into rather a good party as it happens and she seemed to enjoy it. Anyway, she wouldn't say much, but I could tell that she worries about her father for some reason. Thinks he's unhappy. It struck me at the time that he must be about my age. I wondered what it would be like to have a girl like Lila as a daughter.'

'Oh, I see.' Claudia smiled with relief. 'Well, they're particularly close. They're very alike in most ways and when they aren't locked in mortal combat they get on extremely well. Lila's hugely competitive and her father appreciates that . . . Thank you.' The cognac appeared and was placed in front of her. 'This is lovely,' she said, still smiling across at him. He is an attractive man, she thought. Well-groomed, healthy, fit. Nice, square, capable hands. Kind eyes. I really do find him attractive. If he asks me in for a nightcap, I wonder . . .

It was dark now and outside the large windows the harbour lights swam on the flat surface of the water. The restaurant was full and noisy, the waitresses squeezing between the tables with orders, and Claudia was glad that he had chosen such a lively place and not somewhere more intimate. It was exactly right for a first date.

'Dad!' called Victoria from upstairs. 'Can you come up here a minute? I want to show you something.'

'What is it, Mouse? I want to catch the news.'

'Please, Dad, it may be important.'

Peter climbed the stairs to where his daughter waited on the landing. 'There's a really peculiar man hanging around next door,' she said. 'I can see him from my window. Come and see.'

Together they went into her bedroom which was in darkness and stood by her open window. 'Look,' she said. 'He's down there in the bushes by Jerome's drive. He's been there for ages.'

Peter peered through the window. It took his eyes a while to focus and then he saw what Victoria was pointing at. A dark shape humped against the escalonia bush, and then a tiny point of flame as a cigarette was lit.

'There is someone there! You're right, Mouse. How very strange. Casing the joint, do you think?'

'What should we do, Dad? Telephone the police?'

'No point in that, darling. They wouldn't get here until next week. Is your young Jerome in tonight? There are lights on in the bungalow.'

'Yes, I expect so. He usually is.'

'Well, let's give him a bell and tell him to go to the front door and put the outside light on and let that little lurcher out, and I'll go to our gate with Skye. That should get whoever it is on the move, don't you think?'

'I'll come with you, Dad. I'll bring my lacrosse stick.'

They hurried downstairs and Peter glanced into the sitting room where Julia was asleep in her armchair with the television on. In the kitchen he went to get the torch while Victoria telephoned Jerome and then they whistled up Skye and set off out of the back door. As they reached the gate onto the lane, they heard Finn erupt into wild barking and, galvanised into action, Sky shot off into the darkness.

'Get off, you little bugger!' They heard a man's startled voice, accompanied by a scuffling noise.

'Who is that?' called Peter loudly, shining the torch. 'What the hell are you doing?'

Both dogs were barking now and Jerome was shouting too. The man appeared to be trying to make a dash for it and was attempting to shake off Finn who was attached by his needle teeth to his trouser leg. Victoria dodged in front of her father, clutching her lacrosse stick, and with a mighty swipe brought it down on his head. The man gave a cry of surprise, half turned, lost his balance and fell heavily.

'What the bloody hell's going on?' cried Peter, shining the torch into his face.

At that moment Anthony Brewer's car swept up the lane and as it turned into the drive of the bungalow, Claudia saw an extraordinary tableau caught in the headlights. Three people, one of whom she realised was Jerome, were grouped in a state of agitation over a body on the ground. All four turned blind stares to meet the lights and on all their faces she read fear and anger.

Chapter Twelve

Peter Durnford recovered first. What he saw when he moved out of the headlights was that Claudia had ducked down in the passenger seat of Anthony's car and was shielding her face with an arm. Anthony had got out of his door saying, 'What's going on? What's happened?' and the man on the ground scrambled to his feet, shook off Finn and with more curses melted away into the dark.

Victoria began to shriek, 'I hit him! I hit him! I didn't mean to! Not so hard, anyway!'

Jerome hopped into the lane shouting, 'He's got away! Which way did he go?' Both dogs barked hysterically and lights went on in the cottage opposite.

'What the hell's going on?' demanded Anthony loudly.

'It was a prowler, I suppose,' said Jerome, coming back to join them. 'A man hanging around out here, snooping. Tor spotted him, didn't you, Tor?'

'Yes. He'd been there for ages, sort of staring at the bungalow and then going a little way up the drive and then coming back to hide behind the bush. I hit him, though. I hit him with my lax stick!'

'God,' groaned Anthony. 'Assault and battery.'

Ignoring them, Peter went to the passenger door and opened it and crouched beside Claudia in the dark. He realised that she was shaking and very gently he took her arm away from her face.

'It's all right,' he said coaxingly. 'It's all right. It wasn't anything much. Just a snooper. Don't be frightened. We're all here. I'm here,' he corrected. He held the hand that he had caught hold of and slid his arm round her shoulders. She turned and clung to him. Looking anxiously over his shoulder he saw that the others were still not paying any attention. Victoria was showing Anthony Brewer where she had seen the man hiding and they were loudly speculating on what the intruder had been up to.

'You're all right. I'm here,' he whispered, turning to Claudia again. He did not think he had ever seen anyone so frightened. She was shivering now and the hand that clutched his arm was like a vice. He leaned forward and dropped a kiss on the top of her head. Oh, God forgive me, he thought.

Claudia took some deep breaths and made an effort to regain control. Removing herself from his arms, she leaned back in the seat and closed her eyes. 'OK,' she said. 'I'm OK now, thanks. Are you sure he's gone?'

Peter stood up, the intimacy spoiled by her recovery, and looking about him said, 'Yes. No sign. Legged it.'

Claudia got out and closed the car door. Peter stayed by her side and put an arm round her and she allowed it to remain there while she said, 'Jerome? Where's Jerome?'

'Here, Ma. I'm here. Are you OK? God, you look pale.'

'Let's get you inside,' said Anthony, turning to her. Sheepishly, Peter removed his arm and they trooped into the bungalow together. Jerome pushed open the sitting-room door.

'In here,' he said. 'Shall I make you tea, Ma? Isn't that the right thing? With loads of sugar?'

'No thanks, darling.' Claudia was still pale but now very composed. She dropped onto the sofa and sat, knees together, looking at the backs of her hands. Anthony started to tell them about the inadequacy of policing and that although they should report the incident it could wait until the morning. Victoria was demonstrating to Jerome the ferocity of the blow she had delivered.

'Shite!' he said, admiringly. 'GBH at least, I'd say.'

'You don't think I'll get into trouble?' she asked, suddenly alarmed. 'Actually, I think the net bit probably softened the blow. I don't know what came over me.'

Peter still hovered over Claudia. 'Do you have any brandy?' he asked. 'I think that would do you good.'

'No thanks,' she said, looking up. 'I've had plenty to drink. I don't need any more. I'm fine now. It was just a bit of a shock, that's all.'

He would have liked to sit beside her and take her in his arms again, but realised, sadly, that the situation did not call for that level of spontaneous comforting, so he continued to loom over her with a concerned look on his face.

Claudia began to feel hemmed in and wished they would all go. Anthony and Jerome were now discussing window locks and intruder lights. They were all excited, she noticed, talking loud and fast, charged up by the drama.

Eventually she stood up. 'Look, thanks for everything. Thank you all so much, but really, I think we're fine now, and what I'd most like is to go to bed.'

Anthony came to her then and caught her in a hug which made Peter wince. 'Of course,' he said. 'I'll give you a call in the morning.' Claudia rested her head for a moment on the broad chest. How solid he felt. How reassuring. He kissed her on both cheeks and saying goodbye to the others went to the door and stood with it open, waiting to shepherd Peter and Victoria out with him. Peter felt annoyed. Why didn't he just go? There was no need to troop out together. He stood stiffly in front of Claudia, unable to touch her now, especially with Anthony watching from the door.

'Remember, I'm next door. Don't hesitate.'

'Thank you, Peter. Thank you so much. You've been so kind.'

Now there was nothing for it but to leave.

'Come on then, Tor.'

Victoria, who had been out in the lane catching the dogs, was making some kind of arrangement with Jerome. Peter heard him say, 'Early, not long after dawn. Five-ish. Are you sure you want to? I'll see you, then. By the gate. Here, don't forget your offensive weapon,' and he handed her the lacrosse stick with a grin. Then they were ushered out by Anthony, who had the final moment, the last look back at Claudia, the chance to bestow the final reassuring smile, all of which Peter had wanted for himself.

'Come on, Tor,' he said irritably, stepping out into the dark. 'Stop faffing about. Night, Anthony.'

'Good night, Peter. Night, Tor.'

As they walked towards East End House, Skye trotting in front, they heard Anthony's car start and turn round before sweeping past them into the village.

'You know, Mouse,' said Peter as they went in the back door and found the kitchen empty, 'I think we should keep quiet about this, don't you?'

'What do you mean?' Victoria was getting the cereal box out of the cupboard and fetching a bowl and spoon. She still looked flushed and excited.

'I don't think we should say anything. You know what the village is like. The stories that will get around.'

Victoria, standing leaning on the Aga, took a large mouthful and looked at her father over the edge of the bowl. 'What? Not tell Mum?'

'Better not, don't you think? You know what she's like.'

'You mean, she'll make a thing of it?'

'Exactly. Exactly that.'

'Yeah, OK, Dad.' She went on eating and Peter poured himself a large glass of whisky. When he took it to the sink to add some water he noticed that his hands were shaking.

'Are you really all right, Ma?' asked Jerome. 'You did look awfully pale. I suppose it was a shock coming home to all that going on. I daresay it looked worse than it was.'

'Yes, I'm OK.' Claudia sighed. 'Actually, I'm changing my mind about the drink. I could do with one. Have we got any?'

'A bottle of wine, I think. That's all. Shall I open it?'

'No, I've had enough wine. I need something to put a bit of fire back in me. Brandy or something. Like those useful dogs bring to people in snowdrifts. Let's have that tea instead.'

'OK. I'll make it. You're not worried, are you, by the man? I don't think you need be. I should think he's just some pervert who gets kicks by lurking about spying on people. Women. The sort who steals knickers off washing lines. I should think he's been thoroughly scared off by us lot. He won't come back in a hurry.'

Claudia said nothing. Jerome glanced at her. He could not tell what she was thinking.

'Mum?'

She looked up at him. 'It's slightly more complicated than that, Jerome.'

'What do you mean?'

'It's not what you think. Any of you. Don't you realise I would never have been that shaken by just a prowler? That man is much more dangerous.'

Jerome stared at his mother, not understanding. 'You *knew* him?'

Claudia nodded. She slumped back on the sofa and picked up a cushion which she held clamped between her knees.

'Well, who was he, Ma? Tell me! What's this all about?'

Claudia took a deep breath and gripped the cushion more tightly. 'His name is Freddy Hobbs. He is a photojournalist – freelance. I got to know him, I can tell you, because he practically lived in the front garden for three weeks at the time of Dad's arrest. I was even taking him cups of tea by the end.'

'A photojournalist? Are you sure?'

'Positive. Of course I am.'

'Well, what does it mean? Why's he hanging around here?'

'Oh Jerome, can't you see? He's on to us. He thinks there's a story to be had – an exclusive. He'll stake us out, get some photographs and flog them the minute we're newsworthy again. If Victoria hadn't felled him with her lacrosse stick he would have had a shot of me in the car with Anthony Brewer, maybe a goodnight kiss. You can imagine the lies that could be spread about that. Expensive car, new boyfriend. Fraudster's wife's luxury lifestyle.'

Jerome looked at her, dumbfounded. 'Are you *sure*? Absolutely certain? Because you didn't get a very good look at him, did you? You could be mistaken.'

Claudia shook her head. 'I'm not mistaken. I'll never forget his weaselly rodent face.'

Jerome sat beside her on the sofa and took her hand. Finn, jealous, jumped up and tried to climb onto his lap and lick his face. He pushed him away. 'Poor old Mum,' he said. 'This is awful. What can we do about it?'

'I must stop Anthony reporting it to the police. I don't want that. It will just complicate matters. I suppose I'll telephone David Rowntree and see what he has to say, but I don't think there's anything I can do to stop that rat hanging around and taking photographs. We can throw him out of the garden, but that's about all. He can still take pictures from the lane, or wherever else he chooses.'

'Are you surprised that he's found us here?'

Claudia pulled a face. 'Not really, I suppose. It's like you said this evening. I've allowed myself to feel more secure than I should have done. I had just started to function like a normal person again. This is just a reminder that I am not.'

'Oh, Mum!' Jerome pulled her towards him and put his arm round her. 'I'm sorry, Ma. I really am. At least I'm here to share it with you this time.'

They sat for a moment in glum silence and then he said, 'What do you think happens next?'

'I suppose he'll come back. I think if he does, I'll confront him. Ask what he's up to. Why he's still after me. Apart from that, there's nothing else we can do. We'll just have to sit it out. Try to be as normal as possible.'

'Dad's protected from all of this, isn't he? He might be serving the sentence but it's you who has to deal with all this shit.'

Claudia sighed. 'Jerome, I've been trying to tell you that.'

'I'm sorry, Mum. I'm truly sorry. I don't know . . . I thought you were dramatising everything a bit. I haven't been very supportive, have I? Oh, Mum.'

'Oh, it's OK, Jerome. It's OK.' They sat side by side looking at one another. Finn began to whine and tried to duck his head under Jerome's arm.

'You've always been so great, Ma. Always just quietly there for us. Dad was great too, but he was like, you know, rushing about, showing off, being about seven all the time.'

Claudia had to smile at this description. 'Yes, he's always been seven, hasn't he? Even when he was chairman. Can you remember how he loved the big desk and all the gadgets – and the fridge!'

They smiled weakly at one another. Jerome was filled with tenderness. 'I do love you, Mum. I'm sorry.'

'Stop it, Jerome. I haven't cried yet. Don't set me off. Come on, let's have that tea.'

When Claudia went to bed that night she found that she felt strangely elated. It shouldn't surprise me, she thought, that to feel close to Jerome again is much more important than anything that man can do. It was as if a shutter between them had been rolled back; a fence, a barrier gone. She thought of his previously guarded looks, his offhand remarks, his lack of involvement, and was glad in her heart for the transformation of the evening. Together, we're strong, she thought. It will make all the difference to me. We can ride this out together.

She thought of Anthony and Peter and Victoria and their various roles in the drama. Bitter experience had taught her not to trust friends but there was something about those three that made her feel they could be relied upon, that they were more solid and enduring than the fickle London lot.

Peter, silly old thing, had kissed her, she remembered, in a kind of fervour of concern. She was touched by his kindness. Anthony had been all practical advice and level-headedness. One could not help but feel protected by a man like that and when he put his arms round her it had been like taking shelter.

She thought back to the earlier part of the evening. She had enjoyed dinner, enjoyed his company. How would the evening have ended if Freddy Hobbs hadn't introduced his spanner into the works? A little light seduction, probably. Of course she realised Anthony was a man whose specialist subject was women. A sophisticated man who had been round that particular block many times before. And, she thought, smiling into the darkness, he's a lot more grown-up than seven.

Towards dawn she woke with a start and instantly felt clutched by fear again, the euphoria of the evening gone. Please God, help me, she thought, but with everything else going on in the world, she could not, for a moment, see why He should.

Not long afterwards, Jerome was also awake, and judging the time to be right, got up and dressed. He called Finn and went outside. It was already completely light although the sun had not yet appeared in the milky morning sky, and what he could see of the sleeping village was utterly deserted and quiet.

He stopped at the bottom of the short drive where the drama of the night before had been enacted and waited for Victoria. He did not have to wait for long because after a few minutes Finn pricked up his ears and started to whine and then Skye trotted cheerily from the gates of East End House, stopping to lift his leg against the gatepost, followed by Victoria in jeans and wellington boots.

'Hi,' she said. 'Am I late?'

'No, I've only just got here. Come on. Let's go.'

At first Victoria thought that they would talk about the night before. She had hoped to recapture the excitement and to go over the details, to be teased again about her lacrosse stick, but Jerome seemed in an entirely different and more sombre mood. They set off, Victoria's wellingtons making a gallumphing noise on the lane, and there did not seem to be anything to say that was worth breaking the silence for. It was strange, she thought, how different the village was at this hour. The cottages they passed had a closed, secretive look, curtains still drawn shut, cars pulled into driveways, gardens silent and empty, children's toys abandoned on the dewy grass. Then a dog barked and from somewhere a cockerel crowed.

As they passed Waterside Cottage a gaggle of geese set up an alarmed cackle and Victoria had to grab Skye to stop him rushing at the wire netting and causing a furore. A cat crossed the lane ahead, paused to look, and then streaked on and disappeared into the hedge. As they passed Briar Cottage with the 'Honey For Sale' notice at its gate they heard a baby crying from an open first floor window and then a young woman with tousled hair looked out at them as she drew back the curtains, yawning, her mouth an open pink O. It feels a bit like bad manners, thought Victoria, being up and about before anyone else. Like stealing up on someone and watching them asleep

At Church Farm the day had already long begun and black and white cows were making their slow way from milking, crossing the lane and going through the gate into their summer pasture. They also paused to gaze in mild curiosity before moving unhurriedly on. From the dairy yard Victoria could hear a man whistling and the sound of a pressure hose.

Then they were out of the village and Jerome let Finn off his lead and he and Skye set about working up the hedge, disturbing little gatherings of sparrows which erupted, chattering, out of the branches.

'It's not quiet at all really, is it?' said Jerome. 'Listen.' And they stopped and lifted their heads to take in the chorus of songbirds, led by a blackbird perched on a telegraph pole above their heads. Victoria could actually see his sharp yellow beak opening and shutting as he sang, while a line of swallows chirruped from the wires. She would have liked to have commented, to keep the conversation going, but did not feel sure enough about birds not to say something silly. She knew all the commonplace ones, blackbirds, thrushes, robins, but had no idea how to identify them by their songs. Anyway, Jerome didn't seem to want to talk and so they set off again, taking the lane which dropped steadily down into the low-lying and most isolated part of the vale, where the grass was longer and greener and the air was still and damp.

Along the verge Victoria could see Vinnie's hoofprints. This was a way she often rode, liking the empty lanes and the long stretches of bridlepaths, once the old drove roads, she'd been told, which radiated across the vale. They were nearly at the bridge where the lane crossed the old railway line, where Jerome had said they would meet Jena, and they still hadn't spoken. She wondered whether she had annoyed him or, worse still, that he wished she wasn't there, that he regretted having asked her to come. She glanced at him and his profile looked set and stern.

That must be it, she thought. She was always doing things like that herself. Getting involved with something or someone and then later wishing she hadn't. Perhaps she should just go home. Say she had a headache. All the happiness of last night, the closeness, had gone. All the things she had lain in bed and dreamed of in that state of heightened feeling seemed stupid now. In an agony of mortification she lagged behind, pretending she was waiting for Skye who was hunting somewhere in the bottom of a hedge.

By now Jerome had reached the top of the bridge and was looking over the parapet, first one way and then crossing to the other side to look the other.

'She's not here,' he reported. 'No sign.' When Victoria did not reply he turned to look at her dawdling behind and seeing her downcast face he smiled and extended a hand.

'Come on,' he said kindly. 'You do look miserable. Are you worried about going to a young offenders' institute for assault?'

His smile and gesture were enough to transform the morning and Victoria went to join him with a lifting heart. Side by side they rested their elbows on the parapet.

'You're quiet,' he observed, looking down at her.

'So are you. I mean, it takes two to be quiet. I didn't *feel* quiet until you were.' Her face grew hot and she couldn't look at him.

'Silly girl,' he said fondly and with a finger looped a strand of loose hair behind her ear. 'I like your chatter. It cheers me up.'

Later, writing her diary, Victoria imagined her heart, at this moment, as a white bird fluttering up into the sky. It was the only way she could think of to describe how she suddenly felt happy again.

The moment was broken by a clatter of hooves which made them both look to the right. 'Here she is!' said Jerome as up the lane came Jigsaw, flying along, pulling a flatbed cart behind him, with Jena perched on the driver's seat like a monkey. She took a hand off the reins and waved and it was only the steep gradient of the bridge which enabled her to pull up beside them with a lot of stamping feet and snorting from Jigsaw. Finn took off in fright, his whippy tail clamped between his legs, and Victoria had to scramble down the bank to catch him.

'Here, give us yer hand!' said Jena, helping Jerome to haul himself and his disabled leg onto the cart. 'Look, sit there,' and she indicated an old car seat leaning up against the driver's box. 'Are you coming, Vick? Cool. Here, give us them dogs,' and she leaned down to gather up Finn from Victoria and passed him to Jerome, and then took the wriggling Skye who was yapping enthusiastically.

'Here, sit by me,' she told Victoria, and then picking up the reins they were off, racing along the lane, Jigsaw's legs working like pistons, stones flying from his hooves, Jerome hanging on and clutching Finn, and Victoria up on the front seat with Skye on her knees, laughing out loud with exhilaration.

The first thing Claudia did that morning was to telephone

Anthony Brewer and was frustrated to find his answerphone switched on. Damn, she thought. He was the sort of managing man who might well have taken the initiative and already alerted the police.

'Anthony,' she spoke as commanded after the tone, 'this is Claudia. Just to thank you very much for last night and, Anthony, in the cold light of day, I've decided I don't want to do anything about my prowler. I don't think it's worth the hassle and I feel quite safe with Jerome here. I just thought I'd let you know that I'd rather let the whole thing drop. Anyway, thanks again. Bye.'

Now, Peter and Victoria. She considered it unlikely that Peter would do anything without consulting her, but he'd talk, tell Julia, and it would be all round the village. She glanced at her watch. It was still early. She wondered if she could catch him on his way to work. Somehow stop him in the lane. She was mulling this over, staring abstractedly out of the kitchen window, when to her surprise she saw his navy blue estate car draw up outside and there he was, his long, anxious, sheepy face looking at her from the driver's seat.

Running her hand through her uncombed hair she hurried out to meet him.

'Peter, I was just thinking about you. I wanted to thank you for last night . . .'

He had got out and stood by the open car door and now raised a hand to stop Claudia's thanks.

'Nothing. It was nothing. I, um, thought I'd just check . . .'

'The thing is, Peter, I want to let the whole thing drop. I don't think it worth reporting and I'd rather you didn't say anything about it. You see . . .' She couldn't think how to put it. To say, in effect, don't tell your wife. If you haven't already.

'Absolutely. I agree. Much better. No need.' Peter found he had lost the ability to form a sentence. 'Not a word. Not even Julia,' he finished lamely.

'Thank you.' She smiled at him gratefully and noticed his bow tie had white rabbits on a blue background. What a silly man he is, she thought, but essentially kind. A good man. They stood looking at one another and Peter agonised over whether he could say anything else about the evening, but Claudia's quite jaunty mood and the bright sunshine conspired to make such a reference impossible.

'So that's all right then,' Claudia said. 'Thank you for calling in,' and her tone and manner suggested that she expected he would want to be on his way.

'Yes. Righto. I just thought . . . but so glad that you've got over . . . excellent.' He found himself climbing back into his car and closing the door and then pressing the button to further open the electric window so that contact between them could be maintained and shutting it by mistake. Claudia stood smiling. In a fluster he turned on the engine and somehow activated the windscreen wipers which flung themselves across the screen at top speed. Claudia looked amused.

What a fool I am, he thought despairingly as he drove to work. Behaving like a teenager. But what had she said? 'I was just thinking about you.' She was just thinking about me, he told himself, and began to feel more cheerful.

Julia, on drawing back the curtains from Victoria's bedroom window, was arrested by the sight of her husband's car in her neighbour's drive. What on earth is he up to? She thought, but could arrive at no explanation. Right at the back of her mind a very small doubt was raised but dismissed at once. Really, she had no time for that sort of nonsense – not with only eight days until the garden opening.

Nevertheless she stood riveted until she saw Peter hop back in and drive off. He looked rather flustered and agitated, she thought. What *was* he up to? Turning back to the room she was not surprised to see that Victoria's bed was empty. She often went out to have an early ride. Stooping to pick up dirty jodhpurs off the floor the thought came to her that she could telephone Claudia and find out. 'What did Peter want?' she would say. 'I saw him just now. Do tell me, I'm intrigued!'

As soon as Claudia waved Peter off she heard the telephone ringing. It was Anthony returning her call. He was brisk and to the point.

'Claudia, I understand your reluctance to report this incident, but I do think you should reconsider. If this man is more than just a voyeur, something altogether more dangerous, then how would you feel if a woman or a girl, a schoolchild even, was to be attacked and you had said nothing? I'm afraid I see it as your duty to allow one of us to speak to the police. To put it on record. I mean, you've got Valerie living on her own next door, for instance. You know, in a village—'

'Stop preaching, Anthony, please.' Claudia's voice was sharp. 'I actually know what I'm doing.'

'Do you?' he persisted.

215

In the face of his robust opposition she could not see any other way but to say, 'Yes, I do. Believe me, Anthony, that man is no risk to anyone else in the village.'

'How can you possibly know that?'

'Because I know him.'

There was a pause. On the other end of the telephone, Anthony was taking in this piece of unexpected information. 'You know him?' he repeated slowly.

'Yes, I do. There is only one person he is interested in, and that is me. And possibly Jerome,' she added.

'I see.'

'How can you see? Without knowing everything, you can't possibly see. You'll just have to take my word for it, that it is not my civic duty to report what happened. Is that OK? I don't really want to go into it all, but I can tell you that that man was an unpleasant part of my life in a small way before I moved here. I had hoped to have seen the last of him, but that's obviously not the case. All right? Does that satisfy you?'

There was a silence. Then Anthony said gently, 'Claudia, are you sure you don't want to tell me more? Perhaps I can help.'

'You're very kind, but no thanks. I'm sorry if I've offended your Neighbourhood Watch principles, but there it is. And Anthony,' she added, knowing that she sounded dismissive and regretting it, 'thank you very much for last night. I really enjoyed it.'

'We must do it again some time,' he said without much enthusiasm.

'That would be lovely.'

'Wait. Claudia, is this to do with money? If so . . .'

'No, it's not.' Claudia took a breath. She would have to risk telling him more. 'If you must know, that man is a journalist. Is that enough? That's why I would appreciate it if you said nothing to anybody. I really would.'

'I see.' Anthony's voice was thoughtful. 'I would still like you to know that if I can help . . .'

'Thank you. Thank you very much. That's a very kind offer and I will remember it.'

As soon as Claudia put the telephone down she picked it up again to dial David Rowntree's number. He answered at once and she told him briefly what had happened and asked him what he made of it.

David hesitated a moment, weighing up the information and then said, 'I imagine someone local has tipped a newspaper off and he has been hired to do a recce. It's common knowledge that the appeal is coming up very shortly – next week it looks like – and of course that will bring Roger back into focus. The Sunday newspaper has withdrawn their interest in doing a profile, by the way. With the collapse of Arrow Insurance and that huge fraud case in the States, there's enough going on in the City to keep them satisfied.'

'Thank God, for that,' said Claudia. 'What a disappointment for Roger to find he's no longer front page material.'

'Actually,' said David quietly, 'he had decided to withdraw his co-operation. Not go through with the deal.'

'Oh. I see. Why the change of heart? Was it Lila? Something she said?'

'I don't know. Except that if you met him now you might find him rather a changed man.'

Claudia sighed. David was at it again. Always the loyal footsoldier.

'For whatever reason, I'm grateful,' she said, relenting a little.

'I'll tell him. Now as for the present situation, there's not much I can suggest you do. Keep a low profile and be on your guard. You might consider going away for a week or two, until after the appeal.'

'No, I thought of that but I have a job and I'm not running again. I guess I'll just have to sit it out. Thanks, David. Let me know how it goes, won't you? Keep in touch about the appeal.'

'Of course.'

Claudia would have liked to speak to Minna who would have given her the sort of informed support she felt she needed but looking at her watch realised that she would be late for work. Seizing her bag and car keys she ran out. As she locked the front door she heard the telephone start to ring again but left it unanswered. Whoever it was could ring back later.

'Damn,' said Julia, replacing the receiver. The number had been engaged for nearly half an hour and now there was no answer. She'd ring Peter instead but knew he had meetings all the morning and she had to go and make a start in the garden. Tom was coming today and together they still had so much to do. He needed watching, too, preferring to slope off and have a dig somewhere, given half a chance. That was his favourite thing and unless given a specific task, was what he reverted to all the time. The cranesbill geraniums, galegas and alchemillas which had finished flowering needed cutting right back. Thank goodness most of the perennials were showing new bursts of bloom. August was such a difficult month. Changing her shoes and collecting her old felt hat, Julia hurried off into the garden, all thoughts of Peter banished for the time being.

'You guys don't know everything, do you?' laughed Jena as she drove Jigsaw up the track. 'You're always carrying on about books and that, but you don't know any of the things me dad knows. This hedge on the right is one of the oldest round here. Dad's done a survey, see. Look at all the different species. Maple, hazel, plum, holly, sweet chestnut, elm, hornbeam, whitebeam, wild privet, spindle. There'd be elder, too, but Dad took it all out. Elder doesn't do a hedge any good, see. It grows too quick and crowds the other trees and it breaks too easy if stock push at it. This hedge is medieval, he says. You can tell how old it is by counting the different trees. The more there are, the older it is.'

Jerome and Victoria looked at where Jena was pointing and all they saw was an overgrown green barrier of trees running along the top of the bank. Victoria tried hard to distinguish one from another, but gave up.

'This is the parish boundary, see?' said Jena. 'So this hedge was, like, really important. You can tell, too, by looking at the plants. See the dog mercury and the yellow dead nettle?' She looked at her two companions and burst out laughing. 'You wouldn't know them, would yer, if they jumped up and bit yer! Well, there're very slow colonisers, so where you've got them growing like that, all along the bank there, that's taken probably two hundred years or more!'

Jerome looked at Jena in astonishment. He couldn't take in all that she was telling them.

'How do you know all this?' he asked. 'Is it from your dad?'

'Yeah. I go out with him a lot. He tells me.'

'So what work is he doing now? I sometimes see him in the mornings. Hedging or something?'

Jena laughed again at his ignorance. 'Not this time of the year! Hedging and ditching's for the winter. November, he starts. No, he's coppicing now and clearing and sawing up fallen trees. That's when he uses Jigs, see? He takes him out with this cart to move the wood.'

'What about blackthorn hedges? Isn't this part of the country famous for the blackthorn?'

'Dunno about that. There's plenty of 'em. I know that 'cos I jump 'em. Socking great things some of them are with ditches towards and after. Where you get just blackthorn in a hedge, you know it's not so old, maybe just a few hundred years. Blackthorn grows really bushy and that's why it has to be properly cut and laid, and then it makes a great hairy hedge that nothing can get through. That's what the hunt enjoy. A good run across country with a few of them hedges in between. That sorts 'em out good and proper, and Jigs jumps them better than any of them. All them posh ones and all.'

'I know,' said Victoria. 'They're terrifying. You're amazingly brave, Jena.'

Jena's eyes sparkled. 'Nar, it's Jigs. He does it. You only have to point him and sit tight. Here we are. Here's where I live.'

Jena had pulled off the track with its medieval hedge and turned onto the old railway line and there were the vans, two of them, pulled under the ash trees. One of them was a regular old mobile home with a tin chimney and the other was an old school bus, still painted yellow and black. A few chickens scratched around and Victoria took a tight hold of Skye. A goat was tethered on the bank, eating amongst the nettles and brambles. A long open shed with a corrugated roof ran alongside and was filled top to bottom with neatly cut logs; beside it was a saw horse and mounds of fresh yellow sawdust. A chain saw and an axe lay propped on the ground as if Jem Loader had just finished work there. One end of the log shed was an implement store and various saws and axes and scythes and billhooks were arranged neatly against the walls. From the roof, bunches of plants hung upside down in various stages of drying out.

From underneath the bus, the lurcher bitch barked a welcome and three of Finn's brothers and sisters came tumbling out to see the visitors.

'Come on, I'll help yer,' said Jena, jumping down and securing the reins to a post. Jerome passed her down the trembling Finn, who couldn't quite work out whether he belonged here or not and approached the other dogs cautiously before taking off in a wild game of tag, scattering the chickens and annoying the goat, who lowered her head and stamped her foot crossly. Skye whined and tugged at the lead, longing to join in, but Victoria was taking no chances and kept him firmly restrained while she and Jena offered Jerome a shoulder to lean on as he lowered himself down from the cart.

They stood watching the puppies tumbling and romping while Victoria squatted to stroke Meg, the rough-coated bitch who came and leaned against her. 'She's so beautiful and elegant,' she said. 'Like something out of a fairy tale. A dog for a princess.'

'Come on in the bus,' said Jena. 'That's where I sleep. Hagar and Dad and the boys sleep in the van.'

'Hagar? Is that your mother?' asked Victoria.

'Nar. Me mum left when I was a baby. Hagar's Dad's partner. Her real name's Heather but she likes to be called Hagar 'cos it sounds more Romany. She's never a gypsy though. Come off a housing estate in Southampton. The boys are hers – little Rob and Brian. They're not me brothers. Her old man was a lorry driver. Knocked them about and that, so she come here. She's all right, she is.' Jena opened the door of the bus and led the way in.

'Wow! It's amazing,' said Victoria, looking around. 'I never imagined it would be like this!'

'It's all right, innit?' said Jena proudly.

Jerome pulled himself up the steps and entered behind the girls and found himself in an unexpected interior. All the seats of the bus had been removed and every other window boarded over, but it was still very light. Sunshine flooded through the perspex skylights in the roof. A couple of bunk beds had been fitted into the far end, which was cosy with brightly coloured covers and curtains and a striped rug on the floor. Then there was a regular table and chair and shelves all along one side where Jena had some books and ornaments. The end where they stood had a battered sofa and armchair and a piece of red carpet on the floor and Jerome was astonished to see a computer and word processor set up on a steel desk. 'We've got the electric, see,' said Jena. 'We've got a generator out the front. This is where Dad does his work – sends off his results and that to the university in London.'

'What sort of results?' asked Jerome, intrigued.

'He maps out the hedges, counts the species, birds, mammals, butterflies, bats – everything. Hedges is like corridors for animals, see? And you get all these different environments in one – ditch, sunny bank, woodland, stuff like that. They use some of what Dad tells them to plant hedges in towns, like in parks and on housing estates, to get the birds and the wildlife back.'

'It's fascinating,' said Jerome, genuinely interested. 'Absolutely fascinating. I'm totally ignorant of all of this stuff and it's on my doorstep.'

Jena shrugged. 'Most people are. They don't care. Think it's rubbish. Brewer's all right, although he's ignorant. Like most farmers, Dad says. Mrs Pomeroy's the one. She's interested all right.'

'What all this?' asked Victoria, pointing to a box full of handwritten labels.

'That's Hagar's stuff. See, she does herbal cures and that. Flogs them to the magic shops in Glastonbury. Look.' She picked up a handful and laid them out on the table. 'Dill – love. Borage – courage. Bettony – against evil spirits. Briar rose – bite of dog or snake. Elm – childbirth. Dad says it's a load of bollocks, but people buy them. Hagar has to send Dad or me into the chemist to get the aspirin and the indigestion stuff and the Calpol for the boys!' They all laughed.

'Doesn't she believe in it at all?' asked Victoria, rather shocked.

'Yeah,' she does a bit, but she takes the other stuff too, just in case. Do you want a drink or anything? A cuppa tea?'

Jerome and Victoria looked at one another.

'Yeah,' said Jerome. 'That'd be great, Jena.'

'Peter,' said Julia, when she at last tracked him down. 'What on earth were you doing this morning?'

'What? What do you mean?'

'I saw you. At Claudia's.'

'At Claudia's?'

'Peter! Don't keep repeating what I say. Yes, at Claudia's. I saw you at Claudia's. What were you doing?' She spoke pleasantly but in a determined tone.

'I was dropping off a letter.'

'A letter? What letter?'

'The postman left a letter for her with us. By mistake. I dropped it off on my way to work. To save you the bother.'

'You never said anything to me about a letter.'

'You were upstairs when the post came. Why the interrogation, old thing? What's up?'

'Oh, I just wondered,' said Julia, in a changed voice, feeling foolish.

'Ah,' said Peter mildly. 'So it's not the electrodes under the fingernails this time? Really, Julia, you're wasted, you know. You should be working for some South American dictatorship. Now I must go. Unless there was something else?'

Chapter Thirteen

Lila was in love. She did not much enjoy this sensation because for the first time ever she found herself suffering from the disturbing symptoms associated with the condition. What made things worse was that the object of her affection was a continent away and their time together severely limited. She had flown to Paris for another long weekend and he had come to New York on two occasions, but in between the affair was conducted by email and telephone. This did not at all suit Lila, who liked to crack on with things, as she called it, and one of the reasons she knew this must be love was her willingness to tolerate this entirely unsatisfactory situation.

At her co-ed boarding school where she had first gone out with boys, a relationship could be launched, explored and abandoned between breakfast and tea and this was the pace Lila preferred. It was the same at university. If you liked someone you saw them all day and night with the sort of intensity that meant after two weeks you knew them inside out and, in Lila's case, then chucked them, bored and disenchanted.

Now she went through agonies of frustration when she did not hear from him, scanning for new mail every five minutes and nearly exploding with anxiety when a day or two went by with no response, even believing that her computer was not functioning properly and sending for technical support to have it checked. She had seen other girls at work behaving like this and had thought them ineffably silly. It was disconcerting to find herself as badly afflicted.

She continued to see her old crowd and to go out to bars and clubs, but her heart was not in it and it was no longer the fun it used to be when she, along with her girlfriends, was out cruising for a likely man. These days, more often than not, she would end up staring glumly into her overpriced drink and going home early in a cab.

She played sport more frenetically than ever, pulverising

opponents on the squash court and swimming length after punishing length of the pool, ploughing up and down and infuriating the women who were doing a little gentle exercise before going to work and did not want to get their hair wet or their faces splashed.

If she beat herself up physically, Lila reckoned she could subdue how she felt emotionally, only to discover that however hard she tried, however much she made her muscles ache, her heart was still free to lurch from high to low. It's like being seasick, she thought. Like riding a great rolling sea at the mercy of a fickle wind.

Of course, the good times were good enough to hold her, bewitched. On Saturday morning in Paris they had sat in the sun at a pavement café, holding hands, with little cups of espresso coffee cooling in front of them, and Lila was, at last, free of her relentless nervous energy and felt slack and happy and peacefully in love. Exhausted from the week at work, the rush to the airport, the transatlantic flight and a night of lovemaking and too much to drink, she felt dreamy and half-drugged, good for nothing but a long lunch and an afternoon in bed.

Her collection of significant champagne corks was growing, each one embellished with the date the bottle had been drunk, along with all the other memorabilia of a love affair – museum tickets, a red rose now dried into a rather nasty old blood brown, meaningful CDs, books inscribed with special messages and finally, and most telling in Tara's view, she had started to read poetry. She was always leaving a paperback copy of *The Penguin Book of Love Poetry* in the bathroom, its pages wavy with damp.

'Look, Alice,' said Tara, passing over the book she had picked up from the bath rack. 'I can't believe it of Lila. Do you really think she reads this sort of stuff? It's so unlike her. All this introspection and mawkishness.'

'You are horrid, Tara. I think it's lovely for her to have found this man. It's so romantic, zooming off to Paris for assignations,' sighed Alice, who wondered whether Tara was not the slightest bit jealous.

'I suppose "Miss Joan Hunter Dunn" is rather appropriate for Lila,' went on Tara, flicking through the pages and stopping at Betjman. 'Listen.

On the floor of her bedroom lie blazer and shorts
And the cream-coloured walls are be-trophied with sports,

And westering, questioning settles the sun
On your low-leaded window, Miss Joan Hunter Dunn.

That could be Lila, couldn't it? Do you really not know who
her man is?' she persisted, putting the book down. 'Why won't
she say?'

'I honestly don't know. She comes back absolutely brimming
over. You know Lila. Normally she can't wait to kiss and tell,
and I get a blow-by-blow account – oops! That sounds rude! I
don't mean it quite like that. But she says she doesn't want
anyone to know who he is. Yet, anyway. I wondered, maybe, if
he's married. Or famous.'

'Yes, that thought had occurred to me,' said Tara. 'What about
that rugger man? You know, the Princess Di one, with enormous thighs and a very low hairline? The possibilities are
endless. He's obviously well set up, isn't he? I mean, he pays for
all these flights and hotels, presumably.'

'Yes. They're having a holiday together next. In September, I
think. The West Indies or somewhere.'

'Bloody hell!' said Tara crossly. She was sick of scraping along
on her junior fund manager's salary with not a man in sight,
and Lila's good fortune was most irritating. 'Well, let's hope she
knows what she's doing. It sounds to me as if she might be
following the White Rabbit.'

'What white rabbit?' asked Alice, perplexed.

Tara laughed, not very kindly. 'A literary allusion, dearie. To
Wonderland.'

The days before the garden opening at East End House were
filled with frantic activity. Julia gave up cooking meals or
housekeeping and concentrated solely on putting the finishing
touches to the beds and lawns and vegetable garden. She made
Peter tidy the barn and Victoria the yard and paddock. Even the
muck heap was considered not up to scratch and Victoria had to
spend a whole day rebuilding it. 'Before, it was an untidy heap
of horse shit and now it's a tidy heap of horse shit,' she
grumbled to Jerome, 'and the world's a better place, according
to Mum.'

Julia herself was a whirlwind, with her secateurs never out of
her hand. The garden must be well-groomed if nothing else and
the late-flowering plants which would be the focus for the
visitors had to have tidy neighbours. Peter was set simple tasks
like deadheading the roses and irises and columbines while Julia

and Tom tackled the pruning of the summer shrubs that had to have their old flowering branches cut out to allow for next year's growth. The jobs seemed never-ending and Julia was relentless. 'The euphorbias, Tom,' she called. 'We must do the euphorbias!' In the sanctuary of the vegetable garden, Tom kept his head well down and turned a deaf ear.

'It's the same every year,' he muttered to himself. 'Come August, she gets the high strikes. Same every year.'

Victoria was sent out to weed the paths and Peter to trim the edges, while Julia ticked items off her list of things to do. The trestle tables and chairs had to be collected from the village hall – Greg and a tractor and trailer from Manor Farm had been detailed for this task – and Betty was coming on Saturday afternoon to help Star with the teas. Monica and the ladies on the Village Hall Committee had organised the baking of the scones and the little supermarket in Sharston had donated the cream, which would, Julia thought, have to be collected on Saturday. Well, Star could do that on her way through to Court Barton.

Of course everything hung on the weather. Julia had asked Anthony Brewer to get her a long-range forecast from some farmers' station that he subscribed to, and the prospects were only fair. Bright, with the possibility of showers, it said, giving way to more persistent rain in the evening. Showers one could cope with. No gardener minded getting a bit wet, but real English summer rain would be a disaster. Naturally, the number of visitors, and therefore the proceeds, would plummet and the teas would have to be re-sited in the barn.

What else was there? Julia consulted her list. Oh yes, Peter would have to wash the drive gates, which were looking particularly dirty after all the tractor traffic through the village at harvest time, and he might as well do the paintwork on the doors of the house while he was at it. He must put up the Garden Open signs and the arrows for parking in the paddock behind the stables. That would all have to be done on Saturday morning.

She had asked Claudia and Jerome to help. After all, the proceeds were for the Church Fund and they should feel a responsibility to muck in for the community. Claudia could help Star and Betty with the teas – collecting dirty cups and plates and ferrying them in and out of the kitchen to be washed. Jerome and Victoria could be on the gate, collecting entrance money.

She herself had to be on patrol, answering questions and giving advice and keeping an eye out for the wretches who stole cuttings for their own gardens, sometimes even uprooting whole plants to carry away with them. Tom would be a write-off by Saturday. He would have gone off in a grump by then, threatening never to come back. It happened every year, but he always reappeared when the garden needed digging over in the autumn.

Now what else was there? Peter, of course. It was his job to organise the car parking. He set himself up with a deck chair and his old straw hat and spent a relatively peaceful afternoon keeping an eye on things in the paddock, sometimes being fed a sandwich or two out of a picnic basket, and generally welcoming people as they arrived and preventing any major cock-ups in the parking department. Of course, if it rained hard the night before there was the prospect of the grass being cut up and vehicles getting stuck. Julia thought she had better get Anthony to have Greg and the tractor on hand to tow people out if necessary. She must remember to tell Peter that it was strictly no dogs, and no beastly children on bicycles either. She frowned on babies in buggies – they were like chariots these days and driven with scant regard by determined young mothers, sometimes into and over her flowerbeds. A couple of these going round in convoy blocked paths and took up too much space in the tea area. Last year she even had one mother ask her whether she had a changing mat. A changing mat? she'd repeated, not believing her ears and wondering for a moment if it was a type of ground cover. However, she couldn't very well ban babies too. She approved of the sort of fathers who carried their infants slung about their persons – much the most sensible way, in her view, out of the way and far less trouble for everybody else.

Julia consulted her list again. The outside lavatory had to be whitewashed and spruced up a bit. Another job for Peter, but where was he? How could he possibly make the deadheading of the border take so long? She hurried off to find out.

When Victoria went round to the bungalow to tell Claudia and Jerome, on her mother's instructions, what their duties were to be, she detected an absorbed atmosphere which made her feel uncomfortably in the way.

'Oh, hi,' she said when Jerome came to the door. 'Mum sent me to ask if it's still all right about Saturday.' She followed him into the kitchen where his mother sat at the table.

'Victoria wants to know about Saturday,' he said and she saw a look of puzzlement on Claudia's face.

'The garden opening,' Victoria explained, not really believing that one could live just next door and be unaware of the frenzied activity on the other side of the wall.

'Oh, yes,' said Claudia vaguely, running a hand through her hair. 'Damn! I'm working on Saturday. Doing the lunches, so I'm not likely to be back before half past three at the earliest. I'll come round then, though.'

Victoria's heart sank. Her mother would be furious. She would expect Claudia to have made her promise to help a top priority.

'That's fine,' she said anxiously, which it would have to be, although she knew it would cause trouble.

'I can come whenever you need me,' said Jerome. 'What sort of thing will I be expected to do? I don't know the first thing about gardens, you realise, so I must have a purely menial role. Or decorative. I could be a fishing gnome.'

Victoria grinned. 'Oh, that doesn't matter. Mum wants you and me on the gate. You know, collecting the entrance money and giving out the tickets. Could you be round by half past one? Is that OK?'

'Yeah, sure,' said Jerome. Silence fell. Jerome looked at his mother and she looked at the table, and Victoria could tell that there was something going on between them and that she was an unwanted third.

'I'd better be getting back,' she said, nervously twisting her hair up into a knot and then letting it fall.

'Yeah. OK,' said Jerome. Claudia looked up and smiled briefly, but Victoria could see that she hardly registered her presence and that she was absorbed by her own thoughts.

Jerome went with her to the gate, not saying much either, and as she took off back to East End House, Victoria thought how complicated other people's lives were and how little she really knew Jerome. He was only how he *appeared* to her, as a kind of finished product, but all the other stuff, all the complicated family stuff which made people what they really were, she was ignorant of. She realised she had just glimpsed something under the surface that she knew nothing about and couldn't even guess at.

'All right, Tor?' called her mother as she reappeared in the garden. 'All on for Saturday?'

There was no point in putting it off. 'Jerome will come round early, but Claudia can't be here until later, 'cos she's got to work.'

'What? I don't believe it! I especially asked her to keep the afternoon free! It's really too bad of her.' Julia threw down her hoe and put her hands on her hips. This was exactly what Victoria had expected and it went on for some time, the indignation in her mother's voice rising, and eventually including her father and Tom, who loved a good row and came out of hiding to see what the trouble was.

'I don't suppose she has much choice in the matter,' said Peter peaceably. 'If she's a relief cook, I expect she has to work when she's wanted.'

'That's nonsense. She could have asked to have Saturday off.'

Tom went to collect his bicycle from the barn and bent down to fasten his cycle clips. He straightened up and cocked a stiff old leg over the cross bar.

'Come Saturday, them old folks'll be wanting their dinners, same as usual,' he said, 'bloody garden open or not.' With that he wobbled away with Scamp trotting behind. 'That's done it,' he grumbled to himself as he freewheeled down to The Bugle. 'That's it, right and proper. I'm not going back there this side of Christmas.'

Betty was full of it when she arrived at Valerie Pomeroy's.

'That's Tom walked out again,' she said. 'It's the same every year, regular as clockwork. He told Monica he'll not put up with that b— woman any longer. Not a moment's peace, he says.'

Valerie laughed. She liked to hear unfavourable reports of Julia. Petty of her, she knew, but satisfying all the same. 'What's happened now?' she asked, putting the kettle on the Aga.

Betty started to run water into the sink where there was a stack of washing up waiting for her. 'Oh, the usual,' she said over her shoulder. 'The garden, you know. It's open this Saturday. Flat out, she's been. Getting it ready. You can't blame her for wanting it to look nice, can you, but Tom won't take it. Not from her or any other woman, he says.'

'She is insufferably bossy, you have to admit. Are you doing the teas again?'

'I am. Devil for punishment, aren't I?' said Betty. 'Me and Star, as usual. She's bringing that lad of hers to help put up the tables. It's hard work, on your feet all the afternoon, but you see a bit of life. Last year we had that actor from the telly who lives up on Dancing Hill. Ever so charming he was. Came back for a second cup. And the Bishop. The retired one from the Old Forge, and there was Star wearing one of them vest tops with those bosoms of hers bursting out, handing him his drop scones. "Here Bishop," she says, "have some cream with those!" Then she winks at me and bursts out laughing. Bold as brass she was. I didn't know where to look and neither did the Bishop. Mrs Durnford tried to get her to wear an apron, to cover up a bit, but she wasn't having any of it. Threw it under the table.'

Valerie chuckled.

'Greg's not happy either,' said Betty. 'Pat says he's not had a weekend off for weeks, what with the harvest and calving, but Brewer says he's got to be around on Saturday in case it rains and the cars get stuck. Dear, oh dear! Angie says she's not washing up again. Said she was left to do it all last year and Mrs Durnford told her off for smoking in her kitchen. "Do it yourself then," she said.'

'Quite right. Bloody woman,' said Valerie. 'Here, Betty, sit down a minute and have your tea.' She cleared a space on the table for the two mugs and sat down heavily. 'I've some news for you, as well. Christopher is hoping to get a stand-by flight in the next day or two. He may very well be here by the weekend.'

'Oh, that's good,' said Betty, sitting down opposite. 'That's lovely. I'll make his bed up and give his room a turn out. You're not going to the airport to collect him, are you? You're not up to driving all that way.'

'No, he's renting a car. It will be wonderful to see him. It seems such a long time since he was last over.'

But no girls, thought Betty, stirring her tea. That's what really matters, that the girls aren't coming. That's what she'll be thinking.

'We ought to tell Lila,' said Jerome, as he and Claudia sat in the kitchen after Victoria had gone. 'She may want to come over. To be here for Dad.'

'Yes, we should,' agreed Claudia. 'But I don't think there's any reason to fly back. I gather from David that it's just a decision which has to be taken by a judge on whether Roger has leave to appeal against his conviction. It's a sort of first step in a long procedure. To begin with it looked as if there was a fairly strong case to be made for an interlocutory appeal, based on some technical detail about the scope of the original indictment. I don't understand it, Jerome, it's far too complicated for a layman, but the argument was that the judge at a preparatory hearing had wrongly disallowed some evidence which Roger's lawyers claimed was relevant to the case. Now, it seems, after further legal advice, David doesn't hold out much hope. There have to be clear grounds for making an appeal and now it seems this particular evidence would not have affected the outcome of the trial. He thinks Roger's case will be thrown out on Friday. Whichever way it goes, it will bring him back into the limelight and David says we can expect some press interest. Hence the reappearance of Mr Freddy Hobbs. So, Lila should at least be warned. Do you think you could email her from Valerie's? It would be the easiest way. It's so hard to get her on the telephone.'

'OK. I'll ask Mrs P. I'm sure she won't mind. I'm going round tomorrow for a Hindustani lesson.'

Claudia smiled at her son. 'Who would have believed that in a little village in deepest Dorset you could find a Hindustani teacher? It's a bit of luck, isn't it, to find ourselves living next door to such an interesting person.'

'Yeah. She's cool. But Mum, what are we going to do? Shouldn't we have some sort of strategy worked out to deal with the press? After the judge's decision is made public, that Hobbesian bloke may be back.'

'I don't know,' said Claudia. 'I've thought of that, but I don't want to go on the run again and it's not fair to dump on Minna. She's too busy and has her own life. You told me that you were prepared to face up to it, and that encouraged me to think I should do too. David doesn't believe it will be anything like such a big deal this time. He says that the climate has changed, that there have been a number of City scandals since Roger's trial and that he is not such hot news any more. The general public have probably forgotten all about him by now. There's been no sign of Freddy since you lot saw him off, so maybe he doesn't think we're worth pursuing. That's what I hope, anyway.'

She stood up. 'It's getting late. Let's have something to eat. I got some very rustic looking sausages at the farmer's market in Stur today, produced from pigs who lead such a happy life it makes you want to weep. What about bangers and mash?' Turning, she noticed Finn under the table chewing a shoe. 'Finn! You fiend! Jerome, that wretched puppy's got my shoe!'

Jerome pulled the little dog out by his rear end but he was not going to give up so easily and hung on to his trophy, hoping for a contest. He savaged the shoe and growled throatily and they had to laugh.

'He's so naughty,' said Claudia, watching him trotting round the kitchen, head high, shoe in mouth. 'What am I going to do with him when you go to university? It's typical of Lila not to think of the practicalities of me keeping a dog.'

'Mum!' protested Jerome. 'Don't say that. Not in front of him. He'll feel unwanted and become psychologically scarred!'

'Yes, and that's not the only thing he'll be if you don't get my shoe back.'

As Jerome tried to catch the excited dog and Claudia laughed at their antics, he thought that perhaps Lila knew what she was doing after all. He was a wonderful diversion, this wilful scrap of grey fur and needle teeth, and it was good to hear his mother laugh.

Later that night, or perhaps in the early hours of the following morning, Jerome woke from a nightmare which had been so real that he found himself still gripped by terror. In the dark, his eyes sought the familiar shapes of his bedroom, the bulk of the table piled with books, the chair in the corner, the dark rectangle of the door, but he could not rid himself of the vivid image of the crowded bus lurching past where he stood at the roadside. As it went by, he saw his father and Jabeena sitting together, looking out at him and smiling, and although he shouted and banged the sides of the bus, he couldn't make it stop and all the time he knew that the terrible accident was about to happen.

Friday came and went. In the morning Greg delivered the tables and chairs from the village hall, unloading them in a heap on the gravel. Then he reversed the tractor and trailer, and knocked over a staddle stone and ran over a bit of mown grass, leaving distinct tyre imprints. Julia, who had been on the telephone and unable to go out and supervise, was furious. She got straight back on the telephone to Anthony but only got his answer machine.

'Calm down, Mum!' said Victoria. 'It won't take long to stack them and the stone isn't broken. It just needs standing up again. I thought you said Rosco was coming to help. He and I can do it in the morning.'

Star, who was sloshing about on the kitchen floor with her mop, agreed. 'He'll come over first thing,' she said. 'You'll have to pay him, mind, because he'd usually be at his Saturday job.'

Julia was not so easily pacified. 'It's disgraceful,' she fumed. 'I will certainly get hold of Anthony and tell him. He's just thrown them off the trailer any old how, being deliberately unhelpful. I've always thought he was a bolshie young man.'

Oh yeah? I'll tell him that, thought Star, emptying the water in the outside drain and stopping to have a cigarette in the sunshine.

'Mum, he had to load them all by himself, I expect. That must have taken ages,' pointed out Victoria. Star winked at her and she blushed.

'What about the way he's cut up the lawn? That was so careless and unnecessary.'

'We can put the tea table over that bit,' said Victoria. 'No one will notice. Come on, Mum, for goodness sake. It's not such a disaster. Not on a world scale, is it? Think of those awful floods in India and that poor woman on the news, having to give birth up a tree.'

Julia turned on her daughter. 'Victoria, I don't know what's got into you, but I am getting more than a little tired of those sort of remarks. I really am! Is it Jerome who's influencing you? He's one of those too clever by half young men, isn't he? Well, I'm sick of you being a smart-arse at my expense, and I won't put up with it!'

Star grinned and stubbed out her cigarette on the sole of her trainer before posting the butt down the drain.

'Sorry, Mum,' said Victoria. 'I didn't mean to upset you.' She felt genuinely contrite and went to put her arm round her mother who looked as if she might be about to cry. 'Come on, you were going to show me what you wanted me to write on those plant labels.'

Things had simmered down by lunchtime, when Star finished work and promised she would be back in the morning. She'd made a good job of the house, Julia had to admit, cleaning the windows and stripping the kitchen in preparation for the teas. Victoria cut them both a tomato sandwich which they ate outside the back door in the sun. Her mother poured some white wine from the box she kept in the fridge. 'We've earned this,' she said, handing Victoria a glass. 'Here's to Chateau Cardboard!'

After they had eaten, mellowed by the wine, Julia squinted into the sun and said, 'Sorry I flew off the handle earlier.'

'I'm sorry I annoyed you,' said Victoria, and they managed a smile at one another.

'It's too late now to do anything more,' said Julia. 'The die is

233

cast, as it were. I have to say, it doesn't look half bad, does it? I'm quite proud of the garden when I see it like this.'

'Granny would be pleased,' said Victoria and her mother turned to look at her.

'So she would,' she agreed. 'With a fraction of the help she and Grandpa had, I manage to keep it going. No mean feat, though I say it myself.'

But is it worth it? Victoria asked herself silently, and made a vow that when she had her own home she would make sure it had no garden. I'd really like to live in Jena's bus, she thought, and be surrounded by wild stuff. This was not a thought to share with her mother. Instead, looking up at the blue sky, she remarked, 'Let's hope it's like this tomorrow.'

On Friday morning Valerie Pomeroy awaited the arrival of her son, Christopher, who had telephoned to say that his flight was due at Heathrow at ten thirty and that all being well he should be with her in Dorset by early afternoon. It was hard to be patient and she found she could not settle to do anything worthwhile. She went into Sharston to do a bit of shopping – with Christopher staying she would have to make more effort with meals – and bought a piece of lamb which they could have either hot or cold depending on whether he wanted to eat or sleep when he finally arrived. Betty had prepared his room and done a grand job of clearing up the kitchen so that there was space for them both to eat at the table.

She picked up the newspaper but put it down again and went upstairs to her study to check a reference which had been bothering her in an academic paper she had been reading. When she got up there she found she had left the paper downstairs. It was maddening to be so absent-minded. Instead, she sat down at her computer and switched it on. Idly, she checked her emails, hoping there might be something from Guy. Nothing. Flicking through the commands, she landed on deleted items. Skimming down the list to sort out what she wanted to save and what to discard, she found a message she did not recognise. She put it up on the screen and read it before she realised that it was Jerome's email to his sister, sent two days ago.

Valerie sat stunned. Now, of course, everything made sense. She read the message again before pressing the delete button and eliminating it from her computer. Her mistake had been quite genuine and she felt no guilt at having read what had not been intended for her. Instead, she felt a huge wave of compassion for her young friend, and for Claudia. Particularly for Claudia. She remembered the first meeting, that night in the kitchen when she had been so drunk. She remembered how her hand had smoothed Claudia's hair as if she had been one of her granddaughters, and Claudia had wept. It moved her now to re-live that moment of mutual vulnerability. Getting up and going to the window, she looked out across the sunlit garden and over the fields to the distant hills. Yes, now it all made sense. The desire for privacy, the desperate need to find a job and, above all, what she had first noticed about her new neighbour, a kind of uprightness and aloofness, both in bearing and manner. That is her defence, thought Valerie, that determination to stand apart, not to be brought low, and it is a fragile sort of shield against what she must have endured and what she will have to face in this village if the truth gets out. A sense of purpose began to develop as she stood there by her window. Claudia and Jerome would need her support, and by God, they'd get it.

When Claudia got back from work on Friday, Jerome came out to meet her car.

'Well?' she asked. 'Have you heard anything?' She scanned his face, looking for signs.

'David's just telephoned,' he said. 'Bad news for Dad. He hasn't been allowed the right to appeal. It was like you said, the judge didn't consider there were strong enough grounds.'

Claudia sat on in the car, considering the implications. 'How is he?' she asked. 'Did David say how he's taken it?'

'Fairly resigned, he said. Dad wasn't at the hearing but he has since made a statement for the press. They were all there in court, David said, but the result was too late for the evening papers.'

'What statement?' asked Claudia, instantly suspicious.

'David read it to me and I scribbled it down. Come in, Mum, and I'll show you.'

'Does Lila know?' she asked as she got out of the car and slammed the door.

'Yes, I got her at work. She seemed odd about it, rather abrupt, but I think it was probably hard to speak in front of everyone in her office.'

Claudia nodded.

'Here it is, Mum.' Jerome picked up a piece of paper from the kitchen table and handed it to her. She read it with one hand on her chest, as if preparing herself for a shock while Jerome watched anxiously. She put the paper back on the table without commenting. Her face had a strange blank look.

'What do you think, Mum?' he asked.

'I think he's landed us right in it,' she said grimly. She picked the paper up again and read out loud, ' "While it is a disappoint-ment to have lost the right to appeal, I am resigned to serving the sentence imposed by the courts. My intention is to build a new and different life when I leave prison, to restore my marriage, to repay my family for their love and support, and to give something worthwhile back to society." It's utter rubbish. Surely you see through it, Jerome. He's using us, just like he wanted to use me when he was arrested, to create this fictitious idea of a loving family man. It's a sham!'

'But Mum, he is a loving family man! He is to Lila and me. We both feel that. I know he was rotten to you, but he's always been great to us. We've never doubted that he loved us.'

Claudia was silent, her face set, re-reading the paper in her hand. 'How dare he say "restore my marriage"! How dare he, when it was him who smashed it to pieces, who betrayed me in every way possible? He doesn't have a marriage to restore! He conveniently forgets that!'

Jerome shrugged. 'Perhaps he hopes he can,' he suggested quietly.

'Jerome, please! It's absolutely over. Stone dead. He killed it. What does he think I am, that I will believe this sort of lying statement produced by him for his own advantage? I was a fool once, but I'm not any more.'

'OK, Mum. OK. Only you really know the truth.'

'Wait a minute, Jerome. You have the evidence. What more do you need than that? He left me, remember. Moved out and lived with Carla. Where does she come into all this, I wonder?'

'What I meant was that no one outside a relationship can ever really know how things are between a couple. Or why.'

'Thank you, Jerome. Thank you at least for that! I don't have to remind you of how clever your father is, or how manipula-tive. For some reason the idea of resurrecting his marriage is useful to him. I expect it's how he wants to portray himself – contrite and full of earnest endeavour. It makes me sick!'

Jerome saw that it would be wise to change the subject. 'Do you think this will bring the press looking for us again? Wanting you to make a comment?'

'Yes, I do. Don't you? It almost offers them a story.'

Jerome sighed. He could see what she meant. 'David said that any interest would be short-lived.'

'Was that supposed to be a comfort?'

'Just for information, I think. There's some more news as well. Dad is going to be moved to an open prison in Hampshire. Possibly tomorrow, so the rat pack might follow that trail and forget about us.'

'I see.' Claudia put the piece of paper in the bin and turned back to her son. 'Come on,' she said, in a determinedly upbeat voice. 'Let's take Finn for a walk and stop somewhere for a drink. Make the most of this lovely evening.'

'Oh, Mum,' said Jerome, putting his arms round her. 'I wish I could put things right for you.'

Claudia hugged him back. His body felt less bony and frail. 'Do you know, darling, I think you've put on a bit of weight? You're not quite such a scarecrow. Having you well and happy means more to me than anything. You and Lila. Nothing else really matters.'

If I'm well and happy, then I betray what Jabeena meant to me, thought Jerome sadly.

On Saturday it was Victoria who first noticed that there was something odd going on. She and Rosco had spent the morning putting up the tea tables and chairs and pinning down the paper cloths to stop them blowing away. Her mother had swooped down on them twice and rearranged things but she seemed satisfied now with more or less how they had it in the first place. Then they were told to unpack the china and set the individual tables, each for four people. The china proved to be dusty and had to be wiped over, which took hours. A time and motion expert might have had some suggestions to make, Victoria thought as she took each piece out of the cardboard box and wiped it with a tea towel and handed it to Rosco who wandered away to place it in a fairly haphazard fashion on a table. His idea of place setting was a bit hit or miss. He didn't notice when cups were without saucers and sometimes used saucers as plates, or vice versa, and slung knives and teaspoons about any old how. He was so hopeless that it started to make her giggle, and him, too. He looked so funny, padding about in his fashionably baggy shorts with the crotch somewhere round his knees, pulled even lower by an inexplicable heavy chain which dangled in a loop from his pocket, and his outsize trainers and shaved head.

'Here,' she said, tossing him the tea towel, 'you'd better let me do that. You wipe the china.' But they were being silly by then and he started to throw the plates to her as if they were frisbees, and she was such a pathetic catcher that she kept dropping them on the grass until they were both helpless with laughter.

When that job was finally done, Rosco was summoned to help her father to rope off parts of the paddock for parking, and Victoria was sent down the drive to put up the notices to direct the visitors from the lane.

Emerging from the gates of East End House, she was surprised to see a gaggle of men standing about in the lane and several cars pulled up on the verge opposite the bungalow. At first she thought they were visitors who had arrived too early, and then she saw that they all had cumbersome-looking cameras around their necks. They were talking and laughing amongst themselves in a chummy sort of way, passing round cigarettes and using mobile telephones. Victoria stood and watched and realised that the garden was not what they had come to see, and that their focus of interest was next door. As she watched, one of them climbed onto his car bonnet to get a better view, pointing his lens at where the bungalow sat, yellow and ugly in the sunlight.

What on earth was going on? She stepped back out of view and thought furiously. Had something awful happened? Like a robbery or a murder? What about Jerome? Claudia would be at work by now, so perhaps something dreadful had happened to Jerome. She must find out. Throwing down her notices she ran over to the men and seeking the one who looked the most friendly, said, 'What's going on? What are you doing?' They all turned to look at her.

'You a neighbour, darling?' said the friendly one.

'Yes. Yes, I am. I live right there,' and she pointed at the gates. They all crowded round her then, asking questions. 'What's your name, love, Age? How long have you known your neighbours? Can you give us a description of them? Just the two of them, are there? What's the woman like? Has she got a boyfriend?'

'Wait! Wait!' cried Victoria, thoroughly alarmed and frightened. 'What's happened? You must tell me!'

'Don't you know, then? Their old man's in prison, love. Been all over the papers. All we want is some pictures and a bit of a story. What did you say your name was?'

Victoria turned and fled.

★ ★ ★

Jerome was holed up in the bathroom when his mobile telephone rang. He had locked all the doors and drawn the curtains and taken the telephone off the hook when he realised that he was under siege. Now he sat on the lavatory seat summoning up the courage to emerge, not really trusting that none of the bastards had broken in and would confront him in the hall.

He picked up the telephone and pressed the call button. With huge relief he heard Victoria's breathless voice saying, 'Jerome? Jerome?'

'Yeah,' he said, 'it's me. Victoria, do you know what's going on?'

'I've just found out. I was in the lane. Those men, they're all there, with cameras, wanting photographs they said. Or a story. I ran away. Jerome, are you OK?'

'Yeah, I'm OK. Just angry and terrified. I'm worried about Mum. When she gets back from work they'll catch her outside. She'll walk right into them. I'm trying to work out a way of getting out of here. I'm not thinking too straight at the moment.'

'You can't get out at the front. They're all over the lane. They won't be able to leave their cars there, though. Nothing can get through. Nothing big like a tractor.'

'Hang on, Tor. That's given me an idea. It could work. Do you think you could get Anthony Brewer to send a tractor up, some bloody big vehicle which will force them to move? Meanwhile, stick your parking signs up, and suggest they park in your paddock. They're sure to agree, to save all the hassle. While they're doing that, I'll make a run for it. You can give me a couple of rings on my phone when the coast is clear. I'll warn Mum not to come home.'

'OK, I'll do that, but you'll never get out. They'll leave someone on the lookout, and Jerome, you can't run, remember.'

'I'm not going through the front.'

'Where then?'

'Tor, I can't tell you now. I've got a lot to get ready. Can you do what I asked you? If any of it goes pear-shaped, then ring me again. Otherwise I'll expect your signal in about half an hour. Just two rings, remember, and I'll scarper.'

'OK.'

'And Tor? You're a great girl. You know that?'

Off the telephone, Jerome worked fast. He gathered together

the bits and pieces he thought that he and his mother would need to last them for a week or so, jamming toiletries and towels in a plastic bag and tossing a selection of clothes and books in a bin liner. He tried to think things through clearly, but it was so strange to be moving round the bungalow in the gloom, acutely aware of the menace outside and unable to either see or hear what was going on. He didn't dare open the curtains even a crack to look out. He strained his ears for the sound of a tractor and thought he could hear the throbbing of a diesel engine, but couldn't be sure. He went to the back door and thought out his route, praying that he wouldn't be delayed by any unforeseen hitch. Then he hurried back to his room and found a length of Indian cotton and wrapped his head and face in it to disguise his features. Every few minutes he checked the time. He was standing by the door, ready to go, when he got Victoria's signal and in sudden convulsive action he almost fell out into the back garden, Finn's lead round his legs, clutching the bags in one hand and fumbling to lock the door behind him. It took him only a second or two to reach the door in the wall, and in the cover of the overgrown roses he threw the bags over, and put his shoulder to the creaking wood. It stuck, as he guessed it would, and he shoved again. It seemed ages before he had forced an inch or two to give way at the bottom and he scrambled through, dragging Finn behind him. Not waiting to collect the bags he made a one-legged dash across the over-grown grass for the sanctuary of Valerie's kitchen.

Chapter Fourteen

Christopher Pomeroy was slicing onions in the kitchen. The only thing to do with the piece of lamb his mother had forgotten to take out of the oven was to make it into a curry, and he already had some ground spices gently frying in oil, scenting the kitchen with their evocative aroma. He hummed happily as he worked. It was a pleasure to have time to mess about like this, away from the telephone and fax machine, and the incessant bothering of his daughters. He thought fondly of them now, wondering about little Rosie who had cried and clung to him when he left and begged to be allowed to accompany him to England. He had nearly relented but knew that she was better off at home with her sisters and the housekeeper and nanny. Had she come, she would be bored by now, whining that there was nothing to do and no one to play with. She was enrolled in summer school which would keep her happily occupied until he got back and then he would take them all off for a beach holiday somewhere.

He consulted his watch, hoping it was time to have a drink. He could do with a triple g & t, clinking with ice, or a glass of chilled white wine, or a beer. Still a bit too early, unfortunately, and of course his mother was trying to cut down. Yesterday he discovered she had had only one bottle of Scotch in the pantry, which was a good sign and he had been relieved to find that she looked much the same. Not really ill at all. A little slower, perhaps. A little more tired last night than she might have been in the past when they used to sit up together until the early hours, chewing the fat, as she called it.

It was not the time to raise his concerns about her, or the suggestions he had to make about the future. That could wait. Finishing with the onions he chucked them in the pan with the spices and gave them a stir with a wooden spoon. Turning back to the table, he heard the back door bang open with such violence that he jumped, and a figure burst in, a tall veiled figure, so extraordinary that he would later dine out on the description of what he saw before him.

Jerome, who had flung himself headlong into the room, was equally taken aback. The very large man in Valerie's kitchen, with an apron tied round his ample waist, reacted to his sudden entrance by thrusting the point of a sharp knife in his direction and shouting, 'What the hell? Get out! Get out of here!'

'It's me! Jerome! It's me!' he cried, holding up his hands to show he had no malicious intent and pulling off the chech he had wound round his head. Christopher saw a bony young face emerge, with wide-set startled brown eyes and a gentle mouth and knew instantly that this was no malevolent intruder. At that moment his mother appeared, disturbed by the shouting. She took in her son and her neighbour facing each other across the kitchen table. 'What's going on?' she said. 'Christopher, this is Jerome. A friend. What's happened?'

Jerome stood, breathing heavily, not knowing where to start on his explanation.

'Do you mind if I sit down?' he asked. 'I gave my leg a hell of a knock getting through that door in the wall. Then I'll tell you. I'll tell you everything.'

'You don't need to,' she said briskly. 'I know about some of it.' She pointed to the newspaper on the kitchen table. 'It's in there, you see.'

'Tell me again,' said Christopher, 'about the rat pack. Are they out there now?' He indicated the garden.

Jerome nodded. 'Sure to be,' he said. 'They're staking out the bungalow. It was the greatest bit of luck that I got out,' and he explained again the part that Victoria had played.

'She's a good girl,' said Valerie approvingly. 'But now we've got to think about your mother. They'll be looking out for her car and will spot her if she drives in here. We'll have to think of some other plan. Have you been in touch with her at work?'

'No. I didn't have time. I just wanted to get out, to get away. It felt like being in a trap, stuck in there, hardly daring to move.'

'I think Anthony Brewer might help again,' said Valerie thoughtfully. 'If I can get him on the telephone I will suggest that your mother takes the other, longer, route home, by way of Sharston, which will bring her into the top end of the village, and that she goes straight to Manor Farm and that Anthony drives her here in the pick-up. He can cover her up with sacks or something. That way they won't get a glimpse of her and won't know that she's here, next door. What do you think?'

'Fantastic,' said Jerome, 'if he doesn't mind helping us.'

'Why should he?' she asked sharply. 'Do you know her number at work?'

Christopher, who had been out in the garden to retrieve the plastic bags that Jerome had lobbed over the gate and had walked down the drive to get a look at the press men, came back into the kitchen. He put down the bags. 'They're still there,' he reported. 'Milling about, looking fairly bored. About fifteen of them now, I'd say. I wonder how long they'll stick it out.'

'Bloody jackals, aren't they?' said Valerie angrily. 'What a miserable, bloody occupation, hounding innocent people like this.' She caught Jerome's eye and gave him a bolstering sort of look and went out to telephone from the hall. She's totally on our side, he thought. At least Mum will have her support. And the other thing was, she had asked no questions, didn't want to delve into exactly what his father had done or whether he really was guilty – all the sort of things that people generally wanted to know and had a salacious interest in.

Christopher had put the apron back on and was finishing off the curry. He's like his mother, thought Jerome, looking at his wide back, the striped shirt stretched across the well-fed belly. He was very tall, too, so the general impression was of a looming bulkiness. His face was heavy and genial, with good-humoured blue eyes, and he had a loud and ready laugh. His thinning, pale hair was rather long, combed back from his forehead. He bent over the pan, tasting its contents from a teaspoon with one hand and drinking from a glass of beer with the other. He was large, reassuring, unflappable, humming as he tasted and stirred and checked on the rice simmering in another pan. He was taking the whole thing totally in his stride, as if there was nothing unusual happening in his mother's sleepy Dorset village and Jerome found this sense of normality tremendously calming. He began to breathe more easily and to think more clearly.

He wondered how Victoria was getting on. He had telephoned her on her mobile but there was no answer and he left a message thanking her for her help and saying he was sorry to have involved her and that she should get in touch with him as soon as she could. Poor Victoria, he thought, he had really landed her in it and also let her down. He imagined her having to take the entrance money on her own and having no reasonable explanation to give her parents when they asked her what the hell was going on.

'That's that,' said Valerie, coming back in. 'I've spoken to Anthony and he is perfectly agreeable. More than willing to help, as I said he would be. Now I think you should telephone your mother.'

Jerome got to his feet. I've handed over completely, he thought. It's a relief to have Mrs Pomeroy do all the organising. It's a relief that it's not just us any more. Mum, me and Lila versus the rest of the world.

'Take a beer with you,' said Christopher, 'but don't be long or this curry will spoil.'

As far as Julia was concerned, and as she loudly told everyone, her garden opening had been wrecked. By the time she had realised that there was something going on, the press had parked their vehicles in the paddock and were swarming everywhere. Rosco, pocketing a fold of ten pound notes, had shown them where the ladders were kept in the barn and they had helped themselves and had leaned them up against the wall and took it in turns to clamber up and take photographs of the rear of the bungalow, trampling over the flowerbeds and grinding out their cigarettes on the grass.

Julia had tried to get Peter to evict their cars from the paddock but he hastily explained he had charged them a tenner each and he couldn't very well get rid of them now. Meanwhile the wretched men strolled in and out, bought cups of tea from Star and occupied the tables as if they had been set out for their sole use. The worst thing of all was that they *dominated* the afternoon, swamping the proper visitors, the mild gardening women in their flat shoes and cardigans, and diverting attention from the garden and all Julia's hard work. Of course, everybody wanted to know what was going on, and Julia was furious that she knew nothing about it, that she had had no idea at all that she was living next door to the wife of a notorious criminal and had even had her round to supper and introduced her to her friends. She felt as if she was a victim herself, almost as if she had been mugged, she told everybody loudly. The least Claudia could have done was to have taken her into her confidence, after all that she'd done to make her feel welcome in the village.

Of course, now she knew the truth, she wasn't surprised, she told anyone who would listen. There had always been something very odd about Claudia. She had said so to Peter, hadn't she? It just didn't add up, living in that bungalow but with all that stuff in the garage. What stuff? Boxes of stuff. Loot, she realised now. Designer stuff. It was at this point that Peter intervened and told her fiercely to be quiet, to say nothing more. In fact, he took her by the arm and almost marched her inside and into the drawing room where he shut the door and told her not to be so stupid, to say nothing in earshot of the reporters, that she could get herself into very serious trouble if she carried on like that. She had had to shut up then. She had never seen him so angry.

Later in the afternoon, Greg Whittle came down the lane on the tractor, and set up a ring main electric fence round the bungalow, keeping everyone well back off the drive and saying nothing to the reporters who jostled round him like cattle, just grinning in a maddening, local yokel sort of manner.

Peter and Victoria did what they could to keep things going in as normal a way as possible, taking entrance money and parking cars and shrugging off inquiries, but speculation and gossip buzzed backwards and forwards all the afternoon like a swarm of bees. Star loved it, hurrying in and out to fill the tea urn, laughing and flirting and cadging cigarettes from the reporters. Betty listened, not saying much, but taking it all in, genuinely shocked by the news. Whoever would have thought it? Mrs Knight had seemed a nice, respectable sort of woman. Kept herself to herself, and no wonder. She said as much to Mr Durnford and he said, 'She still is, Betty. A nice respectable woman. This makes no difference.' But of course it did. You couldn't pretend otherwise. Betty had seen it all her life. A woman was judged by her family, by the man she married and how her kids turned out. If your kids or your old man got into trouble, you went down with them. People might feel sorry for you, but you were disgraced all right, along with them.

It was a relief to Peter Durnford when the rain set in around four thirty and the visitors started to drift away and the teas were hastily moved to the barn. He got rid of the last car just after five o'clock and then told the reporters that they had to move their vehicles because he was going to lock the paddock gate. There was a bit of grumbling and the less determined decided to call it a day. There wasn't much of a story anyway, they decided, and unless they had a picture in time for the Sunday editions, it was dead in the water. Two or three moved their cars to a wider bit of verge on the Bishops Barton road and then walked back to shelter under the trees by Valerie Pomeroy's drive. The electric fence kept them from straying up Claudia's drive and training their lenses on the blank windows of the bungalow.

'Bleeding waste of time, this,' said one of them to Freddy Hobbs. 'How long are you going to stick it out?'

'Until it gets dark,' he said. 'Then I'm buggering off home. I don't think she's in there anyway, and if she's not, she won't come back tonight. Not now she knows we're here.'

Peter put his back into clearing up. Julia had to give him that. Wearing an extremely old raincoat with the waist tied with orange binder twine, he busied in and out, pulling up the notices and removing the ropes. He decided to padlock the ladders in the barn and with Victoria dismantled the tea tables and chairs and stacked them ready for collection by Greg on Monday morning.

Star and Rosco had gone home after the excitement had died down, calling in to The Bugle on the way, to give Monica an up-to-date report of the goings-on. Betty was left to do the last of the washing up and to pack the china away into the boxes for returning to the village hall. Her feet ached and she felt troubled by the happenings of the afternoon. She wondered where Mrs Knight and that nice boy had gone. She supposed they had had to make a run for it, like chased animals. She thought of Mrs Pomeroy and what she would have to say about it, and meanwhile Mrs Durnford went on and on until her head ached. She had one of those voices which went right through you, thought Betty, and when she wasn't carrying on at her while she was trying to count the teaspoons, she was on the telephone, talking to her friends.

Mr Durnford was different. He seemed quiet and rather upset. A bit like she felt, she thought. He sat at the table with the tea money in a biscuit tin, counting out the float and totting up the takings. What with the car park charges he'd levied on the reporters and the entrance money, they had made a record sum. The vicar would be pleased, but it seemed almost like blood money, she thought. She didn't like to ask what it was that Mrs Knight's husband had done. To hear Mrs Durnford, you'd think he was Jack the Ripper or one of those Kray brothers. Mrs Durnford had shown her the piece in the paper but it was only a small inside column headed, 'City fraudster denied right to appeal'. Nothing very sensational and no picture and it didn't make it any clearer to her what it was he was inside for.

When she'd finished in the kitchen, she wiped down the tops

and changed her shoes and said she'd be off. Mrs Durnford was still on the telephone and just waved a hand in salute. Betty was glad to get out and collect her bicycle. Mr Durnford went outside and walked with her down the drive. 'I wish we could do something to help them, Betty,' he said, miserably. 'It isn't as if Claudia or Jerome have done anything wrong.' That was it though. When you were a wife, you shared the guilt and the shame and the sorrow. Settling her plastic hood over her head she mounted her bicycle and cycled slowly home through the rain.

Peter was in despair. The one thing he might have done for Claudia was to protect her from the intrusion of the press and this he had singularly failed to do; in fact, by the time Victoria had diverted their cars into the paddock and they were swarming in and out of the garden, he felt that he was almost acting as their host. It was maddening that Anthony Brewer had come to the rescue, clearing the lane with the tractor and trailer and then thinking of setting up the electric fence. Peter had seen him driving his pick-up into Valerie's during the afternoon but he hadn't stopped, just swept past with a wave of his hand.

Peter had pored over the newspaper column. Claudia was mentioned, not by name, but as Roger Barron's 'estranged wife', and there was no indication of where she was now living. It was hard on her that she had been run to ground. If anything the revelation about her past had endeared her to Peter more than ever. It lent her a certain heightened drama and glamour. No wonder she had always seemed different, more special than Julia's cronies. Peter thought of her driven out and alone somewhere. He knew she had Jerome but preferred to think of her alone. He remembered how frightened she had been when she had hidden in Anthony Brewer's car that evening and how she had trembled in his arms. If only he could find her he would go at once to reassure and offer her comfort and protection. Julia had incensed him with her stupid condemnation and lack of compassion. He didn't know how he could forgive her. He preferred to stay out here in the rain than go inside and have to face her while he was filled with such intense dislike. He wondered vaguely where Victoria had got to. He hadn't seen her for some time. She would be upset too. She was rather fond of Jerome.

Peter would have been dismayed to discover that had it not been for the bizarre circumstances, something like a party atmosphere prevailed next door at Valerie's. By the time Claudia had been delivered in the back of Anthony's pick-up, covered by a tarpaulin and some half-empty sacks of sheep nuts, Jerome, Christopher and his mother had enjoyed the curry and a couple of bottles of wine.

When Claudia came through the back door, shepherded in by Anthony and brushing the straw and dirt from her sweater, they all got up from the table to greet her. Jerome reached his mother first and put his arms round her and she hugged him back.

'Well done, Mum!' he said, not quite knowing why. Valerie was next. She clasped Claudia's hands and squeezed them between her own.

'My dear!' she said and Claudia felt her eyes welling up with tears which she hastily brushed away with her sleeve. Christopher stood beside his mother, waiting to be introduced, and Valerie turned to do so and he in turn hugged Claudia as if he was an old friend. He then opened another bottle of wine and passed glasses to Anthony and Claudia.

'Thank you all so much,' Claudia gasped, sniffing. 'God, what a nightmare. This is what we had hoped to avoid. The children and me. I'm so sorry to have disrupted your day and brought this nuisance to the village.'

'For goodness sake! You're not a carrier of the plague. It's hardly your fault!' interrupted Valerie. 'Now, you know that Jerome was cool-headed enough to pack up a few things for you? You can stay here until it quietens down. I gather that you don't think the press interest will last for long.'

'That's terribly kind. No, I don't think so. We're not very hot news any more. Roger gets moved to an open prison today or tomorrow and then after that I think he will be a back number, and so will we.'

'Have you seen what's in the paper?' asked Anthony, picking up the broadsheet from the kitchen table and passing it to her. 'It's hardly sensational, is it?'

Claudia read the item quickly and looked up. 'There was much more in the tabloids. I saw them while I was at work. The old people love the most scandal-mongering stuff – you know, all sport and sex. There was one photograph of me, but unrecognisable, I'm glad to say. Taken at least ten years ago, hanging on Roger's arm at a banquet in full fig. It made me feel ill to look at it.'

Silence fell for a moment and then Anthony said gently,

'There's no reason, is there, that you can't just resume your quiet life here when this dies down?'

Claudia looked at him. 'I don't know, Anthony. Will I be allowed to? I'm an incredibly dull person in my own right and very unlikely to be of any interest to anyone but I don't need to remind you of what villages are like. The other thing is that I don't trust Roger not to drag us back into the limelight again.'

'Of course you'll be of *interest* here. That's inevitable, but it will be of a fairly restrained nature, I should say. People will talk for a while and you'll be pointed out as the woman whose husband is locked up. I don't think the village will ever forget that, but you will be accepted for what you are.'

'Villages have changed,' said Valerie. 'They're much less insular now. We have unmarried people living together, children born out of wedlock, even women cohabiting – all unthinkable twenty, thirty years ago. We had a sex-change retired judge living at Higher Holt farmhouse until quite recently, didn't we? He lived with a merchant seaman called Dorothy and they won the Best Single Fruit Preserve every year at the Flower Festival.'

'You make Claudia sound like some sort of freak show,' objected Christopher. 'If I was her, I'd bugger off and live an anonymous life in the city. Preferably in the sun.' He beamed at her cheerfully.

'I've tried that. I moved out of London,' she said. 'It was unthinkable to stay there. I didn't find my London friends very enduring, I'm afraid.'

'They weren't proper friends though, Mum,' said Jerome. 'They were people you knew through Dad.'

Claudia nodded. 'They were all I had,' she said quietly. 'Because of the life we led.'

'Don't go back over the past,' said Valerie briskly. 'You're here now, and you have us. Christopher, you miss my point about village attitudes. It's much more live and let live these days. That's what I meant.'

Only if you're tough, thought Anthony, remembering the talk round the Durnfords' supper table and how Valerie and her drinking had been discussed. He glanced at Claudia. How strong was she? She certainly didn't look physically very robust, but there was a quiet determination about her which he had noticed from the first and also the suggestion that she could stand apart, that she did not need to belong to the crowd or to be widely popular. How much did women need the approbation of other women? he wondered. Valerie Pomeroy not at all, but he believed she was exceptional. Would Claudia ever be accepted here in the country amongst the other much more conventional sorts – like Julia Durnford, for instance – even if she wanted to be? He rather doubted it. And if not, what would the future hold? Valerie Pomeroy didn't give a stuff, but she had lived her life, and she had her academic interests and her professional status. Claudia's position was very different. Were they right to encourage her to stick it out?

Christopher had taken Claudia upstairs to show her and Jerome their bedrooms, carrying the black bags in one hand, the other on her shoulder. He's a familiar sort of bloke, thought Anthony. He's only just met her. Although she wasn't at her best, naturally enough. Very pale and thin, and without make-up she looked her age.

He accepted Valerie's offer of a coffee, and alone in the kitchen said, 'Seriously, Valerie. Do you think she'll last this out? It's not going to be easy, you know.'

'Of course she will. Once the press have gone away, everything can get back to normal. It won't affect her job at the school. Why should it? And I tell you, Anthony, half the people in this village won't ever know. Things are different these days. People move in and out and no one even gets to know their names. Both adults out at work, just coming and going, morning and evening, shopping at the supermarkets in towns, not drinking in The Bugle, not churchgoers. Think round the village. There are as many people like that as there are of the old sort.'

'I daresay you're right. Living like we do, here all the time, particularly in farming, it seems as close a community as ever. I can hardly decide to put the top pasture down to winter wheat and everyone I speak to seems to know. Change a feed merchant, re-concrete the yard, move the sheep – it's all round the county by breakfast time.'

'Exactly. But Claudia's not from your world. It's different for her. She can choose to be as private as she likes.'

'Tell me, Valerie. Did you have any idea of this? Was it a complete shock to you?'

'Yes, completely. Until yesterday, in fact. What about you?'

'Not a clue. It's strange though, I met Roger Barron a couple of times when I worked in London. Fifteen, twenty years ago, I should think. He was quite a character.'

'With Claudia?'

'God, no. At dinners and nightclubs. He always had some

floosie on his arm in those days. They're separated now, you know. Claudia tells me she's divorcing him.'

'Ah. A wise move, I should have thought.'

'Who knows that she's here, Valerie? You, me and who else?'

'Nobody as yet. Jerome didn't tell Victoria where he was going.'

'That's just as well, don't you think? Greg will see her car in the yard but that doesn't matter. I'd leave the pick-up here for her to use again for a day or two but she's already well-known in that.'

'Christopher says he'll drive her to work in his car. Don't worry, Anthony. We'll look after her. And Jerome.'

'I know you will.' Anthony leaned back and looked at his watch. 'Christ! Is that really the time? I must go. I promised to be back to feed the calves. Keep in touch, won't you?' He stood up, wondering whether he would have the opportunity of saying goodbye to Claudia. He would have liked to have had a moment or two alone with her. Her plight had moved him in a way he had not expected and he found that he did not altogether like the idea of leaving her here to be looked after by Christopher.

'Shall I tell her you have to go?' asked Valerie with a shrewd look.

He smiled. She was a knowing old woman. 'I'll just nip upstairs and tell her myself.'

It had been left to Jerome to telephone Lila and tell her where they had taken refuge. Being Saturday morning in New York, he got her at her apartment.

'God, Jerome! What a drama. Is Ma OK?'

'Yeah. A bit strained. The bung is under siege for the time being. Dad is being moved, did you know that? To an open prison in Hampshire.'

'Yeah, I know. I spoke to him yesterday. He seemed OK about the appeal. He's amazingly upbeat about it.'

'I spoke to him too.'

'You did? That's really cool. I thought you weren't in touch because of Mum.'

'Lila, I can't not talk to him, can I? Whatever Mum thinks. I just don't tell her, which makes me feel underhand – you know, deceitful, but I can't see there's any other way.'

'No. If it upsets her, it's better she doesn't know. Is the village in uproar?'

'Don't know. We've gone to ground, so we've no idea what's

going on outside the gates. Reporters and photographers hanging around but not too much uproar, I don't think, although we must have upset Julia Dunghill's garden opening.'

Lila roared with laughter. 'Brilliant. I love it! Poor daughter, though. What's her name? I've forgotten. The rather feeble one with the horse I rode.'

'Victoria. Yes, poor Victoria. I feel really bad about her. I let her down badly. I was supposed to be helping and I'm sure I got her into deep shit with her mother. I can tell you, Lil, she's not actually feeble at all.'

'If I was her, I'd put myself up for adoption.'

'Her father's all right, though. Bonkers about Mum, actually.'

'Not very flattering for Mum although I suppose his taste in women could have improved with age. How's Finn?'

Shit, thought Jerome, I haven't seen him since I came upstairs to this bedroom. 'I hope he's asleep in the kitchen. I'd better go and check.'

'Just a minute, Jerome. There's something I want to tell you.'

'Lila, it'll have to wait. I must go and find Finn. Speak to you soon. Bye.'

Claudia sat on the bed in the room which Christopher Pomeroy had shown her. It looked as though it was normally occupied by one of his daughters because it had a pink patchwork bedspread and a rag doll reclined on the pillow. It faced the hills on the south side of the house and would be bright and sunny, although now the sky had clouded over and hard drops of rain pelted against the glass of the long window. There was a window seat with a padded cushion and rose-patterned interlined curtains which matched the faded wallpaper. A neat little white painted fireplace sat in the centre of a short wall which angled across the left-hand corner of the room. Above the fireplace was a mantelshelf loaded with trinkets and ornaments, and a large old china hand basin with hefty brass taps stood in another corner with a frilled skirt round its metal legs. The carpet was pale green and faded and stained but soft and silky under Claudia's bare feet.

It was a pretty, old-fashioned bedroom, the sort that Claudia and her sister had dreamed of when they were girls. She remembered with distaste the freezing room they had shared in the gloomy Victorian vicarage, with damp patches on the wallpaper and cheap cretonne curtains purchased from a jumble sale. She remembered the matching candlewick bedspreads, the tufted cotton pattern worn thin and bald in places.

It was odd to be sitting here taking stock of this extraordinary day, only a few hundred yards away from her own home and her own bedroom. What she felt most was the kindness and support of these new friends of theirs, who in many ways she hardly knew. 'The kindness of strangers' came to her again, although they weren't strangers, either, just decent, caring neighbours. Neighbourliness in the sense it was used in the Bible. 'Love thy neighbour as thyself,' without all the associations of nosy-parkering and do-goodery. That's what it was, real neighbourliness, and she felt humbled by it.

Anthony Brewer had just come upstairs to say goodbye to her and to promise to help her in any way he could. He had sat beside her on the bed and taken her hand and held it between both of his and she had felt the extreme hardness of the palm and the lumpy calluses on his fingers. He had good, square, brown hands. Then he had removed one hand and used it to gently smooth back the hair from her forehead, and leaning towards her had planted a kiss on her brow. Instinctively she had turned towards him and lifted her face and he took this as the signal to kiss her mouth, his hand moving to cradle the back of her head. It was a wonderful kiss. Claudia shut her eyes and thought of nothing else but the sensation of his tongue and lips touching hers and she responded eagerly. He pushed her back then, onto the pillow, and kissed her more urgently. It could have gone on from there, she thought, had they not been guests in someone else's house and in this innocent girlish bedroom. She had opened her eyes and caught at the hand which was moving over her breasts and held it and smiled up at the serious, preoccupied face which hung over hers.

'No?' he whispered.

'No. not here.' She smiled again. 'Not that it's not tempting.' She felt she should soften what could seem a rejection.

They both sat up and went back to holding hands. 'Claudia, I want to see you. See more of you. You know that, don't you? Will you allow me to?'

She nodded. 'Yes. I'd like it too. When this is over. Your knowing the truth clears things. Thank you, Anthony. For all of it.'

He kissed her again and then got up briskly, straightening his clothes. 'I must go. Dairy farmers have to time their seduction scenes to suit their cows. Milking waits for no man. Keep in touch. Goodbye, darling.' Then he was gone, and Claudia sat on, her sandals kicked off on the floor, the bedspread rumpled. What an extraordinary day this was turning out to be.

Not far away, in East End House, Victoria also sat in her bedroom feeling utterly miserable. It had been a horrible, horrible day. After she had done her bit to help Jerome, she had been completely excluded. She had no idea where he had gone or even if he had got away safely. She had tried to ring his mobile but it was switched off. She did not know how she felt, except miserable. She was shocked by the news which her mother had elaborated on all day, that Jerome's dad was some sort of criminal and was in prison. She couldn't think about prison without a shudder, and she couldn't imagine the shame and disgrace that would fall on a prisoner's family. Up until now she had thought imprisonment was for some sort of lower, sub-class of society; poor, desperate people from housing estates and inner cities. It was hard to believe that it was also for people whose children went to public schools and whose wives looked and spoke like Claudia.

Then there had been the rest of the beastly day to get through, with all the gossiping and speculation. She had heard Rosco talking to the press, bragging about how he knew it all the time and asking them what they'd give him for more information. She had seen him take the money for showing them where the ladders were kept and then pointing out where they could see over the wall into Claudia's garden. She hated him after that and when she got the chance, later in the day, told him so. He told her to grow up, and then to eff off.

Then there was her mother's day being ruined. She couldn't help but mind about that, even though she had driven her round the bend earlier on. It was awful to see people walking about but not talking about the garden, not noticing any of the hard work, or bothering to stoop and read the labels or comment on the planting schemes. Instead the visitors, even the gardening ladies with their untidy hair and moustaches – odd that they were so keen on pruning everything else – were totally taken up with the drama of what was going on next door. Then it rained and that was that. All over for another year and all the hard work gone to waste.

Afterwards her parents had had a row. Her father had drunk a lot of whisky. The bottle was still on the kitchen table more than half empty and her mother had made a cup of tea and gone to bed in the spare room, drawing the curtains against the grey evening. Victoria put the kitchen back to normal and let Skye out of the stables where he had been shut for the day, and fed him and Pushkin. Then, feeling lonely and dispirited, she'd come up to her room. From her window she could see the shut-up bungalow through the gloom, with the white tape of electric fence across the driveway. There were no photographers in sight. She hoped they had gone home, wet and cold and frustrated.

She felt sad that Jerome had never told her about his father and had kept her away from what she thought must be the biggest thing in his life. She felt hurt that when he left the telephone message he hadn't told her where he was. She felt pushed to one side, useful for a bit and then discarded. What had he said? You're a great girl. She was stupid to think that he had meant more than he did, that he felt more than he did. That was how she felt. Stupid and rejected. She picked up her mobile telephone and listened to his message again. She would try his number one more time. She was just dialling when she heard her father calling upstairs.

'Tor! Have you got Skye up there? I can't find him anywhere.'

Jerome knocked on Claudia's door. 'Mum, it's me. Is Finn with you? No? Shit! He seems to have disappeared. He must have got out of the kitchen at some time this evening.' He opened the door and put his head round. His mother was sitting on the bed, her knees drawn up. She looked thoughtful, young and vulnerable. 'Do you suppose he's gone home? Back to the bung?'

'Damn!' said Claudia. 'That was careless of us. Is it safe to go and shout for him? Can we yell through the gate in the wall?'

'Mum, we're supposed to be in hiding. What better way to draw attention to ourselves!'

'Well, what do you suggest?'

'I don't know. He's so disobedient at the best of times. If he doesn't come back for us, he won't come back for anyone else. I suppose we'll just have to hope he's intelligent enough to remember where we are. He'll soon get wet and cold.' With that a shower of rain hit the window like a handful of pebbles thrown against the glass. Claudia looked upset.

'It's a horrible evening. I can't bear to think of him shivering on the doorstep. Can't we ask Christopher to go through and look for him? After it gets dark, perhaps?'

'Yeah, I suppose so. That seems the best thing. He's a very large man to fit through the gap, though. I expect he'll get stuck.

I could ask Victoria to look. Finn knows her.'

'That's a good idea. Does she know where we are?'

'No. I haven't spoken to her since she helped me make a run for it. I left her a message. Do you think it's OK for her to know we're here?'

'Why not? She won't tell anyone, will she?'

'Not if we ask her not to.'

'Perhaps that isn't fair. I mean, asking her not to tell her parents. I don't think we should do that.'

'OK, I won't then.' Jerome went back to his room and dialled Victoria's mobile. It was answered almost immediately.

'Hi, Tor. It's me.'

Of course her first words were, 'Jerome, thank goodness! Where are you?'

'Tor, if you think hard about it, you can guess, without me telling you.'

'What? What do you mean?'

'I've been told not to tell you. So that you don't have to worry about me asking you not to tell anyone else.'

'I see,' she answered slowly.

'But as I said, Tor, if you think about it, you'll be able to guess. Not far away, I can tell you that.'

'Ah! Mrs P's? Am I right? OK, I'm only guessing. Are you OK? God, it's been a horrible day! I've been so worried about you. Mum is all over the place. Really having the high strikes, as Tom would say. She and Dad have had an awful row.'

'About us?'

'Partly.'

'I'm sorry. We've really mucked up your day.'

'Well, it's not me so much as Mum. But Jerome, why didn't you say anything? Why didn't you tell me about your father?'

'I couldn't, Tor. It wasn't fair to tell you. I wanted to, believe me. Mum wanted it kept quiet, you see. She hoped no one would ever know.'

'You thought I'd tell?'

'No, it's not that. I just didn't want you to have to bear the secret. It seemed too much to ask.'

'I see. Well, it wasn't.'

'It wasn't what?'

'Too much to ask.'

'Well, thank you, Tor. Thank you. We've got another crisis now. We've lost Finn. I thought maybe you'd seen him.'

'Oh, Jerome. That's awful, because we've lost Skye as well.

We've just noticed he's gone. They'll be together, won't they? They'll have gone off together.'

'Bugger. I expect you're right. I can't come out to look for them, though.'

'I'm going now. Dad and me are going to have a walk round and whistle for him. If we find them, I'll bring him back.'

'Tor, you're a star.'

It wasn't Victoria and her father who found the dogs. Later, much later, when Jena went to move Jigsaw into the shelter of the high thorn hedge, out of the driving wind and rain, she heard a whimper and saw a flash of grey, and bending down her fingers touched a scrap of wet fur leaning, trembling, against her legs. After she'd made the horse more comfortable out of the worst of the weather, she caught Finn up in her arms and took him inside the bus and rubbed him with a towel. He whined for a bit and took a while to settle, finally falling asleep on her bed in the crook of her bent knees. It wasn't until the following morning when bright sunlight sparkled on the pools of water left by the stormy night that Jena found Skye. The little terrier must have crawled under the van at some time during the early hours. He was muddy and still wet, but as she gently pulled him out she judged he had been dead for some time.

Chapter Fifteen

Summer dwindled into early autumn and in Court Barton the higher countryside lost a little of its greenness and became dusty and dry. For the first time in the year the gateways used by the cattle were rutted and hard and the long warm days spread golden over the hillsides. The lambs were grown as large as their mothers and when they knelt to butt their woolly flanks in greedy demands for milk, they were cuffed away. The heifer dairy calves were now long-legged starlets with great liquid eyes and sweeping lashes, while the unfortunate bull calves had long been despatched as unwanted and unsaleable. The last of the corn had been cut and the harvest reckoned to be a fair one, with yields higher than expected, boosted by the welcome spell of fine weather at the end of August.

The fields of stubble had been scuffled by harrows into loose earth and some winter wheat already sown. Tractors went through the village late into the evenings making the best of the shortening days and there was a culminating sense of the end of the year and preparation for the winter to come.

Horses were got in from grass and early in the mornings the sound of hooves echoed along the lanes as fat, unfit hunters were brought back into work to prepare them for the start of cub hunting. Ron Gripper, the gamekeeper, was out in the misty dawns, checking his pheasants, released now from the rearing pens and running about the coverts as tame as chickens, not yet aware of their fate in the months to come when shooting started.

Boxes of windfall apples appeared by the roadsides with handwritten notices – 'Free – Help yourself' – and Claudia spent happy afternoons collecting blackberries along the hedges which were thick with brambles. She noted where the bitter little sloes were growing on the blackthorn and decided she would come back and pick them after there had been a frost. Pricked all over with a needle and marinaded in neat gin and sugar they would make a wonderful dark and powerful drink for the winter fireside.

For Claudia, Victoria and Jena, about to start a new school year, September seemed a beginning and not an end. Victoria felt a different person, so much had happened in the holidays and although she had been dreading the return to school, she now found that she did not mind as much as she had thought she would. She had lingered over packing her trunk, throwing in the books she had brought home to study and seeking the bits of school uniform which had somehow gone astray during the holidays. She felt so much older, she thought, that was the main difference. Being in love had changed everything. It was like seeing the same old world but through a coloured lens, or observing a special photographic effect casting a new light on familiar objects and making you see them in quite a different way. She realised that she had been initiated into the exclusive world of romance and yearnings so strong that they made her feel physically ill and now she understood what it was all about – the peculiar rituals and obsessive behaviour of her friends – and exactly why she had been so left out before.

Loving Jerome had been such a shock that everything else had been jolted out of focus. It was like a bang on the head, when coloured stars floated across your vision in a dizzy swarm, or the weird sensation after doing a headstand when everything spun and the ground seemed to roll beneath your feet. The world was the same, but your oddly askew senses told you it was not. It was all there in *Wuthering Heights* – it was Cathy and Heathcliffe, it was Jane Eyre and Mr Rochester – and now she could understand it.

When Jena had come round that horrible morning, clattering up the drive on Jigsaw, and told her father what had happened to Skye, it had seemed as if sadness would drain the pleasure from everything. She had cried and cried – it was her fault, after all – and her father had held her and tried to comfort her, but she felt far away and locked in a place where no one could reach her. If only she had paid attention to him, taken a bit of trouble and waited while he ate his supper and then, because she knew he had been shut up most of the day, had taken him for a walk, then it wouldn't have happened. He wouldn't have slunk off on his own and met up somehow with Finn and then the pair of them, egging each other on, would not have gone hunting.

Her father reckoned that he had been hit by a car on the lane and had somehow managed to follow Finn to the camp on the line. He had broken both his back legs, she had discovered, although she wasn't supposed to know, and the thought of him dragging himself through the wet night and crawling under the van to die alone in the cold still made tears start in her eyes and her throat close on a dissoluble lump of grief. She could never forgive herself.

Later, she and Jena had put Jigsaw in a stable and taken Finn round to Valerie's to look for Jerome. As they passed the bungalow, looking a strange and forbidden place behind its tapes of electric fence, there were only two men hanging about outside, one smoking and the other talking on a mobile telephone. They ignored the girls but Jena called out rudely, 'Why don't you just piss off home and leave them alone, yer wankers?' Victoria had to pull her sleeve and tell her to shut up.

'I hate them. Claudio and Jerome haven't done nothing, have they? Why don't they go after all the people who are cruel and mean? To kids and animals and stuff,' she cried fiercely.

Then they were in Valerie's kitchen and they were all there, Claudia and Jerome and Valerie and her son, and Jena was telling them what had happened and they were looking at her with shocked expressions, guilty that they had been relieved to see Finn back and safe. She had cried then. Awfully. Shamingly. She couldn't stop and they had all tried to comfort her.

'Come on, I'm taking you for a walk,' Jerome had said, and he had put his arm round her.

'What about the men? The reporters? There are two of them out there,' she had managed to say.

And he had said, 'Then we'll walk round the garden. That's a very Jane Austen thing to do, isn't it?'

He'd kept his arm round her and they had walked about Valerie's overgrown garden and found a wonky old seat to sit on behind a yew hedge and he had pulled her close to him and made her put her head on his shoulder and let her cry, stroking her hair. Although she felt so terrible, it was wonderful too, and after a bit her grief was more like an indulgence as she felt the warmth of his body through his thin shirt and the delicate bones of the hand that held hers.

When she had quietened down a little, very hesitatingly, he told her about the awful thing that had happened to him in India, about the girl he had loved who had been killed, and they both cried then and she had felt so full of love and tenderness

261

for him that her heart really ached. He kissed her cheek and wiped away her tears and then very gently lifted her chin and kissed her mouth, not with a tongue or any of the awful sucking business you saw on films, but gentle and firm. It wasn't at all like being kissed by her parents or anything like that because it was more lingering and softer, and although she didn't know what exactly, it had a different intention, she was sure.

She had forgotten about Jena, who had had some hot chocolate in the kitchen and then came to look for them.

'Heh! Look at you two! Yuk!' she'd mocked when she saw them sitting like that.

Victoria had moved apart from Jerome and they both thanked Jena for the part she had played and she plonked herself down between them. Victoria had looked at her watch and said, 'I'd better go. Mum'll be back from church and she'll be terribly upset too. You know yesterday was awful for her, with the garden opening and everything.' Then she and Jena had walked back together and Jerome had stood and waved them off down the drive.

That was it, really. They never had another moment like it and Jerome didn't kiss her again, but she cradled the tenderness she had felt in her heart and thought about it all the time – really, all the time. She found she was able to re-live the kiss by gently pressing the tips of her fingers over her mouth and she could look down at her hands and remember how he had held them, and in this way she could make the enchantment last and last, and carry it about with her for ever.

Pony Club camp had come and gone and she had enjoyed it and Vinnie had behaved well, but really she wouldn't have minded if he hadn't because now she had something else.

At her last appointment with the dentist in Salisbury he had promised that the brace could come off her teeth before Christmas and he had made some silly joshing remark about how she could have it removed in time to kiss boys at parties in the holidays, and she had looked at him witheringly. Then it was time to load the car with all her stuff and squash her duvet in a black bin bag and collect the forms for exeats and theatre trips and the art history trip to Florence in the Easter holidays and start to say goodbye to home for another term.

She used to hate the leave-taking but this time it was less painful. She carried Pushkin about with her, a heavy, warm, purring lump in her arms as she went through the house, opening doors and looking in rooms. Jim was still abroad and his bedroom was forlorn and tidy and she shut the door hastily. Her parents' room was just as always, the untidy piles of books and magazines on her mother's side, the jar of cheap night cream which she always forgot to apply, the one earring which had lost its partner. Her father's side of the bed was different – less occupied, somehow; last year's yachting magazine on his bedside table with the lumpy coil dish she had made in pottery class when she was about ten and an empty spectacle case and an old Bible with Gran's maiden name written on the inside cover in sweeping violet ink.

Are they happy? She thought as she sat on their bed in a patch of afternoon sunlight. Do they still feel like I do, or does it all wear off in time, wear down to nothing, so that they can't remember what it felt like to be in love? She knew they were fond of one another in a matey kind of taken-for-granted way, but there was more irritation than love, more argument than agreement, and she couldn't remember ever having seen them kiss – well, not in the way that Jerome had kissed her.

After Skye had died there was an awful time when her mother could hardly speak to her father. It seemed she was taking his death out on him and Victoria felt it was so unfair when, if anybody was to blame, it was her. The fiasco of the garden opening and Skye's loss became one issue and Claudia and Jerome were held responsible for both and because her father refused to come on side and blame them, he was ostracised as well. She was grateful when Pony Club camp started and she was away for five days. When she came home the atmosphere was better, at least between her parents, while the neighbours remained beyond the pale.

She didn't care what her mother said, she continued to visit Garden Cottage, and even went with Jerome to London for the day when he wanted to buy some books from a university bookstore. They had had such a happy time and had gone to Tate Modern and walked along the river in the sunshine. She had taken the camera and took a photograph of him leaning against a wall along the embankment and a friendly American tourist had offered to take one of them together. 'You and your gal,' he said to Jerome, and Jerome had laughed and hooked an arm round her shoulders and she had squinted up at him, and that photograph was the most precious thing she possessed.

When the time came to go back to school she was glad in a way that Jerome was staying in London with some friends and that she didn't have to go through saying goodbye. She left him a little note on a postcard she had bought at the Tate and after much agonising put her school house telephone number on the bottom and wrote 'Ring Me' in a circle, and then turned the circle into the centre of a flower with spiky petals. She had run round to the bungalow to drop it off while her mother was getting lunch ready. The bungalow looked shut up and unloved, with all the curtains drawn tight, which was a precaution Claudia now took after the press invasion. Victoria posted the card through the letterbox and snapped off a sprig of lavender from the bush by the door.

There was nothing to hang around for and her mother was doing steak and chips as a special treat for her last meal at home, so she turned to go. On an impulse, perhaps because she put her hand in her pocket and found an unexpected pen, she took it out and drew a tiny heart on the yellow stone by the door – too small for anyone to notice but like a spell, a good luck charm for her love.

Claudia began the new term with some misgivings. What wild stories, she wondered, would have gone round the village since the press invasion of the summer holidays? Would she have to face a barrage of interest, a gossip campaign, or the cold shoulder of feigned lack of concern? She had been through it all before and was prepared for it again and maybe worse, because in the country people surely had less to talk about. Since the nightmare weekend she had kept her head down, avoiding walking through the village to post a letter and keeping out of the shops in Sharston. Even so, on the Tuesday and Thursday mornings that the wandering local bus came through the village and the little knots of elderly villagers gathered early with their hats and gloves and shopping bags for the trip into the nearest town, she felt all heads turn as she drove past the bus stop and then join in a kind of nodding unison of disapproval. She had seen this reaction, she was sure, in her rearview mirror and imagined the indrawn breath and the clucks of outrage.

As it happened, Valerie had thought it best not to pass on what Betty had brought with her from The Bugle, that Claudia was sitting on a secret cache of money that she and her husband had managed to siphon off and put into bank accounts all over the country. It had been Angie who had heard this from Greg, who'd picked it up in the Nag's Head in Sharston and who had told Monica.

'I don't believe it,' Angie had said, leaning on the bar with a vodka and a bag of crisps. 'Who'd work like she does if they had any money stashed away? You'd go off to Spain or somewhere, wouldn't you? Costa del Bankrobba. Not come down here and pick bleeding mushrooms.'

It seemed the story had grown up around Claudia being seen in the expensive hairdressers in Sherborne. She must have a bob or two if she could afford to go there.

'That doesn't mean anything,' said Monica. 'Not these days. People pay hundreds of pounds to have their hair cut in London, don't they? That Nicky Whatsisname charges a week's wages and it looks as if he's run the sheep clippers over your head.'

'The last haircut I had,' announced Tom from his corner, 'cost me eight pence. That was in nineteen fifty-six. Bloody waste of money I thought it was, too. My Susan's done it ever since.'

'You'd think anything was expensive, you would, Tom,' teased Angie. 'Anything since decimalisation.'

But Claudia, as the last weeks of summer sped past, was largely unaware of the circulation of gossip. She had been busy as a relief cook, had taken Jerome to see her mother in Winchester and done a few day's baby-sitting for Minna while she and Chris went to a conference in Athens. Claudia had noticed, but didn't much care, that Julia Durnford was cutting her, studiously looking straight ahead if they passed in cars in the lane, lifting only one finger from the wheel in a sort of unwilling recognition. Claudia had sent Victoria home with a note and a pot plant after Skye's accident, but had never had an acknowledgement. In a way, she could understand how Julia felt about her. She could see how she was beyond the pale, bringing the gutter press into the village and spoiling the garden opening, and although she could not accept that she was responsible for what happened to Skye, she could see how, if someone was to be blamed, it had to be her. Finn was wild and unbiddable and rather like a wayward boy judged to be a bad influence by other mothers.

Before school started she had thought it best, on Minna's advice, to telephone the office and ask to see Mrs Peck, to explain to her what the situation was. It had been an uplifting moment when the headmistress had looked at her shrewdly and said, 'Thank you for telling me, but I don't think this is relevant, do you? I judge every child on its merits and the staff, too. As far as I'm concerned we're lucky to have you and that hasn't changed. Now, where did I put the new guidelines for

Sarah Challis

nutritional standards for school lunches? I want to suggest a new system for monitoring menu cycles,' and she had scrabbled about on her desk looking for something.

This is what is called moving on, thought Claudia gratefully, looking at the busily occupied figure, dressed this morning in the holiday get-up of jeans and shirt, the helmet hairdo exuding a no-nonsense approach to life, and for the first time ever, she felt as if it was her own worth that mattered. She tried, briefly, to express her thanks, but was cut short. Mrs Peck had no time for misplaced gratitude. 'Now, no thanks to me, please. When I heard you wanted to see me, I thought you were going to give in your notice, so what you have had to say is a tremendous relief. Ah! Here's what I was looking for,' and she pulled out a folder. 'We need to check for foods rich in iron, calcium, folates and zinc. Just a matter of good practice . . .'

In the end it had been far easier than Claudia would have believed possible. After a week with Valerie, during which Christopher ran her to and from work in his hire car, there was no sign of any further interest from the press and the last photographer had disappeared days before. 'We'll move back into Garden Cottage this weekend,' she had announced at supper one evening, 'and we'll never know how to thank you enough for your kindness. Both of you.'

'Nonsense,' Valerie had said gruffly. 'And that will suit us, too, because we're going to London next week, Christopher and I.'

That was as much as she had said, but Claudia and Jerome both knew that their being there had solved something, that there was something amiss, or lacking, between mother and son, and then Claudia had understood what it was. She had picked up the photograph on the mantelshelf in her bedroom and looked at it as she had done many times before in the previous days, and realised that the four girls, the granddaughters, ranged along the edge of a swimming pool, dangling brown legs into the glinting blue water, were the missing ingredient. Claudia gathered that normally they would have accompanied their father to England, but this year, for the first time, the decision had been made to leave them behind. The gap their absence had created had to some extent been filled by herself and Jerome.

She and Christopher had struck up an easy friendship, in fact it was impossible not to like him, and she felt real affection for the big bear of a man. He was openly warm and demonstrative, hugging her frequently, pressing her to his barrel

266

chest, dropping a kiss on her head as he messily prepared supper in the kitchen, a gin always within reach. He had even asked her to marry him.

The thought of the offer made Claudia smile. She had been reading the paper, and commenting on a photograph of a sixty-year-old novelist who had chosen to publicise her new book by releasing photographs of herself in a revealing black camisole. 'Oh dear,' she had said. 'What Lila would call a SOB case. Sad Old Bag.'

'She looks OK to me,' said Christopher, looking over her shoulder, wooden spoon aloft. 'High maintenance, I imagine. A lot of sandblasting and weatherproofing and repointing. But why do women do it? Truss themselves up like that, try to be twenty-year-olds?'

'They need reassurance, I suppose. That they are still attractive. Middle age is a pretty terrifying experience for lots of women. That's why so many of them get themselves photographed in red satin basques, draped about the place with their legs apart, even though what they are respected for is their acting, or their novels or their singing voices.'

'Ah,' said Christopher thoughtfully. 'How would you know, Claudia dear?'

She sighed. 'I went through a pretty low patch when my husband left me for a woman not much older than our daughter. The red satin basque route was a bit of a temptation then.' She looked up and laughed, but Christopher had turned back to his pan on the stove.

'I'd love to marry you, by the way,' he said to the ragout sauce. 'If there was any chance you would accept, I would press my suit accordingly.'

'Christopher! Did I hear you right?'

He turned back to her, his good-humoured face bland and unchanged. 'I expect you did, darling. Why don't you consider it? You would be a wonderful mother to the girls, I can see that, and Ma likes you, which is both saying something, and a huge advantage, and we get on like a house on fire, don't we? Personally, I'm not a great believer in *lurve*,' he said this in a mocking tone. 'Are you?'

'I was. Once.'

'Of course. First time round. Second time, one is much more sensible. Do think about it, darling.'

'I will. Thank you, Christopher. I feel very flattered.'

'Good. Is there any chance you might still consider the

whatever it was – the red satin thing?'
    She threw the tea towel at his head.

Valerie Pomeroy was not unaware of the frisson of attraction
between Christopher and Claudia. It had crossed her mind
before they had met that they would like one another and get
on well. It had been a pleasant interlude to share her home with
them both and Jerome, but she was glad when the week came
to an end. She realised that she had grown too accustomed to a
solitary life and although they were the easiest of house guests –
Jerome being remarkably quiet for a young man of his age,
seeming happy to read and sleep, and Claudia out at work every
day – it was the very fact of their being there which seemed an
intrusion. It was not simply that they were not family, because
she felt the same about Christopher. She found him too noisy
and overbearing, and his bellowing laugh, the gargantuan meals
he insisted on preparing, his wastefulness, his use of her
telephone and fax machine all began to irritate her. I grow ever
more selfish in my old age, she thought. It's different with the
girls because of the love I feel for them. For them I would do
anything, give up anything.
    She would enjoy Christopher more when they were away
together, staying in London where his company had a small flat.
There they would be on neutral territory and they could spend
their days going about their respective business, meeting in the
evening for drinks and dinner and an exchange of news. He had
a sharp and exacting intelligence, her Christopher. It was a
mistake to take him for a softie or a pushover because he was
large and good-natured. He absorbed information and then
when one was least expecting it, he would pounce and skewer
one as neatly as a beetle on a pin. Valerie knew what to expect
from him. He would give her an assessment of her ability to
remain living alone in the large house after her 'do'. What she
did not know was what solution, or proposition, Christopher
would arrive at. He rarely took the conventional view and so it
was hard to be prepared with a defence. She suspected that he
would suggest she sell up and move into what was called
sheltered housing. This she would resist, indeed refuse to do.
While she still had the house and garden she had plenty of room
for the girls, and they had already talked about the idea that the
older two should come over to board in the near future. When
this happened there would be exeat weekends and half-terms
and her house would be their home. True, she might have to

accept that she needed some extra help with catering and so on, but that was not impossible to arrange. And there was Rosie, in particular, to consider. Darling Rosie, who would not follow the others to a conventional school, would need her. She wanted to have a home ready for Rosie.

Anthony Brewer had been marvellous, Claudia had to give him that. He was a man who liked a crisis. He should have been a soldier, she thought, he was so good on strategy and planning. The week she stayed with Valerie he called frequently, finally sending Greg round with her car on the last day and getting him to remove the electric fence from round the bungalow and check that all was in order within and without. He arranged to have a security light fitted which Claudia hated because it flashed on when even a cat or a fox crossed the drive and made her think of a concentration camp or, inevitably, a prison. After a decent interval she would have it disabled.

His interest in her was intensified because of Christopher, Claudia could see that. She realised that Anthony was a man who liked to pursue and expected to be successful. He saw Christopher as a rival and while there was a chance that she might be falling under the influence of another man, he redoubled his own efforts. He asked her out to dinner; she declined while she was staying at Valerie's, but accepted later when she had returned home. This time, because Jerome was away staying with friends in London, she asked him in afterwards and they made love.

It was so inevitable that Claudia was, at first, neither surprised nor disturbed by it. They were both unattached and mutually attracted to one another, and when he finally left at six in the morning, she had turned over, warm and comfortable and happy, and gone back to sleep.

The danger, which she had not seen then, was that to make love so stupendously well and yet to believe that she could remain detached was a foolish error. She floated through a day or two, and then when he did not telephone or call, began to get anxious. Had it been less good for him than it had for her? Had she been a disappointment? It hadn't seemed so at the time. They had dallied a little at first. She had made coffee and he had produced a bottle of cognac. He had kissed the back of her neck as she had waited for the kettle to boil and put his arms round her from behind. She had leaned back into him, enjoying the solid feel of his body and not resisting when he moved his hands up to hold her breasts.

They had laughed at how a bungalow was so ill suited to a seduction scene. There was something distinctly lacking in merely crossing the front hall to a bedroom without any of the significant mounting of the stairs, the invitation to transfer from the public to the private domain, from the general to the intimate. After the preliminaries in the kitchen it had been his suggestion that they should find somewhere 'more comfortable' and Claudia had led the way.

'I've never done this here before,' she announced, pushing open the door. 'It feels very strange.'

'Is that just a question of the elevation?' he'd asked, joking.

'Could be. When I first moved, it took a bit of getting used to, going to sleep on the ground floor. It made me feel vulnerable in some way, and I didn't like all the things which I associate with workaday life being so close – the kitchen with a floor that needed washing, the Hoover, the ironing, that sort of thing. I didn't like lying in bed and being able to hear the fridge switching off and on. Going upstairs to bed, one leaves all that down below, all the tiresome daytime stuff. This feels a bit the same.'

'Ah. I see. Oh dear, I've got an uphill task then. You've made the room charming, though, and I flatter myself that I may be able to take your mind off the Hoover.'

They had gone on to make love – smoothly, like the two grown-ups they were, and Claudia had found that Anthony was all that she had hoped, a sympathetic and enthusiastic lover, and best of all he made her feel totally and wholly desirable. Her nervousness over her less than smooth stomach, the thread veins on her thighs, the distinct droop of her bottom, her much less than pneumatic breasts – all these flaws of middle age didn't seem to matter. He evidently got pleasure from pleasing her, something which Roger had not been too concerned with, she reflected ruefully. A rogering by Roger was exactly that.

The next day she wrote Anthony a little note, thanking him for dinner and alluding coyly to what happened afterwards. Now she cringed to recall her words. They were written while she was feeling cosily appreciated, still tingling with intimacy, whereas now she was caught up by stupid anxiety, fearing that this act of love had meant more to her than it had to him, and by dwelling on what had happened, magnifying it in her mind until she could think about little else. It was utter foolishness, she knew, to allow herself to be at the mercy of a womaniser. Why should she be any different than the numerous other women he had slept with and left behind? To care about him was the way of tears. The truth, she conceded, was that despite her age and world-weary wisdom and years of marital couplings, she was a beginner in this business of casual sex and it seemed that she had misjudged her ability to take the promised pleasure without the complications.

Oh, God, I'm too old for this, she thought after a week had passed. It's bad manners, for one thing. He'd have written a note to thank me if I'd asked him to a drinks party so he should bloody well get in touch after being in my bed. I'll not play games, she decided one afternoon when she got back from school, and she picked up the telephone. She was dismayed when his farm secretary answered, brisk and rather grand, and who clearly enjoyed putting female callers in their place.

'He's been extremely busy,' she announced, 'but I will tell him you rang. Claudia, did you say?'

Shit, thought Claudia, as she put down the telephone. One thing is clear, I must get a grip and stop this nonsense. I haven't come this far to be cast down like a teenager by a thoughtless man.

It was therefore with some surprise and pleasure that she later received a telephone call from Anthony, full of apologies – he'd been in London and terribly busy one way and another, and would she like to come to Scotland with him for a week's stalking. 'What?' she'd repeated stupidly, not taking in this change in her fortunes. 'When? First week of October? But what about my work? I can't get away then.'

'Can't you get a stand-in?'

'Not possibly. It's not that sort of job. I could get away at half-term which is at the end of October.'

'No good, I'm afraid. We're after the red stags and the season finishes on the twentieth of October. Dates are fixed on a tablet of stone. We take the same week every year.'

And a different woman, no doubt, thought Claudia. 'I see,' she said. 'Well, in that case, thank you very much, but no, I won't be able to.'

'Damn. It won't be nearly as much fun without you, er, for a lot of reasons.'

'Oh, really?' she heard herself say coldly.

'There was one other thing, sweetie. Is there any chance you could do our lawn meet for us? Another tradition. We always

have the Christmas Eve meet here at Manor Farm. Have done
for years, but Mrs Walker isn't really up to it any more. It means
quantities of mince pies, sausage rolls, ginger cake, that sort of
thing. Ivo and I take care of the drink. Could you really? That
would be marvellous. We can talk about it closer to the time.
Now, tell me how you are. It's ages since we talked.'

So it is, thought Claudia sadly, but it's going to be no good,
this relationship – if you can call it that. We want different
things.

At the end of the conversation she felt lonely and depressed
and had to talk about him to someone. She telephoned Minna
who listened patiently. 'So let me guess, you slept with him,' her
sister-in-law said before she finished. 'And it was fucking that
fucked it up. Usual story, I'm afraid. You'll have to get tough,
Claudia, if you're going to go on that sort of sexual odyssey. That
sort of adventure leads a lot of middle-aged, recently separated
women into my surgery demanding to be put on anti-
depressants. Now, does that cheer you up?'

Claudia had to laugh. She could always rely on Minna to be
direct.

'The only comfort I can offer,' Minna went on, 'is that time
does make it hurt less. Believe me. That's what I tell them and I
think it's true.'

For Jena, the end of the summer also brought changes. Down in
the low-lying vale, the grass went on growing long and green
and the ditches were still deep and wet. The meadows on either
side of the line were grazed by cattle, now sleek and fat after the
summer, who idled their days hock deep in mud along the
stream, nodding their heads to shake off the clouds of flies. In
the early mornings they stood like ghostly statues in the mist,
trailing silver behind them through the long wet grass. It was a
time of year she loved, when the chill of the evenings reminded
her of the cold of the winter to come, but the days were still
warm and golden.

With the corn cut and the gates open, she was everywhere on
Jigsaw, cantering across the fields and jumping wherever she
could. Soon her father would be using him every day and when
the evenings drew in she would not be able to ride after school.
She needed to make the most of him. He was fit and keen and
once or twice he had jumped her clean off, standing off so
boldly from a fence that she was pinged from his back by the
power of his quarters. The second time she hurt herself and hid

the black bruise on her thigh where she had been thrown into the rails. Her dad had promised her a saddle, but there was never enough spare, not with her new uniform and all the extras she needed for school. Someone had been on at him about a hat, too, that she shouldn't be riding bare-headed. Mr Brewer, she thought it was, and the next time she saw him when she was out riding he had wound down the window of his Land Rover and said, 'I don't want to see you riding without a skid lid. I get an earful every time I see Mrs Durnford and I can't take it any more. How much are they, those crash hats?' She'd shrugged. She'd no idea, and he had heaved himself up out of his seat and fished in his pocket and handed over two twenty pound notes. 'There. Now go and get one, for heaven's sake!' and he'd driven off.

When she was in Stur with Heather, getting her uniform, she'd gone into the saddler's and chosen a helmet, like jockeys wore, and a black silk cover, and brought it home in a big square box. It felt funny, riding in a hat at first, but she knew it was a good idea, especially if she was going to fall off. She'd looked at the second-hand saddles but they were all hundreds of pounds so she'd had to forget that idea.

School wasn't so bad either. She got the bus earlier than before and some of the kids she dreaded were going to a different school, so she didn't have to see them. It was better at a big school. You were split up more and the classes were bigger and there was hardly anyone you knew from before. A few of the bigmouths from the primary were getting picked on themselves now for thinking they were so cool. The older kids didn't like it and soon had them sorted out and taken down a peg. She just kept her head down and no one took any notice. There were a couple of Chinese kids from the takeaway and even a few refugees from somewhere or other who hardly spoke any English, so she wasn't the only one who wasn't, like, normal.

She'd been happy at the end of the holidays with Jerome and Victoria, although it had been horrible about poor little Skye. She'd never seen anyone cry like Vix did. She'd wrapped him up in an old blanket Heather let her have and carried him into the bus and put some wild flowers round his face. His eyes were shut and the lids were dark blue and his lashes were black as if he was wearing make-up. He didn't look as if he died in pain. His face was peaceful, just as if he'd gone to sleep and was having a nice dream. She was glad about that because she had seen dead animals, a farm collie who had been hit by a tractor, an old greyhound they used to have, and lots of foxes, who had died with a snarl on their faces, the lips drawn up and looking ferocious.

Victoria and her father had come to collect him, leaving their car up on the lane and walking down the line carrying a cardboard box to put him in. Vix was still crying. They'd taken him home and buried him in the garden and the next day she had helped to make a tombstone and a cross. Mrs Durnford had come out, looking pale and bad-tempered and she'd scarpered then. She knew enough to know when she wasn't wanted.

Then school had started and she'd hardly seen Victoria again and probably wouldn't until the Christmas holidays. Jerome had gone off to see some friends and to visit his father in prison. It was weird that. You didn't think of posh people going to prison. Then he was starting university so she probably wouldn't see him either.

It was the first time, thought Jena, that she had had any friends.

For Peter and Julia Durnford the summer had rather fizzled out. The holiday they had vaguely planned never happened. Victoria had not expressed any interest in going to Cornwall as usual and inertia had set in about organising anything else. Then there was the garden opening and Pony Club camp and before one knew it the summer had gone.

Julia felt that it was time for a fresh start. With Victoria back at school and Jim abroad until October and then back to university, there was the opportunity to go away together, just her and Peter. Unless he took the days owed to him as holiday he would forfeit them, and she thought it would do them good to spend some time together.

'We're getting a bit rusty,' she explained to Jo Turner at a Pony Club Committee meeting. 'You know, we both need a thorough overhaul.'

'A ten thousand mile service?' smirked Jo, and Julia hooted with laughter. She rather liked slightly risqué allusions to her sex life. Probably because it is almost non-existent, she admitted only to herself. She supposed it was Peter's age. One was always reading about how stressful life was for the present generation of middle-aged men. Professional life was so much more demanding than in the past. Poor Peter worked far longer hours than his father ever had, and although they were so lucky in not having a mortgage, school fees were a terrible burden and Jim was still a considerable expense. They would have to tackle extensive roof repairs before too long, and the horsebox was on its last legs.

It wasn't only the external pressures. She had read a series of articles by the *Daily Telegraph* doctor which suggested that modern man had lost his way and was feeling depressed and confused, and she could really see it, she told Jo, when she looked at Peter. 'He was brought up to believe that he should be a hunter-gatherer,' she explained, 'and be manly and brave and strong. Then a whole different generation of women came along – that's us,' she added, with a dig in Jo's ribs, 'and we demanded something quite different. We asked for men who could be gentle and caring and submissive and share with the housework and the childcare.'

'Wait a minute,' demanded Jo. 'Who is this man you're describing? I've never met him!'

'It's called being in touch with their feminine side, or something like that,' said Julia. 'But then, of course, when we had them domesticated we decided that we didn't like that either. We want them to be a bit wild and exciting as well, or we don't fancy them. So that's why they are so horribly at sea. Anyway, that was the gist of it,' she finished.

Jo laughed. 'I honestly don't think that description fits any of the men I know,' she said. 'Although Peter is just about the mildest, I do agree. Adrian is totally unreconstructed, I'm afraid, but less like a cave man than a wilful toddler. I sometimes think, especially on a Sunday night when I've had a weekend of him, that he ought to be attached to a pair of reins in the hands of a well-trained Norland nanny. One gets so tired of the tantrums and bad behaviour that one would simply not tolerate in one's children.'

Julia giggled. 'You might think Peter is mild and easygoing,' she said. 'But he's not, you know. He's been really quite odd the last few weeks. Thoroughly bad-tempered and moody. That's why I think a holiday is called for.'

'Take him away somewhere hot and give him a really terrific shagging,' said Jo loudly.

Rosemary Vernon's drawing room went suddenly quiet as the committee stopped discussing the pros and cons of allowing the use of spurs, and Julia saw all eyes turn to where she and Jo were sitting. Jo remained as cool as ever but Julia felt her face go red.

'And you might consider the use of spurs,' murmured Jo under her breath.

Driving home that evening, Julia considered the situation more seriously. Something had certainly happened between her and Peter. She had always felt so sure of him before, but this summer they had seemed to move apart and there was all that business over Claudia which had upset them both. For quite ten days after Skye's death, they had hardly spoken. Quite apart from her grief, for she had loved the little dog, her constant companion, she had sulked, feeling badly treated and let down, and for once Peter had not come swiftly to heel. In fact he had remained stubbornly resistant and hostile and the silences between them grew more profound. Julia had moved back into their bedroom but they might just as well have been sleeping apart for all the contact they had. Keeping well over to their own sides of the bed, the space between them felt like a minefield in no-man's land, which neither of them had any inclination to cross. They still had not made love even though as the weeks went by the grievances wore away until they were behaving much as usual towards each other. But something had been dislodged within their relationship, which would not fit smoothly back into place, and it made Julia uncomfortable and uneasy. I know what I'll do, she thought. I'll get some brochures from the travel agent for somewhere like the Gambia or the Seychelles. Somewhere totally relaxing and away from everything, and I'll go on that ghastly cabbage soup diet and get back into a bikini. That should do the trick.

Chapter Sixteen

Christopher's solution, when it came, was a surprise. He introduced it into the conversation over coffee after an excellent lunch at Simpsons on the Strand.

'Now, Ma,' he said, 'listen carefully, and please don't automatically adopt a defensive position, because I think I have got a rather clever idea.'

Here we go, thought Valerie. I knew it. Here comes the bloody sheltered housing. She braced herself in her seat and gave him a stern look.

'I understand and completely sympathise with your unwillingness to move.' A good start, she thought, before he suggests exactly that. 'But you have to accept at your age and with your recent health scare, it isn't sensible to go on living by yourself in a large inconvenient house.'

'Why not?' she demanded. 'I don't in the least object to pegging out on my own, if that's what's on the cards. I do not wish to survive if I have another attack. I will not be resuscitated and then shunted off to some bloody day care outfit and told to sit in the corner and make basketwork trays. You can forget it. It isn't as if I'm isolated in the village. My body is not going to be found three weeks after death, embarrassingly eaten by my pet dog, is it? I have Betty, for goodness sake. She keeps an eye on me, I can tell you.'

Christopher looked over the table at his mother with amusement. She had grown red in the face – the claret and the roast beef helped, of course – and her eyes sparked.

'Now stop it,' he commanded mildly, 'or you'll keel over here, which would be a bore. I'd still have to pay for your lunch. You haven't even heard me out. How old is Betty, by the way? She must be nearly your age. I really don't think you can look on her as a long-term solution.' He took a sip of coffee and unwrapped the chocolate from his saucer. 'The house is far too large for one person. How many bedrooms? Seven? Eight, counting the attic? It does, however, have the huge advantage of being hideous and of no architectural merit. Now, what I would suggest is this. In the quite near future I shall bring the girls back from Hong Kong and will need somewhere to live. I will have to be in London for my work, that much is certain, and they will go to boarding school, as we've discussed. I would rather they had a home in the country and I would like them to be near you. Now this is the gist. I think, if you agree, that we should get an architect to come and look at the house and sketch out some plans to divide it into three separate dwellings, each with its own entrance. The two larger of the three would occupy the ground floor rooms and the main bedrooms, and the smaller would make use of the attic space. In the long term, the girls and I would occupy the largest apartment, while you had the other. The third we could put to good use, installing some sort of woman as a keeper for you and the girls. The ideal person, of course, would be someone like Claudia, a divorcee or widow who needed a roof over her head, a pleasant place to live and who was not averse to doing a bit of cooking and house-keeping when required. I have asked her, by the way. At least, I asked her to marry me and she said she would think about it, but I don't hold out much hope on that front.'

Valerie sat in stunned silence, not quite able to gauge her own reaction to this radical solution. Her dislike of any sort of upheaval and interference had to be measured against her delight at the idea of having the girls next door. Living with her, really. She stirred her coffee thoughtfully.

'You do realise,' she said, 'that I am an extremely difficult old woman and that between us, your girls and I, we would see off almost any sort of helper?'

'Oh, yes, I know that,' said Christopher, motioning for the waiter to bring the bill. 'It would take a pretty unusual sort of person to put up with you, but that is looking very much to the future. For the time being, if you agree and the plans look reasonable and we have a clear run with planning permission, we could get the work done to your satisfaction and let out the upper apartment. That would provide a bit of income to offset some of the costs of the building work as well as giving me the peace of mind of knowing that you were not on your own. Again, we would have to find the right sort of tenant, and again, someone like Claudia springs to mind.'

'She seems rather central to your plans,' observed Valerie drily.

'Unfortunately,' said Christopher, with a wry smile, 'I don't believe I'm central to hers.'

'So you've asked her to marry you?' This was another fairly stunning piece of news.

'Yes. What do you think? She'd be excellent with the girls, wouldn't she? She can cook and you seem to like her. All sound reasons.'

'You make marriage to you sound like a position for an unpaid housekeeper.'

'Oh, come on! I'm not without some attractions. I don't mean physically, like that smug farmer chap, who clearly thinks he's God's gift. No, what I can offer is intelligent companionship, an affectionate and loyal nature and total financial security. I happen to think we'd get along rather well.'

'Do you indeed!' Valerie's tone made it clear that this was less of a question than an observation on her son's extreme presumption.

Christopher laughed. 'There's no one like you, Ma, for putting one in one's place! I realise I have only an outsider's chance, but she didn't turn me down, may I point out. Not down flat, anyway.'

Valerie unwrapped her chocolate and put it in her mouth and surveyed her son critically. 'Are you prepared to meet the cost of all this?' she asked. 'You realise that I don't have the capital to undertake any of this sort of restructuring?'

'Of course. I would have had to buy a property and prices in Dorset are high for family houses. In the long run it would be a very sound investment. I don't envisage any problem with the planners because the house is too ordinary to be listed.'

'Than all I can do is thank you!'

'For the lunch or the proposal?'

'Both. Thank you for both.' Maddeningly and completely out of character, Valerie felt suddenly choked by emotion. Gratitude, she knew, and also a wave of love. Gratitude that Christopher trusted her, a foolish, elderly, semi-alcoholic, with the care of his children. She would not let him down. Love for the large, fair man sitting across from her, and profound love for the four girls who would soon be filling her house with life and laughter.

As the autumn term began, Claudia found, to her consternation, that she was thinking more and more about Roger. She believed this was partly due to Jerome's departure to Cambridge and the fact that she was now alone again with long empty evenings in which to contemplate the past and the future. There was also the emotional state she had got herself into over Anthony Brewer. She did not at all regret the fact that she had slept with him but rather that she had allowed herself to become vulnerable as a result. Minna was right about that. If she was to become a truly liberated woman, independent, and equal to any man, she had to crack this neediness, this yearning to please and relinquish control and be loved as a reward. Anthony did not want her on those terms, that was clear, and she was certain that she did not want to embark on any other relationship while this behavioural response was still so instinctive and strong within her, and yet in the long run yielding such unsatisfactory results.

Thinking about Anthony made her think about Roger. It seemed to her now that when they embarked on married life together, she had fallen naturally into a submissive role because it suited her, and also because it was what Roger expected. Mindlessly, almost, she had continued as a dutiful wife and a devoted mother. Gradually, as the cracks appeared, she had stuck relentlessly, desperately even, to this behaviour because it was all she knew, and because she believed, ultimately, it would have its own reward, its hidden price. When she came away empty-handed, with Roger not only letting her down as a provider and protector, but also deserting her, surely that should have been enough for her to learn that this was not the way to treat or be treated by men?

Interestingly, Roger left her, the accommodating doormat, for Carla, a bright, ambitious, selfish and demanding career woman. How had the papers described Carla at the time? Some American word like 'sassy'. And despite all this past history, here she found herself repeating the pattern with Anthony. Allowing herself to become a victim of this false accounting system. Well, she would not do it. Not again. So she must train herself to treat Anthony with, well, less respect. She realised she had felt flattered that he wanted to go to bed with her and now dishonoured that he had not reciprocated by behaving as she expected in return. In other words, he had not paid up in the coinage of the deal she believed she had brokered. Her problem, not his. A double whammy. Not only had he hurt her, but by allowing herself to be hurt, had made her angry with herself and despondent. Blimey, she thought, getting up in the early hours of a sleepless, chilly September morning to make a cup of tea, Minna was absolutely right. Fucking should come with a mental health warning. It could do your head in if you let it.

Going back to bed with a hot water bottle to warm her feet, she thought about Roger again. He would be sound asleep. Even at the height of their most agonising periods of stress and anxiety, he had slept like a baby. They could have a searing quarrel, give each other a verbal mauling, and five minutes later he would be snoring peacefully, while she lay open-eyed in the darkness, her heart thumping and her guts twisted into knots. She gathered from Jerome that at the open prison he slept in a sort of dormitory with sixteen other men. That, and the grim food would be just like boarding school, which of course he had loved. The lack of privacy, about which other, less robust prisoners grumbled, would not trouble him one bit, and the cold war fought against the bullying warders would be a terrific challenge to him. Again, it was exactly like his boarding school, a particularly spartan and barbaric establishment in Scotland, but without the beatings for punishment.

Lying there, gradually getting warm again, she realised that she felt something unexpected, a sort of grudging affection for the rotten man who lay sleeping somewhere behind barbed wire. I must be in a state of recovery, she thought.

The following afternoon on her way home from work, Claudia called in on Valerie. Now things were, as she thought of it, back to normal, she wanted to keep in closer touch and not only because Christopher had asked her to. After the events of the last month, she considered Valerie a true friend and she wanted to give the latest news of Jerome and also to tell her of a recent conversation with David Rowntree.

They sat, for the first time ever, in the drawing room at the front of the house. It was a mild September afternoon, almost like summer; the windows were open on to the garden and the front door stood wide so that a warm breeze blew through and stirred the curtains. She could hear bees in the 'Autumnal Blue' ceanothus which flowered by the door and the whirring sound of doves softly calling from the Durnford stable roof. She saw with surprise, as they plonked down with their mugs of tea, that there was something of a clear-out going on. Books were sorted into piles and an open cupboard door revealed tidy stacks of manuscripts.

'Goodness,' she said. 'What's this? A sort of reversed spring cleaning?'

'I'll tell you. Rather exciting really.'

She glanced with surprise at Valerie, whom she noticed looked better than usual, her eyes clearer, her complexion less florid. Perhaps she had even lost a bit of weight.

'We have some plans, Christopher and I,' she went on. 'Rather under wraps at the moment, but we're going to divide this place into two. Two proper houses, two staircases, two front doors and the garden split between them. The top floor is going to be a self-contained flat. The larger of the two will be for Christopher and the girls, and I shall have the other. We will let the top flat for the time being and then consider having some kind of living-in home help. It's all decided. I even have some plans here done by the architect. Christopher really cracks on with things, you know. His looks belie him. He is actually a very dynamic man.'

'I never doubted that for one moment,' said Claudia, thinking of the lightning proposal of marriage. 'Well, how tremendously exciting. I should think this solves all sorts of problems in one fell swoop. He talked about needing a home in this country, and it will be lovely for you – and for him and his family.'

'It certainly will for me and I shall serve some useful purpose, I hope. You know about Rosie, don't you?'

'The youngest? I don't think so. Nothing in particular, anyway.'

'She was brain-damaged at birth. A very difficult birth which ultimately killed her mother and left her oxygen deprived. She looks perfect, she's a beautiful child, but she is what they now euphemistically term Special Needs. She, more than the others, requires particular love and attention. She'll prosper here, I think, and there's an education unit in Dorchester which she can attend.'

'Goodness. You have got things well planned.' Claudia paused and Valerie looked at her shrewdly.

'I know what you're thinking. Am I up to it? Betty was exactly the same. The drink and so on. Oh, come on. Let's not beat about the bush!'

'All right,' said Claudia, putting down her mug. 'It did cross my mind. As a possible problem.'

'Yes. Of course I never had the slightest incentive to stop before. Certainly not to please the bloody doctors or that ghastly, bossy, lifestyle woman from the hospital. I always felt it was nobody's business but my own. I mean, I wasn't going to get drunk and go out ramraiding or vandalising the bus shelter, was I? However, if Christopher entrusts me with the care of the girls, that is quite another matter. I haven't had a drink for three weeks.'

'Fantastic! Well done!'

'Oh, for goodness sake, spare me, Claudia. I don't need to be congratulated, thank you very much.'

'Sorry. How can I say it, then? That I'm really pleased? That I think it's marvellous?'

'You can go and get us another mug of tea and tell me about Jerome.' She glared at her visitor.

Unperturbed, Claudia said, 'Actually, I thought you looked well.'

'Thank you,' said Valerie gruffly and leant forward to pat her hand. 'This is a baddish time, this hour of the afternoon. It's when I could most do with a snifter.'

'Ah. Well, I'll go and get the tea and tell you Jerome's news. He's fine, I think. A bit disenchanted by freshers' week, but then I believe a lot of first-year students feel that, especially those who have been abroad for a year and *lived*, as they call it. They can find it all a bit juvenile and sad. There's a terrific emphasis on competitive drinking apparently. You know he wanted to change courses from English to Oriental Studies? The powers that be have agreed and so now he's doing Hindu and Urdu and terribly happy about it. That time in India certainly had a profound effect on him.'

'Hmm,' said Valerie, trying to read Claudia's face. Although in many ways so close to her, Jerome still had not felt able to share with his mother the life-altering experience of Jabeena's death. It would hurt Claudia when she found out that it had been easier to talk about it with a relative stranger, thought Valerie. 'Now what about David Rowntree? Your husband's lawyer, I think.'

'Yes. He telephoned last night to say that he thinks we are through the woods as far as press interest is concerned. After the appeal hearing and Roger moving to the open prison, he thinks things will die right down. He wanted to reassure me that there will be no thunderbolts in the future. Roger just wants to get through his sentence now, as quickly and quietly as possible. He should only have to serve half of it if he behaves himself. However, there was a bit of a sting in the tail.'

'Yes?'

'The main reason for Roger keeping his head down and going quietly is that Carla is expecting his baby. Due in about a month, I think. I don't know why I never thought about such a thing happening, but it hadn't crossed my mind. Roger, of course, has known for some time and is apparently thrilled. I don't know whether I told you that Carla went back to the States. She'll have the baby there apparently. That's where her family is, and it will avoid the English press.' Claudia sat back down, looking slightly defeated.

'I see,' said Valerie. 'Does it make a difference?'

'To me? I've been trying to work that out. Yes, in a way. It's like the final act of the drama for me. My final surrender of him. It was the most binding thing, you see, being the mother of his children. And for Lila and Jerome, I think it makes a huge difference. I'm letting him tell them. I just don't know how they will feel. And funnily enough, it's made me think of Carla a bit, too. I can't help but wonder about her and for the first time consider her position. According to David, she still wants to marry him.'

'What about the statement he made at the time of the appeal hearing? That bit in the newspaper about his family?'

'Oh, that was for effect. I knew it was. Roger is the ultimate showman. It was what he thought would go down best at the time. Now he will want a speedy and uncontested divorce, David says, which is a good thing, and it will also mean that people like my mother, a staunch supporter of Roger's, and even Lila, will see that our marriage really was over and it's not just a case of me deserting a sinking ship.'

'Do you mind about that? How other people see you?'

Claudia made a wry face. 'It may sound shallow to say so but yes, I do, or did, deeply. I really, really minded. I don't so much now, now that I have another life. That's why Minna – Roger's sister – that's why her support was so wonderful. She knew the truth, which nobody else seemed too concerned with. Roger's charm and gloss blinded everyone and I wasn't very good at my own PR, I suppose. Anyway, that's my news.'

'What about Christopher? He told me about his marriage proposal.'

Claudia looked across at Valerie and smiled. 'He didn't mean it. Not seriously. He hardly knows anything about me. It was a joke, really.'

'I don't think so. Don't underestimate him. I've told you that.'

'But we don't love each other.'

'Not so important. Liking is more enduring.'

'You and Frank?' Claudia ventured.

Valerie shrugged. 'Yes. We did love each other. Totally. Quite unusual, I think. We were soul-mates, you see. It made it hard when he died, but even so, I still feel he's my companion. I know exactly how he would respond to things, what his views would be. I often have a little word with him at the risk of someone overhearing and thinking me totally dotty.'

'I'm afraid I feel quite jealous of people who can claim real love matches. I suppose it's what all of us want, and feel we have when we start out on marriage, and then somehow some of us find we don't make the grade. It still feels like a failure to me.'

'You have other things,' said Valerie. 'Other blessings. The good things in life are not meted out equally and the choice of marriage partner is as much chance as judgement, isn't it? I don't think that is a particular stick with which you should beat yourself.'

'I hope not. I mean, I hope I get over feeling like that. I suppose it goes back to upbringing. My father was a C of E parson, you know, and my sister Kate and I grew up with a horror of divorce instilled in us. That reminds me, I was going to ask you about church. You do go, don't you? I'd like to come with you. Would you mind? I suddenly feel the need to hear those Prayer Book words again that were so much part of my growing up. Things like, "Come unto me all that are heavy laden and I will refresh you." Do you think the congregation could cope with me? Would my presence cause a stir?'

'The vicar would be delighted and sod the rest of them. To be fair, I don't believe anyone would turn a hair. You'd be a bit of a curiosity at first, but then so is anyone new. There's a service here in the village every other Sunday. It's Harvest Festival next week. How about that? A full church usually, where you won't feel conspicuous.'

'Perfect. Thank you. Now, I would very much like to help you with sorting your things, if you'd let me. I have time to spare and to tell the truth, I'd like to have something to do. I know I should make more of an effort in my garden but this would be more companionable.'

'I'd be very grateful, Claudia. It's a monumental task and I do not feel much like tackling it on my own. Now where's that cup of tea?'

'What was Christopher's wife like?' Claudia asked later, as they sat with their second cup.

'Karis? She was delightful. Clever and beautiful. You know she was Chinese?'

'I didn't. No. have the girls been brought up to feel more English, or the other way round?'

'I don't think either, in particular. So far, it hasn't really mattered. They've been used to a very international community in Hong Kong and they go to international schools. It will be different when they get here. That's the only thing which slightly concerns me.'

'Have they got Chinese relatives from their mother's side?'

'No. None at all. I am not aware that Karis had any family.'

'Then wherever you are will be home.'

'I hope so. I can't help but remember what it was like when I came here from India. How lost and dislocated I felt, never really belonging, and of course then India was transformed and a lot of what I knew was swept away. It left me feeling homeless and adrift. That was why Frank was so important. He really was my new-found land.'

'I don't think children are brought up like that any more. The world really has become a smaller place. Globalisation or something. Children in the developed world play with the same PlayStation thingummies, watch the same television, see the same films, listen to the same music, wear the same clothes. They share a sort of international culture whether one likes it or not. For instance, the days of British children wearing those little velvet collared tweed coats and reading Beatrix Potter are far, far in the past. I'm sure your little family will fit in with no difficulty at all.'

'I hope so.'

'I think it's much harder to be different in the way Jena is. Have you heard or seen anything of her? Since Jerome has gone and the evenings are dark, I haven't seen her at all, and I worry about how she's getting on at her new school. This weekend I thought I would walk Finn along the line to look for her.'

'I spoke to her father the other day. He isn't the most communicative of men, but I gather she's all right and seems to be happier. One thing he said which did disturb me a little was that he will be selling that horse of hers in the spring. Isn't it a shame?'

'Oh, no! Why?'

'It's obvious, isn't it? He bought it as a two-year-old and it's turned out to be something rather special. He hopes to sell it very well. He says he'll get another youngster and start over again. He said Jena was used to having horses passing through their hands. That's life, he said.'

Claudia stood up and collected the mugs to take them through to the kitchen. She shook her head. 'I can't bear it,' she said grimly. 'Poor, poor kid. Don't children *suffer!*'

Star Bishop enjoyed her holiday. She came back to work in the village with a deep tan and a willingness to show off the white bits which had the lunchtime drinkers in The Bugle choking into their pints. She and Rosco considered they had hit lucky with their choice of resort. The Spanish beach had been packed with sunbathers and there was standing room only in the dirty warm shallows of the sea. A fast four-lane carriageway divided the beach from the high-rise concrete hotels and a smell of cooking oil hung in the polluted, smoggy air through which the hazy sun sent burning rays.

Star emerged from her hotel on the dot of ten every morning, having helped herself liberally at the breakfast buffet bar to hard round rolls, packs of German butter and plastic tubs of French jam. The coffee came in sachets, the UHT milk originated in Holland, and the reconstituted orange juice from Israel. For Star, none of these things were drawbacks. What she cared about was that her room was cleaned every morning by a North African girl called Mimi, the sheets and towels changed and she could get up from the bloody table, as she said, and leave the whole bloomin' lot to be cleared away by somebody else. She loved the sound of pop music which was always somewhere in the air, the flashing lights advertising bars and all-night dancing, the pressing mass of humanity, stripped down to shorts and bra tops and oiled flesh scorched fiery red. She loved the concrete, the noise, the people, the queues, the raucous laughter, the groups of drunken, leering men, and the pervasive promise of sexual adventures to be had if you were up for it.

'Don't get me wrong,' she told her friends when she passed round her holiday photographs of drunken nightclub scenes. 'I didn't have a shag all week, but I could 'ave. If I'd felt like it.'

From ten until two she lay on the sun lounger, then back to the hotel for a beer and egg and chips and a bit of a lie down. Four o'clock saw her back sunbathing, then a shower and a traipse round the shops. Ten o'clock, she and Rosco had their dinner – usually steak and chips and a bloody great ice-cream sundae, and then out they went drinking and dancing. She got back, knackered, at two most mornings and Rosco sometimes stayed out until six and slept until six the following evening.

'Hardly saw the sun, our Rosco,' she said. 'Didn't get up until after dark.'

The best thing, she said, was the laughs, and laugh she did. The hotel lobby and lifts and dining room and bars rang with Star's bellowing laugh. She laughed with the sad-eyed waiters, the flirtatious barmen, the other guests, the taxi drivers, the shopkeepers. She even made tiny, exhausted Mimi laugh, especially on the last morning while she and Rosco were waiting for the coach to take them to the airport and she emptied her purse of remaining pesetas and pushed them into her hand.

'Here, love,' she said. 'Buy yourself something on me and Rosco.'

Now back in the cool of England she still wore her T-shirts and shorts to show off her burnished limbs. 'Touch of the tar brush, there, my girl,' said old Tom. 'T'isn't natural to get that brown. That's mahogany, that is!'

Star dug him in the ribs. 'You'll be saying my hair ain't natural next, Tom!'

'If your hair's natural,' said Tom, wiping his mouth on his sleeve, 'I'm the Queen Mother!'

'That reminds me. They're still away up at East End House, the Durnfords are. Back tomorrow. I'm on my way up there now to give it a going over. You coming, Tom? That garden needs digging.' She winked at Monica and Tom turned away, ignoring her. He'd be back in his own time. He wouldn't be told what to do by any bloody woman and that included Star Bishop, big tits and all.

'I'm surprised they went away, considering,' said Star. 'What with them criminals living next door.'

'What do you mean?' asked Monica.

'You know,' said Star, enjoying a good stir. 'That Claudia woman. Her husband might have got the word around that the house was empty, seeing he's inside.'

'He's not that sort of criminal,' said Monica equably. 'His was fraud, like. Not breaking and entering.'

'Yeah, but who's he mixing it with now? All types.'

'Last time,' said Tom, 'you were blaming the travellers. Saying it was them did the thieving. Now it's that woman in the bungalow. I don't mind who knows it but I like her. She's a nice lady. You shouldn't talk like that. It's not right, and I'll not stay to hear it.' He plonked down his empty glass and stomped out.

Star and Monica looked after him. Star pulled a face.

'He's right,' said Monica, picking up a cloth and wiping the

288

bar. 'You should be careful what you say, Star.'

'Bloody hell!' said Star, pulling down her T-shirt. 'I thought this was a free country.'

'Rosco enjoyed it then?' asked Monica, to change the subject. It had seemed unlikely to her that a teenage boy would go on holiday with his mother and still have a good time.

'Yeah. Got himself a girl. Nice little thing called Susie. Lives in Stoke or somewhere up in the Midlands. Reckons he's in love. Yeah, Rosco had a great time. We got on great, too. Hardly saw him, mind you, after the first day.'

Laughs had not been a feature of the Durnfords' holiday in the Gambia. The weather had been disappointing, overcast and stormy, and Peter had annoyed Julia by reading all day in their hotel bedroom and not making any effort to go out and swim or sightsee. 'You might just as well be at home,' she had complained, to which he had replied shortly, 'Yes, I might,' which was a dig at her for insisting on going away, when he had been reluctant to spend the money.

He had cheered up at times and seemed almost his old self. She had insisted that they had sex, but it could not have been termed lovemaking in any sense of the word. When he had finished, he had rolled off her and over onto his side and gone to sleep. Bloody hell, thought Julia crossly, that was a three out of ten performance, if ever there was one. She'd had a better time cleaning the bath. To make a point she sat up and turned on the light to read her book, turning the pages as noisily as possible and sighing heftily to register her dissatisfaction.

Otherwise she had enjoyed the change and, when the weather improved towards the end of the week, lying by the pool and calling for cold drinks to be brought to her by the charming waiters. After starving for three weeks she now felt justified in relaxing her diet and enjoying the really good food in the hotel. It could have been heaven, apart from the changeable weather and the equally changeable Peter.

Things came to a head as they packed to leave. She couldn't even remember what it was that had irritated her into saying, 'Really, Peter. What *is* the matter with you? You've been a total pain in the neck! Are you unwell or something?'

He had suddenly sat on the bed and put his head in his hands and for a moment she was frightened. He had looked up at her with a miserable expression and said, 'I don't know whether I can go on with this,' in a lifeless tone.

'With what?' she had demanded, uncertain and cross.

'With all this?'

'What, packing?'

He gave a gesture of impatience. 'With living with you. I don't know whether I want to.'

'What do you mean, living with me?' She could not take in what he was saying.

'I don't know whether I can face the rest of my life with you,' he said slowly and clearly.

She looked at him in astonishment, not believing her ears. 'Don't be so silly,' was all that she could think of in reply.

Claudia enjoyed the Harvest Festival at the primary school. The hall was decorated with apples and pears and punnets of squelching blackberries, and two bales of sweet green hay and huge marrows and courgettes and tomatoes. Cabbages, cauliflowers, onions, carrots, beetroots and corn came in supermarket carrier bags, and larger children staggered under small sacks of potatoes. Some children bought packets of biscuits and tinned peas and peaches, but this didn't matter, explained Mrs Peck, because they were going to thank God for the fruits of all the earth and the old people who were going to receive the bounty afterwards would be just as pleased with a tin of peaches as anything else.

Tiny children struggled through the school gates with gaudy bunches of dahlias and Michaelmas daisies from their gardens and a teacher brought a huge sunflower head which had grown accidentally from seed she had put out for the birds. There were baskets of duck eggs, goose eggs, hens' eggs, tiny bantam eggs and even guinea fowl eggs. There were jars of every sort of homemade jam and chutney. The children from the organic smallholding brought clover honey and four naughty boys from Primary Six dragged in a dirty old feed bag containing a dead badger which they had found run over on the road to school.

Claudia tried to continue the theme with her menus for the week, featuring as much local food as possible, with dishes to which she gave names like Barton Pie and Bishop's Bake, and with baked potatoes and cauliflower cheese and blackberry and apple crumbles and baked apples and custard. She and her assistants were invited to attend Friday's service and she watched entranced as the vicar talked to the children about the fruits of the earth, while the little upturned faces shone with optimism and innocence in the front rows and a forest of hands shot up when he asked a question.

Going to the service in the village church was something different altogether and she nearly cried off at the last moment, thinking, why am I doing this? It's running counter to all the decisions I made about living here and keeping a low profile, not getting involved. Then she remembered what Valerie had said about the church being fuller than usual for the harvest service and she thought, damn it, it's now or never. She dressed simply in a dark skirt and an old tweed jacket she wore to work and although it was not far to walk, Valerie suggested that they took her car. 'Looks like rain,' she said to the clear sky. She thinks we'll be less conspicuous, Claudia realised.

She had been into the old church before, sneaking in when the door was unlocked to sit for a moment in the cool, peaceful interior. She had picked up the leaflet for visitors and read that it was a largely thirteenth-century building with a side chapel added in the fifteenth century. She skimmed through the ups and downs of its history, the new tower (sixteenth century), the later chancel windows, the fonts, the pulpit; added to, rebuilt, adapted as the centuries rolled by. Now, as she and Valerie threaded their way through the crowd of people gathered by the door, she was aware of how it still served as a focal point. She recognised many familiar faces and a number of children she knew from school, who tugged at their parents to point her out. There was the usual mix of people that she would have expected, with many grey heads amongst the congregation, but also, perhaps because of the special occasion, a lot of families as well. She was aware of glances being shot in her direction, but after she and Valerie took their seats she no longer felt at all conspicuous and became caught up in the familiar words of the old book of Common Prayer which her father had always stuck to, and the hymns she knew by heart. 'For the beauty of the earth,' they sang, 'For the beauty of the skies.'

When they settled down for the sermon, she glanced about, appreciating all the hard work the Flower Committee must have done with decorating. The church glowed with the ruby colours of fruit and vegetables heaped on every step and sill, an old-fashioned stook of corn leaned against the pulpit and the altar flowers were magnificent. She saw the Durnfords towards the front, Peter tall in a tweed jacket, Julia in a navy jacket and a flowerpot felt hat, and she could not stop her heart lurching at the sight of Anthony Brewer at the end of a pew on the opposite side. She would not try to avoid them, although it was a temptation. She had to get through this with some dignity and scuttling out at the end of the service would not do. As they finished with a rousing, 'We plough the field and scatter the good seed on the land,' she felt her hands tremble and was grateful for the time on her knees as the service came to a close.

Then Valerie took over, cutting a majestic swathe through the people dawdling their way out, greeting the vicar and introducing Claudia in a loud, clear voice, saying, 'So lucky to have her in the village.' The vicar shook Claudia's hand warmly and then the press of people made her move on. Outside the door, Julia was buttonholing people she wanted to 'catch'. She looks older, thought Claudia. The holiday tan was rather unflattering, emphasising the lines which ran down from the corners of her mouth. She nodded at Claudia and Valerie. 'Good morning,' she said briefly and turned to talk to someone behind them.

'She's like the bloody Ancient Mariner,' said Valerie loudly as they walked away down the path. 'She stoppeth one in three.'

Claudia heard a snort of laughter and half turned to see Anthony behind them.

'You are very naughty, Valerie,' he said after greeting them both. 'The village wouldn't function without people like Julia. Now, how about a glass of sherry?'

'No thank you, Anthony. At least not for me,' said Valerie. 'I have some work to get on with. Claudia?'

'Well, that's very kind of you,' said Claudia uncertainly. Did she feel up to another challenge? She wondered.

'Come on, do. Come and meet Ivo,' he said encouragingly.

'Yes, all right. I'd love to. Thank you so much, Valerie, for the escort. I felt in very safe hands with you!'

To his great dismay, Peter Durnford, having hurried through counting the collection money, bolted down the church path to see Anthony Brewer and Claudia walking away together, deep in conversation, and then turn off into the gateway of Manor Farm.

Bugger, he thought miserably. Bugger. Even Victoria coming home for lunch did not cheer him up. He looked at his watch. He had offered to go and collect her from the station, at least that would get him out of the house for a bit. There was nothing for it but to go back and wait for Julia who was talking to the vicar about the cleaning rota for the church brass.

Since his outburst on holiday he had been thoroughly in the doghouse and knew he deserved to be. It was as if he and Julia had strayed off track into completely unknown territory and did not know how to get back on course again. She, understandably, had been tight-lipped and angry all the way home and as a sort of temporary solution he had got drunk on the flight back and slept for most of it.

Since then the matter had not been raised again. Back at the office and in their familiar surroundings he knew it was hopeless anyway. What on earth had he wanted to achieve? He couldn't even remember clearly. He had no hope with Claudia, he knew that. He also knew that he did not want to be turfed out by Julia to live somewhere on his own. There were the children to consider, for one thing, and he couldn't bear to hurt Victoria. The only course open to him was to try to ingratiate himself with Julia and hope that things would eventually settle down. It was an uphill task. She wore her grievance with hostility and brushed off his pathetic efforts to please. She slammed meals down in front of him and they ate in frosty silence. Afterwards she spent the evenings on the telephone to her girlfriends, pointedly finishing the conversation if he came into the room.

The thing was, he did not really feel any differently about her than he had done for years. Mild dislike, affection, loyalty, a mass of contradictory emotions; he couldn't disentangle one strand from another. He didn't know about love. The wild reckless feeling he had had for Claudia, which had so unhinged him and which he thought of as love, seemed to have deserted him now. For a while it had been like a lifebelt thrown to a drowning man and had given him a mad flash of hope, of rescue, and a glimpse of a different life, but it had proved to be a leaky, sinking affair which would not keep him afloat. Maybe love, durable love, was what he felt for Julia. He certainly didn't want to hurt her and was grieved to realise that he had. Not only that, it was bloody boring having to go through this whole performance day after day. He longed for a return to normality and wondered how long she would keep it up. Bugger everything. What a fool he was.

Chapter Seventeen

It was Lila who telephoned Claudia to tell her about the baby.

'Mum, it's been born. Dad's just sent me an email. She's had a baby girl.'

It took Claudia a moment to realise to whom her daughter was referring.

'Carla,' said Lila. 'She's had a girl. They're going to call it Dethany, or Bethlehem, or Bathsheba or something like that. Jesus, Mum, I've got a half-sister!'

Claudia slid down the wall to sit on the floor. 'Takes some getting used to, doesn't it?' she said slowly. 'Everything was all right? Straightforward birth?'

'As far as I know. I can't remember how big she was. Isn't that the thing everyone wants to know? But Dad was pleased, as if he'd landed a decent sized salmon.'

'Well, it *is* exciting for him, I can see that. Where was she born?'

'Here. In New York. Mum, I thought I'd go and see her. Dad has given me the telephone number. A half-sister!' Lila sounded tremendously excited, too. Claudia felt a nasty little drag of disappointment and hated herself for it.

'That would be lovely.' She tried to make her voice bright. 'You can report to him first hand, then.'

'Yeah, that's what I thought. I'm coming over, Mum. In two weeks, but only a flying visit, and I'll go and see him then. I thought I could take some photographs.'

'Can you come on here? It seems ages since I saw you.' Claudia tried to keep the whine out of her voice.

'Mum, I'd love to, but there won't be time.' She hesitated. 'It's a sort of business trip. But I want to come at Christmas. Is that OK?'

'Oh, Lila. That would be lovely, to have you and Jerome.'

'Yeah, I thought so, too. Even the horror bung can be made festive, can't it?'

'Absolutely. You bet.'

'How's Mrs Dynarod?' Lila loved playing with names. 'The ghastly woman next door? Is it still a war zone? Time to call in the UN?'

'Yes, virtually. Victoria and Peter are fine, though. It's only her.'

'And Jena and Jigs? And darling Finn? Can't wait to see them all.'

'They're all fine. Finn's a dratted nuisance, but I do love him. He comes to work with me and sleeps in the car. He's calmed down a lot since I had him de-balled.'

'Mum! You didn't! Poor baby. Look, Mum, I'll have to go. Speak to you soon. Kiss kiss!'

Claudia remained where she was on the floor after putting down the receiver. Lila's position had dramatically shifted, she thought crossly, to one of acceptance. Why, she had sounded enthusiastic about this baby, even though she must realise that its birth meant there was no possibility of going back to how things were. The distressing thing was to find how that upset her – it was like losing another rock in the old landscape. Shit! she thought, I've got to stop this. I categorically do not want Roger back. I used to complain that Lila could not understand, and now she has accepted it, I find it hurtful. And the baby! I mind about the bloody baby! Bethlehem! Surely Lila had got that wrong? You couldn't call a baby Bethlehem. What hurt, of course, what really hurt, was that she had so badly wanted another child, years and years ago, and Roger had said it was out of the question.

Damn! Her eyes started to fill with hot tears. Damn! She felt sorry for herself again. She couldn't help it. It was so effing, effing unfair!

She got up off the floor and stood biting her lip. It was still early. A rotten time which left her with a whole empty space of evening to fill before she could reasonably call it a day. A drink? She went to the fridge and got out a bottle of wine. She would like to talk to someone. Someone who would understand. It was Minna's night for late surgery. Valerie was in London for a few days. She could ring Anthony. Ask him round for a drink. However, when she dialled his number she was put through immediately to the answer machine, and without leaving a message, she rang off. Damn. Perhaps, though, it was just as well to see this through on her own. She would have gone to bed with him if he had come round, she knew that. Maybe that would have meant just another layer of complication to add to how she already felt. She opened the bottle, poured herself a large glass and went into the sitting room. She would light a fire, she thought, and sit with Finn on her knees. Then she would read the novel she was enjoying, listen to some music and make a determined effort to be sensible.

Collecting a handful of kindling from the sack in the garage, she thought of Anthony. He had been sweet to her that Sunday, kindness itself, pouring her two strong gins and then asking her to stay to lunch. 'Just a scratch affair – no roast sizzling in the oven, I'm afraid.' Ivo had been a surprise – tall and dark with a deep, expensive looking tan, and quite ten or fifteen years younger than Anthony. He had a similar manner, relaxed and smooth, and the same attractive voice. He was distracted by the telephone; there had been at least five calls in half an hour, and then had reappeared to say that he was due out to lunch and had come to say goodbye.

After he'd gone, Anthony had kissed her in the kitchen, urgently, pressing his sturdy body hard into hers, backing her against the cupboards. 'Darling,' he had whispered. 'Come to bed?' And she had. She was a pushover, and she had enjoyed every minute of it. They hadn't got up until it was nearly dark and she guiltily remembered poor Finn. Anthony ran her home and in the fluster to find her key, with Finn yelping and scrabbling on the other side of the door, she did not register that he had not said anything about seeing her again. They kissed briefly and he had gone back to his car and the milking. She had opened the door and let the poor dog out, then changed and took him for a run in the dark.

That was how it was going to be, she thought, and now she had adjusted, she could cope. The subject of Scotland had not been raised and she had resisted asking him if he had invited someone else in her place. Of course he had. She could take that for granted. A man of his sort would always find a woman. Now, as she sat by the flaring fire with her drink and a bag of crisps and Finn flat out on the hearth rug, she felt lonely and sad. Roger, a father again. She could not help but remember his elation when Lila and Jerome were born. Now he would be feeling like that again and that was another thing stripped away from her – those most precious first moments of parenthood which they had shared, and which now no longer belonged exclusively to her or her children. Suddenly she thought of Carla in some swish New York hospital, nursing Roger's baby, but with him not only thousands of miles away, but behind bars and prevented from sharing the wonder with her. Poor Carla, she thought. What a shit position to be in, and perversely, feeling sorry for Carla cheered her up considerably.

After the Harvest Festival service, Julia Durnford slammed the joint of lamb in the oven and started peeling the windfalls for the crumble. It was lovely to have Tor home for lunch. For one thing it alleviated the poisonous atmosphere between her and Peter. She glanced at the kitchen clock and wondered whether ten to twelve was too early to have a drink. She decided not and poured herself a glass of white wine from the box in the fridge. Returning to the bruised and wormy apples, she wondered what would come of it all. The blow delivered to her self-esteem by Peter's outburst was as acutely painful as ever. She wasn't only hurt, she was bloody, bloody angry as well. How dared he? She thought, over and over again. Her clear view of their marriage was that Peter was damn lucky to have her. She was a bloody good wife and mother, she knew that. Everyone did. She might not have a career or be like one of those mothers she had come across at the children's schools, who ran businesses and jet-setted about. Peter would have hated that anyway. Not only was she what was acknowledged as being a bloody good w & m, she had also brought all this with her, and she looked out of the kitchen window at the sweep of back drive and the hydrangeas. All this. This house and a place in things, an established position in the district.

Peter was obviously going through this male menopause thing. Jo had told her to take no notice. Keep him on a choke chain, she'd said. Put him into a double bridle and keep him on a very, very short rein. That'll teach him. This is how she treated Adrian, she had confided, when she had discovered he was having an affair with a secretary. She had been very strict with him indeed and had made him buy her a five-figure new horse and take her away to Tobago.

That sort of advice was all very well, but the truth was that she was sick of the unpleasant atmosphere between them and just wished things could be as they were before. Sometimes she had really wanted to go over to him and put her arms round him and say, 'Come on. This isn't getting us anywhere. Let's forget the whole thing.' Instead she seemed trapped in acting in a hurt and resentful way, and the more he tried to placate and put things right, the more she wanted to kick him in the balls.

It would be easier, she thought, if he was like Adrian, who had affairs. Some men were like that. At least she could be a wounded wife. It was less shaming than Peter's simply going off her. Not liking her any more. God, it still made her furious.

Sick of fiddling about with the remaining apples, she shot them into the bucket for the compost heap and took a large swig of wine. He had no right to go off her. No right at all. If anyone was going to do the going off, it should have been her. Why didn't he realise that?

In her heart of hearts, Julia knew that their marriage had to stagger along somehow, that breaking up was not ever in question. What they had to do, she supposed, was find a modus vivendi, some way of making the changed circumstances into a new way of life. It wasn't any good going on as they were now, that was for certain. Something had to change. She just didn't see why it bloody well had to be her.

Peter did not have to wait long at the station for Tor. Her train came in miraculously on time and he got out and went to meet her. She had on an old navy sweatshirt and jeans and trainers and her hair was loose and shiny. She looked very tall and slim and grown-up, he thought, with a stab of something which felt almost like pain. This lovely girl with her luminous pale skin and large brown eyes was his. Her thick dark lashes and clear sweep of dark brows moved him unbearably as she leaned forward to kiss him. Why, she was a beauty, his girl. She was beautiful. He had to gulp hard to quell the emotion he suddenly felt.

'Hi, Dad. You OK?'

'Hello, darling. Yes, fine. And you, Mouse, old thing? How's my best girl?'

'Fine, Dad. How was the holiday? You don't look very brown.'

'Not good weather, I'm afraid. The holiday was fine. Did Mum good to get away.' How easy it was to lie, to allow the easy words to slide out and mask the truth.

'Yeah? Is she OK? She's sounded a bit odd on the phone. Sort of down.'

Peter started the car and they began the drive home.

'I suppose she might be a bit,' he said lamely. 'What with one thing and another.'

'What thing?' asked Tor, turning to look at him. He was glad to concentrate on passing a milk tanker. 'Is it Skye? You know, Dad, have you thought of how much she must miss him? He was really more her dog than anybody's. He was like a best friend to her. Always there. At least, apart from when he wasn't, if you know what I mean. I was thinking, you ought to get her a puppy. Have you thought of that?'

'We did discuss it, but she didn't want to think of it then. Said it was too soon and what with going away on holiday. Maybe we should think again.'

'You should. Why not get her one without asking? As a present. She's always wanted a labrador hasn't she? You could get it trained and all that, and she could take it out shooting with you.'

Peter considered. Poor old Julia. Victoria's words fanned the little spark of affection he still felt for his wife. 'Do you think that would be a good idea? Without asking her?'

'Yes, I do, Dad. Do something unexpected for a change.'

'Bloody expensive, a good gun dog.'

'Dad! Don't be so mean. She deserves it!'

'OK, Mouse, if you think it's a good idea. Will you help me find one? We could try and get her one for Christmas.'

'Of course I will. I'd love to.'

'So how is school?'

'Turgid, but better this term. I seem to get on with people more.' Victoria picked at a hole in the knee of her jeans. She suddenly looked up and shot him a brilliant smile. 'I've heard from Jerome. He writes to me, Dad. The other girls think I'm really cool now. They think he's my boyfriend, and because he's so old and at Cambridge, they're really impressed. It's sad, isn't it?'

'Very sad,' Peter agreed, smiling back at her. His daughter was in love. That was it. That's what made her look so different, so beautiful.

The autumn countryside sped by, the trees now brilliant gold and red, the fields losing their green lushness. In the distance a tractor was combing a hillside with a plough, followed by a flock of circling gulls.

'What's for lunch?' asked Victoria, looking out of the window as they passed a girl exercising a grey horse.

'Baa lamb, I think, Mouse!'

'Oh yum! Good old Mum.'

When they got back to East End House, Tor was out of the car in a flash, leaving the passenger door open.

'God, it's lovely to be home!' she said, turning back to wait for her father.

From the back seat Peter collected the cartons of milk Julia had wanted and together they went into the kitchen. There was a delicious smell of roast meat and the lamb stood on a meat plate on the lid of the Aga. Julia had her back to them at the sink, a tea towel draped over her shoulder.

'Hi, darling,' she called, turning her head.

'Hi, Mum! You look browner than Dad. You wouldn't know he'd been anywhere!' Victoria kissed her mother and stole a sip out of her glass of wine and then bolted upstairs to her room, calling after her, 'Lunch smells fab. I am totally starved!'

Peter hesitated. He got a glass for himself out of the cupboard and the wine box out of the fridge. He went to stand behind Julia who was chopping up a cabbage.

'Refill?' he asked.

'Mmm, please.' Her tone sounded very slightly less chilly. He dribbled wine from the box into their glasses, and putting hers on the cupboard by her elbow, slid his arms round her and kissed the back of her neck.

'Sorry, old thing. I'm truly, truly sorry. I do love you, you know. Very much.'

Rosco Bishop sat on his bed counting his money. He had considerably less than the last time he counted. The holiday with his Mum had eaten into his capital and he'd even had to lend her some for fags on the way home through the airport duty free. Now he wondered whether he was ever going to be able to afford that bike. If he wanted to see Susie, he had to get to Wolverhampton and it cost a bloody fortune and took bleeding hours on the train. He'd done it once, via Bristol, and when he got there it was nigh on time to come back. He'd stayed with her mum and dad in their little redbrick terrace house near Wolves football ground. He'd liked them. Got on well. Her dad had been made redundant from some engineering works and was on the social. Her mum was a taxi driver. They were quiet people with grey hair and lined, worried faces. He was glad that they hadn't met his mum. Not that they wouldn't have liked her, most people did, but she'd have scared them shitless, the way she'd been on holiday. Pissed most of the time and bright red with too much sun and her hair gone into a pink Brillo pad from the pool water.

He thought about Susie, so small and pale and quiet with tiny little hands. He couldn't believe her hands. His mum's were big and red, and so were most of her friends', he'd noticed since he'd got home. He remarked on the fact that women's hands got red and Star had laughed and hit him on the back of the head with the empty cornflake box she was putting in the bin. 'Yeah! 'Cos we spend most of our lives cleaning, don't we? Had mine down the bloody drain this morning!'

Susie's were so small and pale, yellow-white, and the fingers so tiny that they were like little colourless sticks and the nails were tiny pink ovals. He loved looking at them, they were that delicate. When he held one it felt like a little dry leaf in his, that fragile. She was so sweet, little Susie. Never had a boyfriend before and he could believe it. She didn't know nothing. Didn't know how to kiss and he'd been that gentle with her because of it. He wouldn't lay a finger on her that she didn't want, wasn't ready for.

They'd only kissed and held hands and on the last day when they'd been dancing all night in a club, he'd laid a hand on the tiny mound of her right breast and she hadn't minded; he'd even felt the nipple harden, like a little nut or something. They were so lovely, her breasts, like little saucers resting on her frail ribs. He thought with distaste of his mother's enormous pair, or someone like that Mrs Pomeroy with a chest that looked as if she'd got a corgi up her jumper.

Susie had spent the days with her parents on the beach or by the pool and she'd gone a faint brown eventually, the colour of a Nice biscuit. Her fair, thin hair had turned almost white and her pale blue eyes looked even more pale and blue. She was the sweetest little thing he'd ever seen. He thought of the big, coarse girls at school with their heavy bodies, their knowing looks and their shouts of vulgar laughter.

Rosco looked at his money again. It was cheaper to go to Wolverhampton by coach and didn't take much longer. He was planning to go the weekend after next. Her dad wanted to take him to a Wolves match, a home game, and Susie had said, 'It means he likes you, Rosc. He wouldn't offer otherwise.' Meanwhile they had to make do with talking on their mobiles. That was costing him an effing fortune, but he didn't care, and sending text messages. He was going to go there at Christmas when Mr Martin shut up for ten days. He hadn't liked to tell his mum yet. He didn't know whether she'd mind or not.

He rolled up the notes and put them back. Sean was coming round later and they'd go out for a bit of a bevvy. Sean had bought a motocross bike, and after, they might go and try it out along the old railway line. There was a bonfire party in

Sharston they might look in at, but it was really only for kids.
Sean said he'd got some firecrackers off his older brother and
they could let them off somewhere, have a bit of fun, but
Rosco didn't want any trouble. He was nearly off his probation
and now he'd got Susie he didn't want no more aggro. It was
kids' stuff anyway.

Jena was alone in the bus. Not entirely alone, because she had
fetched in Meg the lurcher bitch and Spider the one pup they
had left, to keep her company. From the direction of Sharston
there was the occasional bright burst in the sky and faint sound
of an explosion as the firework party came to its finale, and out
across the vale, where there were hidden farms and hamlets,
the night sky was punctured by showers of colour and a noise
like shells falling. Meg whined and crept closer. She hated
thunder and lightning and tonight, Guy Fawkes Night, was
torture to her. Jena had put cotton wool in her ears tied a thick
woollen scarf round her head to block her ears, but she still
trembled and shook and rolled her eyes in terror. By contrast,
Spider slept peacefully on Jena's bed.

Jena let Meg crawl into the space under the desk where she
was working on some of her father's data. He and Hagar had
taken Robbie and Brian to watch the fireworks and they were
going to bring her back a fish and chip supper. She hadn't
wanted to go anyway, and didn't like leaving poor Meg. Her dad
had asked her to fill in some stuff he was collecting about
vertebrates. It was amazing how many little wild animals used
the hedgerows as corridors and Jena liked to think of them all
safe tonight, crouching in their woody homes, watching the
miracle of the sky erupting above them. What did they make of
it all, she wondered, the hedgehogs and rabbits and voles and
shrews and field mice? And did they remember it from year to
year so that the older ones could say, 'Don't you worry. This
happens every year about this time. It's not the end of the
world'? She was thinking this as she typed into the computer
the number of badger sets, used and disused, and when the
bang came on the door, she nearly jumped out of her skin.

Of course, any other night and Meg would have flown to the
door, barking wildly, but tonight she stayed where she was,
cowering under the desk, and Spider hardly bothered to look
up.

'Who is it?' yelled Jena, her heart thumping, standing just
inside the door, glad that she had locked it.

'It's me! Rosco! Let us in, Jena. It's me and Sean!'

'What you want?' she said, sliding the bolt across and letting the boys in. 'Gave me a fright, you did. What you doing creeping about out there?'

'Not bleeding creeping,' said Sean. 'Came on the bike. What yer doing?'

'Stuff for me dad,' said Jena, saving the work she had done and switching off the computer.

'It's bleeding nice in here, isn't it?' said Rosco. 'Is that where you sleep? Cosy, isn't it?'

'Yeah, I'd be cosy in here with a nice fat tart,' said Sean, laughing. 'You got anything to drink, girl?'

'Nah,' said Jena. 'Don't keep none. No fags either.'

'Where's yer dad, then?' asked Sean, peering out through the window at the dark night.

Jena started to feel a faint unease. She didn't like Sean. She didn't like the way he went round the bus, picking everything up, looking at it. Her stuff. She didn't like him touching it like that.

'He'll be back in a minute,' she said. 'He's just gone out to get some fags.'

'Funny that,' said Sean, ''Cos we passed him, didn't we, Rosco, and I'd have said they was going into Sharston for the fireworks. Got the kiddies with them, hadn't they, Rosc?'

'Yeah,' said Rosco, looking a bit uncomfortable. He didn't know what Sean was up to. Jena was only a kid.

Sean, without being invited, sat on Jena's bed. He pushed Spider off and patted the place next to him. 'Come and sit down, girl,' he said. 'Come and tell me what it's like to be a bleedin' gyppo.'

'Aw, come on, Sean. Leave off,' said Rosco, opening the door and peering out, hoping he might see the approaching lights of the Loaders' old jeep.

'Eff off, pizza face,' said Jena. 'Get bleeding out of here. I never asked you in. Go on, eff off!'

Sean got up and lumbered over to her. He caught her arm and twisted it behind her back. 'Shut up, you!' he said. Pinning the arm behind her back he ran a hand over the front of her sweater. 'Here! You got any titties yet? You goin' to let me have a look? And what about here?' He ran his hand down between her legs. 'How old are yer? Got a nice little pussy, I bet. You goin' to show me, darlin?'

'Sean! What's the matter with you? Leave her alone, you perve. Christ!'

'Aw! She's only a fucking traveller.' Sean let Jena go, and in the split second that he released his hold she brought her sharp little knee up with a violent jerk and shot him a cutting blow to his balls. He let out a cry of acute pain and doubled up, swearing violently. Tears started in his eyes and his face got redder, contorting with pain and anger.

'Jesus! The bloody bitch!' he swore.

'They're coming!' cried Rosco, looking out of the door of the bus. 'I can see the lights,' he lied. 'Come on, Sean, you'll get done for fucking assault,' and he pushed his friend out of the door. 'Lock it! Lock the effing door!' he hissed to Jena as he leapt off the top step.

Out in the dark night, he heard the door of the bus slam behind them. Sean was still groaning, his hands cupped over his bollocks. 'She's bloody done me,' he whined.

'Serves you effing right. What were you doing, mucking around with her like that? She's only a bleeding kid. She could get you put away for that!'

'Who'd believe a bleeding traveller! Where's her dad then? I thought you said you heard the jeep?'

'Must have been mistaken,' mumbled Rosco. 'Come on, mate. Let's get the hell out of here!'

But Sean was still angry and he went round the bus, kicking at the sides and jumping up to thump at the windows with his fists. Rosco had to pull him away to stop him smashing things up outside.

'They'll get you for it,' he pleaded. 'Come on, mate. It's not worth it!'

'Fucking travellers!' yelled Sean. 'Go back to fucking wherever you come from!'

Rosco thought that he had got him away when they went back to the bike together and Sean said in a quieter tone, 'You'll have to drive, mate. She's effing crippled me!'

Rosco got on and switched the key and revved up, with Sean on the pillion seat.

A sudden noise from the bank made them both look up and there was Jigsaw, cropping the grass, tethered to a stake, the white patches of his coat gleaming ghostily in the dark.

'What's that?' asked Sean, peering through the dark.

'It's her horse,' said Rosco, wheeling the bike round and regretting what he had said as soon as it was out of his mouth. 'Come on, Sean. Let's get bleeding out of here!' But Sean had got off and was searching for something in his pocket and then

Rosco saw a flash of a lighter and a little blue flame of light.

'For God's sake, Sean! What the fuck are you doing? Come on!' he yelled, but the next moment Sean was lobbing a flaming object in the direction of the horse, there was a blinding light, a sudden burst of noise like gunfire, and in the blue and yellow and green flares which burst in rapid succession, Rosco saw flashes of the horse running wildly round the stake, neighing in terror.

'Oh Christ! You effing madman! What did you do that for?' He threw the bike down and ran hopelessly to the foot of the bank but the horse was on its side now, the rope caught round its legs, and thrashing about wildly, the whites of its eyes rolling in an agony of fear, while the firework continued to burst in showers of flaming raindrops. Rosco scrambled halfway up but then Jigsaw got to his feet, the rope broken and, wildly plunging, one leg still caught, disappeared into the dark.

'Oh Jesus, oh God!' Rosco half wept in despair. He heard the bike start up behind him and Sean laughing.

'That'll show the bloody bitch!'

'Fuck off!' he turned and yelled. 'Fuck off, will yer. Look what you've fucking done now!' and at that Sean gave him two fingers and drove up the track.

Rosco ran to the bus and banged frantically on the door. 'Jena! It's me! Rosco! Open the door! Jena, for Christ's sake! Your horse is loose!' He saw the curtain on the window by the door being pulled aside and Jena's pale face peering out, trying to see into the dark. He banged again and she opened the door a crack.

Claudia was having an early bath with a glass of wine by her side and her novel on the bath rack. Bonfire night reminded her of the children when they were young and the parties they had been to as a family. She could hear the sound of exploding bangers and the whizzing of rockets even over the concert playing on her little portable radio. The village children must be enjoying themselves at the enormous bonfire she had seen being built on the playing fields behind the council houses. She lay back in the foam, worrying about money. She was only just making ends meet and was concerned about Christmas, which would have to be a very low-key affair. She hoped that Lila and Jerome would understand. She was also worried about her mother, who traditionally came to stay over the holiday and for whom there would now be no room. She could, of course, give her her own bed but it would be hard to manage with such pressure on space. She wasn't sure it was fair on Lila and Jerome. She thought of Anthony and Ivo rattling about in their huge house and Valerie with seven empty bedrooms. Perhaps Valerie wouldn't mind giving Jerome a bed for a few nights. She would ask her.

The banging on the door made her drop her book into the water. Bugger, she thought, fishing it out. The pages had become tea-coloured and stuck together in a wet wodge. There were further bangs and a male voice shouting. She stood up in alarm and stepped out, reaching for a towel. What on earth? Immediate fear clutched at her heart. The children? Something had happened to Lila in New York? Her mother? She pulled on the towelling dressing gown from behind the door and went into the hall. Through the patterned glass of the front door she could see a figure standing in the porch.

'Who is it?' she called, fiddling with the lock. 'What's happened?'

'It's Rosco, Mrs Barron. Rosco. Star's boy. It's Jena. Something awful's happened. You've got to come and see!' There was fear in his voice. Fear and urgency.

Claudia got the door open, clutching her dressing gown round her. 'I was in the bath,' she said, 'What's happened?' He looked pale and shocked and then she saw that there were brown smears on his face and the hand he put to his mouth was covered in blood. 'What's happened?' she cried again in agitation.

He burst into noisy tears. 'It's the horse,' he wept, 'her horse! You've got to come.'

He followed her back into the bungalow while she gathered up the clothes she had shed on the bathroom floor. 'I'll have to dress!' she shouted at him, pushing him into the kitchen. 'Get what we need – scissors, whatever. The first aid stuff is in the cupboard there.' She left him dithering about while she pulled on her jeans and sweater, not bothering with underwear. Running back into the kitchen she found her torch and threw on a coat. Tourniquet, tourniquet, she thought, seeing the blood-soaked legs of his jeans. There's a hell of a lot of blood. She seized a sheet out of the airing cupboard and they ran out of the door, Finn between her legs.

'Car?' she asked.

'Yeah! It would be quicker. He's down the lane. He's been in the wire.' She ran back in for her car keys and thought damn, I should ring a vet, but not wanting to waste time, grabbed her bag and threw it into the back of the car along with Finn. A moment later they were sweeping out of the village and just after the last house where the lane plunged into thick, black darkness, Rosco sat forward in his seat and said, 'Just round this bend. Go slowly!' and then the headlights picked out a dreadful scene.

Jigsaw was lying on the lane, half in and half out the ditch, his head stretched out, cradled in Jena's lap. She was sitting on the ground bent over him, stroking and crooning, covered in blood. Her face was streaked with blood and tears. Leaving the engine running, the headlights on, Claudia threw herself out of the car. She couldn't for a moment take in what had happened and did not know whether the child was hurt as well. Then she realised that Jigsaw had been through the hedge, there were broken rails behind him, and that his chest had been ripped open by the barbed wire which seemed to be caught in his stifle also. Every time he struggled, it went deeper into his flesh. Running the torch over his hind legs she could see a dark little fountain of blood pumping out of one of the deeper wounds. He had quite literally been cut to ribbons. She didn't know where to begin. Keeping him quiet must be a priority. If he moved it would only make matters worse. And somehow they must stop this loss of blood.

'We must get help,' she said. 'Rosco, do you have a mobile?'

'Yeah,' he said dully, sniffing and wiping his nose on his sleeve.

'Ring Anthony Brewer. He'll know which vet to get out.' She ran to get her bag and tipped its contents on the driver's seat looking for her diary. 'Here,' she said. 'Here's his number. Get it for me, and then I'll speak to him.'

She reached for the first aid kit and the sheet. It was all useless. She didn't know how to deal with injuries like this. She began to rip up the sheet and went back to the horse to look at him more closely. Jena had not moved and Claudia could not bear to see the misery etched on her little face. Taking off her coat she put it over her shoulders. 'Just go on doing that,' she said reassuringly. 'That's the best thing. Keeping him calm, like that.'

The wounds across Jigsaw's shoulders were deep. He had obviously breasted the wire, broken through it, but she did not think they were life threatening. Then somehow his hind legs had been caught in the loose strands. She could see the dark glint of the barbs still embedded in the flesh. She passed a strip of sheet under his thigh and tied it as tightly as she could over the wound which was pumping blood. His tail, caught in the hoops of wire, was stained a deep red and the grass on which he lay was sodden with blood. He's had it, she thought. He's bleeding to death. His eyes were closed and Jena was leaning her face against his cheek. Tears began to stream down Claudia's face.

She realised that Rosco had got through on his telephone and was attempting to explain to Anthony. She took the phone from him and, trying not to sound hysterical but her voice choking, said, 'You must come. We're out on Holt Lane just outside the village. You must get the vet. Please. There's not much I can do. Anthony. Please!' She handed the telephone to Rosco and went back to work on the hind leg that she could get at, tying the strips of sheet to hold the worst wounds closed, trying to staunch the blood.

She ran back to the car and pulled out the old rug she used for Finn and threw it over the horse. She couldn't bear to see the heaving of his flanks and the juddering of his legs. His eyes were still closed and Jena hadn't moved. Her streaked, white face lay against his black cheek and her lips moved soundlessly. What can I say? Thought Claudia. What comfort can I give her? He's going to die. He'll die before the vet gets here.

Rosco was walking up and down the lane, she could see his figure dark against the sky, and every now and then there was another burst of coloured stars. She thought she could hear an engine, and then headlights swept round the corner and Anthony Brewer's Land Rover pulled up behind her car and she saw him leap out, torch in hand.

'What the hell's happened?' he demanded. 'Oh my God!'

Working quickly, telling Claudia to hold the torch, he took wire cutters from the Land Rover and cut the terrible strands which imprisoned Jigsaw's hind legs and very carefully pulled them free. Claudia saw his bloodied hands working with precision, his face frowning in concentration. 'How the hell did this happen?' he demanded. 'He's bloody roped up. He's got a rope round his legs as well!'

'He broke free,' said Rosco miserably, standing by, watching helplessly. 'He was tethered, see. He broke loose.'

Jena suddenly sat up. 'He's dying!' she cried, in anguish. 'He's dying! I can tell. He's going away, he's getting fainter. If he dies, I want to die too. I'll kill myself. I will!'

Claudia went and crouched beside her. She put her arms

round her. 'You must keep him here,' she said. 'Talk to him about all the good things. Talk to him about flying over the hedges with you on a summer morning. Talk about the times you've had together. Keep him here, Jena. Don't let him go!'

Jena looked at her with wild, staring eyes. 'I can't keep him,' she wailed. 'He's leaving me! I'll die too, I promise. I'll die too.'

'Hang on to him, Jena. Talk to him! He knows your voice. He loves you. He trusts you. Keep talking to him!' Claudia couldn't stop her own tears streaming down. She could taste the salt in her mouth.

The little girl dropped her face back onto the black and white head which lay in her lap and although sobs wracked her shoulders and caught in her voice, she began a soft crooning. Claudia saw Jigsaw's ear flick a fraction. 'He's listening,' she whispered. 'He's listening to you! Keep it up, darling. You're bringing him back.' I can't stand this, she thought. He'll die, and what then? What then? What will become of her?

Having Anthony there made all the difference. He plugged some of the wounds with wadding and retied some of Claudia's attempts at bandaging but most of all his presence was reassuring, although he shook his head at Claudia over the prone body in a gesture of despair. Twice he used his telephone to instruct the vet on the nature of the injuries and to find out how much longer he would be. Claudia heard him talk about ringing the kennels, getting the kennel huntsman to come out, and thought, my God, they're going to shoot the horse. They can't shoot him with Jena here. She stayed beside the girl, stroking her hair, listening to the quiet singsong voice. She was talking to Jigsaw about spring grass and about riding through the morning mist and seeing the deer, telling him he was the best horse in the land, telling him he was her darling. Claudia found it almost too painful to listen.

Then the vet arrived, a tall handsome young man called Matt, whom Anthony evidently knew well. He worked quickly and quietly, listening for Jigsaw's heart, giving injections, examining the wounds. He was gentle with Jena, patting her shoulder, telling her she had done a grand job, that she made all the difference, and then moving her out of the way while he examined Jigsaw. Eventually he said, 'He's lost a hell of a lot of blood but his heart is still fairly strong. I think we've stopped the bleeding, but my main concern now, apart from the tissue wounds, which I can't really assess in the dark, is the effect of trauma. We need to get him moved somewhere warm and comfortable. If we can get him up, we'll need a trailer.' He looked at Anthony questioningly.

'Julia,' Anthony said instantly. 'Julia will help. I'll get her to come with her box. We'll take the horse to East End House.'

Shortly afterwards another truck arrived and a sturdy man in a cap got out to join the group. The vet looked up. 'Hi, Mike. Don't know yet. It's hard to say. He's got just a whisker of a chance.' Claudia took him to be the kennel huntsman from the local hunt, normally called to despatch beasts humanely and remove their bodies from the everyday scenes of animal death in the countryside. Now, he bent down to work alongside Matt, holding the edges of wounds together, moving limbs with tenderness and care. They are amazing, these men whose lives are spent with animals, she thought, Anthony and Matt and Mike. Not an ounce of sentimentality, but a huge respect for life.

Later, when Claudia was recounting the story to Lila, she had to admit that Julia had been fantastic. She supposed it was the sort of crisis to which she rose magnificently.

Within ten minutes she had arrived with her horsebox and reorganised the vehicles so that she could get as close as possible. With infinite care they rigged up a blanket sling and between them had Jigs unsteadily onto his feet and inched him up the ramp. She had brought straw bales to wedge him comfortably against the partition in the box and because it was such a short distance, allowed Jena to travel with him.

When the convoy got to East End House, the lights were on in the stable and Peter was in one of the boxes putting down a thick straw bed. Julia backed up as close as she could; they lowered the ramp and inched Jigsaw out of the horsebox, the men supporting him down the ramp with their shoulders. He went down on his knees in the straw.

Claudia could not bear to watch. She could only think of the horse as he had been, bursting with arrogance and pride, flying down the lane with Jena, muscles bunched under his beautiful gleaming coat. Under the harsh strip light the full extent of his terrible injuries was revealed and Julia was tight-lipped as Matt went to work, stitching and stapling. She brought bucket after bucket of warm water and finally fetched the warmest stable rugs to make the horse as comfortable as possible. Drugged now, he lay peacefully on the bright clean straw with Jena lying beside him, her arm round his neck.

The child was filthy, Claudia saw, her clothes covered in mud and blood, but Julia made no attempt to move her. Instead she disappeared and came back ten minutes later with a quilted jacket of Victoria's, a duvet and a thermos of hot chocolate and a packet of biscuits. 'You'll want to stay out here,' she said kindly. Jena looked up and nodded. 'Here you are then. We can't have you fainting by the wayside.'

Anthony had gone down the old railway line in his Land Rover to tell Jem Loader what had happened and that Jena was staying with the horse. Now, as Matt washed his hands in the bucket, Julia passed him a towel and said, 'You'd better all come in for a drink. Peter's made coffee and there's a tray of sausages in the oven.' Claudia and Rosco both wondered whether the invitation included them, but evidently it did, because Julia swept them all up. 'Come on,' she said. 'What a bloody awful evening this has been. Jena will be all right for the moment and we can take it in turns to check through the night, Peter and I. I'll do the four-hourly jab, Matt.' She was like a general, thought Claudia admiringly, taking charge, keeping up the morale of the troops and brooking no argument.

When they got inside, the whole crowd of them, Claudia went to the downstairs loo and saw that she looked a complete sight, smeared with mud, covered in blood and wearing no make-up. Not that she cared. She washed her face and hands and went back through to the kitchen and took a large glass of whisky from Peter, who thought he had never seen her looking more lovely. However, he went to stand beside Julia who was leaning against the Aga, holding forth to Matt Digby and Mike about something or other to do with hunting, and very casually draped his arm over her shoulders. Considering how she felt about Claudia and the travellers, she was putting on a bloody good show and he was proud of her.

Chapter Eighteen

When Claudia awoke the next morning, she was immediately conscious of the drama of the night before. She got straight out of bed, found some clean jeans, dressed and hurried round to the Durnfords, half in hope and half in dread of what the intervening hours had brought.

It was a murky, dark morning and the light was on in the stable yard but she could not make out the identity of the two figures leaning over the stable door. As she got closer she realised it was Julia and a man she took to be Jem Loader. They turned when they heard her footsteps, but she still could not read their faces. Please God, she prayed. Please. Let him be alive.

'He's still with us,' said Julia, 'just,' and she moved over to allow Claudia to see over the half door. Jigsaw was still down on the straw, but not any longer lying flat, although as she watched, he groaned and stretched out again. Crouched beside him, still wearing the same clothes as last night, was Jena. The child looked terrible, Claudia thought, and no wonder. Someone had brought her out some warm water and she had half-heartedly washed her face; it was paper-white and still streaked with dirt and blood. Her eyes stared from dark sockets; Claudia had never seen such a look of suffering and sorrow.

'He's just had some water,' volunteered Julia, 'which is a very good sign.'

Jem grunted and shook his head. It was clear to Claudia that he thought the horse was a lost cause. She didn't know what to say and felt helpless and hopeless. There was no role for her now. From what she said, Julia had evidently been out several times in the night, even though Jem had slept on the straw beside his daughter. Now they were waiting for the vet to call again.

'What can I do?' Claudia asked. 'Is there anything?'

Julia shrugged. 'Nothing really. Jem brought some clean clothes for Jena, but we can't get her to move. She should have

313

a bath and a sleep. Maybe we can get her inside after Matt has been. He should be here any moment.' She turned from the door to look at Claudia. 'Don't you have to go to work?' she inquired bossily.

'Yes, I do. But later.' Claudia felt she was being dismissed. 'Well, if there's nothing . . . I'll come back, if you don't mind,' she finished lamely.

Julia nodded then followed her a few yards away from the stables and said in a low, confidential tone, 'Jem Loader found a firework, you know. On the bank where the horse was tethered. This was a deliberate attack. I'm afraid Rosco is involved. We can't get Jena to talk yet, but there might be criminal proceedings.' She gave the last two words deep emphasis. 'I thought I should warn you.'

Claudia was both shocked and taken aback at the news, and also wondered why Julia felt she, particularly, needed to be warned. A moment later it came to her. Of course. She thinks I'll want to avoid anything like that. Anything to do with criminal proceedings.

'But Rosco was trying to help,' she said. 'He came to get me. He was with Jena when she found the horse.'

'Yes,' said Julia with meaning. 'But what was he *doing* there? Why was he down on the line at all?'

Claudia shrugged. Poor Rosco. She thought of his tears and distress. 'Look,' she said. 'I saw how upset he was. Jena will tell you. I don't believe he can have had anything to do with it.'

Julia pulled a face. 'He's been in trouble before, you know. He mixes with a very bad lot.'

'I see,' said Claudia, thinking, well, that makes two of us. 'But this time I can vouch for him. If it helps.'

'We'll see.' Julia adopted a self-important look. 'There's also the cost of all this to be considered,' she went on. 'Vets' fees, for instance, are enormous, and the horse, if it pulls through, is going to need months of box rest.'

'Of course,' said Claudia humbly, although these were issues she had not thought of.

'Somebody will have to pay. Jem Loader can't.' Julia's voice was almost triumphant.

Claudia thought wildly of Anthony. He was wealthy enough. Someone would pay, surely? She knew that she couldn't. Damn having no money. Damn it.

'I thought you should know,' finished Julia. She did not believe in people not facing up to things. 'Anyway,' she added kindly, 'at least you did a good job last night. That's one thing Jena has said.'

'It was nothing. Nothing compared to you,' Claudia murmured, truthfully. 'Well, if there's really nothing I can do . . .'

'Nothing, thank you. Now, I must get on with the mucking out,' and Julia marched back to the stables.

The rest of the day was passed in anxious wondering about Jigsaw. Claudia was on the point of telling Mrs Peck what had happened, but restrained herself. The Loaders were private people and they would not want to be talked about. She imagined Julia on the telephone, broadcasting the events to her friends, and she did not wish to be tarred with the same brush.

As soon as she got back in the afternoon she dashed round to the yard to find out how things were and was greatly relieved to find Jigsaw standing in his stable, although his head drooped, with ears back, and his eye was dull. His hind legs were heavily bandaged right up to the stifle, but the wounds on his chest had been stapled together and left undressed. Jena was sitting in the corner, knees drawn up, still keeping her vigil, still in the same clothes.

'He's drunk two buckets of water,' she said, seeing Claudia. 'He hasn't eaten anything, but the water is what matters. The vet said.'

Claudia opened the door and went in. She put her arms round the girl and felt her stiffen. She's not used to being hugged, she thought, and then she felt the thin arms tighten round her waist in return and Jena started to cry. Claudia let her weep, saying nothing. It's exhaustion, she thought. Sheer exhaustion.

Eventually, she asked gently, 'Do you want to come back with me for a bit? You can have a bath and sleep in Lila's bed. Jigsaw won't miss you now. He needs to rest, too.'

'OK,' whispered Jena, sniffing loudly. Together they walked very slowly back to the bungalow, Jena on legs wobbly with tiredness, Claudia carrying the bag of clean clothes.

The child was too tired to eat and after a bath Claudia put her to bed in an old T-shirt of Lila's, with a hot drink and a hot water bottle. She tucked Jerome's old bear beside her and drew the curtains. Jena was asleep before Claudia had left the room.

She bundled the discarded clothes into the washing machine, together with her own garments, stiff with blood, from the night before and switched it on. Then she sat down to think. First, she had better let Julia know of Jena's whereabouts. She picked up the telephone.

'Julia? It's Claudia. I've got Jena here. She was asleep on her feet. She's in Lila's bed. Could you kindly let her father know, in case he wonders?' She could hear Julia sniff with annoyance. She did not like people taking the initiative.

'Well, I've got other things to do. I don't know whether he's coming back this afternoon.'

'OK,' said Claudia calmly. 'I'll walk round now and leave him a note. I thought of doing that anyway, but then decided I should tell you as well. In case you were worried about her.'

'Oh, I see. Well, I suppose I can do that. I can see if he's about. I've got to go and get Vinnie in from the field in a moment anyway.'

Claudia wondered why she could not have said that in the first place. 'There's one other thing, Julia.'

'Yes?'

'Do you remember the stuff I have in the garage? You said you would like it for a Riding for the Disabled Christmas fair. I just wondered when that was, presuming you still want it.'

There was a pause and Claudia practically heard Julia's mind ticking over.

'Well,' she said finally. 'I'm not sure what the committee will feel. In the circumstances, I mean. We wouldn't want to be involved in any . . .'

Claudia stiffened. 'Handling stolen goods, you mean?' Her voice was tight with anger. 'Well, you needn't worry on that score. There's nothing there that is not legitimately mine, but if you feel like that . . .'

'No, of course not,' Julia blustered. 'I didn't mean to suggest . . .' Her voice trailed off, before starting again in a more accommodating tone. 'Thank you, Claudia. It's in two weeks' time and we'd be glad to have your stuff. I'll make arrangements to get it collected.'

'Thank you, Julia. That's all I wanted to know.' Oh God, thought Claudia as she put the telephone down. She thinks of me like a nasty germ in the water supply. Contaminating everything.

Sighing, she telephoned Valerie Pomeroy and with relief found her just returned from London. She heard out Claudia's tale to the end.

'My goodness,' she said. 'Things have been happening since I've been away. I'm not surprised Julia was so magnificent in the crisis and then foul afterwards. That's her all over. She's exactly like the general you describe. Of the type that excel in war but is a bloody nightmare in peacetime. Then they go around annoying everybody and creating situations. Now what are we going to do about helping that poor child?'

Although no solutions were reached on the telephone, Claudia felt hugely reassured to share her worry with her wise old neighbour.

'We'll think of something,' said Valerie, 'and don't worry about Julia. I know all about being treated like a bad smell. One gets used to it, you know.'

Jena slept round the clock. The following morning as Claudia was getting up, there was a knock on the door and she thought, blimey, not another accident! This time it was Jem Loader at the door.

'How is the horse?' she asked at once.

He nodded, his face difficult to read. 'Not so bad,' he said. 'No infection. Looks stronger. Ate a bit of mash this morning.'

'Thank God,' she said. 'Come in. We weren't introduced the other morning, but I'm Claudia. Our daughters are friends, and you know it's us who have Finn? Look, here he is. Jena's still asleep. Come in, please.' She was aware that she was talking too much, but the man made no effort to speak and some sort of dialogue seemed to be called for, even if it was one-sided.

He stepped into the hall and she had to virtually nip at his heels to get him into the kitchen

'Sit down,' she said. 'I'm just about to have coffee. Can I offer you some? Or tea?'

'No thanks,' he said, looking round uneasily, still standing. 'I've come for Jena.'

He thinks I'm like some sort of social worker, thought Claudia. Some interfering busybody.

'You did get the message from Julia, didn't you? That she was here? She was so knackered and agreed to come back with me. You see, she knows me from the primary.' Jem looked even more disconcerted and Claudia hurried on, 'I'm only the cook. Did she tell you? No, well, she got to be friendly with my son. She spent quite a bit of time here over the summer.'

'Would that be Jerome?' Jem asked. He had a soft Dorset accent. 'She talked about Jerome. Funny sort of name, I said.'

'Yes, yes, that's right. Jerome. He'd broken his leg. Jena was great. Kept him amused.' God, she thought desperately, I'm making this sound like a paedophile ring, or something. She began to make coffee, filling the kettle and looking for the cafetiere in the cupboard.

'Cambridge? Is that right?'

'Yes. He started this term.'

'I'm doing work for London University. Field work. King's College.'

Claudia turned back to him, trying to sum him up. Forty-ish, attractive blue eyes. A nice looking man but with a manner so diffident it was almost painful. 'That's fascinating,' she said. 'Jerome told me. He was very impressed by Jena's knowledge.'

'Ay. She's a grand maid, Jena. She knows near as much as me.'

'She's an amazing rider. I've seen her on that lovely horse.' Claudia, with one hand on the kettle, had a sudden vision of that first week in the village when she had driven into Anthony Brewer's tractor. She couldn't go into all that now. 'I've seen them jumping. Over the hedges.'

'Aye. She's a natural. I don't know as that horse will jump again, though.'

Claudia could see he was not a man given to optimism. 'I don't think we should wake her, do you? I don't have to be at work until nine thirty. I'll see she's up before I leave.'

'She can't go to school. Not today. Not with the horse and all.'

'No. Of course not.' Claudia made haste to distance herself from the authorities. 'What's the plan for the long term, for Jigsaw, I mean? All being well.'

'Mrs Durnford says he can stay where he is. He needs box rest for eight weeks. Jena'll have to do the stable work before and after school.'

'She can change here,' said Claudia quickly. 'Change into her school stuff and get the bus from here.'

Jem Loader considered this, turning his woollen hat round in the brown hands. He nodded without commenting. 'I'm doing some outside work, see. Some hedging and ditching in return, like. The horse won't be worth a bob, even if he pulls through. Scarred like that. Got to see how we can pay.'

'Don't worry. Don't think about that. We'll sort it out. Somehow,' said Claudia recklessly.

It did not take long for Star to hear the first rumours about the injured horse. On Wednesday morning when she was at work at The Bugle, Monica asked her what Rosco had got to say about it.

'Why?' she demanded. 'What's it to do with Rosc?'

Monica back-pedalled. If Star didn't know, she was not going to be the one to tell her.

'That horse,' she said, 'that black and white horse that goes through the village with the tinker's girl. It had an accident Monday night. Went through the wire onto the road. They say it was cut to ribbons. Someone told me your Rosco was there. I must have heard wrong. Got the wrong end of the stick.'

'Why should he be there? He was out with Sean, Monday.'

'That's all right then,' said Monica, peaceably.

'Why? What are they saying?' persisted Star.

Monica hedged. 'Seems the horse was frightened by a firework. Someone threw a firework at it. Bolted it. The kid was on her own, see. Her dad had taken the little'uns into Sharston, to the bonfire.'

'So where does Rosc come in?' demanded Star.

'I heard he was there. That woman from the bungalow, she went to help. She got Brewer out. He called the vet. Julia Durnford's got the horse up her yard now. In her stables. She'll tell you.'

Slowly Star pieced the fragments together but she couldn't make out Rosco's alleged involvement, or who was saying what about him. He didn't say nothing to me, she thought, remembering Monday night. She'd been late back from the pub and he'd been watching a video when she got in. He'd had a bath, changed his clothes and was ready for bed. Hadn't said nothing. She tried to remember if she'd asked him what he'd done in particular, but she didn't think she had. She'd had a bit to drink down the Nag's Head and so she'd made a coffee and sat and watched the end of the film with him.

Instinctively, although she couldn't force it out of Monica, Star knew that they were saying Rosco had been up to no good. That would be the gist of it, she reckoned, and him with only a week or two left of his probation. She felt wild with apprehension. She just couldn't take more trouble, more hassle with the police at the door again, social workers, all that lot down on her, everyone talking, tongues wagging. Just when he'd been doing all right, keeping his nose clean. It was those bloody gyppos, nothing but trouble, they were, and that woman from the bungalow. Her whose husband was inside. How dare she?

Anger and resentment started to gather in Star like a head of steam and by the time she was finished at The Bugle and about

319

to go and start at East End House, she was thoroughly worked up.

Julia was on the telephone in the kitchen when she slammed in with her Hoover and stood waiting for her to finish her conversation, arms folded belligerently.

'I'll call back later, Jo,' said Julia, sensing trouble. She rang off and turned to Star. 'Is something wrong, Star? You look upset.'

'What's this they're saying about Rosco?' Star demanded straight off. 'Monday night and that horse.'

'What are who saying?' asked Julia to gain time, although she knew very well what Star was asking.

'I don't know who. I'm asking you. Someone's talking about Rosco. Saying the horse was hurt deliberate like.'

'Ah,' said Julia. 'Well, Rosco was there, you know. At the time of the incident, and so I suppose people are bound to conjecture . . .'

'How do you know? How do you know he was there?' spat Star.

Julia stared. 'Because he *was* there. I saw him.'

It was Star's turn to stare. She hadn't expected this.

'He came back here afterwards. The horse had definitely been attacked. Jena, the child, said so later and Jem Loader, her father, found the stub of the firework. It's the truth, I'm afraid, Star.'

'Rosco wouldn't do nothing like that.'

'I hope not, but I'm afraid questions are sure to be asked. Claudia, from next door – you know, whose husband's . . . well, she was there first. She can tell you.'

'So it's her, is it? Her who's saying Rosco's done it?'

'No. I didn't say that, Star. Calm down!'

'She works up the primary, doesn't she?' Star demanded.

'Yes. She's the cook. Why?'

'I'll be back,' said Star, picking up her car keys and slamming the back door. Julia heard her car start and the scattering of gravel as she tore out of the drive.

I jolly well hope she will be back, thought Julia, annoyed. She had quite enough to do without cleaning the house as well. She picked up the telephone and dialled Jo's number.

'Sorry about that,' she said. 'A bit of a domestic crisis, I'm afraid.'

'So things are better between you and Peter?' asked Jo, taking up from where they had left off.

'Yes, definitely,' confided Julia. 'Given that we've never been the sort of holding hands and wearing matching anoraks type of couple . . .'

Jo laughed. 'Thank God for that,' she said.

Claudia was just getting the quiches out of the ovens when Star arrived. She saw her car race into the school car park and wondered who was in such a hurry. A mother with a mission, she thought as Star jumped out and slammed the door. A moment later she had arrived at the back door of the kitchen and, without knocking, burst in, her face red and clashing with her pink hair.

'Here!' she confronted Claudia. 'I want a word with you!'

Sensing a scene, Eileen and Susie stopped peeling carrots and watched, open-mouthed.

Claudia stood bemused, a baking tray in her hands. 'You're Rosco's mother, aren't you? Star?'

'Yeah! That's who I am, and that's what I've come about!'

'If it's about the other night,' said Claudia, guessing, but guessing wrongly that Star had heard her defence of Rosco. 'I'm quite prepared to make a statement if there's trouble. As far as I could see, Rosco did everything he could to help. He acted in a totally responsible way and appeared to be extremely upset about what happened.'

Star was like a charging bull suddenly brought up short by a change of direction.

'It appears it was his friend – Sean, is it? – who was the troublemaker. Jena won't say much, but her father thinks the boys found her down there at the camp, on her own. She let them in the bus where she sleeps and they started mucking about. Jena says Rosco tried to stop Sean, who was hassling her. That's all she'll say. Then they left and she heard the firework go off and Rosco came banging on the door, telling her that the horse had bolted. He helped her look for him for over an hour and when they found him, caught in the wire, he ran to get help. That's where I came in. Jena told him to come to me. In fact, as far as Jena's concerned,' Claudia finished, 'Rosco's a bit of a hero. You should be proud of him.'

Star stared at Claudia, open-mouthed. So unexpected was this remark that she found herself speechless. A wave of relief and then genuine pleasure flooded over her.

'I thought, see, he was in trouble,' she struggled to explain. 'I thought he was going to get the blame again. You know, once you've been in trouble, it's what people expect. I just couldn't take no more of it!'

Claudia smiled at her. 'Star, you don't have to tell that to me, of all people!'

'No.' Star realised what Claudia meant. 'I suppose not.' She hesitated. 'Well, I'm glad it was you as was there. I'm glad it was you as stuck up for him. Otherwise, some of those others . . .' She did not know how to express what she wanted to say, that she believed Claudia would be predisposed to be more sympathetic towards Rosco than, say, Julia Durnford. 'Because,' she finished, 'you understand what it's like.'

'I sure do,' said Claudia, with feeling. 'And for you, too. It can be tough on your own, can't it? Dealing with teenagers. But he was great, your Rosco. Like I said, you should be proud of him. Now I would offer you a cup of coffee, but we've got to have lunch ready on the dot and we've still got a fruit salad and cupcakes to make.'

'Rosco,' said Star that evening as she took clothes off the drying rack in the kitchen, and folded them into a pile on the table. 'Why didn't you tell me about Monday night?'

'What about it?' said Rosco, scowling.

'You know, that horse getting injured. I see you come home and washed all your clothes.' She indicated the sweatshirt in her hands. 'Why did you do that?'

'Why shouldn't I? They were dirty. Anyway, what's there to tell?' he said, studiously avoiding his mother's eyes and picking up the free local paper to flick through the pages.

Star folded a pair of jeans. 'Plenty, from what I've heard. I heard you did the right thing for once. Helped that kid. Someone today said I should be proud of you. It's not often I've been told that, is it?'

Rosco looked up, puzzled. 'Who said that then?'

'Claudia, that woman from the bungalow. The one whose husband's inside. She said you did really well.'

Rosco blushed. 'She don't know nothing,' he said irritably.

'She knows more than you think, then. The gypsy kid's talked to her. It was Sean, was it? It was him who set off the firework. They're all talking about it in the village. He did a runner, I suppose, and left you there to hold the baby. Is that what he did, the little toerag?'

'Something like that. Look, Mum, stop talking about it, will you?'

'Yeah, I will, when I know the truth. He didn't touch the kid, did he? I don't trust that lad. He's got a funny streak.'

'Why? What's she said?' asked Rosco, suddenly alert and suspicious.

'Nothing as far as I know. She told Claudia that it wasn't nothing to do with you, anyway.' Rosco looked relieved. 'She said you tried to stop him. So he did, did he?' Star persisted. 'He did muck about with the kid? You'd better tell me Rosc. You'll not get into trouble for it, lad.'

'I'm not having nothing to do with it,' he said. 'I'm not getting Sean into trouble neither. He didn't do much. No one'll believe that kid anyway. She's a traveller, isn't she?'

Star looked at her son thoughtfully. He was right. No one would believe a traveller, but on the other hand it was the girl's word that would get Rosco out of trouble if it came to it. It didn't seem right, really. She was a decent kid when all was said and done. Just wait until she got hold of Sean, she thought. She'd sort him out good and proper.

'I'm going to take Claudia a box of chocs next time I go to the Durnfords,' she said. 'I'm bloody grateful to that woman, and so should you be. That kid, too. I'll take her something and all. They spoke up for you.'

'Leave it, will you, Mum!' protested Rosco. It was typical of his mother that she would overdo it and he didn't want to think about what had happened. The feelings it aroused were like a heavy weight round his neck. He thought uneasily of the money he'd got upstairs, the two hundred quid he felt he had earned. He wasn't so sure now. He just wished his mum would stop going on about it. He wanted to forget the whole thing.

November crept into December and only the sheep now grazed the hillsides, which on some mornings were white with frost. The cattle were yarded up in the farms, out of the weather and bedded down on straw, and when Claudia walked through the village with Finn she could hear the turkeys and geese penned in the sheds behind the farm in Green Lane, where they were being fattened for Christmas.

The hedges, so much a feature of the landscape, which had been so thick and green in the summer, were now dark and bare but threaded with scarlet hawthorn berries and here and there the pretty pink heart-shaped spindleberries. Tangled loops of traveller's joy wound through the thorny branches and a flash of green marked where the glossy ivy with its rosettes of black berries clung and climbed skywards.

Some evenings it was dark by half past three when Claudia finished work and she looked forward to getting home, drawing the curtains and lighting the fire. She had had a load of logs delivered and spent a Saturday morning stacking the sweet-smelling wood into a pile by the back door.

One weekend Claudia packed Finn into the car and drove to Cambridge to see Jerome, staying with an old schoolfriend who was married to a classics don. Jerome was living in a cell-like room in halls of residence and Claudia was disappointed to see how bare and sparse it was. He had made no effort to make it cosy, in contrast to Lila, whose university rooms had always been full of pot plants and stuffed toys and posters. However, Jerome was looking better; he clearly loved his course and was full of plans to return to India. He had put on a little weight and although he was still scarecrow-like, she felt he was on the mend. He had had a four-month check on his leg and the specialist had declared himself very satisfied with his handiwork and did not need to see him again. Claudia sighed. Another thing over and dealt with.

They went out to lunch at an Italian bistro and although she had already told him about Jena and Jigsaw, he still wanted to hear every detail. She explained that the horse was making a slow recovery, still confined to the stable in the Durnfords' yard, and how Jena came every morning and evening, before and after school, to see him and that she was mucking out and exercising Vinnie for Julia, in return for Jigsaw's keep.

'How does that work out?' he asked. 'I should think Julia is quite a taskmaster.'

'Amazingly well. I think all her reservations about travellers have been severely challenged. Jena is as much a perfectionist as she is and the yard is kept immaculately. Of course, Jena gets that from her father, who is a craftsman and pays endless attention to detail. And she rides so well that Vinnie is going better than ever. Do you hear from Tor?'

Jerome grinned. 'At least twice a week. Great letters, actually. She told me about Jigs, of course, but being away at school, she doesn't see how things work out on a daily basis. She said his legs are very stiff and puffy still, but are healing well. Apparently Hagar treats him with herbal stuff and her mother, having poured scorn on what she called witchcraft, has grown very interested in alternative remedies.'

'Yes, she told me that. It's just the vet's bills we're desperate about,' Claudia said. 'They are going to run to nearly a thousand pounds. The practice are being terribly understanding and will accept monthly payments, but it will all have to be found eventually. The Loaders can't afford anything like that sort of money and neither I nor Valerie Pomeroy have any spare cash. We just have to pray that something will turn up. One rather remarkable thing has happened,' she went on. 'Do you remember Rosco? Star Bishop's son? She's the big girl with pink hair who helps Julia in the house.'

Jerome nodded. 'He made a bob or two pointing the newsmen in our direction, according to Victoria,' he said. 'At the garden opening fiasco. What about him?'

'He was involved, indirectly, I think, the night of Jigsaw's accident. There was talk of prosecution but it didn't come to anything. I would have been prepared to speak on his behalf because it was him who Jena sent to find me. You wouldn't think he'd be capable of finer feelings to look at him, but he was terribly upset about the accident. Anyway, he's taken a real interest in the horse ever since and turns up most weekends to see how he's doing. Jena told me that last weekend he brought a girlfriend. A tiny little thing, according to Jena, who never said a word. The opposite of Star in every sense. Anyway, it seems he has given Jena some money – quite a lot – to pay off the first instalment of the vet's bill. Amazing, isn't it? She didn't want to take it, but I think she did in the end because he insisted. She said it sort of cheered him up.'

'How extraordinary!' said Jerome, interested. 'He's only just left school, hasn't he? I remember him hanging about, looking pissed off and bored out of his mind, with a sort of self-abuse hairstyle.'

'That's him. Poor Rosco.' Claudia poured more wine in both their glasses.

Jerome looked at her and thought she seemed more settled, less edgy and strung up. 'And you, Mum?' he asked. 'How about you?'

'Well,' she said, taking a sip and smiling at him. 'I'm loving the job. I really feel part of that little school now, and I'm not so worried about all the nutritional stuff. Mrs Peck has ordered me a computer programme that I'm working through, which is really helpful. The children seem to love most of the food and I sometimes get mothers stopping me to ask for recipes, which is a terrific compliment. I invented something called Bishop's Bake, which is really popular.'

Jerome wanted to steer things onto a more personal level. 'And the boyfriend? How's he?'

'Don't call him that, Jerome!' Claudia protested. 'He's far from being my boyfriend. I see him very occasionally and I suppose we have what is known as an understanding.'

'He's not making you unhappy, Ma?' he persisted.

Claudia reached for the water to fill her glass. She did not want to look him in the eye. 'Well, he did a bit. At first. But I'm over that. He asked me to go to Scotland for a week. I couldn't because of school, but I was flattered to be asked.'

'That's a coincidence,' said Jerome. 'Lila went to Scotland last month. Did she tell you?'

'No. How extraordinary! I knew she was over and I spoke to her a couple of times, but she never said she was going to Scotland. I thought it was just a business trip.'

'I think it was. She took a couple of days off and flew up north to stalk or something grand like that. It seems she has a new, rich boyfriend.'

'How odd! I wonder who she went with. I gathered there was a new man in her life who had lasted rather longer than most of the others. She was in Paris with someone in the summer, wasn't she?'

'Yes, and in the West Indies in September.'

'Goodness, she is living it up. Do you know who it is, Jerome? Has she told you?'

'Not a word. Someone she met in London, I gather. We did meet, though, Mum. Lila and me. We went to see Dad together.'

'Ah.' Claudia paused. Jerome studied her face. Was she going to take this admission as an act of disloyalty? He was relieved when she lifted her wineglass and with a slight smile at his anxious face asked, 'How was he?'

'Thrilled about the baby. Lila took him photographs. Carla is coming over soon, I think, and he hopes to get compassionate leave or something to have a bit of time with it.'

'I see.' Claudia wondered for a moment if she felt upset. She knew that Jerome was watching her to see her reaction. To her relief she felt quite unmoved. It was as if Jerome was telling her about a distant relation. 'What's she called?' she asked. 'It can't be Bethlehem!'

Jerome laughed. 'Did you get that from Lila? She's called Bathsheba. Sheba for short. As Lila pointed out, you couldn't very well use Bath as a diminutive. Sheba sounds a bit like an Alsatian though, don't you think?'

Claudia laughed. 'What was she like? From the photograph?'

'Small and scarlet and rather creased. Cross looking. A bit like Queen Victoria.'

'Not like you then. Not like you and Lila, who were the most beautiful babies,' she said with satisfaction.

Jerome caught her hand across the table and grinned. 'That, Mum,' he said, 'may not be an entirely disinterested judgement!'

Driving back on Sunday evening, round the interminable M25, against the constant stream of headlights coming the other way, and with Finn sleeping on the back seat, Claudia felt happier about Jerome than she had done since his return from India. He had reassured her by his air of involvement in his new life. He was doing a course which he loved, for which she must thank Valerie Pomeroy, and had made friends, to judge from the number of people who banged on his door while they were having coffee after lunch. His interest in events in the village, his attachment to some of the people there and his willingness to be concerned with her own life were all good signs, she felt, and he seemed able to deal with his father's situation without rancour or bitterness.

No, she thought as she switched onto the M3, Jerome was all right. It was Lila who now seemed to be behaving oddly.

The weeks leading to Christmas began to get busy and crowded. There was a school Nativity play in the parish church in Bishops Barton which brought tears to Claudia's eyes, so moving was the innocence and wonder in the shining faces of the children. She had helped with the costumes for the ox and ass, who stood nervously holding hands and nodding their papier-mâché heads wisely beside the little crib in which reclined a large pink plastic doll. Mary, a big dim girl, had been chosen for her rather vacant, sweet expression, and Joseph for his gruff manliness. The shepherds were local farmers' sons, one of whom carried in his arms his own pet lamb, unromantically called Legger. Legger Lamb, see miss, he'd explained to Mrs Peck. The kings were the tallest boys from the top class, including the beautiful Raymond whose mother was West Indian and whose father drove a milk tanker.

The singing was wonderful, with the children all taking part in old favourite carols and one or two incomprehensible new ones, with the parents joining in 'Hark the Herald' at the end. It was perfect, thought Claudia as she filed out into the dark of the December evening, into the still night and the shining stars.

'Listen,' said the woman next to her, holding out a hand. 'A fox!' And across the silver sleeping fields Claudia heard the sharp, ringing bark. 'Him'll be after them turkeys,' the woman said.

Then there was the Christmas bazaar, which coincided with Julia's Riding for the Disabled Christmas fair, so that Claudia had the perfect excuse to bow out of what she realised was the graciously bestowed privilege of being asked to help. 'I can't, I'm afraid,' she had said on the telephone. 'I'm busy up at school.'

'But I wanted you on the cake stand,' said Julia as if Claudia was a Victoria sponge.

Julia then had to come round herself to collect the boxes out of the garage, but not before Claudia had sifted through the contents and pulled out anything she thought would be welcome on the stalls at the school function.

'Whose are these beautiful hunting boots?' Julia, eagle-eyed, asked, spotting Lila's pair of Maxwell's made for her in the days when money was no object.

'Oh, they're Lila's. She's hunting the Saturday before Christmas, so she says. She asked me to look them out for her. I've got her coat hanging inside to air.'

Julia looked puzzled. 'Hunting? Who is she hunting with?'

'Here,' said Claudia. 'The meet is at Manor Farm, isn't it? She's arranged a hireling. She appears to have organised it all from New York.'

Julia frowned. 'Really? Will she be fit enough? I mean a day's hunting here in the vale is quite something, and I presume she doesn't ride in America.'

'Fitness is the one thing you don't have to worry about with Lila,' laughed Claudia. 'She's always fighting fit. Literally.'

Julia shrugged. 'Really? I suppose she knows about asking the secretary and so on. One can't just turn up.'

'I think she knows all that,' said Claudia, amused. 'She's hunted most of her life. She did eight seasons with the Bicester.'

'Oh.' Julia felt her irritation rise. Really, she thought, it was almost as if Claudia was trying to upstage her. 'I must speak to Anthony about the meet. No doubt he will want some help. His dear old Mrs Walker isn't really up to it any more. I must offer to do him some mince pies.'

Claudia just smiled. I'm not going to tell her, she thought. I'm not going to tell her that eight dozen mince pies are already baked and in the school freezer, along with the sausage rolls, and that the ginger and fruit cakes are in tins on the shelf behind her head. Let Anthony explain.

Julia drove away with the stuff and could not resist, when she got home, having a root amongst the clothes. She pulled out two beautiful beaded cocktail dresses, exclaimed at the labels sewn inside, and took them upstairs to try on. To her fury she couldn't get them past her bottom when she tried to step into them, or past her shelf of bosom if she put them over her head. Wretched woman! she thought crossly, throwing them down on the bed.

The week before Christmas was frantically busy. On Monday, Jerome came home on the train and the following day took Claudia's car to Winchester to collect his grandmother. He had tidied his bedroom for her. While she was staying, he would sleep next door. Valerie had asked them all to share Christmas dinner with her. Claudia had agreed readily and gratefully, but explained that her contribution would have to be the cooking, rather than the supplying of food and drink. 'I've made a Christmas cake and a pudding,' she said. 'I'll bring those, and my mother was going to buy us a small turkey. I am afraid things are a bit tight this year.'

'For goodness sake, Claudia!' exclaimed Valerie. 'You are my guests, but in the interests of eating well, I accept your offer of taking over the cooking side of things. I'm a bit erratic on that front. I've already ordered a monster turkey from the butcher in Sharston. Bacon and sausages and a piece of gammon as well.'

'Wonderful!' said Claudia. 'Shall we have it in the evening, then? It's a struggle I don't willingly engage in any longer – that dawn wrestle with an uncooked twenty-pounder!'

'Of course. Much nicer and more civilised. Next year I will have the girls and Christopher and I hope you will be with us then as well.'

On Wednesday, Claudia cooked her last school lunch of the year and prepared for a small staff party in the evening. On Thursday, she had lunch with Anthony in order to have a look at the Manor Farm kitchen with a view to catering for Saturday's meet.

She enjoyed bustling round the old farm kitchen where there was no resident woman to consider her an intruder. She and Anthony had a cup of coffee first, leaning their backs on the Aga rail, laughing and talking about Christmas. Then Greg had come to the door, worried about a steer which was running a temperature, and Anthony had piled on his outdoor gear and gone out with him. Left alone, Claudia began to count baking trays and work out how many she could fit into the Aga in one go. That done, she rinsed the coffee cups and wondered how long Anthony would be. It was then that she saw the photograph. It was pinned to the cork board behind the door, along with a flutter of invitations, business cards and telephone numbers. It was nosy of her to investigate, she knew that, but because she was alone, she couldn't resist a look. It was the invitations she was interested in but then the snapshot caught her eye. It was of Anthony and Ivo, dressed in tweed shooting breeches and flat caps, sleeves rolled up, laughing at the camera, and standing between them, her arm over Anthony's shoulders and round Ivo's waist, looking like the cat that got the cream, was Lila.

Chapter Nineteen

Looking back on that moment Claudia was amazed that she had the strength of mind not to cause a scene immediately. She stood looking at the photograph for only a moment, resisting the temptation to unpin it from the board and put it in her pocket. Then with a thumping heart she went back to stacking baking trays. While her mind was whirling she had to occupy her hands.

What did it mean? Lila. She could not believe what her head was telling her, that on the evidence of the photograph her daughter was involved in some way with Anthony Brewer. Involved in some way? Come on! She told herself. Lila is having an affair with him. Jerome said she had a rich new boyfriend. It all began to fall into place. Anthony's absences from the village – what had Jerome said about Lila's trips to Paris? The West Indies? Scotland?

Now Claudia remembered with perfect clarity how Anthony had given Lila a lift to London and that he had mentioned he had taken her out to dinner. She recalled his words, that the evening had turned into quite a party, that Lila had enjoyed herself. That must have been the start of it. So where did she, Claudia, fit in? Was Anthony really the sort of man who got a kick out of sleeping with both mother and daughter? It was not unheard of. She remembered the well-publicised case of a philandering politician who had bedded two daughters and their mother – maybe the father too, for all she knew. So that was it. Anthony's lack of commitment, his smoothly orchestrated exits and entrances in and out of her life now all made perfect sense. The bastard.

With shaking hands, Claudia ran the blackened old trays under the tap and put them on the Aga to dry. Right. That was it. She was going home. He could forget his bloody lunch. She dried her hands on the roller towel. It was clean, she noticed. Like everything else on this farm, this was a well-run kitchen.

She found a Biro and took a sheet of paper from the pad by the telephone.

'Anthony,' she wrote. 'Didn't wait for you because I've got a headache starting. Sorry to miss lunch. See you on Saturday. Claudia.' That was about as polite as she could bear to be.

She propped the note up against the pepper grinder on the table and bolted out of the back door, across the yard and out onto the village street. She hoped she could get well away before Anthony returned to the kitchen and found her gone. When she got home she really would lie down. She couldn't face her mother or Jerome, asking questions, wanting to know why she was back so early.

There were village children wheeling about the street on bicycles and two on skateboards, all togged up in woolly hats and scarves. Claudia realised that she had come without her coat, left on the back of a kitchen chair, and that the wind was icy, but she hurried on. 'Hi!' the children called. She waved back. A terrier, trotting beside the children, transferred its attention to her. 'Here, Beans!' called one of the boys, and it went back obediently.

Some of the cottages were festooned with coloured lights and the fir tree in the garden of one of the new houses was decked out in winking electric stars. Despite her misery, Claudia noted how pretty everything looked, with Christmas trees lit up in windows and evergreen wreaths nailed onto front doors. Pretty and festive and normal – nice, ordinary, respectable people lived behind these doors. Except for me, she thought. Julia is right. I am contaminated. She remembered the school Nativity service and the innocence of the children's faces which she had found so touching. Here am I, she thought dismally, my husband in prison, sharing the sexual favours of my daughter's lover.

She was nearly home. She hurried past East End House. The last person she wanted to see was Julia. Then she remembered that Julia had taken Victoria Christmas shopping to Bath. Jena was going to get Vinnie in from the field before dark. She had been round to see them that morning, bringing two sacks of holly with wonderful scarlet berries and a great bushy swag of mistletoe. Jerome had made her hot chocolate in the kitchen and she had been full of how the vet had said that she could start giving Jigs short walks, just ten minutes to start with, and how his legs were nearly healed and the hair starting to grow back on his chest.

As long as Claudia kept thinking about these things, she could keep going. Just don't think about the other, she told herself sternly. But what about when Lila arrived on Friday? How could she behave normally towards her? She had to. That was all there was to it. She had to hide the hideous truth from her at all costs.

Thank goodness Jerome and her mother were in the kitchen. Jerome was making toasted cheese sandwiches for lunch, so Claudia was able to put her head round the door and say, 'I came home. Awful headache. I'm going to lie down, do you mind? I'll feel better after a sleep,' and bolt for her room. She drew the curtains and got into bed with her clothes on and lay there stiff and miserable as a board.

Ten minutes later the door opened softly and her mother crept in with a hot water bottle and a cup of tea. Claudia pretended she was asleep, but as the warmth from the bottle seeped through to her, her heart was also warmed by the small act of kindness.

Friday came, bringing Lila on an early-morning flight, bright, bouncing, noisy and beautiful. She appeared at the door wearing jeans and a battered sheepskin jacket, her hair a shining cape on her shoulders, her bag at her feet. 'I got a lift,' she announced. 'From a friend who lives in Dorset. All the way from the airport! Wasn't I lucky!' and then she was off on a whirl, exactly as she had been when she first got home from school as a child, teasing Jerome, chasing Finn who she worked up into a state of delirious excitement, opening her bag in the hall, spilling out clothes and shoes, pulling out presents she had bought in New York to put under the tiny Christmas tree in the sitting room, playing a CD so loudly that her grandmother took out her hearing aid, opening the fridge door to check the contents and then winging off with Jerome and Finn to see Jigsaw.

They were back fifteen minutes later.

'God, Mum,' said Lila. 'What terrible injuries. I just can't believe he's pulled through with that lot. The ones on his chest aren't as bad as his legs. Jena took off the dressings to show me. They're kept covered to stop scar tissue forming. She's so brave, that kid. She looks after him as if he's a baby. We're taking him out for his first walk tomorrow morning. I said I'd go with her. Just ten minutes to nibble a bit of grass. I'd better get my hunting kit ready. The livery people are bringing my horse to the meet, Ma. Just how smart is that, eh? Come on, Jerome, clean my boots for me. I'm suffering from jet lag!'

Some time later the telephone rang and Lila pounced on it. Claudia's heart stopped as she heard her say in a perfectly natural voice, 'Oh, hi, Anthony. How are you? Yeah, I'm fine. I've only been back about two and a half minutes. What? I didn't know she'd been ill. Hang on. Mum?' She turned to Claudia. 'It's Anthony. He wants to know if you're better.'

Claudia did a frantic head-shaking act, waving the palms of her hands at Lila in a silent, 'don't pass me the telephone' mime.

'Sorry, Anthony,' Lila said smoothly, 'she can't come to the telephone right this moment, but she says thank you, she's fine. Much better . . . we'll see you tomorrow. OK. Bye! What was all that about, Mum?'

'Oh, I was supposed to have lunch with him yesterday. Well, only a sandwich in the pub, but I didn't feel well. Awful headache.'

'Oh,' said Lila, unconcerned. 'Poor old you. How are you getting on with the smoothest farmer in the west, anyway? Do you still fancy him?'

Claudia could hardly believe it. She stared at her daughter, who was making toast, poking around in the toaster with the end of a wooden spoon, trying to fish out a crust.

'Not a bit,' she said firmly. 'Someone else has asked me to marry him, as it happens.'

It was Lila and Jerome's turn to stare. 'What? You never said anything! Who?' and in the ensuing laughter and teasing, she was able to steer the conversation away from Anthony. Even her mother sitting, deaf as a post, at the end of the table joined in.

Saturday did not bear thinking about, seeing Lila together with Anthony, and Claudia was relieved that she was responsible for the food at the meet, which meant that she could scuttle in and out of the kitchen with hardly time to take in anything that was going on.

She was there, at Manor Farm, by half past nine, unpacking the car, setting things out on trays. All the port glasses collected from the off-licence needed wiping and Mrs Walker, the elderly daily, heavily upholstered in a flower overall with a green loopy stitched cardigan over the top, and wearing stout sheepskin boots, set about this task. There was no sign of Anthony, who was out farming, Claudia gratefully supposed, although Ivo came in and out, half dressed in hunting clothes. She hadn't realised that he rode, but she gathered from various telephone calls made in the kitchen that he kept a horse at a livery nearby.

Then Anthony arrived, taking off his boots and overalls in the wash house and calling greetings through to Claudia as he scrubbed his hands at the sink.

'Morning!' he said again as he came through to the kitchen and kissed her cheek. 'Would you like a kiss too, Mrs Walker?' he asked playfully.

'I'll slap yer if yer try!' she retorted, delighted.

Oh, spare me, thought Claudia. How he loves to please the ladies.

'Looks a bit grey out there, Ivo. Bitterly cold. You'll need your thermal knickers on today. Should be one hell of a scent, though. God, this looks good, Claudia. Can I have a sausage roll now?'

'They'll be disgusting cold,' she said stonily, refusing to be charmed. 'Wait until I've warmed them up at least.'

Mrs Walker got out a heavy iron pan and began cooking a proper farmer's breakfast, bacon, sausages, tomatoes, fried bread and, last of all, eggs.

'We'll get out of your way,' said Anthony, picking up his plate and the newspaper and going through to the morning room. Claudia heard him on the telephone while he ate, laughing and joking with someone he called darling. Sod you, she thought furiously, slamming the kettle on the Aga to make a cup of coffee.

At half past ten, people started to arrive. She could hear the sound of horseboxes being unloaded in the yard and the clip clop of hooves on the concrete. Watching at the window she saw hounds, a mass of happy grinning faces and waving sterns, stream from the back of the hunt lorry as the kennel huntsman opened the gates to the ramp.

'We'd best keep the kitchen door shut,' observed Mrs Walker, 'or them rascals'll be in here, sure as eggs.'

Anthony reappeared, changed into country squire outfit of battered tweed jacket and cords, and started to ferry cases of port out to the yard, while a crowd of local helpers trooped in to help with passing things round. Claudia sent out tray after tray of cake, piping hot mince pies and sausage rolls. Ivo dashed through, searching for his whip, tall and elegant in his long boots and black coat. I wonder if Lila has arrived, thought Claudia. It was ten to eleven by the kitchen clock. Collecting another plate of hot mince pies, she went out into the yard.

Anthony had set out the table for the drinks in one corner and the crowd was thick around it. Every farmer for miles around must be here, thought Claudia, to judge by the sea of green clothes, flat caps and weatherbeaten faces. A throng of accompanying dogs, terriers of every shape and colour, labradors and lurchers and collies wove round their legs. She spotted Valerie and moved towards her, and then waved at Jerome and Jena who were sitting with a crowd of foot followers on the garden wall. Jerome had found a safe spot to park his grandmother, who was on her third glass of port and looking very pink.

The centre of the yard was a close-packed mass of horses and ponies and riders. There were children in tweed jackets on hairy ponies with tinsel decorations plaited into their manes and large ladies on equally large cobs as safe and wide as sofas. Old Colonel Tincknell, in a red coat faded to a dull orange with age, was out on his mountainous grey, holding up his glass and tipping his hat to greet the ladies. 'He's eighty-eight,' confided Valerie to Claudia, 'and apart from the war, he's never missed a day's hunting. Says he'd hunt his own grandmother if she had a brush. Look, there's Julia doing her best to be lady of the manor.'

Anthony was working his way through the throng, filling glasses and passing food. He stopped to greet several elegant ladies on smartly turned out hunters. He must have said something rousing to one of them – she playfully struck his shoulder with her hunting crop. There was no sign of Lila, but then Claudia saw more riders moving into the yard and there she was amongst them, looking amazingly elegant on a beautifully turned out chestnut horse, her snug-fitting black jacket emphasising her figure and her long fair hair caught immaculately in a net at the back of her neck. Victoria, looking equally smart in a tweed jacket, and riding a neatly plaited Vinnie, was by her side. Instinctively Claudia looked to see if Anthony had spotted Lila's arrival. As if on cue, she saw him turn and his face take on first a look of recognition and then one of total admiration.

No one was in a hurry to move off on this special morning and it wasn't until everyone was pink-faced from the cold or the port that the Master, a handsome young man on a glossy black horse, stood up in his stirrups and called for silence. He made a speech thanking Anthony and Ivo for their hospitality, reminded everybody of the importance of the hunt to the countryside, thanked all the farmers for their help, support and permission to ride over their land and mentioned that the cap collected would go to the hunt servants as a Christmas box. 'Be generous,' he said, 'and Happy Christmas to you all!'

There was a cheer, the huntsman blew his horn and the hounds who had been kept together in the furthest corner of the yard were allowed to burst out and follow him in a bobbing sea of black and tan as he set off up the crowded village street at a brisk trot, his young whipper-in bringing up the rear.

'Are you all right, Claudia?' asked Valerie. 'You look a bit pale and miserable.'

'Thank you! That does sound attractive!' Claudia laughed back, stirring herself. 'No, I'm fine. A bit cold, that's all. It's a bitter morning, isn't it?'

It was after six o'clock before they saw Lila again. She crashed in through the back door, looking happy and dishevelled, her hair loose on the shoulders of her mud-splattered jacket, her boots filthy.

'Had a fantastic day!' she called. 'That was a fab horse and God, this is some country. I've never seen such big places to jump. It really sorts out the men from the boys!'

'No need to ask which you are,' observed Jerome. She cuffed him on the head as she went past.

'I've got to dash,' she informed them, looking at the kitchen clock. 'I've got to be out by seven thirty and I'm longing for a bath. Riding uses muscles like no other sport!'

'Why, where are you going?' asked Claudia, trying to appear nonchalant.

'Didn't I tell you? Out to dins with a load of people. Some I know vaguely from London. I'm going to stay overnight, Ma. Is that OK? You don't mind, do you? It's easier when I don't have transport.'

'Fine,' said Claudia, tight-lipped. Did Lila really think she could keep her permanently in the dark?

'Did you say it was the carol service tomorrow? What time? Three thirty? I'll get back for that, so we can go as a family.'

'That would be nice. Granny would like it, of course. She doesn't see much of you.'

'Are you cross, Ma? Do you mind me going out?'

'Not at all, darling. Why should I?'

'Well, you sound it, that's all,' said Lila, shrugging. 'What did you lot do today?' she asked, unwinding the hunting stock from

337

round her neck and throwing it in the direction of the washing machine.

'Jerome and Jena helped clear up after the meet. Mother was wonderful and did mounds of washing up, and then we had sandwiches in the pub. Anthony had ordered great platefuls for hunt followers. Old Tom Atkins had a field day. Star Bishop was there, saying she was on a diet. She would only have one sandwich but then ate about her own weight in pork scratchings. Then we took Finn out for a walk and that's about it. Not very eventful.'

'And this evening?'

'Supper on our knees and then there's a concert we want to hear on the radio.'

'Very bungaloid! Very old folks' home!' Lila mocked happily.

Sunday was Christmas Eve and Claudia had one or two last-minute things she wanted to do. She had not had time to wrap the little presents she had bought and she started this task after she had taken breakfast to her mother in bed. Jerome was obviously sleeping in late at Valerie's and it was hard to feel at all festive while pottering about on her own in the bungalow. It was a grey, depressing sort of day, with a heavy wet sky pressing down on the village, blocking out the view of the hills and smearing everything with a greasy-looking film of moisture.

When she had finished with the wrapping paper she would light the fire, so that when her mother got up later and had had her bath, there would be somewhere warm and cheerful to sit. Claudia turned on the radio to listen to carols coming from a Methodist chapel in Wales and then *The Archers* started with a lot of emphasis on family gatherings and parties in the village hall. There was even a Christmas Eve meet where two of the characters, involved in a steamy extramarital affair, managed to exchange sucking sounding kisses and heaving, heartfelt sighs when they came up for air. Nothing, however, could match the soap opera quality of her own life, she thought miserably and switched it off again. She would rather listen to Lila's thumping CD instead.

The day fairly dragged by in a horrid sort of limbo and she was short-tempered and snappy with her mother, who insisted on interfering in the kitchen and whose views Claudia found irritating in the extreme. She would keep speculating on what Roger would be doing in prison. She had read somewhere that they had a grand time at Christmas, she said, with extra rations and a proper turkey dinner with two sorts of stuffing. She thinks of him as if he's a sort of prisoner of war and not a crook, thought Claudia crossly. It was something of a relief to get ready for church.

There was no sign of Lila but Jerome had opted to accompany them and had struggled into fairly clean and respectable clothes. At least his dark overcoat covered the holes in the arm of his sweater. The little church was filling up fast when they arrived and Peter Durnford was there, resplendent in a reindeer-printed bow tie, to show them to a pew towards the back. Julia, in a large fur hat, and Victoria were in their usual place at the front, Julia turning round every few minutes to check on how the church was filling and who was there.

There were so many people that it was hard to see the lit Christmas tree and the wooden Nativity scene by the chancel steps. The decorations were simple and perfect for a little country church, thought Claudia, knowing that Julia was responsible for them. The window ledge above her head was festooned with boughs of holly and wreaths of ivy and a simple white candle on a paper saucer stood at the entrance to every pew, to be lit when everyone was seated, before the service began.

Excited children rushed up and down and parents tried to shush their voices and catch hold of their hands to stop them. A squat infant of about two, of indeterminate sex and with a pasty potato face encircled by a knitted woollen bonnet, stood on the seat of the pew in front and stared unblinking at Jerome whilst methodically picking its nose. There was still no sign of Lila.

A stout choirgirl wearing trainers beneath her hassock and a spotty teenage boy began to light the candles and then the main lights went out and a hush fell. From over by the door came the wavering sound of a very young voice singing the first verse of 'Once in Royal David's City', and the service began. Halfway through the first carol, Jerome nudged his mother and pointed to Lila, hovering by the door, trying to see where they were sitting. She was with Anthony, who hooked his hand under her elbow and moved her up the aisle and into seats Ivo was keeping for them opposite the Durnfords. As she entered the pew, Lila knocked over the candle and Jerome grinned. Lila could always be relied on to get herself noticed.

After the service, slightly dizzy from bellowing 'Oh Come All Ye Faithful' at the tops of their voices, people started to crowd out and Claudia saw Lila fighting her way through towards them. She looked tremendously pretty in a white fur hat, which she must have bought in New York, and a smart black coat that Claudia had never seen before. Her cheeks were very pink and her eyes were glittering with excitement.

As soon as she got close she said, 'I looked for you everywhere, but we were late! Did you see me knock the candle over? Nearly set fire to the church! Mum! Gran! Jerome! I have something wonderful to tell you! Wait!' and she caught Claudia's hand and started to drag her through the crowds towards where Anthony and Ivo stood by the door. 'Come on, Jerome!' she cried, looking over her shoulder. 'Bring Gran!'

She was so determined and forceful that Claudia felt herself move through the clustered people, apologising to left and right for such bad manners, and then Lila had them roughly assembled and she dragged off the glove from her left hand and stuck it out in front of them and said, 'There!' in a triumphant voice.

'Where?' asked Jerome, still at sea, but Claudia knew. She had known as soon as Lila had said that she had something to tell them. On Lila's third finger sparkled a huge diamond ring.

'Mum?' she said. 'Isn't it amazing! We're engaged! He asked me last night!' and with a look of intense happiness she hooked her arm through Ivo's.

Of course, as Jerome remarked afterwards, if Lila had wanted the world to know about her engagement, she could not have chosen a better moment. Eventually, the whole of the exiting congregation came to a standstill as the news went round, and then there were spontaneous cheers and congratulations and back-slapping and kissing. Claudia felt poleaxed and only when Anthony kissed her warmly and whispered, 'What does this make us?' was she able to grasp the kind of difference Lila's news did make.

An impromptu party had been arranged and people started to cross the road to Manor Farm where champagne corks popped and laughter and happiness spilled out into the dark night. Ivo made a charming speech about how lucky he felt he was and Lila cried noisily and was then about to start an Oscar-winning-actress type of emotional response when Jerome caught hold of her and told her to shut up. Julia took charge of filling up glasses and embraced Claudia warmly, bottle clasped in one hand.

'Amazing news!' she said, quite genuinely happy and pleased. 'Did you know?'

Claudia shook her head. 'It was a total and utter surprise!' she said as she had done already a dozen times. 'We didn't even know they knew one another!'

'Never thought Ivo would take the plunge again,' said Julia. 'It's great he's marrying a proper girl like Lila,' and by that Claudia knew she meant someone who rode and hunted. 'She can have her wedding reception at East End House, if she'd like. A marquee in the garden. What fun!'

Peter kissed Claudia equally warmly. 'Wonderful!' he said. 'It's wonderful! A happy day for us all! A happy day for the village. Ivo's quite a catch, I believe.'

'I know nothing at all about him,' said Claudia simply. 'We've only just met really. There's a lot to take in. Lots of questions to ask!' but she felt wonderfully happy and relieved.

Victoria, transformed without the braces on her teeth, had drunk a lot of champagne. Now she filled her pockets with sausage rolls left over from the meet and crept out to the washroom where a fat black puppy, as yet unnamed, had taken up temporary accommodation. Jerome found her there, sitting on the floor beside the washing machine. 'He's Mum's Christmas present,' she explained. 'I've got to tear down here tomorrow morning and collect him before she gets up.' Jerome gave her a hand and pulled her to her feet. 'Isn't he just the thweetest thing?' she asked.

'Thweetesth thing?' mocked Jerome, laughing at her. He stood behind her with his arms draped round her neck, rocking her backwards and forwards.

'Don't! I feel seasick enough already!' she said and he let her go, first dropping a kiss on her head. She wished she didn't feel so drunk. She was scared she'd wake up in the morning and find she couldn't remember how lovely it was to be with him again. She turned to him with shining eyes. 'Isn't it a happy, happy day? And it's nearly, nearly Christmas!'

At half past six, Lila said that everybody had to take their glasses and go outside into the yard. When she had everyone out there, shivering and bemused, they heard, coming very slowly down the lane, the sound of the hooves of an unshod horse and round the corner came Jena and Jigsaw, the horse wearing a stable rug, moving stiffly and carefully, but with his head up proudly and his ears pricked. Jena had plaited his mane and threaded it with silver and gold stars and his feet were oiled and gleamed in the dark.

Lila, hitching up her skirt and showing an indecent amount of

long thigh, climbed up on to the old mounting block and shouted, 'I'd like you all to share our happy day with someone else. I want you to raise your glasses and drink to the complete recovery of this beautiful and wonderful horse! You all know what happened to him, and if you don't, well, you should! And this marvellous girl here! My friend, Jena – she simply would not allow him to die, and it's her courage . . .'

God, thought Jerome. Here we go! She's going to lose it – but Lila was ploughing on, flushed with champagne and brimming with emotion.

'Her courage is just an example to all of us! And,' her voice rose happily, 'he's got to get completely better because I want him to take me to the church on my wedding day!' This was followed by a lot of cheering and noise, none louder, Claudia noted, than that coming from the Durnfords, where Julia, glassy-eyed, was searching in Peter's jacket pocket for a handkerchief on which to blow her nose.

Christmas, after that, was bound to be unforgettable, caught up as they all were in Lila's excitement and happiness. Later, Claudia confessed to having seen the photograph and thinking that Anthony was the man involved, which made Lila scream with laughter.

'No wonder you were so boot-faced, Mum! You thought I'd stolen your boyfriend!'

'Hardly!' pressed Claudia, privately acknowledging her daughter wasn't far off the mark.

'Anyway,' went on Lila, 'Anthony's far too old for me. Fifteen years between me and Ivo are bad enough. I have warned him, you know, that when he's eighty and I'm a sprightly sixty-five, I may have to put him down.'

The story gradually unfolded that she and Ivo had met in London the day after she had visited Roger in prison. Anthony had given her his London telephone number and she had felt so low and lonely that she had telephoned when she got back to London and the two brothers had taken her out to dinner. 'That was it!' said Lila. 'Love at first sight!' The plan was that they should marry in the summer, buy a bigger flat in London, and spend weekends at Manor Farm, sharing the house with Anthony, as before.

'I couldn't tell you, Mum,' explained Lila. 'It had to be a secret, what with Dad, and you here in the village and everything. I had one bad moment when I found out that Anthony had asked you to go to Scotland when I was intending to be there too. I wouldn't have gone, of course, if you had been able to go. I just didn't know, you see, how things were between you two. I wasn't going to put a spanner in the works if I could help it!'

'Ah. I see. Tell me, Lila, out of interest, did Anthony take someone else, did he?'

Lila grinned. 'Sorry, Mum. Yes, he did. A rather gorgeous Danish woman who owned a string of dairies. She turned out to be terrifying and amazingly bossy. He must have regretted inviting her after about five minutes. Now, Mum, I want to talk to you about the wedding. We've only got six months to plan it! It's such a shame Minna's only got boys, and Aunt Kate as well. I do want a whole trail of bridesmaids. Do you think Victoria would like to be a grown-up one?'

Three months later on a beautiful blue spring morning, Claudia was stopped on the lane outside her house by Valerie. 'Claudia, you must come in when you have a moment. The builders have made a start. It's rather awe-inspiring seeing the walls come down. Betty is in despair at the dust.'

'They're not knocking down much, are they?' asked Claudia, indicating the council outline of the proposed development nailed to a tree by the gate, amongst the yellow of the daffodils.

'No, it's the kitchen and outhouses which have gone. I can't say I'm sorry. They were always rather dingy and dark. My new kitchen is going to face west and have a lovely view over the hills.' Valerie wedged her large backside on the wall and bent down to stroke Finn. 'Isn't this sun lovely? April is always unpredictable, but when one gets a nice day it can be a real foretaste of summer.'

'The months race past,' said Claudia. 'It *will* soon be summer, with the wedding and everything. When are your girls due to arrive?'

'The end of June, when they break up from school. They will stay with me on my side until their part of the house is finished. It means they can have a hand in choosing curtains and carpets. I can't really believe it. This time last year I was facing the prospect of becoming an increasingly lonely old woman. Christopher had wanted me to have one of those alarms which one wears around one's neck to summon help in the case of a fall in the home. I gather one is supposed to lie in a heap at the bottom of the stairs with one's skirt rucked up round one's waist, showing a lot of knicker and press this alarm device and await rescue. Has it really come to this? I thought. I refused, of course.'

'Of course,' laughed Claudia.

'Now I shall have all the company I want,' said Valerie, 'and the dearest company in the world!' She paused. 'You never, I suppose,' she went on shyly, 'considered Christopher's offer?'

'Yes, I did,' said Claudia, sitting down next to her. Finn flopped on his side amongst the daffodils, the sun hot on his flanks. 'I certainly did. I like Christopher enormously, as you know, but I couldn't possibly have said yes, could I? For one thing, what about the girls? They might have hated me on sight. These things take time, and of course I'm still married. The divorce won't be through for some months yet. However, living next door and giving you as much help as I can in the holidays when you have them all at home means that I shall get to know them pretty well, doesn't it? I hope Christopher might keep his offer open. Allow me a bit more time.'

'I'd be surprised if he didn't! Meanwhile we're going to get that old garden door seen to, aren't we?' said Valerie. 'I showed Robert, the builder, and he's going to replace the rotten wood and put on new hinges.'

'Yes,' said Claudia. 'We must get that door open.'

They sat for a while in silence, enjoying the sun on their faces.

'Christopher has settled Jigsaw's vet bill. Did you know that?' said Valerie. Claudia nodded. 'He said it was far, far cheaper than buying the girls a pony, or even giving them riding lessons. In return, Jena is going to let them ride him in the holidays and teach them all the stable management that girls love. Of course, it will be just a passing phase with them. They never stick to anything, but they're tremendously excited by the thought.'

'Christopher doing that, or rather you persuading him to, it's such a weight off everybody's minds,' said Claudia. 'Julia's letting Jena keep Jigsaw at East End House, isn't she? She's even given her an old saddle. Mind you, Jena earns his keep doing all the stable work and it's much nicer for Victoria to have someone to ride with.'

'Julia's rather pleasanter lately, have you noticed? Less dog in the manger. She never objected to this, you know?' and Valerie indicated over her shoulder to the plastic-covered planning notice.

'I suppose it's not quite the same as building a bungalow on her doorstep,' laughed Claudia. 'But I do agree. She seems happier, I think. She was really nice about Lila's engagement. She might well have been very put out, but of course she takes the line that it was through her that Lila and Ivo met – which is true in an indirect way. Everybody's been kind really. To our faces, anyway. No one's mentioned bad blood or our criminal connections. Roger will be at the wedding. Roger, Carla and baby Bethlehem, it seems. Lila called her that, and it's stuck. My sister is coming over from New Zealand. It will be a wonderful family day.' Again they lapsed into silence, each thinking about the months ahead.

'Jerome's happier too,' said Claudia. 'You know he told me eventually about Jabeena being killed. He told me when he was home at Christmas. I knew there was something not right between us, and it was that. He said you were wonderful, that you helped him come to terms with it. I really have to thank you for that. He very badly needed someone then – and it wasn't me. That hurt a bit, you realise.'

Valerie said nothing but reached out and patted Claudia's hand. Claudia felt her eyes mist over.

'The blackthorn's out,' she said hastily. 'Have you noticed? Tom Atkins told me ages ago, before I'd moved into the village, that when the blackthorn has flowered, the season has turned and the cold days are done. "You can take your vest off then," he said. This morning when Finn and I went down across the valley, the hedges looked as if they had been dressed in white. The winter must be nearly over, we thought. Didn't we, Finn?' and she bent down to stroke his silver ear.